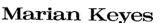

Irish Girls About Town

POCKET BOOKS

New York London Toronto Sydney

POCKET BOOKS, a division of Simon & Schuster, Inc.
1230 Avenue of the Americas, New York, NY 10020

Originally published in Great Britain and Ireland in 2002 by Pocket/TownHouse, an imprint of Simon & Schuster UK Ltd. and TownHouse and Country House Ltd. Dublin. Published by arrangement with Simon & Schuster UK Ltd.

ISBN: 0-7434-8301-4

First Pocket Books paperback edition March 2004

10 9 8 7 6 5 4 3 2 1

POCKET and colophon are registered trademarks of Simon & Schuster, Inc.

Cover design by Christine Van Bree
Cover photograph by Superstock

Manufactured in the United States of America

For information regarding special discounts for bulk purchases, please contact Simon & Schuster Special Sales at 1-800-456-6798 or business@simonandschuster.com.

Contents

Foreword

When established bestselling Irish writers joined forces with up-and-coming new stars to raise money for a good cause, the result was *Irish Girls About Town*, a diverse and memorable collection of stories guaranteed to divert and delight. Originally published in the United Kingdom and Ireland, a portion of the proceeds from each book sold were given to Barnardo's, the United Kingdom's largest children's charity, and the Society of St. Vincent de Paul in Ireland, which works to alleviate the effects of poverty.

Barnardo's supports over 90,000 children, young people, and families through more than 300 projects throughout the United Kingdom. Their work with families covers a wide range of age groups and issues, including homeless teenagers, mothers whose children have disabilities or have been excluded from school, and people who have decided to improve their surroundings through community development initiatives.

The Society of St. Vincent de Paul has over one million members in 132 countries, where it works tirelessly in a wide variety of activities to alleviate the effects of poverty and exclusion. These include providing financial support, running breakfast clubs and homework clubs for needy schoolchildren as well as pre-schools, providing advice/counseling services, giving educational grants, and running 120 "good-as-new" clothing and house-goods shops. The Society in Ireland is also a major contributor to the development of public policy to eliminate poverty.

As with the UK and Irish edition, Barnardo's and the Society of St. Vincent de Paul will benefit from the sale of this edition of *Irish Girls About Town*.

Irish Girls
About
Town

Soulmates

Marian Keyes

So was it a disaster?" Peter begged Tim. "Did they try to kill each other?"

Watched by seven avid pairs of eyes, Tim shook his head sorrowfully. "They got on like a house on fire. They're going to do it again in July."

A murmur of *Isn't that marvelous?* started up.

But Vicky couldn't take any more. In despair, she put her face in her hands. "How do they do it?" she whispered, echoing everyone's sentiments. "How do they bloody well do it!"

Georgia and Joel were born on the same day in the same year in the same city—though they didn't meet until they were twenty-six-and-a-half, while moving and shaking their way around a launch party for a Japanese beer. When Joel discovered the momentous connection, he declared, above the clamor: "We're twins! Soulmates."

Georgia was called the golden girl, an inadequate attempt to convey how fantastically energetic, gorgeous and *nice* she was. In every group of human beings there's a natural leader and she was one. Only a very special man could keep up with her: Joel was the perfect candidate. The kindest and best-looking of his good-looking group of prototype New Lad friends, how could he not help gravitating to Georgia, the deluxe version of her coterie of glossy, shiny girlfriends?

And now she had a soulmate. She *would,* her best friend Vicky thought, with shameful envy. Georgia was always the first. With the first ankle bracelet, the first wedge sandals, she had an unerring instinct for what was good and new and right. Some years back Vicky had tried to trump her with a pair of boots she'd joyously ferried back from New York. *This time I'm the winner,* Vicky had thought, breathlessly ushering her new boots ahead of her. But Georgia had beaten her to it. Again. By wearing a similar pair of boots—similar, *but better*. The heel was nicer, the leather softer, the whole élan simply much more convincing. And she'd only bought them in Ravel.

Soulmates. It was the start of the nineties and new-age stuff had just started being fashionable. Katie had recently bought four crystals and dotted them about her flat, but four crystals couldn't hold a candle to a real live soulmate. It was about the best thing you could have—better than a tattoo or henna-patterned nails or a cappuccino maker. Quickly others followed their example by claiming that they too had found their SM. But it was only a spurious intimacy based on chemical connection, which dissolved just as soon as the cocaine or ecstasy or Absolut had worn off.

"We're twins," Georgia and Joel declared to the world, and paraded their similarities. A crooked front tooth that she'd had capped and that he'd had knocked out in a motorbike accident and replaced. Both had blond hair, although hers was highlighted. Indeed rumors circulated that perhaps his was too.

Within weeks they'd moved in together and filled their flat with a succession of peculiar things, all of which assumed a stylish luster the minute they became theirs. But no matter how much the others tried to emulate their panache it was never quite the same. The liver-purple paint which Georgia and Joel used to such stylish effect in one room in their south-facing flat never survived the transition to anyone else's wall. Especially not Tim and Alice's northeast-facing living room. "I can't bear it," Tim eventually admitted. "I feel as though I'm watching telly inside an internal organ."

Georgia and Joel spent money fast. "Hey, we're skint," they often laughed—then immediately went to the River Café. On receiving a particularly onerous credit card bill, they tightened their belts by buying champagne. Attached to them, debt seemed desirable, stylish, alive.

"Money is there to be spent," they claimed and their friends cautiously followed suit, then tried to stop themselves waking in the night in overdrawn terror.

After four years together, Georgia and Joel surprised everyone by getting married. Not just any old marriage—but you could have guessed that. Instead they went to Las

Vegas; hopped on a plane on Friday night after work, were married on Saturday by an Elvis lookalike, were back for work on Monday. The following weekend they rented a baroque room in Charterhouse Square, draped it in white muslin and had the mother of all parties. Proving they were ahead of their time by serving old-fashioned martinis which made a comeback among the Liggerati a couple of years later.

Close friends Melissa and Tom, who were having a beachfront wedding ceremony in Bali a month later, went into a trough of depression and wanted to call the whole thing off.

Two years later, Georgia once more reinvented the right lifestyle choices by announcing her pregnancy. Stretch marks and sleepless nights acquired an immediate cachet. They called their little girl Queenie—a dusty, musty old ladies' name, but on their child it was quirky and charming. In the following months, various acquaintances named their newborn girls Flossie, Vera and Beryl. Georgia regained her figure within weeks of having the baby. Even worse, she claimed not to have worked out.

Then one day, pension brochures appeared on their circular walnut coffee table.

"Pensions?" asked Neil, hardly believing his luck. Joel had finally cocked up and done something deserving of scorn.

"Got to look to the future," Joel agreed. "You know it makes sense."

"Pensions," Neil repeated, throwing his head back in an elaborate gesture of amusement. "You sad bastard."

"You want to be old and skint?" Joel said with a smile

that was very obviously not a cruel one. "Up to you, mate."

And Neil wanted to hang himself. They were always moving the bloody goalposts.

But most of all it was Georgia and Joel's relationship that no one could ever top. They'd been born on the same day, in the same year, within four miles of each other; they were so obviously meant to be together that everyone else's felt like a making-do, a shoddy compromise. Georgia and Joel fitted together, like two halves of a heart; symbiosis was the name of the game and their devotion was lavish and public. Every year one or other of them had a "surprise" birthday party, "for my twin."

Their friends were tightly bound to them by a snarl of admiration, hidden envy and the hope of some of their good fortune rubbing off.

But as they moved forward into the late nineties, perhaps Georgia and Joel's mutual regard wasn't as frantically fervent as once it had been. Perhaps tempers were slightly shorter than previously. Maybe Joel got on Georgia's nerves once in a while. Perhaps Joel wondered if Georgia wasn't quite as golden as she'd once been. Not that they'd ever consider splitting up. Oh, no. Splitting up was for other people, those unfortunate types who hadn't found their soulmate.

And other people *did* split up. Tom left Melissa for Melissa's brother in a scandal that had everyone on the phone to each other in gleeful horror for some weeks, all vying to be the biggest bearer of bad news, outdoing each other in the horrific details. "I hear they were shagging each other on Tom and Melissa's honeymoon. On the *honeymoon*. Can you believe it!" Vicky's husband left her.

She'd had a baby, couldn't shift the weight, became dowdy and different. Unrecognizable. She'd once been a contender. Of course, never exactly as lambent or lustrous as Georgia, but now she'd slipped and slipped behind, well out of the race, limping and abandoned.

Georgia was a loyal and ever-present friend in their times of woe. Tirelessly she visited, urged trips to hairdressers, took care of children, consoled, cajoled. She even let Vicky and Melissa say things like, "You think that your relationship is the one that won't hit the wall, but it can happen to anyone." Georgia always let them get away with it, bestowing a kindly smile and resisting the urge to say, "Joel and I are different."

People gave up watching and waiting for Georgia and Joel to unravel. The times people said, "Don't you think Georgia and Joel are just *too* devoted? Methinks they do protest too much," became fewer and fewer. People ran out of energy and patience waiting for the roof to fall in on the soulmates and their "special relationship."

But the thing about a soulmate is that it can be a burden as well as a blessing, Joel found himself thinking one day. You're stuck with them. Other people can ditch their partner and forage with impunity in the outside world, looking for a fresh partner, where *everyone* is a possibility. Having a spiritual twin fairly narrows your choice.

And Georgia found herself emotionally itchy. What would have happened if she hadn't met Joel? Who would she be with now? And she experienced an odd yearning, she *missed* the men she hadn't loved, the boyfriends she'd never met.

So acute was this unexpected sadness that she tried to speak to Katie about it.

"Sounds like you're bored with Joel," Katie offered. "Do you still love him?"

"Love him?" Georgia exclaimed, with knee-jerk alacrity. "He's my *soulmate!*"

Then one night Joel got very, very drunk and admitted to Chris, "I fancy other women. I want to sleep with every girl I see. The curiosity is too much."

"That's normal," Chris said in surprise. "Have an affair."

"It's not normal. This is me and Georgia."

"Sounds like you're in trouble, mate."

"Not me and Georgia."

They believed their own publicity and, in time-honored tradition, attempted to paper over the cracks by having another baby. A boy this time. They called him Clement.

"That's an old man's name!"

"We're being ironic!" But their laughs lacked conviction and when they painted Clement's room silver no one copied them.

On they labored, shoulder to shoulder. While all around them people danced the dance of love: merging and splitting, blending anew with fresh partners, sundering, twirling and cleaving joyously to the next one. And shackled to their soulmate, Georgia and Joel watched with naked envy.

It was only when Georgia began questioning her mother on the circumstances of her birth that she realized how ridiculous the situation had become. "What time of the day was I born, Mum?" she asked, as Clement bellowed on her lap.

"Eleven."

"Could it have been a little bit later?" Georgia heard herself ask. "Like gone midnight?" *So that it was actually the following day,* she thought but didn't articulate.

"It was eleven in the *morning,* nowhere near midnight."

Three weeks later when Joel and Georgia split up it caused a furor. Everyone declared themselves horrified, that if the golden couple couldn't hack it, what hope was there for the rest of them? But there wasn't one among them who couldn't help a frisson of long-awaited glee. Now Mr. and Mrs. Perfect would see what it was like for the rest of them.

The "press release" insisted that they were still friends, that it was all very adult and civilized, that they were in complete agreement over finances and custody of the children. Sure, everyone scorned. *Sure.*

But, disconcertingly, Georgia wouldn't join in an "all men are bastards" conversation with Vicky, Katie and Melissa. Not even when Joel began going out with a short, plump dental nurse called Helen.

"Tim has met her," Alice consoled. "He says she's not a patch on you."

"Oh don't," Georgia objected. "I think she's really sweet."

"You've met her?!"

And when Georgia began seeing a graphic designer called Conor, Tim assured Joel that Alice said he was a prat.

"Nah," Joel protested. "He's a good bloke. We're all going on holiday with the kids at Easter."

"Who are?" Tim wanted to pass out.

"Me and Helen, Georgia and Conor."

Everyone declared that it was wonderful they were being so mature about the split and only the certain knowledge that the holiday would be a bloodbath consoled them. Itching to find out just how bad it was, Tim rang Joel the day he got back. Then Tim, Alice, Katie, Vicky, Melissa, Chris, Neil and Peter gathered in the pub, ostensibly for a casual drink. Conversation glanced off the usual subjects—house prices, hair straighteners, Pamela Anderson's breasts—until no one could bear any more. Peter was the first to crack, the words were out of his mouth before he could stop them.

"So was it a disaster?" he begged Tim. "Did they try to kill each other?"

Watched by seven avid pairs of eyes, Tim shook his head sorrowfully. "They got on like a house on fire. They're going to do it again in July."

A murmur of *Isn't that marvelous?* started up.

But Vicky couldn't take any more. In despair, she put her face in her hands. "How do they do it?" she whispered, echoing everyone's sentiments. "How do they bloody well do it!"

———

Since she was first published in 1995, **MARIAN KEYES** has become a publishing phenomenon. Her five novels, *Watermelon, Lucy Sullivan Is Getting Married, Rachel's Holiday, Last Chance Saloon* and *Sushi for Beginners,* have become international bestsellers, selling over six million copies worldwide.

Her latest book, *Under the Duvet,* is a collection of her non-fiction, and her most recent novel, *Angels,* was published in hardback in September 2002.

Marian Keyes lives in Dublin with her husband.

De-Stress

Joan O'Neill

Alex locked her car with unsteady hands, and walked quickly to Julio Cesar's, the new Italian restaurant on the Quays, full of nervous excitement, and anticipation. Nigel had phoned that morning from Brussels, asking her to book a table somewhere quiet, telling her he wanted to talk about their future, taking her completely by surprise. They hadn't seen much of each other recently with him flying back and forth to EU meetings, and now, here he was, about to propose, just when she suspected he was beginning to take her for granted. Typical Nigel to spring this on her without a hint of warning, and wasn't his timing impeccable with her thirtieth birthday looming.

She entered the restaurant with assurance, her hair

pulled back, accentuating her perfect features, her new black Stella McCartney corset dress, that had cost a month's salary, giving her an hourglass figure. Ignoring the group of men at the bar who tried to catch her eye, she made straight for Nigel, already settled into a corner, engrossed in his drink.

"Hi," she said, smiling down on him.

Startled, he looked up. "Alex! You look great," he said, getting to his feet, kissing her cheek.

"Thank you." She sat down opposite him, smiling tenderly at him. "And how was your week?"

"Good. They've offered me a promotion. Head of Committee on Social and Community Affairs," he said, pouring out two glasses of champagne from the cooler beside him.

"Terrific. Congratulations." She raised her glass.

"Thanks. There's one drawback though. It means I'll be based in Brussels for the next six months."

"Oh!"

He looked at her. "It's too good an opportunity to pass up. I have to take it."

"Of course." Alex wondered why she was so surprised. Nigel was ambitious. It was his ambition that had caught her attention that first evening she'd strode into a cocktail party he was hosting, and into his life. He was a Clark Kent lookalike, clean-cut MEP of thirty-five years, who'd whisked her off to an expensive restaurant in Dalkey where he was well known and treated deferentially, to captivate her with his glamor, exuberance and intelligence, and to ply her with champagne.

He'd told her about his job. Influenced by his father, he'd been engulfed in politics from an early age. His charm, politeness and his serious approach to his work had impressed her. He was the epitome of an ambitious politician, sure of himself, confident in fulfilling his wish to become Taoiseach one day. Alex had told him that she was PR for a firm of consultants, a job she loved, which had not impressed him.

Incredibly attracted to him, she'd rushed headlong into a lustful relationship, moving into his apartment in Temple Bar without hesitation when he suggested it only a month after they'd met. They settled down to blissful domesticity, when their separate schedules permitted. Recently they saw each other only fleetingly because socializing played a major part in Nigel's life, and Alex was busy at work. She wasn't invited to Nigel's parents' home anymore. They didn't consider her "right" for Nigel. She wasn't "his class," they thought, pretentious snobs that they were, just because they'd had a fund-raising dinner for Bertie and Celia once in their home.

There would be lots of socializing in their marriage too, Alex had no doubt, especially when they went on the campaign trail. There would be posh parties and dinners with rich, influential people. Alex would have to look her best and happy all the time, going with him from one work function to another. When the babies arrived it would be difficult. She'd have to juggle her time between her family and his career. Depend on his awful parents for baby-sitting, or hire a nanny if need be. Still, she'd be married to the best-looking, most successful politician in Ireland, and they'd have a beautiful home, eventually, in Dalkey or Killiney. That should compensate for the negative side of things.

"As I said, I won't be around much, and . . ."

So that's why this sudden urge to get engaged. So they could establish their relationship officially. Nothing to do with her age.

"Alex!"

Alex pulled herself together quickly. "Sorry, yes, well, at least we have the weekend together to get used to the idea, and make plans," she said cheerfully.

"Lots of paperwork for Monday, I'm afraid," he said.

She touched his hand. "I'll think of something to distract you," she giggled.

"You must be hungry," he said, handing her the menu, put out by her exuberance.

Suppressing her disappointment she said, "God, we're beginning to sound like an old married couple already."

He sighed. "Don't I know."

"It's a natural progression, I suppose."

"What is?"

"Marriage."

His eyes shot up from the menu.

"Don't worry, I find it a frightening prospect too. But we don't have to rush into it. We can stay engaged for a long time."

"But why tinker with an engagement when it's never going to happen?" Nigel said, with a distinct lack of warmth in his voice.

"When what's never going to happen?"

"Alex! Give me a break! I'm not ready for anything permanent in my life, certainly not being buried alive with a family, and when I do start looking for a wife I'll be looking for a Hillary Clinton type, suited to being the wife of a politician."

The waiter appeared. They gave him their orders to

keep things running smoothly, but as soon as he departed, Alex said, "I thought you wanted to talk to me about the future."

"I did. I mean I do," he said, flustered, removing his glasses, polishing them vigorously.

She waited.

"What I wanted to say, what I'm trying to say is, well, we have a wonderful time, great sex and everything, but maybe this is an opportunity to give each other a break. See how things go?"

"I thought things were going fine."

"They are, but let's face it, Alex, our relationship's getting a bit heavy and, quite honestly, I'm not ready for lifetime commitment, and all that scary stuff."

Her heart skipped a beat.

Nigel concentrated on his empty place setting as he said, "Look, I'd make a rotten husband. I'd be no good at that kind of thing, honestly."

She stared at him, openmouthed. "Are you saying that you don't love me anymore?" Her voice wobbled dangerously.

"Alex, cut that out," he said with a threat in his tone that made him blush. "I hate it when you whine. I just need a break, that's all."

Her voice had an unnerving edge to it as she said, "You're a cruel bastard, Nigel."

"I'm sorry."

Flinging down her napkin she jumped up. "Bastard," she shouted, outraged, and stormed out of the restaurant, Nigel in hot pursuit, startled diners gaping after them.

She ran to her car, got in, and tore off, leaving him standing on the pavement, shouting after her. At the apart-

ment she locked the door, went to his cocktail cabinet and
released her temper on his Louise Kennedy glass goblets,
smashing them one after another against the fireplace. Next
went his bottles of whiskey, vodka and gin, then his prized
Venetian glass lamp, a present from a rich aunt. She was
starting on his delft in the kitchen when he pounded on the
door, commanding her to let him in. She ignored him until
she was satisfied that she'd wreaked enough havoc, then she
packed a few clothes and let him in.

"What have you done?" He stood in the middle of the
room, surveying the riot of glass with horror.

"Didn't hurt a bit," she said, taking a deep breath,
ordering him out of her way, Nigel not daring to try to
stop her.

To get his name in the newspapers with any kind of
scandal might hinder his hopes for the future, and already
the upstairs neighbor was poking her head out of the window, inquiring as to the cause of the rumpus.

Alex drove straight to her friend Serena's apartment in
Fairview.

"I've left him," she said, as soon as Serena opened the
door, then burst into tears.

Serena put her arms around her and led her inside.

"Cry as much as you want to," she said, handing Alex
a box of tissues, holding her until the crying stopped.

Eventually Alex blew her nose. "It's the shock."

"I can imagine."

Alex rubbed her eyes with her forefinger and thumb, a
habit she'd had as a child. "I don't know how I'm going to
get through it," she sniffed, wiping away her tears with
the back of her hand. "It was so unexpected. He was

always going to marry me. At least, that's what I thought. Oh, God, I've made a complete fool of myself."

"There, there." Serena held her, stroked her back.

"I've never felt so alone, so unwanted, unloved." Alex closed her eyes to shut out the pain.

"I hate to see you like this," Serena said.

"I'm not exactly thrilled about it myself."

"Do you want to talk about it?"

She shook her head. "I can't put it into words."

"Try."

"Well." Alex took a deep breath. "I hadn't seen much of him for a couple of weeks. He was in Brussels, and my own work was going well. To be honest, when he said he wanted to talk to me about our future I thought he was going to propose."

"Wow! You had no idea this was coming? Nothing specific in his behavior to indicate that the man you loved, and lived with, was suddenly fed up with the arrangement?"

"No."

"There wasn't a hint of anyone else? Not a name mentioned that you hadn't heard before?"

"Absolutely not."

"What about your sex life?"

Alex's head shot up. "What about it?"

"I'm not prying," Serena said defensively. "I'm only asking because I think it might help. Often things in that department can give a clue when two people are not getting along."

"All right, maybe I'd felt neglected, a bit, while he was getting through a backlog of work in the last few weeks, but he was my boyfriend, for God's sake. He came home to me every night. Except when he was away, which was quite a bit recently." Alex studied the carpet, too choked up to speak.

"Then, obviously what he had to say about your future wasn't what you were expecting to hear?" Serena coaxed her.

Alex shook her head. "No. I just remember the tail end of the conversation. Something about him needing a break."

"Bastard!" Serena pronounced. "Of all the cheek! After all you've done for him."

Alex burst into a fresh flood of tears. Eventually, blowing her nose, she said, "I feel so foolish."

"I think you should try to get some sleep. You're exhausted."

"I can't sleep. I'm too restless."

"Come on, you can have my bed, I'll sleep here." She escorted Alex into her bedroom. "At least try to get some sleep. It's very late."

In bed, Alex stared at the ceiling, thinking of him.

Next morning Serena brought her tea and toast. She looked at her friend slumped on the bed, her eyes fixed ahead, staring at the wall.

"I wish I could think of something to cheer you up," she said, sitting down beside her.

Alex pulled herself up slowly, took a sip of tea. "I wish I could forget him." She shut her eyes tightly.

Several days later Serena said, when Alex hadn't budged from her bedroom, "What are your plans?"

Alex shrugged. "I haven't made any yet."

"You can stay here as long as you like."

"Thanks. You're an angel. At some stage I'm going to

have to arrange to get my stuff out of Nigel's apartment."

"I hope that won't make life more difficult for you."

"It has already. I tried to contact him on his mobile, but I only got the answer service. I phoned the apartment. Same thing. I know he's there though. He won't pick up." Alex clamped her hand across her forehead. "He won't see me, I know he won't. He's furious with me for wrecking the place. What did he expect? That I'd steal off like a mouse. After all I've invested in him!"

After a fortnight of listening to Alex's hysterics, having her apartment strewn with tissues, and giving a health report to Alex's boss practically every morning, Serena said to her on the third Saturday morning of her stay, "I have an idea. Why don't you come to Club Anabel's with us tonight? It'd be a bit of craic."

"I don't think I could. The thought of missing him . . ."

"It'd be a chance to forget everything for one night at least. Dress up, get out there, and show the world that you don't give a rat's ass for the fucker."

Alex shook her head and burrowed back down into Serena's bed.

"Come on, Alex, you've got to get out. You haven't left this apartment in a fortnight. You'll get fired if you don't get your act together."

"I can't face the outside world."

"Yes, you can. Beneath that marshmallow exterior you're a strong woman."

Alex sniffed, got out of bed, and stared into her friend's mirror. "God, look at me. I haven't given my appearance a thought," she said. "I've never looked worse."

"You've looked worse," Serena said.

"I have? When?"

"When your dog, Caesar, died."

"That was nine years ago, and I'd had him from a puppy."

"I remember. You were distraught."

Alex sighed. "You're right. I do look distraught, no point in going to Anabel's. Nobody'd give me a second glance."

She hopped back into bed.

Serena rose to her feet. "Have a shower and get dressed."

Serena dressed her up in a strappy white top to show off the St. Tropez fake tan she'd smothered her in, and lent her a pair of tight black trousers and spindly high heels.

"Are you sure I look all right?" Alex asked, twisting and turning unsteadily in front of the mirror.

"Smashing. Come on, you're wasting valuable man-chasing time. You want to get in there and knock their eyeballs out."

How Alex was going to get through the night she'd no idea. She'd been single for exactly a fortnight, and much as she tried to stave off the desperation that comes from being unattached, she couldn't. It was too lonely.

In Anabel's Serena and her friends marched up to the Members' Bar, Alex trailing behind, her nerves jangling, self-conscious in Serena's cling-wrap trousers.

"Get that down you." Serena put a bottle of Heineken in her hand.

Alex drank it down quickly, and hung back while the others trawled around the dance floor, sizzling with excitement and anticipation. The throbbing music, the flashing lights made her head spin. She bought herself

another bottle of Heineken, and watched the girls suss-
ing out the talent in a bid to attract anyone vaguely
desirable, Serena's trousers uncomfortable against her
bladder. She had another bottle of Heineken to pluck
up the courage to go to the loo, by which time she was
bursting.

When she got back to the bar, Serena was waiting for
her.

"Come on and dance," she commanded.

Before she knew it, Alex was plunged into the middle
of the frenetic crowd.

"Don't look now but you've got a secret admirer over
there," Serena said.

"Where?" Alex peered suspiciously through the crowd.

She tried not to stare openmouthed at the tall young
man with black hair and Mediterranean-blue eyes, who was
dancing at full throttle to Daft Punk's "One More Time,"
his biceps, big as babies' heads, jiggling to a rhythm of their
own.

He caught her eye and danced toward her, writhing
around, making her laugh with his wild, jerking movements. She had no alternative but to respond. Waving her
arms in the air, swinging her hips, gasping for breath, she
whirled in all directions, thinking that she must be drunk,
and that what she was doing was positively dangerous in
heels that high.

Suddenly she teetered, and crashed headlong into him.
He caught her in a tight, steadying grip, grinding his
pelvis into her, engulfing her in a blazing heat.

The music stopped. He grinned at her.

"I'm Jake."

"I'm Alex."

He twanged the strap of her top. "Drink?"

Breathless, she cleared her throat, her stomach tense. "I'd love one."

She tottered after him to the bar.

He told her a few personal details, how he divided his time between his job as fitness trainer at Pulsate Sport and Leisure Center, and his rugby training.

"Fascinating," she said, taking a gulp from the bottle. She hated fitness freaks, and she wasn't mad about rugby players either.

She told him vaguely that she was PR for a firm of consultants.

"I've forgotten how noisy these places can be," she shouted, her voice cracking as the noise intensified.

"So what brought you here tonight?"

"My friend dragged me along."

He looked at her curiously.

"To help me forget a bad experience. Sorry, I shouldn't have said that. My brain's fogged up."

He laughed. "How about coming out for a drink during the week for some more 'bad experience' therapy?"

"OK."

He took her phone number.

She searched for Serena, no longer visible in the crowd. Exhaustion was overcoming her, the drink kicking in. God, she was pissed, and her feet were killing her.

Next morning she opened her eyes slowly. Her head was pounding. She put one foot gingerly on the floor, then the other, and staggered into the kitchen.

Serena was drinking coffee, slumped over the kitchen table.

"What a night!" she said. "You must have bruises everywhere from dancing . . . well, throwing yourself around the floor."

Alex put her finger to her lips, "Shh . . . I'm trying not to think about it."

"Still, you scored with what's his name?"

"Jake." Alex smiled, strangely exhilarated as visions of Jake stamping around the floor came flooding back.

"Are you going to see him again?"

"He says he'll phone. Wants to meet me for a drink."

"I'm jealous."

Alex continued to smile. "He hardly knows my name, and at a glance you can see he's far too young for me."

"He's a man, isn't he? And a gorgeous one at that. The trouble with you, Alex, is that you think too far ahead. You want to seize the moment. So what if it doesn't last longer than the next date? It's a chance to get out. Isn't that all you want?"

The following Thursday night Alex met Jake in Sinnot's.

Quietly, over a couple of drinks, he gently barraged her with questions about her bad experience: Was it boyfriend trouble? Had it been really that bad? Did going to the disco help?

She answered all the questions frankly, and finished by saying, "Strange, isn't it? You're going along, leading a normal life, then whoosh, it all goes wrong, and just when you least expect it."

"So what went wrong?" he asked, riveted. "Or is that too personal a question?"

Alex sighed. "It was getting too heavy, at least that's what he said. Collapsed under the strain, I suppose." She took another swig from the bottle. "Only I didn't see it coming."

"You know what you need?" Jake said.

She rested her chin on her cupped hand, looked deep into his eyes.

"I suppose you're going to tell me."

"Exercise."

"Exercise! I'm not fat!"

He laughed. "Burn off that loss. Look, see here." He ran his forefinger across her back. "Your body is tense, especially in your shoulders and neck area. It's because you're allowing the negative effects of stress to paralyze you, and not using it to maximize performance."

"What!"

"It's not your fault. It's the result of your bad experience. Now, I can devise a simple exercise schedule to de-stress you, and get you fit."

"What do I have to do?"

"Come to the gym; we'll start with a swim."

"I haven't been in a swimming pool for years," Alex exclaimed.

"No time like the present. Come tomorrow morning, about seven, when there are no classes in session."

Alex said, "OK. I'll give it a go."

A few cars were parked outside Pulsate Sport and Leisure Center. Alex passed the squash courts and tennis courts, and went straight to the pool. In the changing rooms she put on Serena's swimsuit, a size too small, and went in. The smell of chlorine and warm air assailed her nostrils, reminding her of how much she detested swimming.

Her heart skipped a beat as Jake appeared before her, a Health God, in tiny swimming trunks that left nothing to the imagination, and made her eyes bulge. His Speedo cap had Pulsate written on it.

"You made it." He smiled engagingly at her.

She stood, feeling foolish, clutching her towel in front of her to hide her bikini line, cellulite and legs that needed waxing.

"Come on, get in." He arched his back, and dived in, laughing, breaking the tension. There was something dangerous and exciting about him as he sliced through the water with a smooth, effortless crawl. Turning, he swam back to where she was standing knee deep, shivering.

"I can't swim that well," Alex moaned.

"Hold still," he said, cupping her chin in his hands to align her, his hard body against her fragile one. "Follow that line." He pointed to the black line on the bottom of the pool. "And try to keep your head in the water."

She slogged along, lurching from side to side, gulping in air. Next time her head came up he was sitting at the side of the pool, smiling salaciously at her.

"Good. One more time."

This time he swam along with her at her pace, until she staggered out, collapsing at the aluminum ladder, panting in an effort to catch her breath as she climbed out.

He took her elbow, draped her in a towel, and eased her into a chair.

"I'm in terrible shape," she said, wiggling her finger in her ear to unclog it.

"We'll soon sort you out," he grinned, patting her back gently with the towel.

She looked longingly at the window running off to the side of the pool, *Cafeteria* written on it in red lights.

"I'd love a coffee. Have you got time for one?"

"A quick one. I've got a class in a quarter of an hour."

Hurriedly she showered, dressed, and went to meet him, looking like a drowned rat.

"I can't do it," she said, dragging on her cigarette over her steaming cup. "I don't really like swimming pools."

"We'll try the circuit-training then."

Jake demonstrated the various machines, bench-pressing effortlessly, running on the treadmill, and cycling nowhere on the exercise bike. Alex hated them all.

"Jogging! That's good for stress," Jake said.

"Oh no!" she cried, breaking out in a cold sweat at the very idea.

"It's fun. I'll be happy to put you through your paces, say tomorrow morning in the park, seven sharp."

"Tomorrow!"

"No time like the present."

Serena said, "You could do with it," when Alex told her.

The following morning Alex's alarm went off at half-past six. She stood in front of the mirror and gazed into her bleary eyes and blotchy face, white as a bottle of milk, the challenge of jogging with Jake more of a nightmare than even the swimming was.

Reluctantly she drove to the park, togged out in her very unsexy tracksuit. The early morning air was moist, the haze promising a hot day ahead. Through the trees she could see Jake in his dazzling white T-shirt, shorts and Nike trainers, bending and stretching, sexuality oozing from every pore.

"You made it," he said, smiling engagingly at her.

"Just about."

He came and put his hands on her shoulders. "We'll do a warm-up, nothing too strenuous to start with. Get your body healthy so that it can perform properly."

Alex liked his smooth movements as he stretched his arms to the sky, then lowered them slowly. She did the same.

"That was easy," she smiled.

"Good. Now a simple exercise to strengthen the muscles in the lower leg area."

Taking off his trainers and socks, standing with one bare foot on the edge of a step, he lifted himself up on his toes very slowly and, keeping his back straight, came back down. He repeated with his other leg what he'd just done.

"Now you have a go, nice and slow."

"I've never done this before."

"Good, isn't it?"

He rotated from side to side, put his arms out like propellers, made circles with them.

"Tighten that butt," he called to her. "Feels good, doesn't it?"

Standing on one foot he raised himself up on his toes, and clasped his other foot in his hand.

Alex tried it, wobbled and fell over.

"It's too difficult," she wailed.

He hunkered down beside her. "It's not, you know," he said, solicitously. "You just have to get the basic concept right in your head. Coordination, that's the whole thing. There's nothing complicated about it. Now let's get going," he continued, helping her up, stepping forward. "We'll do the circle. Start slow."

They set off, Jake jogging at a relaxed pace, keeping a smooth pattern all the way, his hair flopping into his eyes, Alex running along beside him, the idea of jogging the circumference of the park unappetizing.

"Gives you a glowing feeling, doesn't it?" he said, raising the pace gradually.

"You could say that," she panted.

Halfway around she fell back, cursing. "I've had it," she gasped, leaning against a tree, wheezing.

He handed her a bottle of water. She took a gulp.

"You're not dropping out?" He stood over her, sweat breaking out on his brow, and around his neck, molding his T-shirt to the contours of his body.

"I need a fag."

"No, you don't."

"Health nut," she gasped, taking another gulp.

He smirked. "Come on."

They jogged a bit further until, crawling on her hands and knees, gasping for air, clammy, disorientated, Alex begged for mercy, and more water.

A large raindrop fell.

Delighted, she said, "That's it. I'm not getting soaked into the bargain."

He walked her to her car. "If you do this each morning, stretching for ten minutes' warm-up, jog for fifty minutes, ten minutes' warm-down, no strain, drink water, you'll get fit, and have something to focus on other than your problem."

"Too much hardship."

Jake laughed. "Hardship's good for you. It lifts your spirits, builds your character, and it'll help you to grow that thick layer of skin that you need to cope with wankers like your ex."

Alex laughed. "What a load of crap!" And got into her car.

They jogged each morning for the next fortnight, during which time Alex moved into an apartment of her own above Serena's, helped by Jake. She collected her belongings from Nigel's apartment, under his secretary's supervision, a task she'd dreaded doing, but managed without too much bother.

She continued to jog with Jake in the mornings. In the evenings she fell onto her sofa, or went to bed too tired to think. He called around the occasional evening she was home early, happy to get engrossed in a video, or eat a pizza from Alex's new fridge stocked with frozen, vegetarian, ready-made meals.

There were no lengthy discussions about her work. He'd no interest in it, which was a refreshing change from Nigel, who was always challenging her after a demanding day.

She said to Jake one evening after a particularly grueling day at work, "I don't think this exercise is working. I still feel stressed."

"You look pretty fabulous to me," Jake said, eyeing her up and down. "In fact, I think you should come with me to the Lakeside Health and Leisure Conference in Galway next weekend. I could show you off."

Weekend! Conference! A tremor went through her. She felt flattered. Then she tried to imagine making love to him, but her fantasies let her down, thinking of him as too young for her. Also, it was hardly worthwhile to interest herself in a situation she would be snatched away from as soon as she was fit. But then, maybe he wasn't romantically interested in her.

She said, "I don't think that's a good idea. I mean it isn't as if we're dating or anything."

"Aren't we?" He put his arms around her, folded her into him, and held her for an instant.

Embarrassed, she moved away. "Jake, I'm old enough to be your . . . older sister."

"I don't care. I like you just the way you are."

"Besides, I'm in love with someone else."

As soon as she said it, she was sorry. Her words hung between them, the atmosphere charged, his stricken look making her feel like a child who'd misbehaved at a party.

"You knew that," she said, trying to qualify her remark, making it worse.

He gathered himself together and stood up. "I don't care. I want you to come."

That night she slept fitfully and, waking up in the morning panic-stricken, rushed down to consult Serena.

Serena said, "You're approaching this the wrong way. He's a man, isn't he? Someone to go places with, hold hands with, if you like. Go. If it doesn't work out, you won't be heartbroken. Besides, it might be a good opportunity to meet Mr. Right. You won't know unless you go."

"I hadn't thought of that."

"You should think of it. You don't want to be alone for the rest of your life. You'd die from sexual starvation for a start," Serena quipped.

"I could bring home a stranger occasionally, to keep the proverbial sexual wolf from the door."

"Or at the door, depending how you look at it," Serena giggled.

Alex decided that rather than deal with the consequences of refusing Jake again, and hurting him further, she'd go, and she told him so next morning in the park.

"Great," he said, taking his mobile phone from his pocket, stabbing the keys to make the necessary reservations.

When they arrived at Lakeside Health and Leisure Center, Jake took their bags into the lobby.

Alex was making her way to the reception desk when he stopped her.

"I've got a room booked for us. We're checked in."

They faced each other.

Alex, ready to protest, but not wanting to cause a scene in public, let him lead the way to the elevator.

In their bedroom she turned to him.

"What's the matter?" he asked as he slid off her jacket and released the clasp that held her hair.

"We can't do this, Jake."

He took her hand. "Oh yes we can." He touched the corner of her mouth with his lips, his breath warm on her face. "What do you think we're doing?" He teased her neck playfully with butterfly kisses.

She opened her mouth to say something. He closed it with tantalizing, feathery kisses.

Shivering, she moved back, shaking her head, gazing at him. "It'll spoil everything between us."

"No, it won't, trust me." His smile was full of knowledge and wisdom beyond his years and beyond that moment; he kissed her again, hard this time, his tongue circling her mouth, his raw, sexual energy pouring into her.

After a long time he released her. "I've been waiting for you," he said.

His eyes, deep and inexhaustible, spoke to her in a clear, uncomplicated way that stopped her in her tracks and possessed her. Reaching for her hand, he pulled her toward the bed.

She went willingly, her lust for him making her shudder.

Early one morning, a few weeks later, Alex was leaving her apartment to go to the park when Nigel's car appeared from nowhere.

He got out and stood looking at her, standing there precariously. The Alex he'd known had been spirited away, and in her place stood this beautiful stranger in white jockey shorts and skimpy top, her hair tied back, her face glowing. It was difficult to define in what way she'd changed, but she looked more mature, definitely more beautiful, and that body!

He went up to meet her.

"Hello," he said, taking a quick glance around to make sure they were alone. "How are you? Are you in love with anyone?" was what he really wanted to ask.

"Hi." She met his gaze, and instantly lowered her eyes with an air of uncertainty he'd never associated with her.

"I heard through the grapevine that you'd taken up jogging."

"It was a welcome distraction." She stood back, displaying friendliness to him, but trying not to show more than a passing interest.

"I wanted to see you, I didn't like to phone. I need to talk to you in private."

"What about?"

"Can I explain?" he asked, taking her arm, leading her back inside.

She looked at her watch. "I have to go in a minute."

"This won't take long."

"If you're quick then." She stood in her hallway, looking at him.

"Alex, it's painful to say this, but I've been miserable since we parted, clinging to the memories. I made a terrible mistake. I miss you."

"Are you being funny?"

"No, I'm deadly serious. I was wrong. I thought we were just going through the motions, neither of us knowing how to end it. But since we split up, I realize that I don't want anyone else."

She could see the remorse in his eyes. He'd come back to her. Amazed, she looked at him for a long time.

Finally she said, a new spark in her eyes, "I made a serious mistake too, clinging on for far too long, and then not knowing what to do when my world came crashing down around my ears. You see, I never expected it to happen to me. It was a shock."

"I'm sorry. It will never happen again, I promise."

"I know it won't, Nigel. Now, I really must go. Jake is waiting for me."

"Jake?"

"He's a fitness trainer." She stood in defensive strain, as if an explanation was due, and she could think of no good one.

"Your own personal trainer, no less!"

Alex looked at the ground. "He's a friend."

"You're seeing each other?"

"Yes."

"He's the wrong type for you, Alex."

"What do you mean?"

"He's bound to be inferior intellectually, financially and socially to you."

She glanced at him. "Listen, I hate to spoil the pleasure of this meeting but I have to go."

He hurried after her.

"Wait a minute."

"Not if you're going to be insulting. I don't appreciate either being put in this embarrassing situation, or your comments, and I really do have to go."

"Look, I'm sure he's a terrific lad, but let's face it . . ."

"You're so patronizing, Nigel. Jake's a kind, caring person, and the sort of person I needed when you dumped me."

"All muscles and testosterone."

"You could say that, but at least he knows how to please a woman, and he's easy to have around too."

"Can't talk to you about your work though?"

"Suits me fine."

"Can't afford your expensive tastes, I'll bet?"

"I've got my own money. Now, I'm going."

"Alex, I came here to ask you to marry me. You can give up your job, come and live in Brussels for a while. You'd love it."

"Ugh! I can't imagine anything worse than giving up my job."

"Surely marrying me is worth a consideration?"

Alex thought for a second. "Yes, it's worse than having to give up my job."

"Alex!"

She was gone, unlocking her car door, turning to look back at him standing gaping after her in his dark, hand-stitched Louis Copeland suit.

She took off at speed, no mercy in her heart for him.

Jake was waiting for her in the park.

"You're late," he said, mischief in his eyes, his body enticing as he came to meet her.

She jogged beside him, her step light, happy to be with him, judging by the envious stares of the other jogging women they passed that she was doing what they could only dream of.

Jake had renewed her spirit, lifted the weight of the world from her shoulders with his exercise regime, and restored her confidence by making her feel loved and wanted. So what if he was nearly eight years younger than she was; she felt reborn, like a teenager.

————

JOAN O'NEILL began her writing career in 1987 with short stories and serials. Her first novel, *Daisy Chain War*, published in 1990, won the Reading Association of Ireland Special Merit Award and was shortlisted for the Bisto Award. It is regarded as one of the foremost Irish novels for teenagers. Since then, she has also become a best-selling novelist for adults with her highly acclaimed novels, *Leaving Home, Turn of the Tide, A House Full of Women* and, most recently, *Something Borrowed, Something Blue*.

The Twenty-Eighth Day

Catherine Barry

I am sitting at the breakfast table with my husband, Michael, the man I normally love, cherish and adore. Only I will not love and cherish and adore him for the next twenty-four hours. I will detest, despise and resent the very air he breathes because I have PMT. I am trying very hard to ignore the loud slurping noises emanating from his corner as he performs an archaeological dig on a bowl of cornflakes. He scrapes the bottom with a metal spoon. The noise is worse than two skeletons fighting to get out of a biscuit tin. I know I have PMT. I know what it is. I know why it happens. I know all about the hormonal imbalance. But all the knowledge in the world will not abate the terrific storm that looms in our normally happy abode. I know that it passes and I know I can't help

the way I feel. All the same, it doesn't stop me from wanting to stick a knife in Michael's eye.

Ellie, my eight-year-old, wanders into the kitchen. Her
blond ponytails are matted in Sabrina's Secrets hair mascara. She has a ton of lipstick on, and none of it is on her
lips. She stands at the table with her new violin. She
places the bow on the strings. The noise that comes out
sounds like a bag of suffocating cats. She's only had three
lessons and she's bloody awful. I try not to cover my ears.

"Hello, munchkin," Michael says to her. Hello, he
says, to *her*. Not a good morning to me. He did that
deliberately. The swine. He'll do everything in his power
to trip me up. Well, he can sing. I'm not going to utter
one profanity or make one mistake this time. It doesn't
occur to me that I haven't exactly showered him with
love and adoration and overt affection, nor does it occur
to me that within five seconds I will have offended every
breathing entity within my radius and not have a clue
why.

"Ellie, have you been at my makeup bag again?" I snap
at the little mite. She is waiting for me to tell her how
good she is on the violin, but my wincing has convinced
her to put it away.

The narkiness is not directed toward her or even him,
but I am powerless to shut my mouth. It will do exactly as
it pleases and I will be completely at its mercy for the
whole day. What I really need is one of those muzzles, you
know, like Hannibal Lecter in *Silence of the Lambs*? I'm
not fit to be let out, let alone speak. I contemplate taking
a large dose of sleeping pills that will knock me uncon-
scious for the waiting duration until the blessed period
arrives. At best, Michael might hold off with the divorce

papers, which is what he threatened me with the last time. He's always saying he will leave home when the next bout of madness comes around. With the daggers looks that are being exchanged at present, genocide seems a more likely outcome. I know by Michael's face that he is aware it's that time of the month. I can't stand the sight of him. His very presence is annoying me. I hate the way he makes those little grunting noises. He looks fat and old and I can't remember one tiny ant-sized good thing about him. Actually, I can't even remember why I married him. Look at the state of him. Smiling away to himself. The great big eejit. Happy he is. The fucking nerve. He's no right to be happy when I feel like a bag of shit. He's doing that to annoy me as well. The "I'm a happy, normal, well-adjusted, balanced human being" thing. As opposed to "You're a crazed lunatic with a potentially lethal kitchen utensil and I'm pretending not to notice that my life is at stake."

I play with the frying pan and conclude it would be better to use it for the purpose God intended. I fry some eggs and then realize nobody eats them in our house. I nonchalantly throw them in the bin and wonder what I'm supposed to be doing. The atmosphere is so tense, you could stick a dinosaur tooth in it.

"Ellie, check if your PE gear is in your bag and take that muck off your face immediately," I snap.

She grumbles.

"Now," I command.

One glare from the cave woman with the bulging eyes and mad hair sends her running. Ellie and I both know that the PE gear is in her bag but it doesn't stop my mouth from stating the obvious. She checks what she already knows is there and wanders back in and gives *him* a hug. Michael kisses her and they have a little cuddle. They're conspiring. They're in it together. I'm on to them though, I'm not stupid!

"Ellie, what do you want for breakfast?" I ask wearily.

"Honey Nut Cheerios in the flower bowl with the pink spoon," she answers.

I can't find the flower bowl or the pink spoon. I bash and bang around the kitchen looking for them and then it dawns on me he hid them deliberately. I may be completely off my trolley, but I ain't dumb. I slam down a ginormous bowl that I usually make sherry trifle in. I fill it with cornflakes and pour too much milk in it. It dribbles over the side and looks like it's alive. I plunge a tablespoon into it.

No one in their right mind is going to challenge me about it.

Michael gets up. Any minute now and he will be off to his nice job, sitting at his nice desk, talking with nice adults—nice blond, buxom female adults—and having a fine dandy day. What have I got to look forward to? A trunkload of laundry and having my elbows immersed in parazone for the next three hours. The highlight of the day will be an over-the-wall chat with Mrs. Bucket next door. The one with the house that looks so perfect I swear little elves are doing the cleaning during the night. It's always spick-and-span, the perfect display house for magazine articles like "Superior decors for inferior feckers" or "How to make you feel even more crap about your nonexistent domestic skills."

She amazes the hell out of me. The house is a palatial work of art but *she* looks like something that just crawled out of a wheelie bin. She has no dress sense or personal hygiene standards. There's no need for any woman to be sporting designer stubble and go around smelling of Jeyes fluid and hamster droppings. And that kid of hers. That snotty little four-year-old torment drives me insane. Why can't she wipe his nose instead of the kitchen table, just occasionally? Why doesn't she do something about the two streams of green slime that permanently ooze from his nostrils? I don't know why he gets these delusions every time he sees me coming. His face lights up and his hands go out expectantly. For some strange reason he seems to think I might have a surprise for him. Oh, I would love to give him a surprise now. Yeah. A good kick up the . . .

"Betty, we've no teabags again." Michael's voice brings me back.

He is standing beside me and hasn't brushed his teeth yet. He smells like a Kellogg factory and it makes me sick. If he goes to kiss me, I will spew. No need to worry. He leaves the sentence unfinished and we both glance at the calendar hanging on the wall. Michael has ringed the twenty-eighth day in a big fat black felt pen. I don't think it's a particularly funny gesture. He doesn't have to go through this hell every month. He doesn't know what it's like to be a woman. PMT, periods, pregnancy, labor pain, hysterectomies and finally the long-suffering menopause, after which we hurtle onwards to certain death. At least there's something to look forward to. It's a relief to know that really.

"You forgot, didn't you?" he barely whispers.

Michael nods at the calendar again. Does he really think I'm sane enough to handle a comment like that?

Does he value his life at all? Does he not realize we are in the kitchen and the carving knife is within arm's reach?

"How could I forget?" I roar at him, tearing the calendar off the wall. How insensitive can he get? I think to myself; *I know I have PMT.* I know I'm away with the fairies. Does he want me to put a sign on my back or something? AWAY WITH THE BIRDS. BACK TOMORROW.

"Huh?" he stares at me, utterly confused.

He's pretending to play dumb. He's noticed the carving knife and my itching fingers dangerously drumming nearby.

"I'm talking about the . . ." he fades off.

I give him the deranged look. The one that should permit any husband the right to commit me to the home for the bewildered. He steps back in abject terror. All he is short of doing is thrusting a crucifix in my face and screaming: "Come out! Come out, whoever you are! I command you to leave this woman's body immediately!"

I can't say I blame him. I feel as if the devil and all his distant cousins possess me. I am being tormented and tortured by some unknown force I cannot touch or feel. It's like somebody else has taken over my body, mind and soul. There is a demon spirit inside me, telling me to do inappropriate things, prompting me to say hurtful, offensive words, urging me to be the meanest bitch that ever walked the earth. I wish they would all fuck off and find someone else to haunt. I'm a zoo of multiple personalities and there's no more room at the inn.

If it gets any worse, there may be murders committed and I start praying for Michael to get the hint and leave. He does. He turns away, looking sad and offended. What has he got to be hurt over? The great big sack of self-centered self-pity! I hear the door shut quietly, but the noise echoes through my brain like an orchestra of crashing cymbals. My sense of sound is heightened and I already have that familiar throbbing, tense headache. It feels as if someone has tied a band around my head and is squeezing it tighter and tighter. I need some Anadin Extra but can't remember where they are.

Ellie is at my side, tugging at my dressing gown. I hate it when she does that.

"What?" I ask, irritation spilling out.

"Mam, I'm late and you're not even dressed," she pleads.

"Right." I remember now.

I have to get dressed. I climb the stairs wearily and walk into my bedroom. There is a dirty cup and a magazine lying on the floor. But I do not see that. My eyes are affected as well as everything else. It looks like the Dunsink Dumping Ground. I don't know where to start. I feel overwhelmed. I'm so confused. I try to think about how I will cope with all the things I have to do even though I know I don't really have anything more to do than I did yesterday. I cannot bear the dirty room that isn't dirty.

I go looking for clothes. Confusion. Oh, please don't give me choices today! I cannot decide what to wear. My pajama top is stuck to me from sweat, always a sign that I am in the war zone. I can't be bothered taking it off. I dream of climbing into bed as soon as I have left Ellie at school and want to aspire to minimal effort as my goal for the day. I pull on a pair of jeans but the zip won't go up. I normally look about three months' pregnant anyway, but this morning I look like I am three weeks over the estimated date of delivery. My stomach is bloated and full of wind. I pull the jeans off and pull on a dirty pair of black tracksuit bottoms. I look in the mirror and die with the shame. My face has erupted. I am covered in spots and pimples and they are really sore to the touch. My hair is greasy and limp despite having been washed only yesterday. I look like a turned-out bread and butter pudding with a few raisins thrown on top. I look fat, dumpy and ugly. I feel fat, dumpy and ugly.

I race down the stairs, pulling Ellie behind me and telling her to hurry up when it is me that is delaying everything and she has been ready for over half an hour.

"Right. Get a move on, Ellie." I nudge her out of the door.

"Mam?" she says, bringing her eyes down to my feet.

"What now?" I ask, exasperated, and it's not even 9 A.M.

I look down myself and see the problem.

"You're wearing your slippers," she sighs.

"I knew that. Get in the car," I snap.

Actually I didn't know that, but I'm not giving in, no sirree, not by a long shot.

I open the gates and the boot of the car and throw her stuff in haphazardly. We get in, I reverse out onto the road and only then does it become apparent that I left my bag on the roof of the car. I jam on the brakes and the contents spill out onto the road. An irate woman in a jeep swerves to avoid me and beeps several times in succession. Those stupid-looking military monsters. What are they doing buying jeeps, for God's sake, when the road has a ramp every ten yards? They gaze down at you from their mile-high position of presumed power and bully their way along residential streets and block the whole road outside the schools. I mean, it's not exactly fucking *Out of Africa* in Donaghmede, is it?

"Yeah. Yeah!" I shout after her. She probably has it too. The PMT, that is. Imagine if all the women in the world had PMT at the same time. Nothing to imagine really. No need for red buttons or any of that rubbish. And you can certainly shelve your retirement plans for that cottage in Connemara. There won't be any Connemara. Let them all out at 8 A.M. and the human race, as we know it, would be extinct by 8:15 A.M. (give or take a moment or two).

As soon as I have dropped Ellie off at school and battled my way through the intimidating tanks overtaking me on the ramps, I collapse into my bed. My back is aching. A slow, dull ache that will nag all day. If I bend down at all, I feel like I have been weight-training. I lie in the bed feeling sorry for myself and start to feel guilty. I could have been nicer to Ellie. I never even kissed her goodbye. Michael never kissed me goodbye either but then again, he doesn't love me and he doesn't care about me. If he did, he wouldn't have put me through the cornflakes thing. I bet he's having an affair with someone. They're probably swapping cornflake particles behind the water dispenser as I speak. I pine in grief-stricken silence.

I get up and decide to go to the shops. There are no teabags as per usual and I am determined Michael won't get the better of me. I write "teabags" on the back of my hand just to be on the safe side. My back is really killing me. I need to get some Anadin for it. Besides, I had better pick up his suit or there will be another outburst of unwanted temper. I make a quick cup of watery coffee, remembering Michael didn't bring me any in bed this morning. How selfish and inconsiderate! Typical. He ought to know I need to be pampered. He definitely doesn't love me. *No one loves me . . .*

I look around the kitchen and the breakfast things are still sitting on the table. All of a sudden the skirting boards look manky dirty and the curtains need a wash too. Those carpets are awful-looking and the walls need a lick of paint. The whole house is a filthy, dirty mess and I'm a failure. I can't stand it. I can't stand the house. The four walls are closing in on me. I have to get out of it, now.

I sniffle my way to the supermarket, determined not to leave it without what I came in for, but I am sidetracked almost instantly and decide to visit my favorite Boots store. I am immediately drawn to the "pick and mix smartie counter" (the medicinal aisle, for those of you more emotionally balanced individuals). Mmm, yummy tablets. Some nice little red ones, oh and some blue ones; hey, they look cute. Yes. Now, starflower oil, vitamin B6, evening primrose oil, Waterfall tablets for the bloated tummy, strawberry-flavored Remegel for the excessive flatulence that is sure to arrive after I binge on a shopping bag full of high-calorie, fat-saturated, sugar-loaded goodies. Feminax for the agony of period pain and Anadin Extra for the headache. Not forgetting some cream for the facial explosions. Oh, and St. John's Wort and some "calm" drops. No, wait. I see something more interesting. I put back the calm drops and pick up another bottle called "Serenity." I choose that one instead because there are more letters in the title and "serenity" sounds a damn sight better than calm. I'm not either. Who am I kidding? I wander up and down the other aisles, grabbing unwanted items and throwing them in the trolley. I stand at the shampoo counter for ten minutes, trying to figure out why I am there. I know there is something. Oh yes. Sanitary towels for the onslaught. I pick up a packet of Ultra Always. With wings. With wings? What next? Boeing 747s with chilled champagne, free newspaper and window seat? I wish . . .

I notice the security assistant sidle up beside me. He is watching me like a hawk and I know he has me down for a thief or a drug addict. Not surprisingly, as I arrive at the checkout with a trolley load of drugs and a huge bag of doughnuts. (There's also a padlock in there. I've no idea why I am buying a padlock, so don't ask . . .) I look like a strung-out junkie who has just won the full house on *Telly Bingo*.

I start to hum to myself.

"Telly Bingo Friday night, Telly Bingo Friday night . . ."

The security assistant is right beside me. He discreetly covers his mouth with his hand. He is whispering into one of those walkie-talkie things. I imagine his alarmed plea for assistance: "Guys, we've got a real live one here. A member of the tutti- frutti club, if I ever laid eyes on one. The lift doesn't go all the way to the top, if you get my gist. I suggest calling in backup. All SWAT teams on red alert. Over."

I pay up and get out fast before the men in the white coats come and straitjacket me. I arrive home about lunchtime, exhausted and with my back aching. I'm dying for a cup of tea and the sugar cravings, which have been bugging me since early morning, have reached fever pitch. I put on the kettle and get out a nice clean mug. Then I realize. I forgot the bloody teabags. What's new?

I settle for coffee again and curl up in front of the telly. Sally Jessy is on. Great. Just what I need. The show is about reunions. There are women sitting in a row on the stage claiming undying love for men they haven't seen in twenty years and have not been able to contact. Hey presto! The men appear from backstage and they run into each other's arms. I'm not able to cope with the emotion of it. I'm in bits. I can't stop crying. It's like a waterfall. I try to get ahold of myself but it's no use. I am crying for Ireland. I switch channels. I start watching a program about the Eskimo fishing industry. A guy has his head in a pool of water. It's no use. I'm still sobbing my eyes out. I ravage the last of the jam doughnuts and feel full of wind. I take some Remegel to deal with the fallout. I'm miserable and lonely and depressed. Only six more hours and the whole thing will be over. Only six more hours and I will once again be human and it will be safe for others to approach me without putting their lives in danger.

I amble back up to the school to collect Ellie at two o'clock. I have a bit of a scuffle with a particularly nasty jeep that tries to ambush me out of a parking space, but I win hands down because I'm faster and driving a smaller car. Hah! The jeep is forced to park on the curb and causes an obstruction. I'm delighted with myself and shout something about the "outback" as I pass the driver up on her stilts. It's the only thing I have enjoyed today so far, but Ellie is clearly mortified and dubious about this strange woman who is supposed to be her guardian and mother. After all, she is in the passenger seat and there's a fruit and nut driving the car. She clunks her seat belt in and gives me a sideways glance. Am I really that bad, I wonder.

When we get home, I try to help her with her homework. I watch her concentrate hard on doing her joined writing. I just watch. I think about her growing up and wish there was some way I could fix it for her that she sidesteps it all. It won't be long before she becomes a woman herself and starts getting breasts and periods and boys will be ogling her. I don't want her to have to go through any of this. I can't bear the thought of letting her go. I push the stray blond strands of hair that fall on her face behind her ears so she can see better. She smiles at me and melts me for a second. I smile back. She's beautiful at eight. What's she going to be like at fourteen? Oh God. I kiss her head lightly and I start crying again. I can't help it. She stares at me in bewilderment. I get up and try to tidy the house.

For the rest of the afternoon I work like a dervish. I don't know what's come over me but I have to clean everything. Cookers get pulled out, skirting boards get washed, the Hoover is going constantly and the can of polish is almost empty. The house is spick-and-span but I'm still finding stupid things to do. It's like I'm preparing for the Pope's visit. I remember, my mam used to do this when she was due a period. "Homing," they call it. Getting ready. Getting ready for a baby. Only there's no baby. I made certain of that. Ellie is enough for us both at the moment. I think about Michael and glance at the clock. He'll be in for dinner soon. We have to get through the whole evening together. How are we going to manage it? I'll do the usual, I suppose. I'll have a long, hot bath, shave my legs, moisturize my whole body, paint my nails (and the bathroom if necessary) and hope that when I'm through he's snoring his head off. Any better suggestions?

The mouth will have its way no matter what, and all I can think of doing is locking myself in the bathroom for a couple of hours. It's completely insane.

I manage to string together a rather meek-looking dinner of chops, potatoes and vegetables. Michael strolls in, looking tired and hot. He nods at me and sits down at the table. As soon as he starts to eat, I go to exit.

"I'd kill for a cup of tea," he sighs.

Fuck. The teabags. I hide my hand behind my back.

"I was just about to have a bath," I try.

"Go ahead. I'll get them at the corner shop," he says quietly.

That's odd, I think. He's not fighting with me. He's not pouncing on me like he usually does about my interminable forgetfulness during PMT. I get in the nice hot bath and immediately my back feels the benefit. I am up to my chin in bath oil and bubbles and I am playing some soft dolphin music to try and calm my grating nerves. I can empathize with the dolphins and I'm sure they can identify with me. I look like one myself, that's probably why.

I take over an hour in the bath. I can hear Michael taking Ellie to bed. Thank God. I am not in the humor for reading *Harry Potter and the Chamber of Secrets* tonight. I am in my own chamber of secrets and feel like my body is a passenger on a coffin ship. I wade backward and forward in the slippery bathtub and when my skin begins to wrinkle I reluctantly climb out. I set about doing my beauty regime with deliberately prolonged attention to detail. I even paint my toes and give myself a facial scrub before applying the spot cream. I take ages drying my hair.

When I finally tiptoe upstairs I can hear Michael snoring. Yippee! I've won! I creep past Ellie's door, which is slightly ajar. She is asleep on her back with two huge chunks of cucumber on her eyes. Another one of Sabrina's Secrets, I guess. It makes me laugh. I paddle over to the side of her bed and kiss her lightly on the forehead. I remove the wedges of cucumber and she mutters something about "Hagrid." It's been a hard day for her. Tomorrow will be different. I can already feel the niggling first cramps of period pain in the base of my abdomen. It's on the way. I can sense it. I slip in beside Michael, who is too deep in sleep to even notice he has company. I am relieved. I drift off myself and dream I am the Captain of the Quidditch team at Hogwarts School of Magic; well, come on now, at least it's innocent . . .

When I awake, the cramps are in full swing. I already have a sanitary towel on and can feel the first trickling of my period as it arrives at last. I'm in physical pain now but I would still welcome it any day in preference to the black cloud that sits over my head in the days leading up to it. I immediately feel better. I turn over to hug Michael, but he's not there. I glance at the clock. It's late and I missed him. He must have taken Ellie to school. The pet. Suddenly, I am in love with him again and wonder how I could ever have harbored such ill will toward him yesterday. I miss him now and want to kiss him and hug him and tell him I love him. I feel guilty about it again, the mysterious illness that destroys my relationships once a month. I'll have to call him, or do something special for him today. Perhaps I'll make a nice meal this evening?

I get up and go downstairs to find the kitchen immaculate. The little darlings. They knew I would be tired and sore. Evidence of Ellie's help is everywhere. I can see she tried to fold some tea towels, but gave up when they refused to become square-shaped.

There is a cup and a saucer and a spoon laid out. Inside the cup is a teabag. I put the kettle on and then see the small card that's lurching against the side of the salt cellar.

I pour the water into the cup, swirling it around as I read the card.

"Happy Anniversary, Betty. Enjoy the cup of tea."

Happy Anniversary? Oh shit. It all comes back to me. The memory part of my brain is working again. The twenty-eighth day was our tenth wedding anniversary. I think of Michael leaving this morning and how horrible I was to him yesterday and all the time he was trying to tell me something else. I burst into tears I feel so overwhelmed with remorse and guilt.

I am still swirling the teabag but it's making an awful racket.

It sounds like there's something metal stuck in it.

I haul it out.

There is something in it.

A beautiful solid gold eternity ring.

I slip it on my finger and it fits perfectly.

"Oh Betty, shame on you," I sniffle out loud to myself, recognizing the voice.

It's me. Betty. I'm back in my own body. I've survived intact but I'm none the wiser for the experience. The whole thing seems comical now. I am laughing and crying at the same time. I reach for the phone to call Michael, but just before I do . . .

I look to the calendar. I get the big black felt pen. I put a big X through the twenty-eighth day. Just in case I forget to remember, next month.

———

CATHERINE BARRY lives in Dublin with her two young children. The author of numerous poems and short stories, her first novel, *The House That Jack Built,* was published in 2001.

Thelma, Louise and the Lurve Gods

Cathy Kelly

he taxi driver thought Becky was a bit of all right.
"Got any room for me in your rucksack, love?"
he said, winking back at us and showing an expanse of
nicotine-stained teeth. As if a 29-year-old blond babe
would be even vaguely interested in some fat slob who'd
never see fifty again and who had the remains of his
breakfast on his beard.

Becky gave him her "drop dead, moron" look, a fierce
glare which usually made even the cockiest bloke gulp
and start examining his cuticles. Not this bloke. Mr.
Missing Link just grinned even more.

"Bet your friend isn't so choosy," he said eagerly, giving
me the eye.

It was the story of my life. Guys who'd been given the

cold shoulder by Becky Hill (twice voted the girl "most likely to succeed" in St. Mark's Community School) always assumed that her not-so-stunning red-headed friend would be so desperate for male company that she'd give them a mercy snog. Whoever said there were advantages to being best friends with a supermodel lookalike was wrong.

"I like a girl with meat on her," slobbered the driver, admiring the size 12 denim shirt I was bursting out of in the hope that I looked a bit like either Thelma or Louise.

Becky's blue eyes narrowed to deadly slits. I recognized that look. Missing Link didn't.

"OhmiGod!" she roared. "I think I'm going to be sick. Please stop the cab!"

The thought of having his sticky, filthy upholstery made even more sticky and filthy prompted Missing Link to slam the brakes on faster than Michael Schumacher on the chicane at Silverstone.

Becky winked at me. "Ready Suze?" she whispered.

I nodded. Once the car was stopped, we dived out, clutching our rucksacks and running away.

"Oi, come back here!" yelled the outraged taxi driver. "You owe me money!"

"He catches on fast," giggled Becky as we risked life and limb by running across the road, onto the central reservation, and then over to the other side.

"It'll take him at least five minutes to get up to the next junction and come back," she crowed as the taxi driver waved his fist at us menacingly from the other side of the road.

"I'll get you little bitches!" he roared.

"Oh yeah? We'll report you to the police as a pervert first!" Becky roared back.

At that precise moment, a clean and respectable taxi, as opposed to Missing Link's ramshackle Cortina, cruised along. Becky flicked back her long, streaky blond hair, angled one tiny black-leather-clad hip forward and gave the piercing wolf whistle she'd mastered at the age of twelve. The taxi backed up.

Of course, if it had been me, no taxi would have appeared and I'd have been stuck on the Shannon airport road for another half an hour until the Missing Link man turned up with the police and had me arrested for non-payment of my fare. Then again, if it had been just me, I wouldn't have got out of the original taxi in the first place and would have endured sexual harassment all the way to the airport. But that was the difference between me and Becky.

Becky grabbed Life by the throat and shook it: I was the sort of woman who'd politely ask Life if it minded my breathing.

The airport was jammed with harassed families maneuvering overpacked luggage trolleys around and trying to hold on to Granny, little Clare's hand and the bag with all the nappies in it. Your average preholiday hell.

Becky and I grinned at each other in delight. Our holiday was going to be a million miles away from that. We weren't going to be ordinary tourists—we were going to be travelers for twenty-one glorious days. Forget a week in Benidorm or two in Greece with nothing more thrilling to look forward to than which sun lounger to lie on. We were trendy travelers who wouldn't be seen dead in a touristy joint and shunned the idea of comfortable, normal travel. We were Stateside Twenty-Oners.

In case you haven't heard of this, I'll explain. Unlike

your average holiday, a Stateside Twenty-One holiday is a trip into the unexpected: twenty-one days in the U.S. where the travelers are given a car, a map, hotel vouchers and a designated meeting spot twenty-one days later, from where they're flown home. Some people fly into Los Angeles and their meeting point is Denver. Others go for New York with Atlanta as the final destination.

It had been my idea to sign up for the trip. When I'd read the piece on the Internet about the cool new way to experience the buzz of travel without spending months away, my pulse raced. This was just what I was looking for. A one-woman odyssey into the heart of America where I would be my own boss, traveling at my own pace through the recesses of the country where the tour buses never reached. All this with the added safety factor that there were five hotels on the tour that I had to use, so people would be keeping an eye out for me and if I was kidnapped by a serial killer, Mum and Dad would soon hear about it and I'd be rescued, preferably by some hunky FBI person with big muscles and a gun. Or would it be CIA? I can never remember.

Anyway, this trip was the answer to my dreams: my dreams being how to get out of my BORING life.

Boring is the only way to describe being the telesales manager in a double-glazing firm in Limerick. Mind you, since Paul and I got disengaged (my mother hates it when I say that but how else are you supposed to say it? "We've broken it off" sounds like something painful that involves a sudden snapping noise and male howls of agony), I am slightly less boring.

Because being the sedate, double-glazing telesales manager fiancée of a bank official has got to be up there at the top of the Boring-ometer. I think there's some kudos about a broken engagement, a sort of mysterious, tragic thing in a Marlene Dietrich way. Me, heavy-lidded in a cocktail bar somewhere with a handsome man gazing deep into my eyes as I twirl the olive in my martini and languidly purr, "There was a man, long ago, a man I thought I could marry—" Sorry, daydreaming again. My mother said it'll be the end of me.

"You're always in a fantasy world, Suzanne," she says in a worried voice. "You want to spend more time in the real world, love, for your own sake."

If you ask me, the real world is not all it's cracked up to be. Give me Fantasy World with George Clooney any day.

In the real world, Paul and I had the house (two-bed town house), the beige three-seater with two armchairs (complete with fabric protector in case of stains), the savings plan, and the wedding booked for next summer. We were *that* organized. Even our sock drawers had those divider things in them so that Paul's fawn argyle socks wouldn't dare get squashed up beside his best black ones. Our holiday plans never varied from two weeks somewhere hot that wasn't more than four hours' flight away (Paul hates flying) and our idea of total, untrammeled excitement was not having a Chinese takeaway on Friday nights but . . . shock, horror . . . having a pizza instead.

Do you see where this is going? Yes, Boring City. So when Paul and I parted mutually (this is what we've told everyone because he's so sorry for what happened and promised never to reveal anything about his one-night stand with that slut in New Accounts. If he does, he can kiss goodbye to his share of the money from selling the furniture), I moved home to my family and decided a hol-

iday was in order. Not a two-weeks-anywhere holiday, but
something exotic to wrench me out of being dull as a
dodo. An adventure.

"An adventure!" yelled Becky over the phone when I
told her about my plans. Becky has nearly burst my
eardrums on several occasions. She says it's her job and
that she's always yelling because she has to talk to clients
on mobile phones in bad signal areas. She's a booker in a
model agency, the same agency which wouldn't hire her as
a model because they sadly told her she didn't have what it
took to be a photographic or a catwalk model. Personally,
I think Becky has just what it takes but she's remarkably
OK about it all and says that she just didn't photograph
right.

She photographs better than me. I'm five foot four,
built along curvy lines (which is shorthand for saying that
I'll never need one of Marks & Spencer's maximizer bras
but am an ideal candidate for their tummy-flattering
knickers) and have the sort of Celtic complexion that
looks great on the Corrs but not so good on women with
less visible bone structure. My hair is my best bit, I suppose: long, wavy and the color of molten bronze, as my
father says fondly.

Well, Becky said she was boring too. How can she
think that when she was going to wild model parties every
night of the week during those years when I was stuck at
home with Paul, circling interesting documentaries in the
TV guide? Anyway, she was determined to go with me.

"We could be like Thelma and Louise in a soft-top
sports car," she said excitedly.

"I think it'll be more on the lines of a jeep thing," I
pointed out, in case she got too carried away with visions

of the two of us belting down the interstate in a green
Thunderbird with the wind in our hair.

Becky grinned. "Suze, you've got to have a spirit of
adventure," she said.

She was right. Thelma and Louise it was. Which is
how we ended up in the airport with rucksacks filled with
denim garments, and me wearing lots of silver jewelry like
Susan Sarandon, ready to board the flight to New York.

I spotted them first: two gorgeous guys alone amid the
throngs of couples and families. They were stocking up
on magazines in the bookshop, talking to each other and
laughing and generally having the sort of great time you
have when you're among the world's top ten percent of
hunks. One of them had cheekbones you'd cut yourself
on. Dark-haired, melting dark eyes, with a bod to die for.
You know the sort of thing: big shoulders and proper
biceps that stick out all the time and not just when he
flexes them in desperation (like Paul's). His friend was
taller, leaner and a paler version: the same cheekbones and
the same bone structure but with chestnut collar-length
hair and a lopsided, sexy grin. He looked like the clever
one; it was the intelligent glint in those expressive eyes.
Brothers or cousins, definitely.

Being me, I turned away and looked at my watch
again. I was off men, for understandable reasons.

Then Becky spotted them. She's very good at spotting
blokes. She claims it's because she's on the lookout for
possible male models for the agency but I know it's
because she has an insatiable hunger for men. I used to
have an insatiable hunger for men too, but when I met
Paul I stopped looking, naturally. When Paul went off
with that slapper, the only insatiable hunger I was left

with was for Mars Bar ice creams, which are not good for your backside on a long-term basis.

"Suze," she hissed. "Get a look at those two guys."

"Cute," I said dismissively.

"They're not cute, they're lurve gods," she drooled. She was just starting to sashay over to them when our flight was called.

"We'd better board," I fussed, stopping her mid-sashay. Becky never bothered being on time for things but I did.

"You're worse than my mother, Suze," she grumbled, but she followed me all the same.

"There'll be loads of time for men in America," I said consolingly.

On the plane, Becky picked at her meal (the secret of staying thin, obviously), drank two Bacardis and fell asleep, while I ate every last forkful of my meal, had my dessert, had her dessert, drank four vodkas, watched two films, half-finished a detective novel, and wondered if I'd ever want anything to do with a man again.

"Suzanne, there's plenty more fish in the sea," my mother said stoically when I arrived home after the breakup, complete with four suitcases and a face swollen from crying. "I admire you so much for deciding that you'd made a mistake. In my day, we'd have been too scared to end an engagement. Modern women know their minds and that's great."

I burst into tears again, wishing I could tell her what had really happened, but not wanting to humiliate myself by doing so.

Mum hugged me and then made me tea and toast with honey, my favorite comfort food when I was a teenager. We went through a lot of honey when I was a teenager.

"You'll be back in the dating game in no time," Mum assured me.

"I don't want to," I sobbed. "I hate men. They're all bastards."

"I know but sure, they have their uses," Mum said kindly. "Look at your father. He did a great job putting up those shelves in the kitchen, didn't he?"

That was a month ago. The house Paul and I had bought was up for sale, I was still in my old bedroom at home (there wasn't much room for me there, actually, seeing as it was full of things from the house—Paul was not getting his hands on the stereo system I'd spent a year paying off), and Paul had phoned me four times in the last week begging me to reconsider.

"Hang up on him!" said Becky in outrage when I told her he'd had the temerity to call me at work. "Tell him you'll nail his kneecaps to the floor if he bothers you again. No, better still, tell him *I'll* nail his kneecaps to the floor!"

Becky was very loyal and I suspected that nothing would give her greater pleasure than to nail any part of Paul's uptight anatomy to the floor. His knees would not be top of the list, either.

I felt a bit groggy and uncoordinated when we got to JFK. Becky was bright as a button thanks to five hours of sleep.

"Look!" she squealed in my ear as we emerged into the arrivals hall and spotted the two lurve gods ahead of us. "Those gorgeous guys. Maybe we should ditch our plans and just follow them."

"Yeah right," I grumbled. "And forfeit all the money we've already paid for the holiday."

"I thought you wanted an adventure," Becky said.

"Not tonight," I said. "I want to climb into a nice hotel bed and fall asleep."

Becky smirked. "If we hitch up with those two blokes, there's no reason why hotel beds can't be involved."

After a certain amount of grumbling as we dragged our rucksacks along, we finally made it to the Stateside Twenty-One office, which was close to all the rental car agencies. There were lots of those sports utility jeep things around. Becky was a little miserable to see no signs of any Thelma and Louise–type sports cars parked nearby.

"I'd hoped we could do a deal and maybe upgrade to something sexy and sporty," she said as we hauled our luggage up the steps. "I really wanted to feel the wind in my hair as we drive through Utah."

"You can hang your head out of the window like a dog," I suggested. I *was* tired.

Inside the office was a bored-looking young woman who was sitting behind a high counter, chewing gum and talking at the same time. Guess who she was talking to? Yes, our lurve gods. Beside me, I could feel Becky adopting her model pose of stomach in, boobs out. My stomach was already painfully in thanks to my too-tight jeans, and my boobs always stick out, so no action was required on my part.

"Hi," Becky said throatily to the guys.

Both lurve gods smiled, displaying lovely teeth. I'd been wrong with my previous assessment: they weren't in the top ten percent of hunks, they were definitely in the top five.

"Are you Suzanne O'Reilly?" the girl behind the counter

asked Becky, not bothering with the whole "hello" business.

"No, *I* am," I said.

"Now you're all here, we can process your tickets," the girl said.

"Now we're all here?" I repeated. "What do you mean?"

"There's four people to every sports utility vehicle," she said, as if she was talking to a moron.

"Four people?" I repeated, probably intentionally making it look as if I *was* a moron.

"Yeah, four people to every vehicle," said the taller and, to my taste, sexier lurve god. The one with the glinting, intelligent eyes. He did not sound pleased. "It's in the small print apparently. We thought we got our own car but it seems that we're sharing with you two."

Becky's face grew radiant.

"Great. Hey, it'll be fun," she beamed at the other lurve god with an unmistakable I've-just-won-the-lottery smile. "I'm Becky Hill."

"I'm Tony Stewart," he said, also with an I've-just-won-the-lottery smile. "And this is Liam, my cousin."

Liam didn't look too pleased, probably because it was obvious that Becky fancied Tony, which left him with me. The expression of irritation on his face was the sort of look that's not good for a girl's morale.

"There must be some other way of sorting this out," I said to the girl behind the counter in my firm but confident voice, which I have honed over two years as the telesales manager. A managerial tone of voice is very important, as they told us on the management training course. "I'm afraid this isn't satisfactory. We were led to understand that we got our own vehicle and if this isn't the case,

then your company is guilty of misrepresentation, which
is illegal. If you don't have the authority to sort this out,
we'll need to speak to the manager or whoever is in
charge."

The girl looked as if she couldn't give two damns either
way. She kept chewing. A dentist with a loaded drill
couldn't get the gum out of her mouth. "It's like, seven
o'clock on Saturday, like, there's nobody to talk to. If you
wanna complain, you'll have to wait for Monday."

I dragged Becky away from batting her eyelashes at
Tony and we went outside for a confab.

"This is terrible," I said. "I vote we stay in New York
until Monday and come back and get this sorted out then."

"Suze," Becky wailed, "it'll be fun. Think of the adventure we can have with them. It'll be much more fun with
four of us."

"No way, Becky," I said.

Becky gave me a poke in the ribs that winded me. "It'll
be fun," she said between gritted teeth. "Please, pretty
please. We haven't got any choice, Suze, we're stuck with
them."

She was right. I felt like crying. My dreams were going
up in smoke. Instead of a male-free holiday where I could
wash Paul out of my hair, I was going to have to spend
three whole weeks with two strange guys, both of whom
had drooled over Becky as if she was Cindy Crawford's
better-looking sister. Nobody was looking at me. Mind
you, denims always make my backside look enormous. It
was going to be like being fourteen all over again. Me,
Miss Wallflower at discos despite all my best efforts at
looking cool, and Becky with boys clustering around her
in the manner of bees and a honey pot.

"Cheer up, Suze," Becky begged.

How could I cheer up when I could see through the glass doors to where Liam was gesticulating wildly at his cousin, obviously making the point that there was no way in hell he was going to end up stuck with me the entire holiday. I could even imagine the conversation: "Forget it. You get the good-looking one and I get the short, ugly one. No deal."

Iron entered my soul. Tough bananas. He was going to be stuck with me.

We went back in. "You'd better record our complaints," I said to the girl behind the counter. "I'm getting a discount when this is over, I promise you."

She gave me a look that said this was pretty unlikely. "Sign here."

It took an hour and a half to get to the New Jersey town where Tony had read about this "cool hotel Bon Jovi goes to." I sourly pointed out that any hotel where rich rock stars congregated was going to be a bit out of our price range but he and Becky chorused, "Lighten up, Suze!"

"Fine," I said tightly.

Liam, who was driving, looked just as irritated as I did. I was sitting in the front of the utility vehicle, while the love birds were sitting in the back, bonding. Liam and I were not bonding.

Via Tony, I discovered that they worked together in the family estate-agency business and lived in Dublin. Tony was the younger at the age of twenty-eight, while Liam was thirty, and Tony's sister, a trainee travel agent, had booked the holiday for them.

"If I'd booked it, I'd have realized we'd have to share a

car," Liam said grimly, "and we'd have booked another holiday instead."

Charming. For a good-looking guy with a movie-star profile and lovely long fingers that rested lightly on the steering wheel, Liam could be a real pain in the ass. He had really long legs too, I noticed, legs that looked pretty good in soft canvas jeans, not that I cared either way.

"But isn't it fun that it's worked out this way?" Becky said happily.

When we got to the Bon Jovi hotel, I asked Tony where he'd read the crucial bit of information that led him to believe it was a nice place.

"In a magazine," he said, staring at the seedy one-story building with delight.

"Was it a very old, out-of-date magazine?" I knew I was being a bitch but I couldn't help it. We'd driven for ages off the beaten track to find this place and now that we were there, I realized it looked like the sort of premises that even cockroaches would boycott. The only good news was that it was cheap. That was the deciding factor. None of us had money to spare and we were all ready to stop somewhere for the night, so we checked in.

"Let's all go for something to eat," said Becky enthusiastically as soon as we'd dropped our rucksacks on the twin beds in our crummy room.

"The only place I'm going is to bed," I said, inspecting the sheets for wildlife. It was that sort of place.

"Spoilsport," she said.

"Trollop," I answered. "Wake me in the morning."

It took Tony and Becky until the second night on the road to reach first base.

We'd driven to Atlantic City and found a small, pretty

motel that we all liked the look of because it was fake
fifties. Our room was full of veneer, frilly curtains, ice-
pink bed covers and a squashy purple couch that could
have come straight out of the *Happy Days* set.

Dinner was in a steakhouse down the road where
there was a beer promotion. By the end of the night,
none of us could remember how many dollars a giant
jug of beer was, but we got through seven jugs before
we ran out of budget. Booze was certainly easing the
tension between us all. Well, the tension between me
and Liam, actually. Becky and Tony were about as
tense as a couple of carefree teenagers and could be
heard screaming with laughter as we all walked home:
them arm in arm, myself and Liam walking about a
yard apart. When the other pair started running hys-
terically back to the motel, Liam and I kept walking
along in not-very-companionable silence.

I wasn't surprised when I opened our door and found
no sign of Becky. She was clearly in Tony and Liam's
room. Well, if they wanted a *ménage à trois*, that was their
business.

I switched on the TV and was trying to find something
to watch from the zillions of cable channels, when there
was a knock at my door.

Liam, rangy and vexed-looking, stood on the thresh-
old. "Can I come in?" he asked.

"Don't tell me," I said, letting him in. "Live sex show
in your room?"

"Something like that."

The *Happy Days* couch was quite small really, and
when we both sat on it we were quite close together. I
kept stealing glances at Liam's profile, wondering if I

was so horrible-looking that he couldn't be bothered even making a move on me. Not that I wanted him to or anything. But if he tried to chat me up, I'd have the satisfaction of telling him that I had taken a vow of chastity and would never look at a man again. Or something like that.

At half-twelve, I said I was shattered and was going to bed.

"Can I stay?" he muttered, eyes glued to the TV.

I nodded.

"I'll sleep on the couch if you'd prefer me not to use the bed." He looked wary.

Thanks, I thought. Obviously I was so repulsive he preferred to be as far away from me as possible.

"Sleep on the bed," I snapped. "I'm not expecting you to hop on me in the middle of the night." Chance would be a fine thing.

I woke up next morning and rolled over to see Liam lying on his back, half-covered by Becky's pink bedspread. Either he'd been away somewhere hot recently or he used sunbeds but his body, his perfectly sculpted body, was a golden caramel color.

Wow. He sure was gorgeous.

I gazed longingly at the hard, muscled shoulders and at the taut six-pack stomach. I thought briefly of Paul's untoned belly and how he used to drool all over the pillows at night. Liam was not the sort of person to drool. In fact, the only person around here who was drooling was me. I clambered out of bed and threw myself into the shower. It didn't help.

Even when I closed my eyes, I could still see Liam in all his gorgeousness. There was no doubt about it: somewhere inside me, the anti-men icicle had melted. How typical that I'd start getting over Paul with a man who clearly wouldn't touch me with a bargepole.

I dressed in the bathroom, averted my eyes as I walked past the sleeping Liam, and then marched over to the other motel room.

"Let's all get up and get going," I yelled, sounding like a holiday camp rep with a lust for power.

We soon got into a routine. We booked three rooms every night: one for me, one for Liam and one for Becky and Tony, who couldn't keep their hands off each other. Every morning, we'd have breakfast together and plan the day's driving. We wanted to see Kentucky, Tennessee and go to Memphis, obviously. We were all keen to visit Graceland and see just how madly tacky it all was. Then, it was down to New Orleans, over to Houston (Liam was eager to visit the NASA space center) and finally, back up to Atlanta. Or at least, that was the plan. We had lots of conversations about how we were going to do all this because there was a lot of driving involved. Well, Liam and I had long conversations about how we were going to do all this, because the other pair were too deeply in lust to think about anything else. Every day when we reached our destination, Liam and I set off sightseeing while Tony and Becky slammed their hotel door and did their own personal sightseeing.

"They're missing everything," I said to Liam one evening as we walked around downtown Nashville and found ourselves in a little club where you could dance and listen to lively country music all night.

"Yeah," he said, surprising me by pulling me onto the dance floor to join all the cowboy-boot-wearing dancers, "it's their own loss. We might as well enjoy ourselves, Suze."

And we did.

Liam and I started a diary which we wrote up every morning.

We'd sit side by side and laugh as we wrote our own versions of the previous day. Tony and Becky were so late getting out of bed, that we had normally finished our breakfast by the time they joined us.

I had great fun teasing Liam by writing descriptions of our various budget motels in what I called "estate agent speak."

"Let's see," I said the first morning in Memphis as we sat in a pancake house waiting for our giant breakfasts to arrive. "Compact and simple accommodation with a comforting police presence."

Liam laughed uproariously. "Don't forget to write that the police presence is due to the fact that the area is so bad, the cops have to drive past twenty times a night."

I giggled. "The decor is Zen-like . . ."

Liam laughed again. I loved hearing him laugh. When he did, his face crinkled up in a sexy sort of way and he looked utterly adorable. "What do you mean, Zen-like?" he asked. "You should say that there's no furniture in the room apart from the beds, which are probably nailed to the floor."

"I thought estate agents needed to be inventive," I teased.

"Not that inventive. You have a great imagination, Suze."

Breakfast arrived.

"I'll never get used to these portions," I sighed, looking

at the huge plate in front of me. "I'll look like a hippo by the time we get home."

"You look great," Liam said with his mouth full. He smiled at me before turning his attention back to pancakes the size of dinner plates.

In between bites, he started talking about what we were going to do that day, but I wasn't listening really. I was in a daze thinking about Liam saying I looked great. Granted, I'd got a bit of a tan and it made me look healthy and glowing. And now that I'd made friends with Liam, I was relaxed enough to abandon the big, floaty shirts that hid my bum and had started wearing my little strappy tops, which did suit me, I have to say. With my long hair rippling down my back and with my new American jeans slung low on my waist, I looked as good as I ever had. But for someone as Grade A gorgeous as Liam to say so, well . . . that was something else.

There was no sign of Becky and Tony by the time we'd finished, so we walked back to the motel and knocked on their bedroom door.

Becky opened it. She was paler than I was, thanks to the fact that she and Tony spent far too much time in bed to actually get a tan.

"We're going to Graceland now," I said. "Are you guys coming?"

"Er, no," she said and grinned at me.

I shrugged. Tony might not be the brightest bulb on the Christmas tree but he was obviously fantastic in the bedroom department.

Graceland was incredible. Even if you'd never been an Elvis fan, there was something very moving about seeing his house. It was sad too.

We felt a bit subdued after seeing the King's home, so we decided to head for Beale Street and have some fun. It was a bit touristy, we realized when we got there, the sort of place that had lost its real character and was now just a must-see destination on the tourist map.

"It's like walking down a film set," I said as we ambled down the street, drinking in the sights and listening to the mellow music coming from B. B. King's club.

"I know, but we'd be furious if we'd missed it," Liam said.

That was exactly what I'd been thinking.

We found a tiny restaurant that advertised the best steaks in town and plonked ourselves in the corner. Liam ordered a steak that was so big we burst out laughing when it arrived.

"Y'all enjoy yourselves and ask me if you want anythin' else," said the waitress with that lilting Memphis accent.

We smiled at each other. I loved America. Everyone was so nice and I was having so much fun. The only dark spot in the future was the fact that we only had seven more days to go and then it would be back to normal life, normal life without Liam, life where I dressed in boring office suits, placated irate customers over the phone and limited my chocolate biscuit intake to two a day.

"I might never wear a suit again," I commented, stretching out my denimed legs and admiring my cowboy boots.

"It's funny, but the first day we met, I could just see you in a suit, all starched up and bossing people around," Liam said, finally giving up on his huge steak; "but not anymore," he added quickly. "Now," his eyes roamed over my curves, "I can't imagine you all buttoned up at all. You're perfect as you are."

I balled up my napkin and threw it at him. "Stop it," I said, embarrassed. "You're such a big tease." Well, he had to be teasing, didn't he?

New Orleans turned out to be my favorite place on that whole magical trip. I adored the atmospheric French Quarter with its overhanging lacy balconies, shutters and shady courtyards. Liam and I were like children as we rushed along, desperate to see everything. I insisted we visit a voodoo shop, while Liam wanted to go on one of the cemetery tours.

"You can go on your own." I shivered. "I've seen *Interview with the Vampire*."

He laughed and squeezed my arm. "I'll hold your hand, scaredy-cat."

We had sugary doughnuts in a café on Jackson Square, half because we were hungry and half because the combination of humidity and heat was so overwhelming that it was impossible to spend too long in the outdoors without rushing into a shop for a blast of air-conditioning.

I'd never experienced such humidity before. My little white T-shirt was literally stuck to my body and Liam's wasn't much better. The upshot of this was that we had to keep stopping for liquids. After trailing around Decatur and Chartres streets, we got out of the heat in a little bar off Dumaine and ordered mint juleps, the traditional Southern drink.

Liam loved his but I hated mine. "I thought it would be sweet," I said with a grimace.

Liam smiled and ordered me a Long Island Iced Tea. "I thought you were sweet enough already," he said softly.

Afterwards, we wandered off looking for the voodoo shops. Before we found one, we came upon a little old Creole lady on a street corner, with a sandwich board beside her proclaiming her skills as a seer.

"You want me to tell the pretty lady's fortune for ten dollars?" she asked.

"No," I said, blushing.

"Yes," said Liam with a grin.

He handed her the money and she took my hand in hers. I looked into her eyes and was disconcerted to see that she was blind, with the milky white pools of cataracts covering the iris.

"You have to make a choice," she said softly to me. "You have love. Do not waste time. Life is too short."

That was it. Liam thanked her and we walked off. I felt a bit dizzy what with the heat and what she'd said.

"You OK?" he asked.

I nodded. "It's strange, what she said," I mumbled. "About a choice."

"Do you think it's between me and your ex?" Liam asked.

I stared at him.

"Becky told me," he admitted. "I wanted to know why you were so hostile all the time."

"I wasn't," I protested. "I didn't think you liked me and . . ."

He stopped and faced me, tracing the damp line of my collar bone lightly with his finger.

My skin, already hot, burned. "What made you think that?" he said, his voice as soft as a breeze.

"I don't know," I said. "I thought you preferred Becky."

He sighed and gave me an exasperated look. "Come

on," he said in a normal voice. "Let's go back to the hotel and rest. We could sunbathe by the pool and come back here tonight for dinner. We've only got a week left and I want a bit of a tan before I go home."

I felt cheated that the moment had been broken. It was my own fault for mentioning Becky. He liked me and I'd ruined it all by reminding him about Becky.

Back at the hotel, I put on my bikini, got my book and my sun lotion, and met Liam out by the pool.

He was sitting on a lounger with a can of beer and he looked moody.

"Hi," I said shortly, doing my best not to look at that lean, brown, nearly naked body clad in khaki shorts. I rubbed sun lotion on my front and lay there for half an hour, brooding and feeling sorry for myself. Half an hour was long enough for one side, I decided, unless I wanted to go lobster red. I readjusted my sun lounger and took a surreptitious look at Liam. He looked as if he was asleep. Probably dreaming about Becky, I thought crossly.

I sat up and creamed the backs of my legs before trying to rub lotion onto my back. It's impossible to rub anything on your own back, so I cursed a bit under my breath.

Suddenly Liam appeared beside me.

"For God's sake, give me the bottle," he said in exasperation. "Lie down, I'll do your back."

Gulping, I lay on my front. "I only need a tiny bit, you don't need to do my legs," I bleated.

It was bad enough that he had to see my un-Becky-like flesh in its entirety, never mind rub sun lotion into it.

"You don't want to burn," Liam said, his voice suddenly unsteady.

His hands felt warm and delicious, spreading the lotion gently over my shoulders. It doesn't mean anything to him, I reminded myself miserably.

It must be like rubbing sun lotion into his sister's back. Utterly platonic.

"Do you have a sister?" I asked.

"Sister?" he said, puzzled. "No. I've only got brothers." I could almost hear him smiling. "I've never met anyone like you, Suze, your mind works in mysterious ways."

His hands slid over and back across my spine, firm movements. Then I could feel him unfastening my bikini.

"You don't need to—" I began.

"Hush," he said, pulling the shoulder straps down. I obligingly raised my body and he whipped the bikini away. My heart was beating like a drum with excitement. I could hear Liam breathing more heavily, I could smell his aftershave, hot and lemony.

The slow rhythmic strokes slipped down to my rib cage, circling and circling, rubbing lotion in. His touch was exquisite; it was like finding someone who can play your body like a grand piano after years with someone who hammered away on it like they were playing a wrecked old upright piano. Paul's fingers had never electrified me like Liam's did.

Suddenly, I couldn't take it any longer.

I turned over, clutching my towel to my chest, not caring that he could see every untoned inch of me. His dark, handsome face was close to mine, his pupils large with desire as he stared longingly at me. It was the most erotic moment of my life. No, correction, that was when he moved to sit nearer to me on the lounger, and gently ran one finger along my collar bone, sending ripples down my spine.

"I wanted to do that from the first night I slept in your room," he said huskily. "You fell asleep and I watched you for ages."

I could only stare at him.

"But I thought you liked Becky," I began stupidly.

"I don't fancy Becky. I fancy you," he said, his voice gentle. "And you've got to stop thinking you're some sort of second-class citizen just because you hang around with her all the time. She's lovely but so are you. I'm crazy about the way you bite your lips when you're thinking, I'm crazy about the way your hips sway when you walk, I'm crazy about those sexy little tops you wear . . . I'm just crazy about you."

At that moment, I pulled him close and our lips met. I wanted to taste him, to devour him, and it seemed as if he wanted to do the same to me. Our bodies were pressed together and it suddenly occurred to me that we'd better leave the pool area or get arrested for lewd behavior if my towel slipped.

"Will we go upstairs?" I said, astonished at my own bravery.

He smiled. "Absolutely. There are a lot of breathtaking sights I've wanted to explore for a long time." He playfully twanged the elastic of my bikini bottoms as he spoke.

I grinned back and wrapped the towel around myself. "Will this be the quick, budget five-minute tour or a long, drawn-out one?" I whispered.

"It's definitely going to take more than five minutes," he promised.

* * *

I was back at work on Monday morning over a week later. Although my own world had shifted on its axis after the holiday, in the office nothing had changed. My desk was still piled high with the same old queries; Antoinette, the new junior, was still spending most of her time flirting with Danny, two desks away; and the air-conditioning was still broken, making it a nightmare to work in the sultry August weather.

It was nearly lunchtime when Paul phoned me.

"Suzanne," he said plaintively. "I need to see you, please. We've made a terrible mistake."

I said nothing. It was funny, you see, but I'd spent so long mentally telling Paul what a complete pig he was, that when I was actually talking to him, I'd run out of insults altogether. And besides which, you don't want to scream at your ex-fiancé when you're in the office. Not my office, anyway. Reuters doesn't have as efficient a news service as this place. One word from me about Paul's dalliance and I might as well have taken out an advert in the *Limerick Leader* telling all and sundry that he'd slept with a stick insect named Maura.

"Please talk to me," Paul begged. "You mean everything to me and it was all a big mistake and since you've been away, I've missed you so much." He paused for breath before starting again. "Suzanne, we can't throw it all away. We have a house, a life together, a future and a history. We've been through too much to end it all."

"Yes, we have a history," I agreed calmly. I'm used to sounding calm in the office.

It was all the encouragement he needed. "Yes," he repeated eagerly. "We've been together so long, Suzanne, we can't throw it all away for one meaningless fling."

"Are you sure it was just once?" I said politely. We'd never actually discussed whether he'd had a one-off with Maura or a series of passionate encounters in his car on the bypass.

"Yes!" He sounded very convincing. "She meant nothing to me, it was a mistake, I never meant to hurt you, honestly. Please let's try again."

"You want to start again? I don't know, do you think we could? Would we just end up torturing each other over the past?" I asked him.

"I love you, I want to be with you," he said frantically.

"We have to meet," I said decisively. "As soon as possible, don't you agree?"

Even over the phone, I could hear Paul breathe a sigh of relief. I could just imagine him smiling. He had a lovely smile. It was the thing I liked most about him, the thing that other women admired. Paul wasn't tall or well-built but he was certainly attractive, with Nordic blond hair and cool blue eyes.

We arranged to meet on Friday. Paul was eager to meet immediately but I said no. Friday, it would have to be.

I don't know how I got through the week. I thought about Paul a lot, naturally. Well, we'd spent years together and you can't throw all that away lightly, can you?

On Friday, at ten past six, we met up in The Den, a big modern pub near my office. Paul got the drinks and we sat down beside each other. He looked pale and tired, to be honest. I took his hands in mine. He was smiling, those blue eyes were glinting with delight. I looked at his familiar face and at the blond hair I'd loved running my fingers through. I thought of how sweet he could be on weekend mornings when he'd sometimes bring me a cup of coffee in bed and we'd read the papers and chat. We'd been together since we were twenty, a lifetime. He'd been there for so many of the big things in my life: my graduation, my twenty-first, Granddad's funeral, you name it, we'd been there together. It had been perfect, until he'd ruined it all by sleeping with that bitch.

"Will you marry me, Suzanne?" he said softly.

I smiled and kissed him gently on the cheek. He smelled of that musky, expensive aftershave I always bought him at Christmas. It cost a fortune. Last Christmas, he'd bought me bubble bath. Really cheap bubble bath and not the dear stuff I'd actually asked for.

"No, I won't marry you," I said. "You blew it, Paul."

His face was a picture. Shock, astonishment and disbelief fought for control of his features. Disbelief won by a narrow margin.

"B-b-but you love me, Suzanne. You're heartbroken about me, I know you are," he stammered.

"I *was*," I corrected him. "I got over you."

Paul stared at me, shocked.

"I don't believe you," he said. "You're just trying to hurt me, to make up for my fling."

"I'm not," I said. "I'm in love with someone else."

"You're just saying that!" Paul raged. He was getting red-faced and angry now. Pale-skinned people can go amazingly red in the face. His eyes were no longer warm and kind: they were a strange combination of enraged and astonished. Paul couldn't believe that I was turning him down. He'd thought that all he needed to do was snap his fingers and I'd come running. Well, it *had* worked in the past. But not this time. Things had changed. *I* had changed.

I got to my feet. "I'm not just saying it," I said kindly. "It's true."

I looked over to the bar where Liam was standing, looking ruggedly handsome in a very nice gray suit, his face anxious as if he was dying to rush in and punch Paul for daring to hurt a hair on my head. I smiled at Liam and he walked over. If Liam looked good in jeans, let me tell you, you've got to see him in a suit. Those big shoulders were made for Italian tailoring.

You see, I *had* thought about Paul a lot since he'd rung me. We'd been in love once and it had seemed like a good idea to get married. But not anymore. I'd spent a whole week thinking of how he'd bossed me around, how we'd never gone anywhere thrilling for holidays, how he'd always picked what we watched on the telly. And then I thought about Liam, lovely Liam, who couldn't bear to be away from me and who was running up an enormous bill on his mobile phoning me night and day. Sexy, funny Liam, who liked me for who I was rather than for the sort of person he could mold me into.

I suppose I forgot to mention how well Liam and I got on after New Orleans. Well, we had a lot of stuff to write in the diary but it would have been so X-rated that we'd never have been able to show it to anyone else, so we left it out. But the things that boy can do with an ice cube. (The air-conditioning was dodgy in the motel in Houston, so we had to improvise.)

Paul's eyes nearly popped out of his head as he stared at Liam, my own personal Lurve God. He stood up, which was a mistake. Beside Liam, Paul looked scrawny and badly dressed. Liam also looked as if he could flatten Paul in a second, so Paul sat down again and took a deep slug of his beer.

"You can't be serious, Suzanne," he said weakly, but I could tell his heart wasn't in it. He knew serious competition when he saw it.

I patted him on the arm. "We'll talk about the house," I said confidently. I took Liam's hand and we walked out of The Den. We were picking up Becky and Tony and the four of us were driving to Kinsale for the weekend. We wanted to get a move on to beat the traffic. You see, Liam and I were keen to do some sightseeing.

CATHY KELLY is the author of five novels: *What She Wants, Someone Like You, Never Too Late, She's the One* and *Woman to Woman,* all of which were Top Ten bestsellers in the U.K. *Someone Like You* won the Parker Romantic Novel of the Year Award in 2001.

A former journalist, Cathy is now a full-time writer and lives in Wicklow, where she's working on her sixth novel.

Your Place or Mine?

Gemma O'Connor

The in-comers were thinly spread over the valley. They came from far and wide and had little in common except a rampant romanticism which somehow got them through the shock of realization, as season followed season, that what they'd bought were less dwellings than rough indications of some future longed-for comfort. The locals wryly watched as the eccentric foreigners tried to push back the ravages of time and the long dereliction of the scattered houses. The pattern did not vary: teased apart from what seemed, at first, a paltry enough purchase price, the new owners remained jubilant until the sun went in and the full impact of each picturesquely crumbling ruin engaged their horrified attention.

The Murphys were perhaps more optimistic than

most, and because they were so engaging, the Irish couple's heroic attempt at ordering the chaos was bemusedly watched by their French neighbors with something approaching indulgence.

They arrived with their three young children in July when the weather was sweltering and the problems resulting from the lack of indoor plumbing soon threatened their cheeriness. By way of encouragement their nearest neighbor, one Philippe Thorel, took to sauntering across the fields bearing gifts of flowers or vegetables or an occasional bottle of lethal home brew.

On the third such visit he invited them to walk the shared boundary of his farm and their tiny parcel of land. He spoke in patois—which they could just about understand, or thought they could—all the while making a great show of racking his brain in remembrance of a long forgotten *source* which, unsurprisingly since the earth was parched, did not materialize. As he trotted away, he waggled his head in admiration and disbelief at their naivete, then halfway across his field he turned back and, with some embarrassment and much good humor, pointed out that the back wall of their cottage belonged by rights to him. His grin widened impishly at their obvious dismay.

"Regardez!" he cried, describing the length of crumbling masonry with a broad sweep of his hand. "See how it rises out of the field passed down to me from my mother's eldest brother?" He shrugged. "My field, my wall—but only on this side. Of course." Having caught them on the hop, he charmingly assured the Murphys that this would not, of course, make any difference to their good relationship. Then he adjusted his beret to a jauntier angle and wandered off. He never uncovered his

head. It was fully two years before they discovered his bald shiny pate.

Elizabeth and Dan eyed each other and smiled uncertainly, bravely dismissing the tinge of fear that his information might have some vital importance obscured by their ignorance of both patois and the finer points of local law. But, during the following couple of days, they stole off separately and secretly to the *Mairie* to ask the import of this half-owned wall. The *notaire* patted Elizabeth's arm in avuncular fashion and murmured imprecations against the intractability of peasants who frightened themselves and all about them with their lunatic claims where none existed. And though the Murphys accepted his verdict, somewhere in the recesses of their minds the seeds of not quite belonging took root and, even if dormant, lingered. Imperceptibly a germ of vulnerability struck and began to grow. Perhaps the little house was not really, not truly, theirs at all?

The in-comers came randomly from this country and that. Few were French, though one or two, with remote local connections glossed over by several generations in Paris, saw the possibilities of the valley's beautiful granite walls and pantiled roofs. So that when the older generations built new, warm, comfortable, hideous villas alongside the family pile, they swooped in and bought the old ruins at knock-down prices. No DIY for them, for they knew that local skill in every craft came cheaper than what they might botch themselves. Soon new windows and doors, floors and finally a shroud of gray rendering transformed the picturesque decay. Not spoiled, exactly.

The true foreigner having exhausted his meager funds with buying would, as year followed enslaved year, scrimp and mend and add small comforts, but the houses remained essentially the same: untamed. The locals watched these naive guardians of their building stock with nodding approval, patiently waiting for the moment when, the effort proving too much, the dwellings would once more revert to them—not improved beyond recognition but just enough to add some simple comfort to their unambitious wants. Meanwhile *les 'ippies,* as they were dubbed, provided a welcome diversion to the unchanging rhythm of the farmers' lives, with their exuberant offspring, gay clothes and suspect morals—it was the early seventies after all.

The Murphy children were enchanted with country life and quickly became willing seasonal slaves to cow, calf and vineyard, up at six and swapping their meager but growing store of basic French, mostly rude words. They were different from the farm children, their pale gold limbs gleamed in the sun and as summer raced along their hair turned from gold to almost white. They looked alarmingly free measured against the confining blue overalls of the weather-beaten farmers and their black-clad wives who spoke affectionately of them as *les mignons,* or *les p'tits irlandais.*

Because the in-comers filtered in slowly and remained scattered and separate they appeared unaware that they were part of a steadily increasing group. For the most part they thought that in this place, *their discovery,* they were the only outsiders—or one of two or three at most. For did it not take discernment to see the charms of countryside so remote, so sleepy, so unendowed with lake or river or even hill? Just rolling pasture and woodland with here and there a tiny man-made *plan d'eau,* which by August would sport a thin brown film of Ambre Solaire on its surface. The wealthier tourist would, by and large, pause only briefly to sniff at the campsite aromatically draped around the southern end of the largest of these pathetic little ponds before driving further south.

And so it worked out that the scattered strangers, unknown to themselves, were of a kind: romantic, young and stretched for ready cash; except for a tall, blond family who settled in a nearby village, whom M. Thorel declared to be *Sal Bosch*—his capitals were unmistakable. Then one morning Liz overheard the great blond woman trying to make herself understood by Mme. Beausoleil, the butcher's wife, in sparkling BBC. Liz, acutely aware of her five foot nothing and scruffy clothes, was too shy to speak, and the Valkyrie eyeing the Irish girl's red-gold hair and clear freckled face neatly turned the tables with a gay *"auf wiedersehen"* to which Lizzie insouciantly mouthed "pet" as she smiled sweetly into Mme. Beausoleil's inquiring eyes. She was swept with an unreasonable fury that the Englishwoman, so obviously well-heeled, should also have had the wit to find the best butcher for miles around.

"Une allemande?"

"Malheureusement, Madame," Liz lied treacherously, appealing to old enmities, realizing that Madame would thereby continue to reserve her choicest morsels for herself and her pretty children who now tumbled through the door with their hands held out for the proffered slices of garlic sausage.

"Hey Mam, you see her car? Wow!"

But for once Liz didn't respond, being preoccupied with the thought of how little she wanted to be patronized by money, or worse, by style. For a second or two she felt thoroughly put out that her small private world had been invaded, that she was no longer special. Odd, how conveniently she had forgotten that the real reason they had chosen that particular valley was simply that the cost of property was so low. True, the prices were steadily creeping upward but, six years before, the asking price for their own cottage was precisely what it would have cost them to replace their battered VW Beetle with a spanking new camper van. When this plan was first mooted, Liz, alarmed at the notion of campsites and sanilavs and sleeping five in such a confined space, took one look at the van's cramped interior and persuaded Dan to come to France, just to look.

They installed her mother to look after the children and took the Rosslare–Cherbourg ferry on a freezing, wet January day. It was a long grim crossing and when at last, holding their churning stomachs, they staggered into a dockside Bar-Tabac for an early morning hit of coffee, they admitted that it was all a terrible mistake; a wild-goose chase. But seven hours and a boozy lunch later, when eventually they arrived in their chosen *département,* the sky was blue and their spirits high. The sun had gleamed on the pinkish granite of the little house, which sat snugly into the incline, sideways to the track that led past, and at right angles to a magnificent stone barn. Practicalities were ignored; they were immediately seduced. The grass must have been recently grazed because the impression, which swept them away, was of a triangular kempt garden. When they next saw it, six months later, as proud new proprietors, the grass and nettles formed an impenetrable barrier around the door, but on that sparkling January day they'd stood entranced as the small fat farmer had twinkled and shrewdly named a price a few hundred francs above the cost of the van. They'd eyed each other uncertainly. It was at this point the estate agent had his brainwave. He looked at his watch pointedly and announced he had to go to watch the match—France was playing Ireland—surely they wouldn't want to miss it? The Murphys were soon squeezed into the back of his car with the farmer bunched between them.

Dan's natural exuberance took over with the second bottle of wine. "We will have a bet," he announced. "If Ireland wins, we'll buy the house." Liz was amazed. Neither of them was remotely interested in rugby. The Frenchmen roared with complaisant laughter and explained patiently that the Irish had not beaten the French for fourteen years. Impossible, unthinkable.

Ireland won. The farmer called for champagne and, hardly thinking beyond the moment, the Murphys shook hands on the deal. And seamlessly, almost without pause, before they'd time to change their minds or even consult, they found themselves sitting in a bemused *notaire*'s office while he, pityingly, inquired if they were quite sure they knew what they were doing? In reply they grinned at each other confidently and joyously signed away their leisure time for seven years. Afterward they went off and got hopelessly and joyously drunk, making love in the rattling bed of the Hôtel du Commerce to the almost certain diversion of the old lags in the bar below noisily toasting the vendor's good fortune. Had the voices traveled upward the celebrants might have heard:

"Empty for six years, you say?"

"Oh, but no. Seven, eight . . . At least." Gleeful Gallic shrug. "I can't remember how long . . ."

"Is it safe?"

"As houses." Sage nods. Bursts of laughter.

But the Murphys knew that despite the drawbacks the bargain was, undoubtedly, in their favor. With three young children to amuse, the summers passed happily enough—food plentiful, the wine, even if barely drinkable, cheap enough to ensure a lifelong quotidian habit, long after the house was no longer theirs.

And so the children flourished in the country air and Farmer Thorel came with his gifts of fruit and flowers. By the second year, tired of sharing the earth closet with wildlife, nettles and a nomadic herd of cattle, they managed to build a bathroom. It was at this point that Louis Bertrand entered the picture.

"Not the full shilling, but willing," Mme. Legrand, from up the road, opined confidently.

Louis was installed as jobbing gardener within an hour of his name being mentioned. Dan's instructions were smilingly listened to, but Liz, eyeing their new retainer, felt a faint shiver of apprehension. His yellow teeth seemed overlarge in the round flat face. Like tombstones, she thought suddenly.

The villagers watched with approval. *Pauvre Louis*—so hardworking, so hard up, and so good to his widowed mother. The dowager Madame Bertrand herself soon arrived, to approve the appointment, with a gift of gigantic *cèpes* cradled in her black spotted pinafore. She talked nonstop but since she hadn't a tooth in her head, Liz could only pick out the odd word—vipers in the wood . . . poor Louis . . . her widowed state . . . tenants all their lives . . . the poor children.

"Children?"

Liz thought some calamity had befallen her own little

dotes but even as her hand flew to her mouth they charged into the newly pebbled courtyard and announced gorily that they'd just watched a calf being born, thus relieving Madame of the need to explain further. So it was only much later that Liz discovered to her surprise that the children referred to were Louis' own, apparently held in some orphanage, some institution, though nobody explained why this should be so. Or if they did she didn't understand. M. Thorel muttered something about their mother dying young, gesturing and miming the act of drinking as he spoke. The children had found her, he murmured, his eyes sliding from hers as he tapped his forehead. Whether he was referring to the lunacy of the children or parent was left unclear. Confused, Liz wondered why she felt foreboding rather than pity.

Year on year, the Murphys planned the reconstruction of the little house—a new floor, insulation, a new ring main—and year by year the resident rat shrugged, moved out for the weeks of their summer sojourn, then returned at the end of the holidays with his friends and relations in tow, and spent the winter undoing whatever had been achieved. Louis, as regular consultant, laid down ever increasing amounts of poison, always mentioning *rat* in the singular when he produced an annual token body. He determined new ways of keeping others at bay but the rats had had longer years to perfect their means of ingress, and continued to persist and, presumably, multiply.

As time went by, Louis Bertrand became ever more indispensable. Under his inspired care the garden flourished. The neighbors came to marvel and praise him, several in-comers tried to poach him but he remained faithful to the Murphys. His skills as a handyman were prodigious. Pantiles dislodged by winter storms would be quickly replaced, mattresses aired, a basket of fresh eggs to welcome them. The cottage no longer appeared chill and neglected when they arrived, as if the promise of their yearly visit was enough to chase damp and dust. They assumed that Louis must sometimes light a winter fire and clean up, but thoughtlessly did not inquire. Why should they? His ministrations were a godsend.

In truth, after the first couple of years, the novelty of DIY wore thin and each succeeding summer Dan and Liz did less and less—barely enough to keep the cottage from further deterioration. They spent more time in the garden, reading in the shade of the old cherry tree, plaiting the annual crops of onion and garlic, watching for the great white barn owl to swoop out of the barn as twilight fell each evening.

Each year they added bits and pieces of furniture, some from home, the occasional bargain from the village *brocante*. It was there, among the other junk, that Dan found a decrepit old rocking chair one morning when he went off to the *boulangerie* for bread. He returned home in triumph with it tied to the roof of the car.

"Bargain," he said.

"Oh, I can see that," his wife replied skeptically.

"When it's repaired, cleaned up . . ." he laughed, "it'll look grand." And he was right, it did.

After he stripped away layers of darkened varnish, Liz sewed bright cheerful cushions. When it was finished, they rearranged the living room where it took pride of place. The children loved it for it easily held all three. After supper Dan would doze over a book in its capacious embrace and the sound of the gentle creaking quickly became synonymous with their contentment. At home, during the long winter months, if the cottage was mentioned, Liz would picture the chair rocking gently with Dan or the children smiling up at her. It became a symbol of the place.

One day, when she was alone in the house, she came downstairs to find Louis standing at the door with a couple of lettuces in his hand. At first he did not notice her and when she turned to follow his gaze she saw that the chair was moving, not much, almost imperceptibly, as if someone had recently vacated it. It seemed to mesmerize him. His head moved back and forth in time to the slight clicking on the bare floorboards. And suddenly she imagined him sitting in it. He was standing at the door and yet for that vivid instant she could see him contentedly rocking to and fro, to and fro, smiling and nodding at her. She shook herself and called out, *"Ça va, Louis?"*

He gave his shy smile and held out the lettuces and together they walked down to the vegetable garden to plan the next year's planting. Did she imagine his speech more mumbled and more difficult to understand than usual? Was he avoiding her eye? Whatever the reason, she began to feel uncomfortable with him. When she remarked as much to Dan, he shrugged impatiently and said that they could not manage without Louis. Louis Bertrand was the key to the success of their summers, he was gentle and hardworking and wouldn't hurt a fly. "Remember the garden before he came to work for us? The leaking roof?" he asked. She did not reply, unable to make sense of her disquiet.

Over the following winter Louis made a splendid cover for the old well and had it working in time for their summer arrival. With great excitement he showed his new system for watering the sloping garden, explaining how much better the vegetables were as a result. He dug his hands into the warm earth to pull the new potatoes for their first meal. The byre door was opened to reveal a great store of garlic spread to dry. Before he left he said the well water was not yet fit for drinking and warned the children from climbing up to wind the great iron wheel.

They'd been putting a little money by and at the beginning of their sixth summer they decided to begin a phased development of the barn. As soon as the builder's merchant delivered a consignment of sand, cement and breezeblocks, the huge white owl whose residence it was began a sustained pelting of their battered car with regurgitated mice to protest his territory.

For days they sat under the cherry tree and talked through stage one of the conversion—a splendid staircase. Looking at the elaborate drawings, their eldest boy, Shane, remarked nonchalantly that the village garage had a small cement mixer for sale. Secondhand. Cheap. Dan disappeared on the instant and returned with it strapped to the roof rack, clattering through the village to general amusement. It looked lethally red in the hot sunshine. Their neighbors asked each other why it was *les irlandais* did not employ the local tradesmen? Of course nobody actually mentioned this to Dan or Liz because they were well liked and their whims were indulged, but among themselves they wondered if the foreigners realized how gimcrack their amateur renovations were?

The children were enchanted with the cement mixer, and they weren't the only ones. On the first evening Louis came to admire it. Watching through the kitchen window

Liz saw him shyly draw his hand over the gleaming surface. He spat on his sleeve and lovingly polished away a bit of dirt.

"Try it," she called. "Turn it on."

But Louis only shook his head and shuffled off down the garden as if ashamed that she had seen his longing. As she watched, the fugitive image of him in the rocking chair drifted fleetingly across her mind. She drew her soapy hand through her hair and called the children away from the well.

The grape harvest was late that last year, but it was clearly going to be a bumper crop. An unexpected postcard from Mme. Legrand asked if the Murphys could come; her husband, Maurice, was unwell and not able to manage alone. Dan and Liz were both very fond of the self-sufficient Legrands, who had never before asked for help, and decided to fly over for the weekend. Being off-season, fares were low and they had no difficulty hiring a car. In the flurry of arranging childcare, Liz forgot to write to Louis announcing their arrival—neither he nor the Legrands had phones. They set off assuming that somehow or other the information that they were on their way would osmose through the settlement or that Mme. Legrand might mention in passing that she'd asked them to come. In any event they didn't really give it a second thought. What did it matter? No need for Louis' usual offerings of eggs or fruit for supper, with just the two of them they could as easily eat in the village.

They were in high good humor as they drove up the incline out of the village. They paused, as they always did, at the top of the hill to catch their first sight of the cottage. Usually they saw it bathed in strong summer sunshine, now only the pinkish stone of the chimney reflected the dying light.

"Well, what do you know, Lizzie," Dan said. "Mme. Legrand must have told Louis, after all. He has the fire lit. Great." As he stretched out his hand and patted his wife's knee, the engine stalled and the car coasted silently down the deserted road before coming to a gradual halt a couple of hundred feet from their garden fence.

The door of the cottage was open. The Murphys rolled down the windows and sat contentedly admiring the profusion of late roses draped romantically around the dark doorway and held hands. The scene was idyllic, even from that distance they could catch the scent on the mild evening air.

"Glad we came?" she murmured.

"Hmm." He leaned across and kissed her, then pulled away, startled by a sudden clanking from the garden.

To their amazement the cement mixer was trundled out of the barn by a tall gangly youth who threw a pail of water into the revolving drum, then went to the well and took a second pail from a heavy, rough-looking girl whom they now noticed for the first time. Mesmerized, they watched the pair move deliberately from mixer to well, stopping from time to time to drink before splashing the water into the drum. Even in the fast fading light everything about them proclaimed their ease and familiarity with the place. After a while the girl went toward the cottage door and slipped inside.

"I thought the water wasn't safe to drink," Lizzie remarked softly.

"Apparently it is."

"Who are they?" she whispered.

"I don't know but I'm bloody well going to find out." Dan touched her cheek. "Why are you whispering, honey?"

"I don't know," she murmured. "Something. I don't know."

As Dan opened the car door, the lights in the cottage were suddenly switched on and through the open doorway a movement caught her eye.

"Dan. Look. Oh Dan."

The rocking chair was moving violently backward and forward, the familiar creaking carried toward them a second or two before a shout from the girl brought the boy plodding across the courtyard. He pulled the door after him as he entered. By now the light had faded but Dan was out of the car in an instant, hurtling toward the cottage. Liz caught him up as he threw open the door. A delicious smell of roasting meat wafted toward them, new bread mingled with the perfume of fruit. The table was set for four but only the boy and girl sat facing each other at either end. Now they turned to stare curiously at the intruders from beneath identical furrowed brows. There was no doubt whose children they were; they were the image of their father. From the rocking chair Louis smiled inanely. Creak, creak, squealed the floor. No one spoke nor moved. The motion slowed, then stopped. Without turning his gaze, the boy put out his hand and set the chair rocking again, then grinning oafishly he motioned the couple toward the empty places at the table.

When they did not move the girl rose, fetched five tumblers from the cupboard and solemnly filled them with purple local wine. Her movements were laboriously achieved, her slow-witted face grimacing intently as she concentrated on her task. Still nobody spoke.

The boy, young man rather, bent over his food and chomped noisily, watching intently as the girl took a glass to Louis. She held it out but he did not move nor did his fixed expression change. Then with surprising deftness she threw back his head and poured the wine roughly into his open mouth. The head fell forward as the dark liquid dribbled down his chin, staining the coarse material of his overalls. His daughter turned triumphantly to the Murphys, who still stood openmouthed at the door, as if expecting their applause. With a sharp cry her brother pushed her aside and rearranged Louis against the cushions, then set the chair rocking gently again. Louis smiled on.

Liz let out a little scream. Dan grabbed her and pulled her backward. She clutched at him blindly as they fled toward the car. Behind them, the door of the cottage slammed shut. Dan turned the ignition over and over but couldn't get the car started. Liz kept tearing at his shaking hands, shouting at him to get them away. The lights in the cottage went out as the great white owl emerged from the barn. Then without warning a figure rose out of the gloom in front of them. A hand tapped softly on the windscreen, then another and another. Dan screamed mingled prayer and abuse as he hopelessly turned and re-turned the flooded engine.

Liz slipped forward onto the floor, whimpering pitifully, as the door was wrenched open and rough hands grabbed her shoulder and dragged her out of the car. Before Dan could move, the other door opened and Mme. Legrand's arms anxiously encircled him.

"Hush," she said softly. "Come quietly. The *gendarmes* are waiting to go in. We never guessed you'd show up. You never before came for the harvest . . . I wasn't thinking straight, I shouldn't have written," she gabbled, "but with Maurice not well I couldn't manage on my own . . . I didn't know . . . *suis désolée.*"

Later, at her own fireside, her tale was told resignedly, haltingly, as she made sure each lumbering sentence was properly understood. She explained that for the previous three years, the twins were released into their father's care for increasing periods, but only during the autumn and winter. It was then that Mme. Legrand shamefacedly confessed her failure to mention that their cottage had been in effect Louis' and the twins' home for the greater part of each year. The scheme seemed elegant in its simplicity. It was only after she had sent the postcard that she remembered that the Murphys alone were not aware of the arrangement.

"I just forgot. By now we'd become so used to it. After all, the house was empty for so much of the year, and he loved it so . . ." her voice trailed off.

Carelessly, the previous week, she had mentioned the postcard to Louis in the twins' hearing, and only realized too late that Louis had not explained to his offspring that the house was only his when the owners were absent. "The twins would have to go back to the institution, just for a few days—in case you turned up." She let out a deep sigh. "He said they wouldn't like it. He was afraid they'd cut up rough. Poor Louis. He never could manage the pair of them . . . even before they . . . his wife . . . their mother . . ."

Too late, old Mme. Bertrand's lamentations made sense. But even the kindness of the Legrands could not console the Murphys for their failure to learn the common language of their neighbors properly. What did they know of the place after all? They were outsiders. There was simply no gainsaying it. Tolerated but not really trusted. When had anyone told them that Louis' wife had been smothered by her own children pouring wine down her insatiable throat? Had it been said? Repeated? Misunderstood?

Had they ever really had possession of the cottage or had they merely been on sufferance? Passing strangers, part-time keepers of *chez-Louis*.

———

Dublin-born GEMMA O'CONNOR is the author of five highly acclaimed suspense novels, most recently, *Walking on Water*. Others include *Sins of Omission, Falls the Shadow, Farewell to the Flesh* and *Time to Remember*. She has also written several works for the stage based on literary themes and personalities.

A Good Catch

Mary Ryan

essa listened to the step on the stairs, then the door opening across the landing, and saw the momentary spear of light under her own door. It was hard to get to sleep with the shuffling and whispering that went on when Nora Murphy had visitors; not that *much* noise was made, but Tessa was a light sleeper. Tonight there had been a spurt of loud laughter from Nora's room which had even disturbed poor Quentin. She had heard him fluff his feathers in the dark.

It seemed to Tessa that red-haired Nora had a great many men friends. Sometimes when she went to the bathroom she would meet one coming up the stairs. One of them had even tried to pat her bottom, but she had given him a sixpenny look and that had quelled him.

Tessa wore curlers when she went to bed—to keep the frizz at bay—and kept a net over them. She was doing a novena in Clarendon Street for a husband but, so far, one had not presented himself even though she went to dances and rugby hops on a weekly basis. At dances the fellows would barely look at you and then ask the girl beside you to dance. Tessa knew she wasn't a beauty; she was shortsighted and wore glasses like bottle bottoms, but her legs were good and she had fine clear skin. She put plenty of Yardley's Skin Food on it before retiring to keep it nice. Faint lines had appeared around her eyes and she paid particular attention to this area in her nightly beauty routine.

Tessa was a typist in the Civil Service, a job with a weekly pay packet and a pension, if she stayed until she was sixty. She would have to resign if she got married, but she wouldn't mind that. She would then have someone to keep her and that would be great. Her sister Eileen had warned that marriage wasn't all jam, that you never had five minutes to yourself between the cooking and cleaning and washing and ironing and the kids getting sick, but Tessa knew all the same that anything was better than being an old maid and having everyone despise you. She could see her little home in her mind's eye, with its gleaming kitchen and cozy sitting room with a blazing hearth. Like the old ditty her mother used to intone tunelessly:

> *. . . With a nice warm fire*
> *And a neat hearth stone*
> *It's very very cozy when a man comes home.*

It had been Eileen who had told her she'd never find a fellow as long as she stayed with the nuns in the hostel, that she should get a room or flat for herself and catch herself someone with a few bob. Eileen's husband, Mike, had come in from the milking in the middle of that conversation and had said to his wife in a whisper, "Sure that *óinseach* isn't fit to look after herself . . ."

The cheek of him! Tessa thought, although a small frisson of dread rose up in her at the prospect of being alone.

Tessa was desperate to get married. It would be such a relief getting away from that boring job in the Service, eternally typing other people's memos, with Miss Higgins of the scrawny neck and pinched mouth down on top of you if you relaxed for a moment. Sometimes she heard the clacking of the typewriters in her dreams. And it would be great to be away from the fear, the sick feeling every morning in case she made a mistake or anyone complained about her work. Once she hadn't been able to read Mr. Cummisky's longhand and had typed a few wrong words. He had come to the typing pool roaring like a bull, "What is the meaning of this rubbish, Miss Higgins?"

Tessa had been summoned to him like an erring child, and had overheard her supervisor confide that sometimes she thought the girl wasn't the full—

Tessa saw that Mr. Cummisky enjoyed his power very much and this had made her more frightened than ever.

Men were bigger and stronger and had all the best jobs. You had to please them and then you were all right. And although pleasing people and worrying about their opinion was a strain, it would be all right in the end if you made a good catch.

* * *

Tessa had been in her new bedsit (found by answering an ad in the *Evening Press*) for a week now and barely knew the other occupant of the upstairs, who had introduced herself when Tessa had arrived the Saturday before with her cases.

"I'm Nora . . . let me help."

Nora had carried one of the cases up the stairs. She was looking peaky, Tessa had thought, although she was pretty and wore a nice blue dress and lots of black eye makeup slanting upward at the edges like Cleopatra. Tessa had tried the same look once, but had scrubbed it off. She was nearly thirty, after all, and it really didn't suit her. She preferred the sort of thing they had worn in the fifties when powder and lipstick was all a decent girl would put on her face. Anyway, in the hostel, the nuns did not approve of makeup.

When the cases were safely deposited, she had surveyed her new home. The small bedsit had faded beige wallpaper, and a small corner kitchenette. There were no pictures on the walls, just a mirror and a calendar that said June with the year 1962 printed over it and beneath it a photograph of Glendalough. Tessa had suddenly thought of Eileen, who had instructed her to let her know that she had arrived safely.

She'd rooted in her handbag for some pennies for the phone.

"Where's the phone?" she had asked Nora.

"Downstairs, in the back hall."

She had found it, put in the money, dialed Eileen's number and told her the place was fine, and that she'd met a nice girl.

"Great," Eileen had said and reminded her that they would be expecting her for dinner on Sunday week and were looking forward to hearing all the news.

When Tessa had returned to her bedsit, Nora had invited her across the landing for a cup of coffee. Tessa had thanked her effusively. She had been delighted to be making a new friend so quickly. She'd thought Nora's room was very cozy with a pink bedspread and deep-pink lampshades to match. On the table in the corner was a birdcage with a little yellow canary inside, picking at seeds.

"Isn't he sweet!" Tessa had enthused, going over to the cage and staring in at the bird in secret distaste.

"He's worth ten of them any day," Nora had replied with a sudden mirthless laugh.

"Ten of whom?"

"I'm only jokin'."

Nora had made coffee with Nescafé and boiled milk and had opened a packet of fig rolls.

"What do you work at?" she had asked.

When Tessa said she was in the Civil Service, Nora had not pressed her further. "What do you do yourself?"

Nora had hesitated and then said she was an actress.

"How exciting!" Tessa had exclaimed enviously. "I was at a play once in the Abbey—*Playboy of the Western World*—do you work there much?"

Nora had made a sudden grimace, compressing her lips.

"Isn't that a grand name for a play?" she'd said with a strange little laugh. "I don't do much work in the Abbey."

"All the same, you must have such an exciting life . . ." Tessa had gushed.

And Nora had said that you got used to anything.

"I hope you won't mind me having . . . my friends in?" she'd added. "I'll try to make sure they don't make much noise."

"Not at all," Tessa had said, hoping that maybe Nora would introduce her to some of them. They might be bigwigs in the theater business. You never knew.

As Tessa had been about to leave, Quentin had huffed his feathers and some seeds and assorted dried droppings had fallen out onto the floor. The bird looked out at them levelly. Tessa had laughed. He had such a funny expression, she'd said, he really was a dote. And Nora had asked if she would like to take him for a while.

"Just for a week or something. My boyfriend doesn't like him. I'll get all his seeds and stuff of course."

And Tessa had said, yes, of course, although her heart sank.

"What's his name?"

"Quentin!"

Tessa had thought this was an odd name for a bird, but she said nothing. Before leaving the room she'd noted with approval the statue of St. Anthony in his brown habit, which was standing on the window ledge, half hidden by the curtain. It had been a relief to know she had such a nice neighbor who took her religion seriously.

She herself always went to Confession every Saturday and Mass and Holy Communion every Sunday, and sometimes during the week as well if she got up early enough. On a Retreat in the hostel, the Redemptorist priest had told the girls to enjoy life, but never to commit a sin. So on the infrequent occasions when a man had asked her out, she had made it plain from the start that there was to be no hanky-panky, that she was a respectable girl.

Once, eight years earlier, she had gone out with a fellow she knew from home, who had given her dinner with wine and Irish coffee and afterward had kissed her in the car and touched her in places he shouldn't, and for a moment she would have given her immortal soul for him to go on and on and on, but she had realized he would think nothing of her and that she would be ruined, and so had drawn back from the brink, opened the car door and fled.

And now, whenever thoughts came into her head, the sort that shouldn't enter the head of a decent girl, she prayed and asked Our Lady to help her, as the Redemptorist priest had advised them to do. If this didn't work she would simply have to tell it again in Confession, something she hated, like going to the dentist. She only liked Confession when she could go in triumph with a clean spiritual bill of health and know that the priest must approve of her because she had nothing to tell him, at least nothing dirty like that.

The morning crept into the room and Tessa stretched and got up, intending to go to eight o'clock Mass. She washed in the small bathroom at the top of the stairs. When she returned to her room she wondered if there was any point in inviting Nora to accompany her to Mass. It was a fine morning and it would be nice if the two of them could walk together to the church, and she would make them tea and toast when they came back.

She was dying to find out from Nora which of her theater friends had been to see her the night before, and if they were practicing for a play. She knew that the nuns would not have approved of Nora having so many men friends, but that was probably part and parcel of theater life and anyway she was sure that Nora would not do anything wrong.

So she got dressed, struggling into her roll-on, and adjusting the suspenders on her new seamless nylons. The door of her room was shut, but not latched. She heard it creak and turned to see a man standing in the doorway. He had a raincoat over his arm and was wearing a dark blue blazer. She wasn't wearing her glasses and could only see him fuzzily.

"Hello, sweetheart," he said, stepping into the room. "Nora didn't tell me about you!"

Tessa was too speechless to answer. She pulled a towel, the nearest thing she could find, around her and tried to find her voice. The man didn't seem to mind her embarrassment, although she was standing there in her underwear. He came to her, pushed her gently back against the wall and the towel fell to the floor. She could smell his breath, stale cigarettes, and his unshaven chin rasped against her cheek. She felt as though she had a big bubble in her throat and words couldn't get past it. What incensed her more than anything was the way the man thought he could do what he liked, walk into her room like that and . . . assault her.

He ran his hand down her bare arm and then leaned back to look at her appraisingly as her color came and went. Quentin spilled some seeds onto the floor and the man turned and said, "So that's where you've got to, my ol' son!" and Tessa didn't like the tone of his voice.

"Get out," she croaked. "I'm a respectable girl!"

"Course you are, darlin'!" he murmured, smiling, but his eyes were hard as flint. "Got a bit carried away like . . . I apologize . . . Wrong room. It isn't every day a bloke meets a lovely girl like you!"

Tessa stared at him from large, myopic eyes.

"Tell you what," he continued, "I'll take you out for a drink tonight, to make it up to you."

"I don't drink," Tessa said nervously, although the words *a lovely girl like you* rang in her head. "Please go away."

She was still a bit frightened but, as he seemed sober and not about to attack her, not as frightened as she had been. Close up she could see that he was kind of handsome and that his raincoat had an Austin Reed label.

"If you're looking for Nora, she's across the hall . . ."

At that moment she heard Nora's door open, and then the latter appeared in the open doorway in a pink nylon dressing gown. She stared at Tessa's visitor warily.

"Introduce me to your new neighbor, Nora my love," he said pleasantly.

Nora looked from him to Tessa and hissed, "You fucking bastard . . ." The man's eyes narrowed.

"I said," he repeated in a quiet, chill voice, "to introduce me to your neighbor, Nora." Nora looked at Tessa and said dully, "This is Tony . . . this is Tessa . . ." and Tony said to Tessa that he was very pleased to have met her and was sorry for having barged in. Then he put his hand on Nora's arm and drew her from the room, shutting the door behind them.

Tessa could hear them whispering on the landing, and heard him say something about only one punter last night, did she think she was on holiday, and Nora whispered, "For God's sake, it's Sunday and I'm still not over it," and then he replied that it was her own fault and that she had to pull herself together . . .

The voices petered out as they returned to Nora's room and after a while Tony's steps went downstairs and out of the front door and Tessa ran to the window and looked down after him, squinting as she tried to focus on the hazy figure walking to the big red car that was so often parked under her window, and driving away.

She sat down on her bed.

"Whew," she said, getting up after a moment to fish around for her glasses so she could glance in the mirror at the "lovely girl." She thought she looked flushed and rather well, but it annoyed her that she could never really see what she looked like, because without her specs she was blind as a bat.

When she was dressed, she knocked on Nora's door and when there was no response she pushed the door open and found Nora sitting on the edge of her bed, her head in her hands.

"Nora, are you all right?"

Nora raised her head. Her face was streaked with tears. "Fuck off, Tessa, and leave me alone . . ."

Tessa was shocked, but stood her ground uncertainly. "How about a cup of tea? It would make you feel better!"

"Christ!" Nora muttered. But she made no further demurral as Tessa filled the kettle and plugged it in.

"Tony . . ." Tessa said diffidently after a moment, "is he rich?"

"God," Nora replied, "if he isn't, it's not my fucking fault!"

Tessa frowned. She disapproved of the language and began to think Nora must be quite common after all. "Is he in the theater?"

Nora looked at her as though she were mad. Then she burst into bitter laughter. "Of course he's in the fucking theater. He gets other people to do the acting."

"So he's a director?" Tessa pressed. "He seems to be doing well for himself, he has a lovely car. Has he ever done any work on telly?"

Nora said yes, he was doing well for himself and no, he hadn't done any work on telly as far as she knew; and while Tessa made the tea her tears dripped down her face and she wiped them away with her forearm.

"Are you going to marry him?" Tessa then asked, because it had occurred to her that Tony might have been in Nora's room before, and had probably even spent several nights there, as his car was so often outside in the morning. Even if they had been rehearsing their scripts all the time it was still pitching it a bit fine.

"We were engaged once," Nora said in a strange still voice, and then she put her head down and sobbed, big noisy sobs that shook her and wet the sleeve of her dressing gown.

Tessa put her hand awkwardly on Nora's shoulder. "He's broken it off, is that it?" she whispered, sorry for Nora, but glad too in a way, because maybe he would prefer *her* now and he was obviously a good catch.

Nora raised her blotched face to Tessa, her eyes red and angry. "I told you to get lost," she cried. "Just bugger off and mind your own fucking business!"

Tessa froze. This was too much. And to think I imagined she was nice, she thought. It just goes to show you.

"If that's the way you want it . . ." she said huffily and turned to the door just as Nora threw her mug of tea at her. It hit the door jamb and broke, steaming tea dripping onto the linoleum.

"It is the way I want it . . . it *is* . . . it IS . . ." she howled in a tempest of tears and Tessa scurried across the landing to safety, shutting and bolting her door. She would have to leave this house, she could see; Nora Murphy was obviously a bit unhinged. And she can have her canary back too, she thought, eyeing Quentin, who was raising his tail to relieve himself. Poor Tony. It was no wonder he had broken off the engagement.

That afternoon Tony returned. He knocked politely on Tessa's door and asked if Nora was there. Tessa said she didn't know where she was, that Nora's door had been wide open when she'd got back from Mass and there had been no sign of her since.

Tony was looking great, freshly shaven, wearing a silk scarf and shirt and tie.

"Looks like she's gone away," Tony said, shaking his head, and Tessa went across the landing into Nora's room. Everything was left in a mess, but her clothes were gone from the wardrobe.

She turned sympathetically to Tony. "But she can't be really gone . . . What about Quentin?"

"You can wring his—" He glanced at Tessa's shocked face. "I'm sorry . . . I'm just a bit upset, my love—"

"Of course," Tessa murmured sympathetically. "Would you like a cup of tea?" she added. "This must be quite a shock for you."

* * *

As he sat at Tessa's table and drank her tea Tony produced a silver flask from his pocket and put a drop from it into her cup.

"It's the best thing for shock," he insisted when she said she didn't drink, adding, with a sad, quirky grin, that *he* had good shock absorbers which was why he didn't need any.

He looked so sad that Tessa thought it would be rude to refuse. So she sipped the tea and after a while she began to feel light and a bit funny. He took her hand and led her to the armchair by the gas fire and put her on his knee, and she let her head drop onto his shoulder the way they did in the pictures. It felt wonderful. He gently removed her glasses and asked what a lovely girl like her was doing in this little bedsit. And when she asked him if he would like another cup he wouldn't let her stir, but left her sitting in the armchair while he got up himself and poured two more cups of tea. She thought he put another drop from his flask into hers but she couldn't be sure, and then he stood for a moment with his back turned looking down at Quentin. He was so kind that she took the fresh cup of tea and swallowed it and when she said she thought it had a really queer taste he just put her head back against his shoulder and stroked her arm.

Quentin burst into song, so loud it almost brought her back to her senses, but then the bird seemed to doze off just as suddenly.

"You're the nicest and prettiest girl I've met in a long time," Tony whispered after a while, during which time Tessa had been feeling very sleepy and fluffy and not too sure anymore about anything. "I've been looking for a nice girl like you. Tell you what we need to cheer ourselves up—bit of a party!"

Tessa looked up at him, fuzzy with happiness. She knew her hair was in a mess, but she didn't care. She could see that he liked her for herself. She had forgotten all about Quentin, who now lay upside down on the floor of his cage, thin yellow legs kicking straight up into the air.

"With some of your theater friends?" she asked and he looked into her large, half-blind pupils and laughed and said yes, of course, his theater friends . . . two of them he could think of would be delighted . . . would she be nice to them? And she said she would, of course.

"You know," she murmured after a while, as Tony nuzzled her hair and examined her now and then with curiously detached eyes, "you're really as well off . . . about Nora, I mean. When I think of the language she used this morning . . . just like a tart, if you don't mind me saying so. You don't want to marry someone like that!"

Tony started, stared at her intently for a moment, and then nodded gravely. After a moment he said that it was very sad, but that that was the way things had gone with Nora and she wasn't being nice to his friends anymore and he couldn't marry someone who was rude to his friends, now could he?

Tessa replied, although her voice seemed to come from a distance and sounded slurred, what a shame it was for someone to turn out like that, so bad tempered and foul tongued and St. Anthony and all in the room.

That night Tessa lay hunched up in the couch beside her sister's fire and listened to the low conversation. They thought she was asleep, she knew, but she was trying desperately to precisely piece together what had happened. She only dimly remembered Mike's arrival—the way he swore at her that she was the right eejit and that she was coming home with him and that he was sending her back to the nuns tomorrow.

"The bloke downstairs told me where her room was and, as I went up, there was this fellow coming out, dressed fit to kill, and I asked him is this Miss Tessa O'Reilly's room and he looked at me hard, like, for a second."

"That was Tony," Tessa murmured miserably.

"So you're awake, miss," Mike said. "Well, your admirer said he was a doctor, but he slithered off down the stairs in a very unmedical manner." He turned back to Eileen. "Begod but he had her doctored all right, lying back stocious on the bed—"

"I was not stocious," Tessa intervened in tears. "I was just a bit sleepy . . . and you left poor Quentin behind."

"Quentin?" Eileen demanded, on a note of rising hysteria.

Mike hooted that he'd seen the bloody canary but thought it was dead and that anyway one drunk bird was all he could cope with, and his large bulk shook in his chair. Tessa wept silently. She hated Mike; he had such a dirty mind and now he had to go and spoil the one little chance she'd had.

————

MARY RYAN is the bestselling author of ten novels, including *Hope, Glenallen, Whispers in the Wind, The Promise* and *The Song of the Tide.*

She is based in Dublin.

About That Night

Sarah Webb

I'm never going to meet someone," Shona wailed. "Never, ever, ever."

"Would you get a grip," Kate smiled. "The whole airplane can hear you."

"I don't care," Shona said petulantly. "I'm hungover to shit, I'm sure I've forgotten to pack something important, and I know there'll be no single men at this bloody wedding. I'm pissed off."

Kate sighed. "Listen, Mick's our friend. We're going to his wedding as his emotional support, not to find men."

"Emotional support, my ass," Shona said. "He just wants some Irish mates there to go drinking with, that's all."

Kate smiled again. "Too right. Anyway, I'm sick of you. I'm going to read my magazine."

"Charming," Shona muttered, even though she knew her friend was only joking. She read the glossy copy of *VIP* magazine over Kate's shoulder.

"He's cute," she said, pointing at the photograph of a bronzed man who was wearing a white shirt and funky glasses with pink lenses.

"Dylan Higgins," Kate read. "Hairdresser to the stars."

Shona sighed. "He's probably gay."

Kate held the magazine up higher. She happened to know that not only was Dylan Higgins not gay, he was having an affair with one of the girls from Louis Walsh's new band, Starpuppies. But, as a client had divulged this in the strictest confidence, she was keeping it to herself. Shona had a mouth like a foghorn and didn't know the meaning of the word discreet. If she told her, the news would be all over Dublin in no time. "Do you mind, I'm trying to read," Kate said.

"You're not being very nice to me today," Shona complained.

Kate ignored her.

"You know that wine we were drinking last night, the white," Shona continued, unabashed. "What was it called? It was nice."

No reply.

"It had a kind of nutty taste," Shona carried on. "Went well with the pasta. Where did you buy it? The wine, I mean."

Still no answer.

"Are we nearly there, do you think? How long is this flight?" Kate glared at Shona and thrust the magazine at her. "Here," she said. "Now shut up, will you?"

"Touchy, touchy." Shona smiled. She knew if she

annoyed Kate enough she'd get the magazine off her friend. It worked every time.

When they were children she had nagged Kate so much about borrowing Kate's dark-pink toweling sundress with the halter-neck top, that Kate had finally weakened and given it to her. Shona never wore it again after that, but it had made her feel good just seeing it in her wardrobe.

"Would you look at Nat and Colm," Shona nudged Kate and whispered. She nodded at the couple in front of them. Nat was resting her head on her boyfriend's shoulder and Colm had placed a gentle kiss on her head. "They've been together for ages, you'd think they'd be sick of each other by now. Get a room," she said loudly.

Nat lifted her head, turned around and stuck out her tongue. "Jealousy will get you nowhere," she smiled. She licked her tongue down the side of Colm's face. "Yum, salty," she grinned.

"Get off, you mental case," he laughed.

Nat swung her chocolate-brown hair back off her face and beamed. "So what have you two planned for the Cowes boys then?" she asked. "I hope Molly's warned them about you both."

Molly Booth was Mick's English wife-to-be. A stunning almost-six-foot blonde, she had perfect sallow skin and a toned body to die for. Once a professional athlete (she'd won a silver for Great Britain in the Sydney Olympics), she was now a sports presenter for the BBC. Which is why *Hello!* magazine were going to be there. And why Kate and Shona had spent weeks looking for the right outfits, not to mention shoes, hats (for Kate; Shona was doing something artistic with feathers, apparently, if she could only remember to buy some), getting their hair cut (Kate and Shona) and highlighted (Shona), having manicures, pedicures, waxes in all the right places and, yesterday, getting glowing instant St. Tropez tans.

"We're going to behave impeccably," Shona said, digging Kate in the ribs. "Aren't we, Kate?"

"Of course," Kate smiled.

The two girls had been talking and fantasizing about this wedding for months. All they needed now were some warm, friendly Cowes men to make it all come to life.

Colm laughed. "Yeah, right, like you behaved on that rugby weekend in Scotland in March."

Kate and Shona had disappeared for the night with "Scotty" and "Drew," fine, strapping Welsh men. How they'd managed to find Welsh men in Edinburgh they couldn't quite remember.

As they got off the plane they were all hit by a balmy waft of air, which smelled deliciously like vanilla.

"It's hot here!" Shona exclaimed.

"Mick told us that last night on the phone, thirty degrees," Colm grinned. "Were you not listening?"

"I thought he was only joking," Shona admitted. "Making Cowes sound better than Dublin."

"Why would he do that?" Nat asked.

"You know," Shona said, walking along the steaming tarmacadam, "trying to make us jealous. And to make himself feel better about leaving all his friends and settling down in some godforsaken holiday village in England."

"Shona!" Kate said, slightly shocked. "That's not a very nice thing to say. I'm sure Cowes is lovely."

"Maybe," Shona muttered. "But it's not home."

Kate put her arm around her friend. "You'll miss him, won't you?"

"Yes," Shona admitted. To be honest, it wasn't that she missed him exactly; more that it didn't suit her. "He shouldn't have gone meeting a bloody English girl. Why couldn't she have lived in Dublin? It's not fair."

"You know Molly's job takes her all over the place," Kate said levelly. "It wouldn't have been practical for her to live in Ireland. Anyway, stop being so negative."

They walked into the baggage reclaiming area and took some U2-like shots of each other, shades on, standing in carefully chosen poses.

After they'd collected their bags they found a taxi.

"We're going to the Cowes ferry, please," Colm said to the taxi driver.

"Been dropping people to the ferry all day," the taxi man said. "Going to the Booth wedding?"

"Yes," Nat smiled. "Mr. Booth-to-be is a friend of ours."

"Mr. Booth?" the driver asked in confusion.

"Mick Connolly," Colm explained. "But we all call him Mr. Booth. It really annoys him."

The taxi driver didn't really understand but he thought it was best to let it go. Mad Irish people—he was quite used to them.

They drove through Southampton, Colm chatting to the taxi driver about the new football stadium and the girls half listening and looking out of the windows. It really was a beautiful day—the sun was splitting the heavens and there was a welcome breeze moving the leaves and alleviating the stifling heaviness of the heat.

"Here we are," the driver said after ten minutes. "The ferry terminal. Enjoy the wedding."

* * *

"It's so exciting," Nat said as they sat on the ferry. "I can't wait to see Mick. I bet he's bricking it."

"I don't know," Kate smiled. "Maybe he'll surprise us all." Shona stared out of the window at the large yachts sailing by. She was feeling decidedly queasy. She didn't like ferries one little bit, even small ones like this. She was usually all right standing out on deck in the fresh air, but this ferry seemed to be sealed in. It was making her feel claustrophobic. In fact, this whole thing was making her feel most odd—the wedding, England, seeing Mick again. She hoped there wouldn't be a scene. Molly was pretty straitlaced. Then again, it might liven things up a bit. If Molly only knew about Kate. Frankly, she was amazed Mick had asked Kate at all in the circumstances.

"This place is excellent!" Shona said, dumping her bags unceremoniously on the floor of the Rawling's Hotel room and collapsing on the double bed beside the window. "I hope you don't mind sharing with me. They only had two rooms left when I called and Nat and Colm took the other one. I thought it would be nice for us all to stay in the same place. Molly and Mick are staying here tomorrow night too, after the wedding."

"It's fine," Kate smiled, sitting down on the narrow single bed. "It's like being in college again. Remember?"

Kate and Shona had been in Trinity together and had shared elegantly high-ceilinged rooms in Front Square, complete with an original Picasso drawing borrowed from the college collection, which never ceased to impress their guests.

"How could I forget?" Shona laughed. "The best year of my life."

"Really?"

"Absolutely," Shona said. Nothing like having your own personal slave in the form of your best friend and never lifting a finger. She missed it now—she hated washing up, and as for Hoovering . . . "Now I must show you what I'm wearing tomorrow."

"Mick!" Shona screamed. She threw her arms around her friend, attracting the attention of the whole hotel. "It's so good to see you."

Mick smiled broadly. "I'm so glad you could all come."

"Wouldn't have missed it for the world, mate," Colm smiled, slapping him on the back.

Nat gave Mick a hug. "Good to see you," she smiled. She kissed him on the cheek.

Kate smiled gently at Mick. "Hi," she said.

"Do I not get a hug?" Mick asked.

"Of course," she said, putting her arms around him.

He squeezed her tightly.

"Thanks for being here," he said in her ear. He stood back and grinned widely. His eyes were sparkling and he had an awesome tan. He laughed. "This is so great!" he beamed. "The old gang, all together again. And I'm getting married!"

"Has it sunk in yet?" Colm asked. "The whole marriage thing."

"Not really," Mick admitted.

"Right," Colm murmured. He knew Nat was quite keen on the idea, at least he presumed she was. They'd been together nearly two years after all and, as she kept telling him, she was nearly thirty. In fact, he knew, from happening upon her driver's license in her wallet, that she was actually thirty-three, but he was much too polite to mention it. Besides it would mean admitting that he'd gone through her wallet, which wouldn't look good. Not good at all.

They all sat down beside the heated outdoor pool. The water was a bluer-than-blue color, deliciously inviting. Luckily Mick had warned them to pack their togs.

"How are you feeling, Mick?" Kate asked as she peeled off her T-shirt, exposing her bright-pink tankini top. "Are you nervous?"

"I'm not sure," he smiled. "I think so. Nervous but excited. Much better now that you guys are here."

"Are you not supposed to be off doing wedding things?" Shona asked. "Blowing up balloons or something."

"I'm off the hook until this evening," Mick said. "There's a wedding practice at six and then I'll meet you guys at the pub after. Except Colm, of course. I'll need him."

Colm was Mick's best man.

"So we can stay here and sun ourselves until then?" Nat asked.

"Yes," Mick smiled.

"Excellent," Nat grinned. "I can work on my tan."

Shona looked at her enviously. Nat was already an amazing honey color. She was also a natural beauty who would look good dressed in a bin liner, and to top it all, a really lovely girl. Colm had met her on a scuba diving holiday in Portugal and had been instantly smitten. Shona liked her, of course, you couldn't help but like Nat, she was a primary school teacher for heaven's sake, but she was a little jealous of Nat and Colm's relationship. It made her two-week "relationships" look dysfunctional in comparison. And besides, it meant that Colm didn't go on the piss as much anymore. What with Mick away and Colm in dotage, Shona was suffering a bit of a hiatus in her previously healthy social life. Kate was fun but she didn't drink enough for Shona's liking. In fact, although she was her best friend, Kate was a bit, well, boring to tell the truth. Although, in light of recent events, Shona wasn't so sure.

As Nat and Colm canoodled in the pool, Shona settled into her third Sea Breeze cocktail. Kate was sipping a glass of chilled white wine.

"This is heavenly," Kate said.

"The drink?"

"Well, yes, that too," Kate smiled. "The sun, the pool, everything."

"Um," Shona murmured.

"What's up?" Kate asked. "You're very quiet."

"Nothing," Shona said. "Just a bit tired from the traveling, that's all." She took a long sip of her drink. "Do you think those two will be next?" she asked, staring at Nat and Colm, who were having freestyle races in the pool.

"Wouldn't be surprised," Kate said. "They're great together. I've never seen Colm so happy."

Shona frowned, stopped looking at the pool, concentrating on her drink instead. "They make you tired just looking at them," she complained. "Competitive swimming's far too energetic for this time of day. Hey, you two," she yelled at them. "You're missing valuable drinking time. Your cocktails are getting warm."

Colm and Nat swam over and held on to the side of the pool beside where the girls were lounging.

"Hand them over," Colm smiled. "We'll drink them here."

"I don't think you're supposed to drink in the pool," Nat said, scanning the notice on the wall. "Look—no eating, drinking, or kissing in the pool."

Colm leaned over and kissed her. "Born to be wild, that's me," he laughed.

"Who's that?" Kate asked Jenny. She was sitting in the Pier View Pub with Shona, Nat and some of Molly's gang, including her best friend, Jenny, waiting for the boys to come back from the wedding rehearsal.

Jenny smiled. "That's Molly's cousin. Nice, isn't he?"

The Irish girls looked him up and down.

"Not bad," Shona agreed. "How tall is he?"

"Tall," Jenny laughed. "Over six foot, I guess."

"Interesting," Shona said. "What's his name?"

"Oliver. We call him Ollie. Molly and Ollie."

Ollie glanced over and caught her eye. He held up his glass, toasting her. "Hi," he grinned. He had long dark hair tied back in a ponytail, and a black Celtic tattoo snaked down one of his arms, peeking out from his short-sleeved, red-and-white, dragon-patterned shirt.

Shona looked away.

"Not my type," she said. "Bit rough looking. And the pony-tail's very eighties."

"Shona," Kate warned.

"He's a really nice guy," Jenny said, a little miffed. Ollie was a friend of hers and frankly she thought Shona would be lucky if he looked twice at her. After spending the last few hours with the Irish contingent, at Mick's request, she'd found them all great company, except Shona. She hadn't taken to her at all.

"No," Shona decided, giving Ollie a final once-over. "Too scruffy."

"What are you talking about?" Kate laughed. "Shona loves a bit of rough, don't you? Remember Bert, the builder?"

"Shut up," Shona muttered. She'd been very drunk that particular night.

"At least he wasn't called Bob," Nat giggled.

"Ollie's a painter," Jenny said.

"Really?" Shona asked. "What does he paint? I'm very interested in art, especially modern art. I studied History of Art in college."

Jenny laughed. "Ollie's not an artist, I'm afraid. He paints houses."

The girls laughed, all except Shona, who felt a bit stupid. How was she supposed to know he was a tradesman?

"How are my favorite girls?" Mick said as he walked into the pub.

"How did it go?" Jenny asked.

Mick groaned. "Well, you know what they say—bad rehearsal, great wedding."

"Do they?" Nat said.

Colm gave her a look. " 'Course they do. It'll be brilliant tomorrow, Mick. You'll see."

"Where's Molly?" Kate asked.

"Having dinner with her parents," Mick smiled. "I'm free for—" he stared at his watch "—at least another hour or two."

"Excellent," Colm grinned. "Let's get the pints in, so."

* * *

"I'm sure I got a bad pint last night," Colm groaned. They were sitting outside Rawling's, attempting to eat breakfast.

Kate and Nat had gone for the full fry-up, but Colm and Shona were suffering.

"Try some toast," Kate suggested gently, pushing the plate toward Shona.

Shona picked a piece up gingerly and began to butter it.

"Marmalade?" Nat said.

Shona glared at her. "I don't like marmalade."

"I was only trying to be helpful," Nat said. "No need to snap at me." She looked at Colm. He was staring at the water in the pool.

"Be nice, Shona," Kate said. "So what are you wearing today?" she asked Nat, trying to steer the conversation onto safer ground.

"A white and pink dress," Nat said. "And a white hat. It was a bugger to bring over on the plane so I'm going to keep it on all day. What about you?"

"Red dress, quite plain really."

Shona snorted. "Plain, my ass. Pay no attention to her, Nat. It's a slinky little number covered in beads by Louise Kennedy, no less. She got it in the sales last year. Plain, my ass."

"You already said that," Kate said. "Anyway I've worn it loads of times, I'm sure everyone's seen it by now."

"So, I'm saying it again. Plain, my ass."

"What are you wearing, Shona?" Nat asked nervously. She didn't want to annoy her again. Not that asking if someone wanted marmalade should annoy anyone. Still, they were Colm's friends and she had to be nice to them.

That was unfair, she thought to herself. She liked Kate. And Shona wasn't too bad, Nat supposed. She was just a bit scary when she was in one of her moods.

"A blue trouser suit with a sequined top. Whistles. It took me ages to find. Cost a bloody fortune."

"It's stunning," Kate added kindly.

Colm stood up. "I'm going to have a quick dip before I get changed. It's nearly twelve."

Kate squealed. "You're not serious? We're supposed to be at the hairdressers' at twelve."

Colm smiled. "Better get a move on then, hadn't you?" He jumped into the pool, splashing the three of them.

"Bastard," Shona muttered.

Nat and Kate looked at each other anxiously.

"I hate it," Shona complained. She stopped in front of a shop window and stared at her own reflection. The local hairdresser had obviously ignored her request for it to be blow-dried "flat with lots of texture." Shona had been much too engrossed in the latest issue of *Cosmopolitan* to notice, and by the time she'd raised her head it was too late. "It's fucking puffy," she moaned. "I hate puffy hair. I won't be able to put my feathers in it now."

"It's fine," Kate said. Nat was keeping well out of it. "It'll settle down later."

Shona wasn't convinced. "I should go back and make them do it again. Bloody culchies."

"We don't have time," Kate said. "Come on." She walked on ahead.

Shona glared at Kate's back. "It's OK for you, your hair always looks good." Kate had long, naturally curly brown hair. She usually left it alone, tying it back off her face. Shona had a high-maintenance blond bob, Geri Halliwell style. Which, seeing as her hair was naturally mousy-brown with a wave, wasn't the easiest of styles to maintain.

"Oh, shut up and move it," Kate muttered irritably under her breath. She was getting a little sick of playing mummy to Shona.

"What?" Shona asked.

"Nothing," Kate said. "Just come on, would you?"

"This is the life," Shona purred.

She was sitting under a white parasol on the wooden deck of the Bellevue Hotel. White satin ribbons had been tied to the wooden posts of the deck and they fluttered gently in the breeze. White rose trees stood like soldiers at the entrance to the large marquee off the deck.

"More champagne, darling?" Colm asked Nat in his best plummy accent.

"Please," Nat said, shading her eyes from the sun with her hand and smiling warmly up at him.

Shona held out her glass. "Me too," she said.

"How about you, Kate?" Colm asked.

"I'm fine for the moment, thanks." She was watching the people from *Hello!* magazine setting up their equipment. There were two young male assistants both dressed in a "uniform" of black jeans and black T-shirts, a cameraman, who was actually a tall, angular woman with tightly cropped white hair, also dressed in black, and a large woman in her fifties holding an official-looking clipboard, who had more than a passing resemblance to Christopher Biggins, round red plastic-framed glasses and all.

Shona was doing her best to get noticed by the photographer, turning her chair sideways so that they could see more of her face and laughing like a drain, head thrown back and hands gesticulating wildly.

"Can I have the wedding party, please?" the clipboard lady said, ignoring Shona. She was well used to her type and made a point of never including them in any pictures. Pity, really. The other girls at her table were very attractive.

Mick squeezed Kate's shoulder gently as he walked past her to pose for the waiting photographer.

"That's it," the photographer said. "Molly, can you rest your hand on Mick's cheek. Big smiles. Lovely, lovely."

When the photographs were over it was time for dinner. Everyone was ushered into the huge marquee. Rather than split everyone up, Mick and Molly had left groups of friends together, so Shona, Kate and Nat were at a large round table beside the top table.

"They could have made more of an effort to find some decent men for us," Shona complained as she sat down beside Kate. "There's five girls at this table and only three men. It's not on." To Shona's right was Ollie, and also joining them at the table were Jenny, Ollie's brother, Leo, a 22-year-old student, Molly's uncle, Richard, and his partner, Karen.

Kate shrugged. She actually thought they were at a brilliant table. Ollie and his brother were charming and great fun, and Jenny was lovely too. In a way she wished they hadn't put Shona beside her though, they saw enough of each other back in Dublin and she would have liked to get to know some of the others better.

As the plates were cleared away, Mick's dad stood up and gave a short but touching speech about how delighted they were to welcome Molly into the family. Colm followed next.

Halfway through his tale of a particularly drunken night in college, when Mick, himself and the rest of the rugby seconds team had lifted, heaved and pushed some poor unfortunate lecturer's mini between the rugby posts in College Green, Shona nudged Kate obviously.

"Remember that night, Kate?" she said loudly.

"Shush," Kate whispered.

When Mick stood up, Shona began to giggle.

"Why are you laughing?" Kate asked crossly. "Apart from being drunk, that is."

"Listen to you, Miss Sobriety," Shona sniggered. "You're not always such a goody two-shoes, are you?"

Kate stared at her. "What are you on about?"

"The stag night," Shona said smugly. "I was there, in the club with Mick and the stag party. I saw you."

Kate winced. She could feel the blood drain from her face and she felt faint. She took a sip of water and concentrated on Mick, who had just started to tell the story of the night he'd met Molly for the first time.

"I was in the Lansdowne Hotel with Colm and some of the Clontarf lads," Mick was saying. "Ireland were playing France and they'd just lost 9–10. Molly was sitting beside us and smiled at me, leaned over and said, 'Bad luck, they'll win next time, you'll see. That David Humphreys has an awesome kick.' I was a goner. A beautiful woman who loved rugby." Everyone laughed.

"That's not quite how I remember it," Colm interrupted. "You were trying to chat her up the whole way through the match, but she was having none of it. She wanted to concentrate on the game."

Mick laughed. "Thanks for that, Colm. Anyway, that's all I have to say really. Again, thank you all so much for coming and enjoy the rest of the evening."

Everyone clapped warmly.

"He could have mentioned his Irish friends by name," Shona sniffed as she held her glass out for yet another top up from the waiter.

Kate gripped her own glass tighter. It was going to be a long evening.

"What are you thinking about?" Nat asked Colm. They were sitting at a table in the marquee, watching the dancing.

He pulled her hands toward him and kissed them firmly. "You," he smiled. "And how lucky I am."

"You're sweet," Nat smiled back.

"Nat?" Colm began.

"Yes?"

"How do you feel, about marriage?"

Nat looked at him carefully. "Why?"

"Just wondering."

"To be honest, I really like things the way they are," she said after a short pause. "I don't feel ready for that sort of commitment yet."

"Really?"

"Yes."

Colm beamed at her. "I love you, Nat."

She leaned over and kissed him on the cheek. "The feeling's mutual."

"Would you like to dance?" Ollie asked Kate. "Mick told me you're a great dancer."

"Did he now," Kate said. She wondered anxiously what else Mick had said.

Ollie was a superb dancer and he threw her around the wooden floor with controlled abandon. She hadn't enjoyed herself so much in a long time. When a slow number came on, he said, "May I?" held out his arms and pulled her toward him. They moved together to the dulcet tones of "Moon River," one of Mick's favorites, Kate recalled.

Halfway through Frank Sinatra's "Let's Face the Music and Dance," Kate heard Shona's voice cutting through the air.

"Cooee, love birds, I'm coming to join you."

Shona barged her way onto the dance floor and grabbed Ollie by the hands. "My turn," she said, looking at Kate and daring her to protest.

"I don't think . . ." Ollie began.

Kate gave a half smile. "It's OK," she assured him. "I'll see you later." She walked into the bar and ordered a double vodka and Red Bull.

"Hello stranger," Mick said. He lowered his weight against the bar. "Saw you dancing with Molly's cousin. Nice guy, isn't he? You two look great together."

"He's dancing with Shona now," Kate said, trying to keep her voice level.

"Attacked him, did she?" Mick grinned. "Never the most subtle is our Shona."

"No," Kate said. "I guess not."

There was an uncomfortable silence for a few minutes. Finally Mick said, "I haven't told anyone, about . . . you know. Anyway, no one else saw you."

"Thanks," Kate said. "I appreciate that." She took a long swig of her drink.

"Steady on," Mick said.

Kate finished her drink and put the empty glass down on the bar. "Except for Shona," she said eventually. "She saw me. She let it slip at dinner."

Mick raised his eyebrows. "Nice timing. I knew we shouldn't have let her come on the stag night. I don't know why she wanted to go anyway." He grinned. "Actually, I do know. She was looking for a man."

"What's new?" Kate smiled.

"But Shona won't tell anyone, will she?" Mick asked. "She's your best friend."

"I hope not," Kate said. "But you never know with Shona."

Ollie stood beside Kate, who was outside on the deck, leaning against the balustrade. "Hello again," he smiled. "I was looking for you. Nice view."

The sea stretched out in front of them, flickering lights of yachts and boats illuminating the water in places. Shona had been wrong about Cowes. It was beautiful by day and by night. Strains of ABBA's "Waterloo" drifted out from the marquee.

"Where's Shona?" Kate asked.

"Inside with some Olympic boxer," Ollie smiled. "Huge guy. Molly introduced them. Would you like to dance again?"

"Love to," Kate said.

Shona was on the dance floor with the boxer. She waved and staggered toward Kate and Ollie.

"Kate's a great dancer," she slurred at Ollie. "You know why, of course? Gets lots of practice. She's—"

"Shona!" Kate interrupted but it was too late.

"—a bloody lap dancer. Works in Lap Land's in Dublin."

Kate ran outside. Stupid cow, why did Shona have to ruin things like that? She sat down and stared into the distance.

"Kate?" Ollie sat down beside her. "Are you OK?"

"Yes," she said. "No, I don't know."

"Are you really a lap dancer?"

She nodded. "I was up to my tonsils in credit card debt after traveling to Australia. My day job wasn't paying that well, this guy I know from college owns the club and . . ."

"You don't need to explain," he said gently. "I know how it is." He looked at her. "And that Shona's a friend of yours?" he asked.

Kate shrugged her shoulders.

"Some friend," he said.

Kate looked at him carefully. "Listen, I'll be back in a minute. I have to go inside."

"I'll wait for you here," Ollie smiled. He took her hand and kissed it gently. "Don't be long."

"I won't," she promised.

"Shona," Kate said. "I've got something to say to you."

"Yes?" Shona smiled. Her arm was draped around the boxer's thick neck possessively. "What?"

Kate took a deep breath. "I'm sick to the teeth of you. From now on we are no longer friends."

"What?" Shona said, wrinkling her nose.

"You heard me," Kate said. And with that she walked away.

Ollie, as promised, was still there when she returned.

"I don't mind, you know," he said.

"Don't mind what?"

"That you were a lap dancer. It doesn't make any difference to me."

"Really?" she said, looking at him carefully.

"Yes," he smiled. "A few years ago I used to be a strip-o-gram."

"No!" Kate laughed.

"Don't sound so amazed," he laughed. "I was a bloody good stripper."

"I just can't believe she told you," Kate said. "Just like that."

"I think she may have been a bit annoyed," Ollie said.

"Why?"

"She tried to kiss me," he admitted. "I told her I wasn't interested."

Kate laughed. "That must have annoyed her all right. Anyway, I've given up the lap dancing."

"Why?"

"Dublin's too small," she smiled. "You never know whose stag party might end up there. And they made me a partner in the accountancy firm. I don't think the other partners would approve."

Ollie laughed. "Come on." He stood up and held out his hand. "Let's dance."

"As long as you keep your clothes on," Kate smiled.

"And you stay away from the poles," Ollie laughed.

"Deal," Kate smiled.

SARAH WEBB lives in Dublin with her eight-year-old son. She writes half the week and works for Eason the other half as the Children's Marketing Manager, which she loves. As well as writing bestselling novels such as *Three Times a Lady* and *Always the Bridesmaid,* Sarah appears regularly on RTÉ's children's program *Den 2.*

She also reviews children's books for newspapers and magazines and is currently working on her fifth children's book and her third adult novel, *Something to Talk About.*

Sarah attributes her energy and enthusiasm to having a child in the house and to yoga which, unfortunately, are not always mutually compatible.

This story is dedicated to Tanya and Denise—her partners in crime—and to Jamie and Shirley "Robertson."

The Cup Runneth Over

Julie Parsons

I could never adequately explain the attraction I felt for Declan McDermott. He wasn't an obvious object of desire with his graying hair, lined face and gold-rimmed glasses. But to me he was just that, an object of such desire that from the first moment I saw him I was smitten.

It was mid-October. The end of an Indian summer. The weather had been beautiful since the beginning of September. Warm days with cloudless skies. The same skies at night so the harvest moon hung huge and golden just above the trees and the stars were bright and silver in elaborate decoration around it. And just enough of a chill to make you shrug your shoulders into a shawl and find an extra blanket for the bed.

I had enrolled for a night course in the History of Art at the local university. Declan McDermott, Dr. McDermott, was our course tutor. Registration evening was a huge affair. There must have been literally hundreds of students crammed into the echoing lecture theater for his introductory talk.

I had never been to university before. I had left school when I was sixteen and gone to work in my father's haberdashery shop in a market town in West Cork. I was a natural saleswoman with flair, style and a sophisticated sense of design. Soon the town was too small for me. So I left and went to London. It was the swinging sixties and I swung with them. Mini skirts, then micro skirts, then maxi skirts—I wore them all and soon began to make them for myself. One thing led to another and by the time I was in my early forties I had my own label and my own shops in London and Dublin. A failed marriage and two disastrous affairs had left a sour taste. But I had money in the bank, an apartment in Marbella and a house in Dalkey. Plenty of friends, two Siamese cats and an extensive wardrobe of couture clothes. But I had no love.

Declan would provide that. I knew it as soon as he stepped up to the podium, cleared his throat and began. His subject was the early Italian Renaissance, in particular the work of Raphael. As he spoke, a succession of images were projected on the huge screen behind his head. St. Sebastian, his body pierced with arrows. The Three Graces, their breasts, buttocks and bellies round, tactile and sensuous. A series of Madonna and child, each one more beautiful and perfect than the one which preceded it. And as his voice, gentle and tender, beguiled me and I shifted on the hard seat, feeling the soft wool of my skirt against my thighs, I knew that this was a moment that would change my life.

We didn't meet that evening, or for a number of weeks afterward. Declan's classes were popular and crowded. There was always a throng of students between him and me. And I found myself unusually intimidated by his intellect, his knowledge and the aura of wisdom that hung ineffably around him.

However, I was patient and determined and my patience was rewarded. A list of topics for essays had been posted on the noticeboard and I picked one which I was sure had been set by Declan himself. The title was "Figures in the landscape—the relationship between man and nature in the paintings of Raphael." I seized upon my task with the same kind of gusto with which I would have set about designing a new collection for my shops. All other tasks were relegated to second place. Up at six every morning, to bed late every night, I labored long and hard over my cherished subject. And the more I studied the paintings the more fascinated I became with Declan. I could see his angular face and long limbs in the body of Christ taken down from the cross in the painting *The Deposition*. I saw his strength of purpose and his nobility in the figures of St. Michael and St. George slaying their dragons. And in the self-portrait, painted in 1506, I saw the young Declan, his skin smooth and sallow, his brown eyes wide, his lips full and sensuous and a clear unlined brow which I longed now to touch and kiss.

We met in his office. I sat on an upright chair, my legs crossed. My skirt was tight and knee length. My tights were sheer and black. When I leaned forward my breasts pushed out through the white linen of my blouse.

Declan leaned back in his swivel chair. His fingers tapped rhythmically on the title page of my essay. I craned my neck to see the mark written in red ink in the top right-hand corner.

"You've done well," he said, the first words he had ever spoken directly to me. "I've given you a distinction. Congratulations."

I tried to speak but for some reason the words stuck in my throat.

"Aren't you pleased? You should be." He held out the pile of typed pages. As I took them from him our finger-tips grazed. I swallowed hard and tried to moisten my lips. I noticed his expression was puzzled.

"Are you all right? You're very pale." He leaned toward me and touched me gently on my knee. He smelled very clean, almost antiseptic.

"Look," he pulled away, "we have to be so careful now with our women students. Can't afford any whiff of impropriety. But how would you fancy a drink to cele-brate your wonderful achievement?" He glanced at his watch, smooth, gold against the dark hairs on his wrist. "I'll be finished here soon. Meet me in the hotel across the road, say fifteen minutes? How would that be?"

What did we talk about that first time? I don't remem-ber any of it. Oh, of course I had rehearsed my conversa-tion with him many times before. Lying in bed, with the light off and the radio on. Sitting in traffic on my daily commute into town. Daydreaming and doodling over next spring's line. But when it came to it I could remem-ber nothing of the carefully prepared presentation of myself and mў life.

Not that Declan seemed to notice. It was apparent very

quickly that all he wanted to do was touch me. He squeezed close beside me on the upholstered bench beneath the hotel's plate-glass windows. We drank, at his insistence, champagne. He paid for it. It went straight to my head, and to his too, I do believe. Soon his shoulder was pressed against mine in such a way that as we moved my breast brushed against his upper arm. When he spoke he gazed into my eyes and when I spoke he inclined his ear toward my mouth as if the noisy bar necessitated such closeness. When closing time came he insisted on driving me home. His face in the street lights was excited and animated. When we pulled into the driveway of my house he had barely switched off the ignition before he kissed me, holding my head tenderly with both his hands. I pulled away first, and he followed me out into the moonlight. We stood staring at each other, then without a word I opened the front door. I stepped into the hall and without a word he followed me and closed the door behind us both.

When dawn broke we were still awake. His body was beautiful, supple, fit and gently muscled. When he touched me, angels sang and the sun bent down to shine in through my bedroom window. It was love, for me at least. But when I pulled his head to my breast and whispered the words into his ear I realized there was a problem. Declan, like most men of his age, was married.

"Tell me about her," I asked, as I ground coffee for breakfast and scrambled eggs.

What was there to tell? She was an academic too. Her specialism was microbiology. They'd been married for twenty years or so. No children, he said. No interests in common. Not now.

"It's just habit really," Declan said, looking rueful. "I've thought about leaving her, but I couldn't do it. She'd be lost without me. She's shy, awkward with people. She's dedicated to her work. Oh don't get me wrong," he held out his cup for a refill, "I do love her. I've always loved her. But she's not the woman she once was. She's still wonderful," he paused, "in her own way."

Jealousy smote me like an iron bar.

"Where is she now?" I asked, pulling my kimono more tightly to me.

He took my hand across the breakfast table.

"Visiting her mother. They're very close. She goes to see her twice a week, and quite often she stays over."

And so began our regular evenings and occasional nights together. It was bliss. I threw myself into my studies, determined to show Declan the true extent of my talent. My life was transformed. Suddenly someone to share my daily trials and tribulations, my triumphs and successes. We talked on the phone, hourly it seemed. Even when Declan was at home with his wife he somehow contrived to call me, our whispered clandestine conversations filled with amorous suggestions and love. Everything about the world was different now. I even looked like a different woman. My friends and colleagues commented. My figure was fuller, more voluptuous. I wore clothes which accentuated my femininity. Sweaters and blouses that molded themselves to my body. Vibrant colors, blues and purples which complemented the sheen of my dark hair and eyes and the rich blood red of my lips. Life was full, my cup runneth over. I had everything I had ever wanted.

Or almost everything. There was still the nagging problem of Declan's marriage. Since that first morning together we had not discussed it. It was on the tip of my tongue from time to time to raise the thorny question of the dichotomy between Declan's oft-proclaimed passion for me, and his feelings, obviously not as passionate, for his wife. Or wife in name only, as I thought to myself as we shared yet another intimacy.

It was a misty November day some weeks later that I found myself driving down the street in which Declan lived. I had been taking the cats to the vet for their regular yearly checkup. They lay curled together in their basket on the backseat of the car, occasionally rending the air with complaining yowls. Did I get lost? Hardly. I had traveled this route through south County Dublin countless times. And yet before I knew it I saw the sign, Abbeyglen Park. And I realized where I was.

The McDermotts lived in number twenty-four. I knew this because I had looked Declan up in the phone book, not long after our first encounter. Idle curiosity, I suppose. So there I was, inching past his late Victorian redbrick, noticing the front door painted a fashionable black, cream linen Roman blinds clothing the windows and two neatly clipped bay trees in terra-cotta pots on either side of the front steps. And then as I slowed almost to a stop the door opened and a woman emerged. She was small and dainty, her face heart shaped, her features delicate. Her blond hair was cut short, lying sleekly against her head. She was wearing a long dark skirt and boots fashioned from soft black leather. She paused, wrapping a shawl made of some kind of wool or mohair, the color of crushed raspberries, around her shoulders, then picked up a leather briefcase and walked past me to the car parked just outside the gate. Declan's car, I saw with a pang. The car in which he had driven me home that first incredible night.

I followed her. She drove to the university, to the science department on the other side of the campus from where her husband had his office. The office where on more than one occasion, excited by the proximity of his colleagues passing to and fro outside the locked door, he had lain me on the dusty cork tiles, undressed me and stopped my mouth with his kisses. I parked beside her in the car park, all discretion vanquished. She got out, locked the door, greeting and being greeted warmly by passersby as she walked up the flight of steps to the swing doors. I walked too, more slowly, but still keeping her in my sights. Her office was down a dark corridor that led toward the laboratories. Her door was open. The nameplate gleamed whitely in the gloom. Dr. Dervla McDermott, it read. I hovered. She looked up from her desk.

"Can I help you?" she asked, her voice warm and friendly.

"I think I'm lost," I replied.

She stood up and came toward me. She smelled very clean, almost antiseptic.

"What a beautiful shawl," she said, her hand reaching out to touch the fine wool and mohair wrapped around my neck. "And that blue is exquisite. It's the color of dragonflies' wings. Do you know," she paused and looked back toward her chair where her shawl was lying, "I think it's the same as mine. Just a different color."

My eyes slid past her to the large photograph, framed on the wall. She and Declan stood together. They held each other's hands and gazed into each other's eyes. They looked young and beautiful. They looked in love.

She cleared her throat.

"You were saying, you think you're lost?"

"Yes." I stepped back from her. "I was looking for Dr. D. McDermott, is that you?"

"Oh," she gestured toward the picture. "Was it the male doctor or the female? Me or my husband? People are always making that mistake."

Somehow I made my excuses and left the building. I drove home in a daze. Declan's words filled my head: "Shy, awkward, lost without me. Not the woman she once was." Over and over again they repeated, drilling into my consciousness, and at the same time I saw her grace, her elegance, her beauty, her confidence and her raspberry-colored shawl. Just like the blue one he had given me to celebrate our first month as lovers.

We met that evening at my house. I wanted to say something but I was conscious how pathetic I would sound. Going to his house, following his wife. And who was I to say or know how she seemed to him? Perhaps she was shy and awkward. Maybe she was lost without him. It was possible she was not the woman she once had been. Who ever knows what really goes on within a marriage, I thought as he kissed me and wrapped me protectively in his embrace.

Afterward, while he slept I tried not to think of him with her. I could see the way her small body would fit with his. I could imagine their conversations, elegant, academic, intellectual, far removed from my chatter about fashion, styles, trends and balance sheets. But most of all as I watched his eyelids flicker, his eyeballs roll in their sockets, heard the soft grunts escaping from his mouth as his dreams deepened in their intensity, I thought that he was with me and not with her. That for all her beauty and intelligence, tonight he slept in my bed, while she, the dutiful daughter, was back once more in the bed of her childhood.

But somehow, as the days shortened and the chill of December seeped into my bones, I found it less and less easy to be resigned to the situation. Dervla, as I soon came to call her, was becoming as fascinating to me as her husband. I tried to keep away from her. I tried, but failed. Somehow there was always time within my busy schedule to detour on my way into town, to drive by the house at 24 Abbeyglen Park. She often worked from home. If I parked under the lamppost diagonally across from the house I could see her blond head, bent over her desk in the top window on the right. She shopped locally in the smart delis and bakeries of which her part of the city abounded and I regularly followed, keeping a discreet distance as she filled her wicker basket with loaves of wholemeal bread and delicacies such as hummus, taramasalata, black olives and Parma ham.

She knew a thing or two about clothes as well. Her taste was what one fashion magazine had described as designer boho—that *faux* casual mix of draped skirts, woolens, scarves and shawls, all of top quality, with beautiful boots, shoes and bags made from the most exquisite leather. A couple of times I saw her neat blond head coming out of shops that I too frequented. And I suppose it was inevitable that I would chance upon her in Grafton Street, and that she would have a carrier bag with the logo of my shop emblazoned upon it. I watched her pass by, barely able to contain my excitement. What had she bought? What of mine would soon be in her wardrobe?

But it was not she who had bought it. Janet, my sales assistant, remembered the couple well. They were all over each other she told me. Couldn't keep their hands to themselves. And as for the purchase. It was a dress I had designed myself. Black jersey, with a crossover bodice that both revealed and contained the breasts and a calf-length skirt designed to emphasize the length of leg.

Jealousy again draped its green flag around my shoulders. The man had paid, Janet said, by credit card. I hurried to the till to look for the slip. How could he have done that? Brought her here, to my place. Perhaps he wanted to tell her about me? But he would hardly have chosen to do it here, just yards from my workroom where only last week we had met and made love, leaning back against some huge rolls of cream linen destined for next summer's dresses. Of course he knew my movements. I had given him a copy of my schedule. So he would have known I was out of the shop this morning, visiting customers. Could he be that cruel that he would have brought her here behind my back, I thought, as my trembling fingers slipped through the sheaves of shiny paper. But then I stopped dead. He had not done it after all. The name on the receipt was unfamiliar. The signature was not that of my beloved.

"Are you sure this is it?" I asked Janet. "Are you sure they were together?"

"Together," she replied, raising her circumflex eyebrows to heaven. "They were so together you'd have needed a Stanley knife to separate them. It was positively embarrassing."

There was champagne on ice when next Declan came. He was tired. The end of term was near. I made him din-

ner and ran his bath. I washed his back, soaping and rins-
ing his smooth skin with infinite care as he talked of
exams and essays and the tedium of staff meetings. I
barely listened as he told me of the proposal he was sub-
mitting for a sabbatical, three months in Florence, an
international research project on his beloved Raphael.

With sudden clarity I could see a bright future for
both of us. They would separate. They would sell 24
Abbeyglen Park. They would divide the spoils between
them. He would move in with me for a while and then
we would move together to a house that we would fashion with exquisite care and attention to detail into our
home. He would love the apartment in Marbella. His
long university holidays would be spent there. I would
delegate more responsibility to my assistants and join
him, working long distance by fax and email. His academic friends and my rag-trade buddies would enjoy each
other's company. There would be dinners and lunches.
Visits to the theater and the opera. Weekends in London,
Paris, Rome, perhaps even a trip on Concorde to New
York. He would show me the cultural sights of the city
and I would take him shopping on Fifth Avenue. The
cats would have to go. Already they made him sneeze and
cough. But maybe in their place we would get a dog, a
poodle or a Yorkshire terrier. We would go walking on
the beach and in the mountains, coming home cold and
wet, to a roaring log fire, a casserole in the oven and a
bottle of Burgundy. This time life would really be perfect. All I needed was incontrovertible proof of her
betrayal. And that would be that.

But how to get it? Of course, I realized, the nights with
her mother; that must be her opportunity as well as ours.

But following her during the daytime was one thing; sacrificing my time with Declan was something else. A private investigator was what I needed.

I have always been a resourceful kind of woman. And ruthless with it. Once in London in the early days local gangsters tried to extort protection money from me. I hit back with my own paid thugs. They weren't expecting it from a woman. A valuable lesson learned. Confounding expectations became my trademark. I'd had problems here in Dublin too. Spies within my business had threatened my exclusivity. I had needed to find out who the traitor was. The investigation had been thorough. The punishment, dismissal without notice, was swift. I had taken precaution against such betrayal again. Security cameras were placed strategically in my office and in my home too. Now I would turn to the same investigator again. We spoke over the phone. I gave him the details from the credit card receipt, the relevant names, addresses and physical descriptions. Then I sat back and waited.

It was a week from Christmas. Declan had told me we would not be able to meet from Christmas Eve through to New Year's Day. He and his wife would be busy with family obligations. He was concerned, I could see, for my happiness throughout this time.

"I'll phone every day," he assured me. "Don't worry, I'll be thinking about you." He kissed me tenderly.

"And," he said, "I'll make it up to you afterward. She's going away to a conference in Brussels in mid-January. Poor thing. She hates traveling. She's terrified of flying. She was going to pull out, but I convinced her it would be good for her career to make the trip."

How interesting, I thought, that he sees her vulnerabilities, that he understands the insecurity beneath the polish. That she is such a different woman with him. I nodded and told him not to worry. I would have plenty to do. And so would he, I thought to myself. The investigator's report would soon be on my desk. I would act upon it swiftly and then Declan's Christmas would be very different than he imagined. In anticipation I ordered extra of everything. Champagne, wine, the German wheat beer he liked chilled before dinner. I told my sister that I would not be joining her and her family as usual. I gave no explanation and she did not ask. Sleep eluded me as I lay in my bed and planned.

It was large and heavy, the envelope that waited in my in-tray. The contents were damning. The sainted, insecure, vulnerable Dervla McDermott had been involved with a professor of genetics called Michael O'Brien for the last year and a half. He worked in a provincial university, but came to Dublin twice a week as a guest lecturer in one of the smaller colleges. There were photographs, grainy, black and white, of intimate scenes between the two. They met in hotels and occasionally in an apartment in Temple Bar. He was married, with a plump stay-at-home wife and four children. He's not the first, the report said. Discreet inquiries conducted with staff in the hotels they visit suggest that the subject has had a number of previous attachments. There were other revelations too. Dervla it seemed was something of a party girl. There were suggestions of more exotic encounters, threesomes and the like.

I sat back in my chair and took a deep swallow of coffee. Poor darling Declan, I thought. Cheated, abused, deceived by this woman. No wonder he turned to me for comfort. He would need me more than ever when he saw what I had discovered. And I would not fail him. I carefully selected the best photographs and put them into a fresh envelope. I deliberated. Should I send them anonymously? I decided I would not. Declan needed to know how resourceful I could be, and the lengths that I was prepared to go to prove to him my love. The note I wrote was short and to the point. "Declan," it read, "I thought you might want to know what kind of woman your wife really is. Remember how much I love you and want you. For ever." And I signed my name beneath it.

It was two days before Christmas. The post was impossible. I would deliver it by hand. It was raining as I drove from the city to the university, the clouds so low it was as if they would swallow up the whole world. But I sang as I negotiated the traffic, and my step was light as I took the stairs to his office, two at a time. He was out. His secretary was in, a glass of wine on her desk, a paper hat askew on her head.

"He'll be back later," she said. "They've all gone for a drink in the bar. A tradition, you know, at this time of the year."

"Of course," I replied, laying the envelope down. "But you will make sure he gets it, won't you? It's important."

"Oh you mature students," she tut-tutted, "always so conscientious about your work. The younger ones could learn a lot from you. Don't worry, dear," she picked it up, "I guarantee you, I'll give it to him myself as soon as he comes in."

Like a child waiting for Santa Claus to fill her stocking I lay awake that night. He had said he would phone so we could say our happy Christmases. But the phone was silent. Christmas Eve came and went. Christmas Day, St. Stephen's Day and still no word. In desperation I phoned his mobile. His recorded voice rang in my ear.

"Can't take your call. Leave a message and I'll get back to you." I phoned again and again. It was sale time in the shop. Every day was more hectic than the last. But surrounded by mobs of people I was still all alone.

Finally I could take no more. I drove the familiar route to Abbeyglen Park and stopped as always beneath the lamppost diagonally across from the house. The Roman blinds were down. There were two pint bottles of milk on the doorstep. I sat and waited, light-headed and sick with apprehension. Eventually I got out of the car and approached the house. It was cold, beginning to sleet. I wrapped my wool and mohair shawl more tightly around my neck. I walked to the door and put my finger on the bell.

"They're away," a voice behind me said.

I turned. A teenage girl stood in the gateway.

"Oh," my voice was hoarse in my throat.

She walked toward me, her short blond hair sleek against her head. She took a key from her pocket.

"Yeah," she said, "they've gone to Italy, skiing for a week. Lucky things. They won't take me any longer. They say I'm old enough to look after myself." She put her key in the door and opened it. She turned back to me and held out her hand. She smelled clean, almost antiseptic. "Can I do anything for you? Do you want to leave a message? They'll be home the day after tomorrow, but Dad will phone sometime so if it's urgent I can pass it on."

Urgent? What was urgent? I stood outside the fashionably painted black door and saw my reflection in its shiny surface. So unlike the pretty girl who had closed it in my face, with her mother's blond hair and her father's wide brown eyes. I walked slowly back to my car and drove away. I was dry eyed, calm. The betrayal was all so clear to me now.

I could never explain to anyone the attraction I felt for Declan McDermott, with his graying hair, lined face and gold-rimmed glasses. No doubt the head of his department felt the same bewilderment when he looked at the photographs and the videotape he received in the post. Dr. McDermott, course tutor for the evening class in the History of Art, having sex with one of his students. They used to call it conduct unbecoming. Now they call it sexual harassment. Either way it's a sacking offense.

I had wrapped the video and the pictures in gold embossed paper and put them under the Christmas tree with Declan's other presents. I hadn't told him about the cameras in my office and my workroom, in the hall and on the landing. Or hidden in the light fitting in the bedroom. I thought he'd appreciate the surprise. I'm sure he would have been proud of my progress through the rest of the course, even though he wasn't there to see it for himself. I'd learned a lot from him. Not least a lifelong love of the paintings of Raphael. I keep a copy of the self-portrait of 1506 above my desk. To remind me how important it is to confound the expectations of others. In every way.

JULIE PARSONS was born in New Zealand but moved to Ireland at an early age. She worked for many years as a radio and television producer with RTÉ, and is the author of three internationally bestselling and critically acclaimed thrillers, *Mary, Mary, The Courtship Gift* and *Eager to Please*.

Julie Parsons lives outside Dublin, with her family.

Carissima

Maeve Binchy

*W*hen Brenda's great friend Nora had lived all those years in Italy she had written long long letters. Always she began with the word *carissima* . . . It had sounded a bit fancy, Brenda thought, a little over the top.

But Nora had insisted. She spoke Italian, she dreamed Italian now. To say Dear Brenda would sound flat and dull.

Carissima . . . dearest was a better way to begin.

And Brenda wrote back faithfully. She charted a changing Ireland for her friend, for Nora who lived in the timeless Sicilian village of Annunciata . . . Brenda wrote how the waves of emigration were halted, how affluence came gradually to the cities, how the power of the Church seemed to slip away and change into something entirely different.

Brenda wrote that young people from different lands came to find work in Ireland now, girls who found themselves pregnant kept their babies instead of giving them up for adoption, young couples lived together for six months or a year before their marriages.

Things that were unheard of when Brenda and Nora were young.

Nora wrote about her friends in this village. The young couple who rented the pottery shop. Signora Leone.

And, of course, Mario.

Mario who ran the hotel.

Nora never wrote of Mario's wife, Gabriella, or their children.

But that was all right.

Some things were too huge to write about.

Brenda wrote about a lot of things, how she had met this guy they used to call Pillow Case but was most definitely called Patrick Brennan these days, how they had fallen in love and worked in many restaurants. She told how the good fortune of running Quentin's had fallen into their lap and they were rapidly making a great name for themselves.

She wrote about the people who came and went— staff, and those like Patrick's brother Blouse who had stayed and flourished there.

But Brenda didn't tell the deepest secrets of her soul either.

She made no mention of their great wish to have children, the long, often humiliating and eventually disappointing road of fertility guidance. That was too hard to write about.

But Brenda was very helpful in that she acted as a spy for Nora O'Donoghue by going to see Nora's family. Hard, unforgiving people who regarded Nora as a sinner and a fool, someone who had disgraced them by running off after a married man.

They were so uncaring about Nora's life that Brenda urged her friend to forget them.

"They have forgotten you unless it suits them," she had written to Sicily. "I beg you don't listen to any pleas they may have when they are older that you should return and be their nurse."

"Carissima," Nora had written, "I will never leave this place while there is a chance that I can see my Mario. I wish they could share my happiness. But perhaps one day they will be able to."

Nora's Mario died, killed in an accident on the mountain roads which he drove across so fast. The village implied that the Signora Irlandese should now leave and go home.

Brenda would never forget the day Nora had appeared at Quentin's, long dress, wild hair, her face mad with grief for the only man she had ever loved.

She still called Brenda *carissima.* They were still best friends.

The long years apart, well over two decades, had changed nothing between them.

And when Nora found a new love, Aidan the teacher up in Mountainview School, she and Brenda clutched each other like teenagers. "I'll dance at your wedding," Brenda promised.

"Hardly, there is the little problem of his first wife," Nora had giggled.

"Come on, Nora, drag yourself to the present day . . . there *is* divorce since 1995."

"I managed for well over twenty years without marriage first time around. I can do it again." Nora wasn't asking for the moon and stars.

"You do what you like but I'm not giving up on it," Brenda threatened.

Patrick said that it was amazing they found so much to talk about.

He was never jealous of their friendship but often said that men just didn't have conversations like that about every single aspect of life.

"You are the losers," Brenda said.

"I agree, that's what I'm saying," Patrick said unexpectedly.

Nora went every week to the hospital where her elderly father lived in the geriatric ward.

Rain or shine she wheeled him in the grounds. Sometimes he smiled at her and seemed pleased, other times he just stared ahead.

She told him about any happy things that she remembered about her childhood. Often these were difficult to dredge up.

She didn't tell him about Sicily because already it was fading in her mind like a brightly colored photograph left in the sunlight.

So she told him about Aidan Dunne and Mountainview School and the Italian classes. And she talked pleasantly about her sisters Rita and Helen, even though she hardly saw them at all.

The news that she had moved into a bedsitting room with a married Latin teacher had horrified them all over again.

Really Nora seemed to be a scourge sent to lash their backs.

Nora called to see her mother every week.

Age had not improved her mother's temper or attitude.

But Nora was determined to remain calm.

Years of practice had given her a skill at being passive.

And it was easy to call in for an hour and listen to her mother's list of complaints if she could go back on the bus to good, kind Aidan who was so different and saw nothing bad in the world.

The day of her father's funeral was bleak and wet.

Brenda and Patrick came but they decided against letting Aidan take part. He might be like a red rag to a bull.

Some of her students from the Italian class came to the church, an odd little group that certainly helped to boost the numbers.

"I'd ask you back but I don't honestly think that my mother would be able for . . ."

No no, they insisted, they had just wanted to pay their respects.

That was all.

Nora's mother found fault with everything.

The priest had been too young, too swift, too impersonal.

People hadn't worn dark clothes.

The hotel they had gone to for coffee, just the family, had been entirely unsuitable.

She brooked no conversation at all about Father. Did not care to hear that he had been a kind man and that it was good that he was at peace. Instead there was a litany of his mistakes, which were apparently legion, and the main one was his never having taken out a proper insurance policy.

"And now of course you'll all go off to your own homes and leave me alone for the rest of my days," she said.

Nora waited for the others to speak.

One by one they did.

They told her that she was in fine health, that a woman in her seventies was not old these days. They reminded her that her flat was very convenient for bus stops, shops and the church.

They said that they would all come to see her regularly and now that there was no longer a matter of visiting Father they would take her on different outings.

Their mother sighed as if this was not nearly enough.

"You only come once a month," their mother said.

This was news to Nora. It had always been implied that the visits from her sisters and sisters-in-law were much more frequent.

It meant then that she, with her weekly visit, was indeed the best of them all.

She noted it without allowing her face to change.

Rita and Helen were quick to explain.

They were so *busy* and, honestly, others must remember how hard it was with *families* and running *proper homes*.

The implication was that Nora had all the time in the

world and no responsibilities so should play nursemaid and be glad to do so.

Nora, who worked harder than any of them; Nora, the only one of them without a car, who did the awkward shopping, and visited four times as often as the others did, always bearing something she had cooked for her mother.

It was grossly unfair of them to make *her* of all people feel guilty.

And she had promised Brenda Brennan that she would never weaken.

But Nora had also promised herself that she would be polite and courteous to the family, she would not return their hostile bad-mannered attitude.

So she blinked at them all pleasantly as if she hadn't understood the direction of their conversation.

She could see it driving them all insane.

Still, what the hell, she was not going to lose her dignity on the day of her father's funeral.

And after all she had Aidan to go home to. Aidan, who would make her strong tea, play some lovely arias in the background as they talked and who would want to know every heartbeat of the day.

Then tomorrow she would meet *carissima* Brenda and tell her the story again.

She looked at her sisters, brothers and their spouses.

Not one of them had a fraction of the happiness she had.

This gave Nora great confidence and strength and made it easy to put up with their taunts and very obvious suggestions that she abandon everything and go to look after her mother full-time.

"I'll come around to see you tomorrow," Nora promised as she left. She kissed the cold parchment of her mother's cheek.

Did this woman miss the man they had buried today? Did she look back at times when there was passion and love?

Maybe there never had *been* any passion and love.

She shuddered at the thought. She who had found it twice in one lifetime.

She saw Helen and Rita looking at her oddly.

She knew that her sisters often talked about her with their sisters-in-law. It didn't matter very much.

"Will you be around at Mother's tomorrow also?" she asked them pleasantly.

Helen shrugged. "If you're going, Nora, there's not much point in us all crowding in," she said.

"And anyway I'll be there next week," Rita snapped.

But she could still hear them reassuring their mother.

"Nora'll be in tomorrow."

"Aren't you going to be fine tomorrow? Nora will do any jobs for you."

"Nora has nothing to do, Mam, she'll do all the shopping for you when she comes to see you."

It would be like this always.

But it didn't matter.

None of the rest of them had known happiness like Nora had.

It was only fair that she should give something back.

"Did you end up paying for their coffee and sandwiches yesterday?" Brenda asked her friend Nora.

"Brenda, *mia carissima* Brenda, don't you always have the hard word?" Nora laughed.

"That means you did," Brenda cried triumphantly. "Those four kept their hands in their pockets and you, who have no money at all, paid."

"Don't I have plenty of money, thanks to good people like you?"

She went on washing and chopping vegetables in Quentin's, where she was paid the hourly rate.

"Nora, will you stop and listen to what you're saying. We pay you a pittance here because you insist it will all mount up to take Aidan and yourself to Italy, and then those selfish pigs make you spend your few pounds on *their* bloody sandwiches. It makes my blood boil."

"Brenda *carissima* . . . you of all people must not boil. You know they call you the ice maiden, you know you must be cool and calm. To boil would be a great great mistake."

Brenda laughed.

"What am I to do with you? I can't make it up for you, which *might* stop me boiling. You won't take what you call charity."

"Certainly not."

"Well, swear one thing. Now. Swear here and now that you won't listen when they tell you that she needs a full-time carer and that you are it."

"They won't!"

"Swear it, Nora."

"I can't. I don't know the future."

"I know the future," said Brenda grimly. "And I'm very sad that you're not going to swear."

* * *

It happened sooner than even Brenda could have believed.

Only weeks after her father's funeral, Nora found herself being told that her mother had failed terribly.

They didn't get in touch with her at home because the little flat she shared with Aidan Dunne was still out-of-bounds territory for her brothers and sisters. Some of the letters were sent to Mountainview School, some care of her mother.

Helen directed hers through Quentin's restaurant, which was why Brenda became suspicious.

"Tell me. I demand to know what are they asking you to do now?" she begged.

"You are really a very difficult friend, *carissima*," Nora laughed as she polished the silver, another little restaurant job she had managed to wangle to help top up the Italy fund.

"No, I'm so helpful and so good for you. Just tell me what they want."

"Mother is walking around in the night. It came on her suddenly. She can't bear being on her own apparently."

"Your father was in hospital for over three years, she had some time to get used to it."

"She's so old and frail, *carissima*."

"She's seventy-five and as fit as a flea."

They looked at each other angrily.

"Are we having a fight?" Nora asked.

"No, we couldn't have a fight, you and I. You know all my secrets, where all the bodies are buried," Brenda said ruefully. "But believe me I tried to persuade you not to run after Mario, and as it turned out I was wrong. You had the life you wanted. However, I'm not wrong this time, and that kind of pressure was nothing to what I'm going to put on you now. Before I have to shake it out of you, what have they asked?"

"That I spend some nights in Mother's place." Nora sounded mutinous. "It's not much to ask, I mean—"

"How many nights?" Brenda's voice was like steel.

"Well, until they get a full-time carer—"

"Which they won't."

"Oh they will eventually, *carissima*."

"Don't *carissima* me, Nora. They've asked you to go in every night, haven't they?"

"For a very short time—"

"And Aidan?"

"He'll understand. I'd want him to do it if it were one of his parents."

"Listen, that man had one Class A bitch of a wife already, don't let him have a second wife who turns out to be as mad as a fruitcake."

"We owe it, we who have so much happiness, and isn't it like a bank? You have to give something out if your account is overflowing."

"No, Nora, that's not the way it works."

"It is for me and for Aidan, too. I know it will be."

There was a silence.

Nora spoke again. "It's not that I don't have the guts to refuse them. I do. Plenty of guts. I know my mother disapproves of me, and my brothers and sisters do, but that's not the point."

Brenda knew with terribly clarity that this *was* the point. This family wanted to destroy Nora's happiness.

Nora had spent too many years in the hot sun of southern Italy, it had affected her judgment, softened her mind. It was going to lose her the love of that good man, Aidan Dunne.

"Will you promise me one thing . . ." Brenda began.

"I can't make any promises."

"Just do nothing for a week. Say nothing to anyone for one week. It's not long."

"What's the point if I'm going to do it anyway?"

"Please. Just to humor me."

"*Bene, carissima* . . . just to humor you then."

Brenda Brennan called a friend who was a matron in a hospital.

"Kitty, can I ask you a very small favor? There's a nice bribe of dinner for two in the restaurant."

"Who do I have to assassinate?" Kitty Doyle asked eagerly.

"Do you like having me around your flat, Mother?" Nora asked.

"What kind of a question is that?"

"I just wondered. You don't smile, you don't laugh with me."

"What is there to smile and laugh about?"

"I tell you little jokes sometimes."

"Ah, don't start going soft in the head, Nora. Really now, on top of everything else."

"On top of what else?"

"You know."

"Can I bring Aidan to meet you, Mother? I've met all his family."

"You haven't met his lawful wedded wife, I'd say."

"I have, actually. I met her up at Mountainview School and I met her up at her house, you know, where Aidan used to live. I painted the Italian room so that she could make it into a dining room when she sold the house."

Her mother showed not the slightest interest.

"Would you like me to paint the kitchen here for you, Mother?"

"What for?" her mother asked.

"No, let's leave it," Nora said.

"Your mind is a million miles away, Nora," Aidan said that night. "Is something worrying you?"

"Not really."

"Tell me."

"I'll tell you in a week," she said.

"There's nothing wrong, Nora? I can't wait a week. Tell me, tell me."

"No. It's not illness or anything, it's just a problem. I promised I'd wait a week. You sometimes wait before you tell me things. Believe me, it's nothing sad," she said, her hand on his arm.

"I love you *so* much, my beautiful Nora," he said, tears in his eyes. "And I too will have news for you in a week."

"I'm not beautiful, I'm old and mad," Nora said seriously.

"No, you foolish fifty-something, you are beautiful," said Aidan, and he meant it.

Back in her mother's flat, Nora assessed how much she needed to bring with her. Sheets, a couple of rugs that could be easily stored when they were not in use on the sofa.

She would have to have a sponge bag, a change of shoes and some underwear that she could store in the bathroom cupboard.

She must get a stronger electric lightbulb.

Maybe she could do some embroidery at night when Mother was asleep.

It would be *so* lonely without Aidan and he would be lonely too. But there was no point in trying to get him under her mother's roof.

The protest was too strong.

Brenda had been to see Nora's mother yesterday.

As always Mrs. O'Donoghue sighed and said it was such a pity that Nora hadn't turned out like her friend. Properly married, earning a decent living.

"Very selfish, of course, she and her husband, not having family just so that they could get on in their careers."

"Perhaps they tried and the Lord didn't send them any children," said Nora, who knew just how hard they had tried.

Her mother sniffed.

"And I hear Helen was here."

"She hasn't been here for days," Nora's mother said.

Hard to know which of them to believe.

Helen had said she was leaving a letter for Nora on the dresser.

Nora read it. The usual stuff about how Mother was failing every day, some accommodation must be reached, the rest of them had proper homes and families . . .

There was also another couple of letters.

They were about Mother's health. Nora took them down to read.

One was a typed letter from a Ms. K. Doyle, matron of a large hospital, responding to a request to know about the availability of in-home carers.

Nora's heart soared.

She always *knew* that her sisters must have planned for her mother's care. But it was good to see it proved.

Ms. Doyle had offered them several options, but suggested first that their mother's health should be properly assessed so that her needs could be established. Then, oddly, there was a photocopy of the letter that Helen must have sent back. Nora stood there reading.

Thank you for your concern. I am at a loss to know exactly who it was that contacted you, possibly my sister, Nora, who has been abroad a lot and is very unbalanced. She doesn't realize that our mother is a very strong, fit 75-year-old, well able to look after herself. Like all elderly people left on their own she sometimes suffers from the need of company. But now that Nora has, we think, returned to Ireland permanently, she might well spend overnights with my mother, which would get her out of another unsuitable situation and kill many birds with one stone.

So there is no question of us needing any carers now or in the foreseeable future.

I am sorry that you have been bothered in this regard by my sister who undoubtedly meant well but who, as you can see, has little grasp of the situation. I am surprised that she asked you to reply to me, but glad that I was able to set you right on this.

Nora has always been a great problem to this family.

We don't suggest that she live full-time with our mother as Nora has no social skills and is unable to be a companion for anyone. Still the nighttime company should surely benefit both of them.

Thank you again for your courteous and helpful letter.

Nora sat for a long time with the letter in her hand.

Surely her sister had not intended her to read it.

It must have been left in error. It *must* have been.

Helen would surely not want her to see what she had written. That Nora was unfit, without social skills, that Mother was fit and strong, needing no caring, that the family was trying to rescue Nora from an unsuitable situation.

But if Helen had not left her this letter in the high shelf of the dresser, then who had?

For a long moment, Nora thought about her friend Brenda. Dear, dear Brenda *carissima,* who had been so loyal over the decades, and who had asked her to wait a week. Just one week.

But even Brenda couldn't have set this up.

This was a real person. Ms. K. Doyle. Her name was on the hospital's headed paper.

This was Helen's handwriting.

Not even wily, cool Brenda could have accomplished this.

* * *

Nora went back home to Aidan.

"My week is up so I'm telling you that I'm going to spend every single night with you until I die," she said.

"This was what was worrying you?" Aidan was puzzled.

"Yes. I thought I might have to spend every night on my mother's sofa."

"We'd have been very uncomfortable on a sofa," he agreed.

"No, you'd have been grand. You'd have been here," Nora said, stroking his face.

"I wouldn't have been at all grand without you," he said softly.

"What was your news for me?" she asked.

"I saw Nell about the divorce. She said fine, that we're far too old to be getting married at our age, but fine."

"She is right, of course," Nora said thoughtfully.

"She is *not*," said Aidan with spirit. "Was this big decision about your mother's sofa easy to make?"

"In the end it took about ten seconds," Nora said. "I have to tell just one more person, and that's *Carissima*."

"Will she be surprised?"

"You have no idea with Brenda Brennan," Nora said. "She'll be pleased but I will go to my grave wondering whether or not she's surprised."

———

Dublin-born **MAEVE BINCHY** taught in various girls' schools before joining *The Irish Times,* for which she still writes occasional columns. Her first novel, *Light a*

Penny Candle, was published in 1982, and has been followed by more than a dozen bestselling novels and short-story collections, the most recent of which is *Scarlet Feather.* Maeve Binchy was awarded a Lifetime Achievement Award at the British Book Awards in 1999. She is married to the writer and broadcaster Gordon Snell.

The Ring Cycle

Martina Devlin

very time Tara opened her jewelry box the ring winked provocatively at her. No matter how deep into the velvet recesses she prodded it, she was conscious of the wedding band's glinting superiority. It exuded a complacency that repelled her. Vexed her, too, with its implicit challenge. "I've fulfilled my destiny, what have you to show for yourself?" Imagine a discarded ring making you feel inadequate. Even a circle of gold, with its monopoly on sentiment, was still no more than a lump of metal. Not even intrinsically desirable if you judged it dispassionately.

Tara reached into the casket and slid her fingertip into the circlet, deliberately using the middle digit—superstition precluded contact with the wedding band finger. It dangled just below the nail, neither fish nor fowl. No longer conferring marital rank and never likely to fool anybody as costume jewelry. Once a wedding ring, always a wedding ring.

It had to go.

She extracted the silver initial chain she'd opened the casket to find and frowned as she fastened it around her neck. That ring had cluttered up her jewelry box for a year and nine months. And she'd had enough of its territorial ambitions—it was as though the jewelry box existed solely to accentuate its charms. Her bangles and beads were diminished by its attention-seeking sparkle. If it were human it would have invaded a series of European statelets by now. Instead of which it had annexed her jewelry box as its personal fiefdom.

Irritated, Tara shook it off her finger and the ring clattered onto a hand mirror that lay on her dressing table. She suspended breathing, waiting for a crack to spider out from the force of the impact. That was all she needed, seven years of bad luck. Although the ring had already brought her nearly three years' worth.

The mirror remained intact. Unlike her composure. For the question of how to dispose of it nagged at Tara. She considered digging a hole in the garden and burying it, a miniature crock of gold for someone else's rainbow end. Then she contemplated slipping it into the St. Vincent de Paul box in the nearest church—it might pay some senior citizen's gas bill. Or she could reinvent it as a bird's toy and dangle it from a hook in the cage belonging to her grandmother's pet. Joey could head-butt it for his budgie kicks.

She lingered over the prospect of posting it back to her

ex-husband, imagining him opening it as he shoveled in his breakfast prunes—he was obsessed with his bowel movements and prunes were a ritual. Tara had realized she was on a slippery slope when she had taken to conversing with the pips he would arrange end to end along the lip of his bowl. She'd empty them into the bin with encouraging cries of "Don't forget to pull the parachute string, boys"; or sometimes she'd adopt a mock-censorious tone and complain, "Stoned again—it's a bit early in the day for that." He'd caught her once and had reacted as though she were the nutter instead of him.

Tara fantasized fleetingly about sending him a packet of prunes with the ring secreted inside one, that should give him something to chew over. However, common sense intervened and she abandoned the daydream, since renewal of contact wasn't advisable.

Not when their last encounter had resulted in a solicitor's letter. Nettled by his hectoring attitude as they'd attempted to agree a financial settlement, she'd turned to strangers in the pub and confided that her companion picked his toenails in bed. With a fork.

The canard had the nutter bulging with fury.

"Trollop," he'd snarled.

"I admire and respect you too," she'd responded.

No wonder the ring had the capacity to glimmer so obscenely at her, thought Tara, shaking herself to loosen these unsettling images of the past. That band of gold had witnessed some unbridled behavior—episodes that cast an unflattering reflection on both herself and the nutter. And at least he had insanity as an excuse.

But the riddle of disposal remained unsolved. What did people from collapsed marriages do with their defunct wedding rings? Tara flopped onto the bed, catching sight of last week's *Sunday Independent* still lying on the floor beside it. She could always write in to its problem page—but it seemed so trivial compared with the trauma other letters were saturated in. She imagined the exchange.

Q. *"Dear Patricia, I have a piece of jewelry with unpleasant associations and I don't know what to do with it. Please advise."*

A. *"I suggest you throw it away. Now get a life—and some perspective in it."*

Except she couldn't just sling it in the dustbin. She could junk the marriage but not the ring. You'd imagine, she thought bitterly, daytime chat shows would address the conundrum of how to devise a final resting place for a wedding ring once the marriage was interred. Countless people must puzzle over it. She couldn't be the first.

Tara harried her brain cells for some evidence they were earning their keep—at this rate she'd be stuck with the ring for another couple of years. Perhaps a change of scene would help. She mooched along the corridor to the living room, a skinny figure aware her dark roots needed rebleaching but foiled because her hairdresser had eloped to Mexico with her carpenter boyfriend. Who wasn't even Mexican. Tara didn't know what business a 38-year-old woman with her own salon had eloping but she presumed it must hinge on romance. The carpenter's undivorced wife and four children in Tullamore may have had some bearing on it as well.

The salon had a brazen "Closed until further notice" sign on the window and she hadn't the heart to find a new hairdresser, even though the inching reemergence of her natural color was overruling more than a decade of blond ambition. If Sheila of Sheila's Shears had bothered to give her any advance warning of the runaway nuptials she could have had a complimentary wedding band for her trousseau. And Tara could have had a scalp overhaul. But Sheila probably thought a slightly used husband was enough for starters, never mind a slightly used ring.

Tara pushed her hair behind her ears, reassuring herself it was only her imagination that it felt less blond to the touch, and switched on the television set for the men's singles semifinal about to start at Wimbledon. The television commentator was describing, with misplaced pride, how people were willing to pay an exorbitant sum for a bowl of strawberries and cream because it was traditional. Tara didn't believe tradition was an appropriate reason for anything. An excuse, maybe, but never a reason. As the commentator began deconstructing the cost per strawberry, she hit the mute button on the remote control.

The camera operator must have lost patience with him too because the next shot panned across the crowd and a woman's features swarmed onto the screen. She looked familiar to Tara, all triangular face and cat's eyes, and she wondered if they'd gone to school together. She was always mistaking television newsreaders and *Fair City* extras for classmates and it invariably unnerved her when she realized the error; imagine turning into an eccentric old lady at the age of thirty-one. She was braced for it in principle but hoping for a few more years' grace first— although her mother wasn't sixty yet and she'd been erratic for decades.

Still, Tara was convinced she'd definitely seen this tennis fan before. She reactivated the sound in the hopes of a clue. But the commentator, instead of identifying figures in the throng, was chattering about weather conditions and reeling off statistics about how many times rain had suspended play in the last ten tournaments.

"We also had play interrupted by gale-force winds in . . ." he was saying when Tara's powers of association clicked into place and she connected the woman with Vivien Leigh from *Gone With the Wind,* a film which was a favorite of her mother's. The resemblance was striking.

And Tara should know because while other children were raised on Disney classics, she'd been subjected to endless repeats showing the Southern belle stamping her feet and being swept into manly arms. Tara's name was no coincidence—if the plantation estate in the film had been called Drumcree she'd be wearing a silver D around her neck instead of a T, so unswerving was her mother's devotion. Tara's father had been cajoled into growing a pencil mustache. It had done nothing to increase his resemblance to Clark Gable.

But even as her mind hopscotched about, inspiration struck in its usual lopsided way. Tara remembered how Scarlett O'Hara and her prissy companion whose name she could never dredge up had made some grand gesture with their wedding rings. She rubbed at her calf, noticed her stubble had grizzled into a beard and made a mental note to buy some wax strips. There was a lot to be said for Mizz Scarlett–length dresses. Apart from the corsets. Now, what had they done with their wedding rings? Of course: they'd given them away to be melted down for the war effort, to buy food and clothing for their brave Confederate boys.

She could do something similar. Maybe not to aid soldiers, her marriage had been enough of a battlefield, but she could certainly put the money toward—she pondered—toward famine relief in Africa. That's exactly what she'd do with it. Converting her ring into famine funds would salvage something positive from the wreckage.

Tara's conscience had been pricked by a charity appeal she'd seen the previous day in which GOAL invited viewers to buy pigs for Ugandans; suddenly the idea of her ring reconfigured as trotters and a curly tail held irresistible allure. The RTÉ report had told of an entire generation wiped out by AIDS—so that grandparents who had expected their offspring to keep them in their old age were now child-rearing all over again. A goat or a pig would ease their burden. Pigs were particularly thrifty because they'd eat anything, according to the voiceover.

It had struck a chord from childhood with Tara. Her grandmother used to say a pig would eat the hand of God and Tara would marvel as she looked at the Sacred Heart picture on the chimney breast, with its scarlet teardrop indentation on each palm. Imagine chewing through that. Granny seemed to approve of pigs despite their voracious appetites. Or possibly because of them, for leftovers on children's dinnerplates were up there with the Seven Deadly Sins as far as Granny was concerned. Tara wondered if she could stipulate to GOAL that a pig must be bought with her donation. She had nothing against goats, they could dole out as many of them as they liked with other people's contributions, but the prospect of that malevolent circlet of gold transformed into a squealing little creature with a snout was tantalizing.

And the nutter would never know.

She twirled her silver initial on its chain. Her cloud-burst of inspiration so elated her that she forgot to watch the tennis match she'd taken a lieu day off work especially to savor and adjourned to the kitchen to plug in the ket-tle. She didn't hear the thud of balls or the spectators' gasps emanating from the gray rectangle in a corner of her living room. Instead the Edward Lear poem about an owl wooing a pussycat percolated through her memory banks, for it featured a pig and a wedding band too. A masterly combination, she was persuaded.

Tara chanted so softly the words could scarcely be dis-tinguished above the hiss of water heating, "And there in a wood a Piggy-wig stood, with a ring at the end of his nose . . ." She broke off. The pig sold its ring for a shilling in Lear's rhyme—she was sure her ring was worth more, although how much more she couldn't guess.

She watched her kettle adhering to the watched-kettle principle and mulled over how to turn a ring into money. The charity probably didn't have facilities for melting down wedding rings so she'd need to circum-vent that procedure. There was always the classified ads in the evening paper but that might take up to a week and it was illogically—although no less vitally—impor-tant to her to reconstitute the ring as cash immediately.

Tara savaged her lower lip and was rewarded with the answer: a pawnbroker's. Whatever sum she was offered by the pawnshop owner could be dispatched to Uganda to buy a pig. Wedding bands didn't cost much to begin with but they had to have some commercial value. Girls still wed, didn't they? Not all of them had fiancés who could afford a ring from Weir's.

She spooned sugar into her mug, but left out the milk because she never allowed herself both, and studied her ringless hands. Shame she didn't have an engagement ring, that might have run to a litter of piglets, but the nutter hadn't bought her one. Instead they'd put the money toward a deposit on a house. A house neither of them lived in now—it had been sold after they went their separate ways. The parallel lines solution. Sometimes it struck her as bizarre that she didn't even have an address for a man to whom she'd been married for a couple of months shy of three years. For all she knew, he might eat cherries now for breakfast instead of prunes. Mostly, however, it was a relief no longer to find herself distorted by the prism of his contempt. To wonder, as she had in former times, if she were the nutter instead of him.

"A man who won't buy his wife an engagement ring won't buy her roses," her grandmother had predicted long before the universe they'd constructed had tilted on its axis.

"It was a joint decision," Tara had lied, defending the nutter because she loved him and was ashamed for him. Ashamed for herself too.

Tara drank coffee and wrinkled her nose, trying to remember where she'd seen a pawnbroker's. They weren't exactly thick on the ground.

She hunted out the Golden Pages and looked up the Ps, not really expecting an entry that said Pawnshops: Bring Your Unwanted Wedding Rings Here and yet uncertain how else to locate one. To her surprise there was an entry, immediately after Paving Centers and before Popcorn Machines. There were four to choose from and she decided to try her luck with the first on the list because it was close to her office. Strange how she'd never noticed it before and yet she walked down that street at least five times a week to buy takeaway cappuccinos.

The ring was an oppressive weight in her pocket on her way into work the next day. She handled it constantly during the morning.

"What's that you're futtering with?" asked her friend Kim, who sat facing her in the accounts department of a firm which sold bathroom appliances to the retail trade.

"It's the ring I wore when I was married to the nutter."

Kim reached for it and automatically tried it for size on her wedding-band finger.

"Are you unhinged?" Tara was scandalized. "I never had a day's happiness wearing that—it'll bring you nothing but bad luck."

"What about the day you won £1,000 on the Lotto," objected Kim. "And the time you were named Employee of the Month and we all made you buy the Friday afternoon cream cakes to pay you back for being such a toady. You looked as though you were having a fabulous time in your honeymoon photos. And then there was—"

"Enough," interrupted Tara. "I may have had the odd day's happiness. But the good times were few and far between. And happened irrespective of the nutter."

Kim rolled the ring back to her and it nosedived over the edge of the desk. "If you were so miserable with him, what are you doing carrying his jewelry around in your pocket?"

"Trying to find a way to get rid of it." Tara bent to

retrieve the circlet. "I'm withered with seeing it in my jewelry box."

Tara wasn't ready yet to admit she was planning to pawn and never redeem it. Even as an act of charity, it might be misconstrued. Nobody used pawnbrokers anymore—it reeked of the Dickensian.

"So bin it," suggested Kim. "There's one at your feet—it'll be emptied in a couple of hours and hey presto, it's out of your life."

Tara knew that was the obvious solution but, while it had the quick fix merit, it struck her as sordid. Prune pips went into rubbish bins, not wedding bands. She pulled a face to convey reluctance.

"Or if you really wanted to twist the knife you could lob it into a pooper scooper and then make a deposit in one of those special bins for dog droppings on Dún Laoghaire pier," continued Kim, animation spiking her voice.

Tara was aghast: her friend had a lurid imagination.

"Remind me never to get on the wrong side of you, Kim. I'd probably wake up to find a severed donkey's head on the pillow next to me. What I want is to do something constructive with the ring."

"If it were me I'd have it turned into another piece of jewelry, maybe earrings," suggested Kim.

She had a penchant for earrings and wore three in one ear, four in another. She changed them every day, to Tara's amazement—she must have a massive collection. Not to mention limitless time in the morning.

"That would never work, I'd know it was my wedding ring tricked out in new clothes," she objected.

"Why don't you just give it away?" Kim was losing interest in the wedding ring—it was too plain for her taste. Not so much as an inset diamond or a pattern traced on the gold.

"Nobody wants it. I offered it to my mother, my grandmother and my sister who lives in Boston and they all laughed at me. They don't want the bad luck. Would you like it? Naturally no. Why court misfortune?" Tara's tone was no-nonsense, the one she used on staff who attempted to claim expenses without accompanying receipts. "Wedding rings should always be shiny and unscratched."

Her briskness evaporated. "Like dreams," she added.

Kim rolled her eyes and pretended to immerse herself in paperwork.

The pawnbroker's was sandwiched between a video rental shop and a Mod Miss boutique whose mannequins looked ready for pensioning off. It had the customary trio of gilded balls above its sign and she made a mental note to check the reason on the Internet. Its interior was dim and smelled of clove rock sweets but, incongruously, an invisible radio played a song by The Corrs. A girl with Pippi Longstocking plaits scarcely out of her teens sang along as she dandled a baby against the counter, not bothering to acknowledge Tara's presence.

Tara pretended to examine some watches in a glass display case to postpone the moment when she'd be obliged to produce the ring. Evidence of failure. Unless you were in a particularly buoyant mood and could convince yourself it was proof that mistakes could be rectified. And rings could be removed. Still, she felt uneasy about flogging off her wedding band. She could claim she'd inherited it but that left her looking unsentimental as well as mercenary. Imagine trading in your grandmother's wedding ring.

"Think of the pig," she exhorted herself. "Faint heart ne'er won pink piglet."

The girl sniffed when she proffered the ring, nestling in the palm of her hand. "No market for those fellows, nobody wants a secondhand wedding ring."

"Oh."

Tara was instantly downcast. So much for her grand scheme. But she felt obliged to speak up in the ring's defense—Tara was allowed to reject it but this girl hadn't earned the right.

"It's eighteen carat," she said.

The girl flicked another glance, still inclined to label it surplus to requirements. But some coagulation of urgency and wistfulness in Tara's demeanor made her pause. "Suppose I could let you have a tenner for it."

Tara hesitated; she hadn't a notion how much pigs cost but they had to sell for more than ten euros.

"Take it or leave it," snapped the young mother, returning her attention to the baby.

"I'll take it."

Tara experienced a qualm as she turned away from the counter. She and the nutter had held hands as they had shopped for their rings, whirling with plans for their future life together. They'd bought a matching pair in a backstreet jeweler's that was now a restaurant so trendy it declined to take reservations. After their shopping expedition they'd celebrated with cocktails in the Clarence. Just one apiece; they were saving to furnish their dream home. She sighed, remembering how he'd kissed her fingertips one by one in the Octagon Bar, indifferent as to who saw him. That was in his pre-nutter days, when he was sane enough to think her a goddess.

She was halfway up the street when she could bear the pangs no longer. She galloped back to the shop and threw the note on the counter.

"I've changed my mind." Her heart was jackknifing and the baby had started fretting in the interval.

The girl scowled and muttered something about time-wasters but reached beneath the counter and returned the ring, jogging the child in a way that seemed unlikely to alleviate his whimpers.

There was a spurt of euphoria as Tara dropped the ring into her pocket and curled her fingers around it. Protecting it. But by the time she was back in the office the dominant emotion was exasperation. She was still saddled with it. And she'd forgotten to pick up a lunchtime sandwich. Plus she'd have to buy GOAL a pig out of this month's pay packet since her conscience insisted she owed it one.

Meanwhile this wedding ring was a pig in a poke.

She decided the only way to be free of it was to drop it into water. Maybe into a wishing well—and she could wish that whoever found it would have more luck than her. Or she could take the DART out to Howth and fling it in the sea, perhaps the waves might wash away the rancor attached to it. Then she remembered the Floozy in the Jacuzzi and her impulses signaled solution—this was just the place. She'd whip over to O'Connell Street after work and heave in the ring.

Heartened, Tara produced her checkbook and made out a check for GOAL, then scribbled a note that she'd like her pig named The Nutter if its Ugandan owners didn't find that too much of a tongue twister. As she purloined a company envelope from the stack on Kim's desk, she hoped the pig wouldn't be a picky eater like its alter ego. Although a pig with a discerning appetite rather defeated the purpose.

After work she strolled over to the statue, scattering indiscriminate beams on whoever she passed. The end was in sight and she felt like whooping. There was even an air of benevolence, as though she sanctioned Tara's decision, from the reclining stone figure in its waterlogged nest. It was meant to represent the spirit of the Liffey, Anna Livia—although Tara's obsessional mother claimed she had a look of Scarlett O'Hara.

Unusually there was scarcely a soul around: no tourists, no shoppers, no office workers, no gurriers, just a few street urchins trying to fish out the cigarette ends floating in the fountain. Tara allowed herself the luxury of believing they were civic-minded eight-year-olds before acknowledging they probably intended to dry off the butts and smoke them. She perched on the rim of the sculpture, waiting to choose her moment. It came as a garda walked along the pavement toward the General Post Office and his arrival scattered the boys.

Tara took a steadying inhalation of exhaust fumes in lieu of oxygen and tipped in the ring. She watched its post-dive ripples for a moment, nodded to Anna Livia in a sisterly fashion and headed for her bus stop. A giddy whoosh of liberation suffused her and she hummed as she skirted the GPO pillars to drop the GOAL letter into a postbox.

"Excuse me, missus."

There was a tug on Tara's jacket tail and she looked

behind to where a small boy wearing a Bart Simpson T-shirt was holding out her ring between his thumb and forefinger. She could see a couple of butts leaking tobacco shreds tucked further back in his hand. "I think this must have fallen off your finger when you were washing your hands in the Floozy," he piped up.

For a millisecond she considered denying ownership—but wound up mumbling her thanks and pressing some loose change on him. Although he'd probably only buy cigarettes with it.

"You don't want to go around losing wedding rings, missus, it could be taken the wrong way."

And with these sage words the child hurled himself into the teeming traffic.

Tara was so dejected she hailed a taxi rather than wait for a bus. At least that would give her something to be truly depressed about because the traffic was virtually stationary so it was a complete waste of money. What would Scarlett O'Hara do in her position? For starters she wouldn't care about the taxi meter's inexorably mounting tally. She'd probably just roll down the window of the cab, toss out the ring and never spare it a second thought.

She went so far as to stretch her arm out of the window as the car swung around the side of the Rotunda hospital before withdrawing. With her track record she'd bounce it off someone's windscreen, winding up with a glazier's bill—and a boomeranging ring.

She returned it to her jewelry box when she reached home, where it blinked in a particularly smug fashion at her.

"I'm not through with you yet," she advised it, but it

was bravado and the wedding band's complacency was undented.

That night Tara dreamed she erected a Christmas tree in the communal front garden of her block of apartments in Clontarf, flying a flag that invited people in possession of unwanted wedding rings to hang them from its branches. A grown-up version of the trees where children leave their soothers for Santa Claus. She spotted nobody approach it but the spruce was weighted down with gold offerings by the Feast of the Epiphany. Worn, scratched rings, gleaming new ones, yellow-gold and orange-gold and gold so pale it verged on silver all clung to her tree. The dream was so vivid that Tara awoke convinced she smelled pine needles.

Dazed and still focused on the ring tree, she forgot to double-lock her door on the way to work. When Tara came home that night, a little intoxicated from the Bacardi and cokes she'd shared with Kim in the pub near work in honor of the weekend, she found the door ajar.

Bile bubbled along the base of her throat, threatening to erupt at any moment, as she tottered a few steps into her apartment. Her eyes told her she'd been burgled but her brain refused to accept the data. She was positive there had to be some mistake—she'd wandered into a neighbor's flat by mistake or a practical joke had been played on her—even as she registered a dust-free space in the living room where her television and video recorder once stood.

She scouted through the rooms, brain still teeming with improbable explanations fueled by the fact nothing else seemed to have been taken. The bedroom was her last stop and at first she fancied it was intact. Then she realized her jewelry box was missing.

And with it, the wedding band.

It seemed fated. Tara's nausea was replaced by a soothing sense of relief. Granted, it was an extreme solution but the ring was gone and she'd never see it again. Her numbed face cracked into a smile. It hurt a little but it was still a smile. Except then she had to sit down on the edge of the bed because suddenly her legs would no longer support her.

Her pragmatic streak reasserted herself rapidly in the aftermath of the shock and she was consoled by the knowledge that televisions and videos could be replaced, her insurance would cover the loss. As for her few items of jewelry, none of them were valuable and she was wearing the pieces she was most attached to—it was a shame, but she could live with it. The apartment could have been asset-stripped, she'd heard appalling stories about obscenities scrawled on walls. Whereas she appeared to have escaped relatively lightly.

Tara rang the guards and a locksmith, and while she was waiting for both she called her mother for some sympathy. The older woman wanted to race over that night and spend it with her, or failing that insist she return home to Bray for the evening.

"You're unnaturally calm, angel," she told Tara. "The shock might hit you at any time—it's only delayed. I don't like to think of you on your own."

However Tara, although luxuriating in the commiserations, was adamant. She needed to have her door fixed and the gardai would be taking a statement. She'd run herself a hot bath before she went to bed and yes, Mum, of course she could manage—lightning wouldn't strike twice in the same night.

Her front-door buzzer sounded at ten o'clock the next morning. Tara, who'd confounded her mother's predictions by enjoying a sound night's sleep and had only just surfaced, released the lock. Although she'd have preferred an injection of caffeine before facing her visitor's clucking-hen routine.

Her mother had brought fresh bread rolls and oozed condolences as she rooted in the cupboard for jam to spread on them.

"I'd feel so violated if it happened to me," shuddered Tara's mother. "You're not safe in your own home anymore. Mind you, these apartments are a honey trap—sure nobody knows their neighbors."

Tara's stoicism was no act. Her television set was ancient so that was no great loss and although she was sorry to be parted from her charm bracelet, she still had her Swiss watch and the initial chain. The wedding ring was gone, she'd never know where, and that suited her perfectly. A suspicion of a chuckle rumbled in her throat, which her mother interpreted as courage in the face of adversity.

"You're in fine fettle for someone who's just been burgled," she remarked over the coffee cups.

Tara gave a shrug. "Possessions, Mum. If you're not careful they'll end up possessing you."

"I think you're being so brave, angel." Her mother patted her hand. "Your father and I are very proud of you. If I lost my jewelry I'd be devastated—some things are irreplaceable."

Tara dipped her head, seduced by her mother's image of herself as an uncomplaining victim. She felt a constriction across the bridge of her nose as moisture gathered in her eyes and she started to view herself as a casualty of fortune. Its random prey.

"Oh, I nearly forgot"—Tara's mother rustled in her mock-croc handbag—"this envelope was poking out of your postbox as I came through the entrance hall. I thought it might be important so I brought it up—it was hand-delivered." She produced a brown envelope with the apartment number printed in blue ink but no name.

It rattled as Tara opened it. The noise was caused by her wedding band.

It tumbled out onto the kitchen table, spinning dizzily. Tara felt light-headed, too, looking at it. She checked the envelope but there was no explanatory note. Except none was necessary—it was obvious she'd been burgled by the only thieves in Dublin with scruples. They probably believed the circlet had sentimental value.

"Angel, how wonderful," exclaimed her mother, extending a finger to halt the ring's pirouettes. "This is just like *Gone With the Wind.*"

Tara raised jaundiced eyes to her mother's excited ones.

"Scarlett and Melanie have their wedding rings sent back by the general because he says it's a sacrifice no Southern gentleman could ever ask them to make. Such a chivalrous gesture. And your burglars have done the same. You must be thrilled."

"Thrilled," repeated Tara, monotone.

"I've always believed, angel, that every cloud has a silver lining. Or even a golden one. And this is proof." Her mother was radiant as she stood to make another pot of coffee.

Tara regarded the ring, which seemed to shimmer as it refracted the morning sunshine. It was at it again, winking at her.

Born in Omagh, County Tyrone, MARTINA DEVLIN now lives in Dublin, where she works as a reporter and columnist with the *Irish Independent*. She won a Hennessy Prize for her first short story and has gone on to write two novels, *The Three Wise Men* and *Be Careful What You Wish For*.

The Unlovable Woman

Annie Sparrow

*M*illie Jones sat in her armchair and cried. She sobbed loudly, cradling herself like a lost child. Her whole body ached from the pain of loneliness, which was her constant companion, usually benign, yet occasionally it rebelled and rose up to torment her.

He doesn't love you, Millie Jones. No one loves you, Millie, she told herself. *You're a sad, lonely person who at forty-six is still alone. One day they'll find your body in your apartment and the state will bury you in a little plot. Weeds and hardened thistles will grow over you. Passersby will say, "Is that where the unlovable woman is buried?" and coach tours will visit, buying overpriced plastic souvenirs of shriveled and withered hearts.*

Millie stared fearfully into space. The futility of her future loomed before her, cast in stone.

There was nothing to love about Millie Jones.

Herman Feltz was the latest man to tell her so. He was a fifty-year-old besuited German, cleanly shaven with cropped brown hair and exceptionally polished shoes, who traveled the world selling one product or another. She didn't understand what exactly and he never elaborated, but he had approached her at a poetry reading in the Writers Center in Dublin and after polite introductions, when she confessed to her own humble attempts at writing, his eyes dilated with admiration.

Within an hour he had invited her back to his hotel for a drink and after intelligent and interesting conversation, during which he listened so intently to her, something she wasn't used to, he invited her to his room.

And she went.

As she lay on the bed, she watched him undress her, throwing her clothes all over the floor. He then undressed himself, carefully hanging his suit in the wardrobe, putting his tie on a hanger, his shirt in a plastic washing bag and his shoes neatly next to several other pairs, forming an exact straight line. He finally glanced at himself in the mirror and then got on top of her.

For fifteen minutes Millie Jones was loved. For those few moments she was no longer alone as she delighted in his bare skin touching hers. She filled her lungs with the smell of his expensive aftershave and she smiled, seeing how he was enjoying her company. Catching a glimpse of herself in the mirror opposite, she felt that she looked younger than her years. Her hair was cut short and dyed medium brown, and she'd managed to keep herself reasonably slim. But up close the lines of experience were encroaching on her face.

When it was over Herman Feltz got up, put on a robe and poured himself a fresh orange juice from the minibar. Looking suddenly preoccupied, he said, "I have an early appointment tomorrow but let's meet up in the evening . . . Discuss more poetry."

Millie Jones beamed a smile at him, scribbled her telephone number onto the back of a matchbox, quickly dressed and left.

As arranged, the following evening she waited at the top of Grafton Street, in a shop doorway to avoid the constant rain. For the first half-hour she checked her watch several times, but eventually she stopped and just stood there, shoulders bent, gazing downward into the flooded gutter. A few years ago, she would have gone to his hotel, wondering if she'd got the wrong meeting place. Not anymore!

On a cold, rain-drenched Monday night in February, Millie started the two-mile walk back to her one-bedroom apartment in Rathmines, where she'd lived for the last seventeen years.

At least the rain hid her tears from the passersby; she still had some pride.

That night, sitting in her armchair, her tears eventually stopped. She sat, hunched, motionless and anesthetized, yet her face was taut, revealing a strand of bitterness that had etched its way onto the lines under her eyes.

Early next morning Millie entered the offices of Dublin Corporation, where she had worked for twenty years:

heartache or no heartache, the mortgage had to be paid.

She was now a supervisor in the Housing Section, where her team processed claims for various schemes and benefits. For four days of the week they sat at desks and computer terminals, inputting data and taking telephone calls, but every Tuesday it was their turn to man the front desk for the day. Everyone hated the front desk. It was nicknamed the "Abuse Desk" as angry people, made even more angry by the long waiting time, could scream abuse, venting their whole life's frustration.

It was a thankless job, underpaid and stressful. Yet surprisingly most of the staff had been there for years. In the canteen at coffee breaks, everyone spoke about leaving, but very few did. Misery had become a familiar friend.

Feeling extra fragile, Millie made her way to the front desk with trepidation and a sick stomach. At nine-thirty the doors opened to the public and in they flocked, racing to one of the five booths.

Soon a dark-haired man was sitting in front of her. Their hair color was the only feature she usually took note of. She had learned it was easier to deal with the public by seeing them as case numbers not people. When she first started the job, she had really cared about everyone, taking on board all their problems, dealing with every case personally and working the longest hours of any member of staff. But over the years, drained by everyone else's fragmented and problematic lives and her own non-life, she stepped back, erecting a protective armor around her so strong that no angry outburst or sob story could penetrate it.

"Hello," said dark-hair in a friendly manner. "Can you give me an update on my application for the shared-ownership scheme?"

"What's your reference number?" she asked, not really expecting him to have it. None of the public came prepared.

"546698."

Surprised, Millie entered it onto her computer screen and the case file for a Ronnie Littlebrick came up. After checking various details she said, "We're still awaiting confirmation of your earnings."

"I recently changed jobs."

"You'll need to fill in a new form. Your employer needs to fill in Appendix One and the tax office Appendix Three." She passed him them under the protective glass barrier.

"I'm now self-employed."

"We'll need a set of audited accounts."

Dark-hair paused. Millie braced herself.

"The thing is, I'm not sure if I'm still eligible. If I tell you my new circumstances could you let me know?" he said with a smile.

"Just complete the forms. We need full and complete information before any decision can be made."

"I'd prefer to converse with a human being," he continued without giving her a chance to interrupt. "I've recently set up my own practice as a Spiritual Teacher and Clairvoyant."

Hearing this, Millie finally focused her eyes on him fully. He had an open and friendly face with shoulder-length dark hair and dark eyebrows framing large, bright green eyes, plus full lips, which were curved up in a smile. He was around forty and looked strangely futuristic in a long leather coat over black trousers and emerald green shirt.

"Over the years I've built up a good client base, so four weeks ago I took the plunge, left my job and started up a small practice. Is it still worth me filling in the mountain of forms?"

"Your profession is irrelevant to us, but you have to be able to prove your current income for the last six months. I suggest you reapply in five months' time," she said in an autocratic, unfriendly manner.

"Well, thank you for your help anyway." He seemed to hesitate, glancing over at the door then back toward Millie. "I hope you don't mind me saying this, but I sometimes pick up things around people, get messages for them. I believe I have one for you."

She had already exited out of his file on the computer and now stared back at him with a guarded, suspicious look.

He leaned forward and lowered his voice to a whisper. "Everyone is lovable. Even Millie Jones." With that he gracefully stood up, pushed a yellow piece of paper under the glass barrier and walked away.

Millie froze. Her whole body stiffened as she watched him glide out of the main entrance, the tails of his leather coat flowing up behind him in the wind, finally disappearing out of sight. She suddenly grabbed at her chest for her name badge, but she wasn't wearing it; it was in her desk. An uneasy feeling descended on her. She bit her lip and looked down at the yellow piece of paper. It was an A5 leaflet stating, *Ronnie Littlebrick, Clairvoyant and Spiritual Teacher. Love is in the palm of our hands.*

"I wanna know why ye stopped me bleedin' rent allowance?"

Millie jumped and looked up. A bleached-blond-haired woman with black roots was scowling at her. She instantly put the yellow piece of paper in her pocket.

"Do you have a reference number?" she asked.

"No I bleedin' don't."

That evening, back in her armchair at home, while listening to the Love Zone on the radio and sipping her third glass of wine, Millie stared at the yellow piece of paper in her hand.

Do I now look that desperate that even strangers can see how I crave for love?

He'd probably been into the office before and seen her name badge, she thought. He was probably a charlatan, preying on lonely old women. She suddenly pressed her hand against her heart, wondering how she had become a lonely old woman. It seemed OK to be a lonely young woman. One could seek solace that things would change in the future. But the future had arrived and she was still lonely, searching for love from anyone who showed her the least bit of interest. She knew sex didn't mean love but, for a few minutes, it eased her unbearable burden, and she glimpsed togetherness. That wonderful, probably elevated fantasy of togetherness.

Out of curiosity and also boredom, she decided to telephone Ronnie Littlebrick and make an appointment. But looking down at the yellow leaflet she realized it didn't have a phone number, just an address: 17 Millbank Lane, Dublin 6W.

That was strange. How were you supposed to book? Gulping down the rest of her wine, she decided to look at his file on the computer at work tomorrow; that would have it.

* * *

The next day she arrived early, at eight, and logged onto the computer system. She couldn't remember his reference number, so she did a name search on "Ronnie Littlebrick," there could only be one of those. But strangely no match came up.

She frowned. She knew she had seen the file on-screen yesterday. Standing up, she went and checked the manual files where all the correspondence was kept on each application.

But again there was no sign of a Ronnie Littlebrick ever having applied.

Both confused and intrigued, she went up to her friend Fergus who worked in the computer room. Since the installation of the new computer system a year ago, for security reasons every file logged into by a member of staff was recorded on a daily transaction report to which the managers had access. With some persuasion and the promise of a drink, Fergus reluctantly logged on with his security code. He typed in her user ID, and although refusing to print the report, allowed her to view the file numbers and names of the applicants she had logged into yesterday. It should have been the first file she worked on but it wasn't there. Instead up came the name of Jackie Murphy, the bleached-blond-haired woman she had served next.

"Fergus, I logged onto a file about five minutes before this first entry," she said.

Fergus glanced up from his desk and stared at the screen. "You can't have. Not under your own ID."

"But I did."

He shrugged his shoulders. "For some reason it hasn't

logged it." Hearing some footsteps on the stairs outside he quickly exited out of the program. "I'll get shot if I'm caught giving you access to this."

Millie nodded, thanked him anyway and went to leave. Reaching the door she quickly turned back. "Oh sorry, how's Penny?"

His eyes instinctively lowered. "A bit better," he said in a forlorn manner.

She gave him a sympathetic look. "Tell me over lunch."

Fergus nodded and smiled.

Millie left his room and stood at the top of the stairs, gazing into space. It was probably some computer error, she told herself. It was always crashing and doing odd things, plus manual files were always going missing. But throughout the day, the curious Ronnie Littlebrick constantly occupied her thoughts.

That evening after dinner, Millie put on her coat and boots and having checked her Dublin street-finder map, set off down her road. Being February it was already dark and a light rain was starting to fall. She wasn't sure that she was going to actually knock on the door, but she felt compelled to have a look, see if the house even existed.

After twenty-five minutes she eventually turned off the main road between Rathgar and Terenure, and walked down three residential roads before coming to the narrow entrance to Millbank Lane, which was tucked in between two houses. Millie started to feel nervous as she began walking down it. Run-down, Victorian terraced houses lined either side and some of their windows were broken and had been boarded up with corrugated iron.

It was dark and full of shadows, so she walked in the middle of the road, which was still cobbled in parts, as if the Corporation had somehow forgotten its existence.

She stopped for a moment, debating whether to go home, but something propelled her forward down the little street. Eventually, right at the end, stood number seventeen.

So there it was. Now what?

Millie looked around. This place was spooky. Not that she believed in ghosts, or God for that matter. She used to have so many beliefs, but over the years every belief she'd had had been cruelly exposed as untrue.

It was freezing and Millie suddenly questioned what the hell she was doing there. Was she mad? She turned and started walking home.

"Millie Jones."

Millie jumped. Her heart was banging loudly. She slowly turned back and saw Ronnie Littlebrick, still wearing his leather coat, standing in his open doorway, with a beautiful and welcoming smile. "I'm so glad you came." He then disappeared into his house, leaving the front door open.

Millie glanced down the empty street and then back toward the open door. This was crazy. Don't go in, she told herself. He was probably some madman, ready to attack her. She walked three paces away but stopped. Her face screwed up. Go home, she kept telling herself. Yet she turned and began walking, slowly and tentatively, toward the little house. Her fists were clenched as she stood for a moment in the doorway, peering inside.

"Come in, Millie," she heard, from the front room.

She bit her lip then quipped, "How much do you charge?"

"Much less than the price you're already paying."

Her eyes narrowed, but after glancing behind her once more, she stepped inside, leaving the front door open.

Ronnie Littlebrick was sitting in a blue armchair, gazing into an open, lit fireplace, which, together with a small lamp in the corner, was the only source of light. Yet it was a pleasant room with yellow walls and fresh-cut flowers stood in several vases, filling it with a beautiful sweet aroma.

"Please sit," he said, looking up and indicating the armchair opposite.

Millie perched herself on the edge of the chair, keeping her eyes on him the whole time.

If he tried anything she'd kick him in the balls and run for the door.

He laughed slightly and she eyed him cautiously. He was around mid-forties, she guessed, but depending on the flickering light from the fire, he looked either younger or older by turns.

"How did you know my name?" she asked firmly, crossing her legs.

He gazed back into the fire and smiled. When he didn't respond she persisted, "Look, what's going on? If you're a clairvoyant you might as well get on with it. I've got things to do at home."

He looked over at her. "No you haven't, Millie Jones. You have nothing to do but feel sorry for yourself and dream of dreams, yet you won't allow them to enter your life. You won't allow anything to enter your life. You're happy in your unhappiness. It's what you've come to know. Anything else scares you."

Millie scowled. "Is this your message for me? How much do I have to pay for that?"

Ronnie leaned back in his chair and smiled again. "You can have that on the house."

"This is all too strange for me. I think I'll leave."

"But you haven't asked me your question yet."

"I don't have a question."

He stared right through her. Millie glared at him for several moments. He was a tall, slimly built man, possessing a masculine elegance. His stare was so intense that her eyes slowly lowered and she said in a less hostile manner, "You said everyone is lovable. Your leaflet states *love is in the palm of our hands*. But . . . well . . . I don't see any love. I'm still alone. Others find it. Why not me? I don't understand. Where is it?"

He stared over at her for at least a minute without saying anything. Eventually he nodded. "Millie. Sometimes we search and search but never look."

She frowned. "Is that it?"

"It seems it's all you want at this point. Come back when you're ready for more."

Millie jumped up and shook her head. "If I wanted riddles, I could have done *The Times* crossword." With that she marched out, pulling the door shut behind her.

The next day at work Millie couldn't concentrate. She had woken up exhausted, having had a strange dream all night. In it, she was standing at an Autobank, which was in the outside wall of Ronnie Littlebrick's house. She was trying to get some money out and after putting in her card and typing in her four-digit code, instead of money, sand started pouring from the machine. Soon it was all around her feet, turning into quicksand, and she started to sink slowly. There was a large queue of people behind her but instead of helping they just stood there laughing.

She'd woken in a sweat, actually trembling with fear. Each time she'd fallen back to sleep the same dream came to her. Eventually she had got up and made herself some tea.

As she now tried to input an applicant's details into the computer, her mind wandered off again to Ronnie Littlebrick and what he'd said. What a bizarre man he was. What a bizarre incident.

As usual at lunchtime she met up with Fergus in the canteen and they ate their sandwiches together, while discussing the latest gossip at work. He was a fairly shy and gentle man in his late thirties, with blond curly hair and large, kind, hazel eyes. He was happiest in jeans, however, two years ago when the management had introduced a dress code, he had invested in a couple of navy suits, which Millie always felt he looked out of place in. Over the last four years they had become good friends.

After lunch they went for their thirty-minute walk around Stephen's Green, which they did at least twice a week, both enjoying the fresh air and the break from the office environment.

Although she hadn't planned to tell him about the incident with Ronnie Littlebrick, she found herself relaying the whole story. It wasn't like she had many other people to tell. Over the years she had lost touch with a number of her old friends. They all eventually got married, had kids and busy lives. Whereas Millie's life had stayed the same. They promised to keep in touch but, one by one, they lost contact.

So Fergus got the full story of the strange Ronnie Littlebrick and Millie's subsequent dream.

Fergus was annoyed that she had entered his house. "That was stupid and dangerous," he said. "I can't believe you went there. If he contacts you again, you'll have to report it." In a calmer voice he added, "I think I should drive you home for the next few days."

Millie laughed. "No. I'm fine."

"I insist, Millie. At least for the rest of this week anyhow."

Eventually she agreed, if only to make Fergus happy. He was a bit of a worrier.

They continued on their walk, then just before the entrance to the office he stopped and stared at her. "Is that how you feel?" he asked. "That you're unlovable?"

Millie suddenly blushed, realizing what she'd said and how personal it was. "Not at all. That's what *he* said to me."

"You know you're welcome to come walking with me and Penny on a Sunday. Come down to the cottage for a weekend."

"Don't worry about me. I'm happy being on my own."

He looked at her as if he wanted to say something else but remained silent. She offered him a smile and they walked inside.

That night the strange dream returned. This time she started to recognize some of the people who were standing behind her in the queue. One was John Keogh, her boyfriend for two years when she was twenty. He'd wanted to marry her but she always knew she needed more. He had little ambition and was more than happy to go into his father's gas and plumbing business. However, he ended up marrying Rose McIntyre, another girl from school. When her father died, they inherited two farms, four houses, and over half a million in cash. John Keogh ended up a millionaire. Not bad for someone with no ambition! And here was she, overambitious but nothing in life to show for it apart from a one-bedroom apartment.

Another face she recognized was Dave Jennings. She would have married him at the drop of a hat. He was intelligent, handsome, wealthy and enjoyed life to the full. Yet after two years of dating he broke her heart by ending it one night. He'd fallen for someone else. The hurt tore her apart and it took over two years to put the fragmented pieces back together. Through a chance encounter with his sister a year ago, she found out that Dave Jennings was a gambling addict and was now unemployed, penniless and living in a hostel.

Who could predict the future? she thought.

In the dream both these men laughed as she sank lower in the quicksand, screaming for help.

The next evening she drank nearly a whole bottle of wine, determined to sleep without any interruption. But again the dream invaded her mind and more faces became recognizable, mostly past boyfriends and old friends.

On Friday morning she went into work and headed straight for the coffee machine.

"Are you OK? You look dreadful."

She turned to see Fergus beside her.

"It's that dream again. It's awful. I feel like I'm being haunted. Maybe Ronnie Littlebrick is a wizard who's put some spell on me." In her exhausted state, part of her was beginning to believe it.

Fergus shook his head. "There's no such thing as wizards."

"I'm thinking of going to see him again. Ask him what he's done to me."

"Millie, what's got into you? Don't go anywhere near that guy. Maybe he just said a few things that hit home."

She stared at him, knowing what he meant. "So you think I'm desperate for love too. Do I really look that pathetic?"

"Of course not. In fact you look the total opposite. Tough and not always approachable."

"Good. I'd hate to look needy."

Fergus gazed at her and sighed. "Everyone wants to be loved, Millie."

Her eyelids lowered but within a second she shrugged her shoulders and picked up her coffee.

"Maybe you should have taken the day off, called in sick," he said.

Her eyes lit up. "Good idea. I'll tell them I'm not feeling well and I can go to see him this morning. It won't be so scary in the daylight."

Fergus protested but Millie was determined. He settled on offering to drive her there at lunchtime. "You're not to go alone," he said. He added that she still needed some sleep and so should go home and he'd collect her from her apartment.

Millie agreed, yet as soon as she left the offices she started walking in the direction of Terenure.

Within half an hour she was walking down Millbank Lane. Although it was light, with each step she took her stomach tightened, her heart quickened and her legs felt weaker. *What am I doing here?* she thought. She screwed her face up and shook her head. What was she hoping to learn? There's nothing to learn, she told herself. Life is hard. Life is very hard. Some lucky people are born happy, everyone else has to put up with this miserable place. Dreams are merely frustrating mental torture. Hope is eternal folly. And people like Ronnie Littlebrick preyed on the considerable sadness that pervades the human race.

With a sudden air of defiance, she turned on the spot and marched away. Loneliness was acceptable. It had been around so long it was now a part of her. Take that away and what would it leave? So many of her friends had been colonized and enslaved by so-called love, lost to somebody else's illusion. Not her! And some charlatan like Ronnie Littlebrick could go and make some money out of someone else.

"Millie. So glad you're back."

She stopped in her tracks and slowly turned to see Ronnie Littlebrick a few paces behind her.

She stood staring at him, blank-faced, unsure what was going on.

"Come in, Millie," he said with his huge, heartfelt smile and she found herself following him back into his little house, sitting down in the armchair opposite him, next to the lit fire. For a couple of minutes she sat there, gazing at the flames and neither of them spoke.

Millie then sat back in her chair and looked across at him.

"How are you?" he asked.

"Exhausted. I've been having a strange dream and can't sleep."

He smiled. "That's good. That's very good."

Her eyes narrowed.

"Tell me about it," he said, sitting forward and giving her his full attention.

When she had finished retelling her dream, including the bit about her past boyfriends, Ronnie Littlebrick smiled again and sat back, looking contented.

"It's all so clear," he said.

"Not to me."

"It doesn't take a genius to work it out."

She screwed her face up. "I'm so very tired, please just tell me what's going on."

"Some people pursue the wrong goals, which can make them stuck in life. Money for money's sake will never bring peace of mind. So many people aren't truly living."

"I could have told you that. I know I'm not living."

"When you change, things will automatically change around you. The fact is, Millie, you have to learn to care again. It may seem easier in the short term not to care. It may initially protect you, but it also imprisons you. Care again, Millie. Care about the people you meet through your work. Care about yourself. Care about life. How can love enter your life when you're all closed off to it? You need to open your heart. The fear of being hurt is no valid reason to close it. True love can be painfully revealing. Many turn away from that."

Millie sat in her chair, gazing into the fire. For a brief

moment she felt tears form in her eyes, but she quickly composed herself. "I suppose I have shut off from people. So if I learn to care again, I'll find someone?"

"Love comes in many forms."

"But I want it in the form of a person, a partner, lover, hopefully husband."

Ronnie Littlebrick smiled. "I suppose you're one of these people who want it to come knocking on the door. But even if it did come knocking, would you recognize it?"

She frowned. "Of course I would."

At that moment several loud knocks were heard on the front door. Ronnie Littlebrick stared calmly at her, not moving. She eyed him suspiciously.

"It's time for you to go," he said with a smile. "Time for you to embrace life . . . if you dare."

"Is that your next appointment? Can I book for another time?"

He laughed. "I can see subtlety doesn't work on you. The magic of life can be lost in blatant and harsh neon signs."

"I need a neon sign to tell me what to do."

The knocking on the door became louder, as if the person was becoming impatient.

"It's time for you to go. You have all you need to know. I don't need to tell you anything else. Open your eyes as well as your heart."

Millie slowly got up, feeling dissatisfied, but she thanked him anyway, especially as he refused any payment, which confused her even more. She walked into the hall and the banging on the door was now continuous and intense. She opened it and was surprised to see a fraught-looking Fergus standing there.

"You said you wouldn't come on your own," he said, sounding angry. "Are you OK?"

"I'm fine," she said, stepping outside and closing the door. "Sorry, but I had to come. Don't worry, though, he's harmless."

"You should have waited. I've been really worried, telephoning your home for ages. I had to pretend I was sick also, so I could leave early."

Millie laughed. "Well, that will start a rumor at work, both of us going home."

"That rumor's old hat. They've been saying it for years, since we first started having lunch together."

"Really! How come I never knew?"

"Because . . . because people don't always talk to you, Millie."

They were nearing the end of Millbank Lane, which was where Fergus had parked his car. It was a ten-year-old, beat-up Volvo, which Millie hated traveling in. It wasn't as if he hadn't got the money to buy a new car, but he chose to spend his money on holidays and traveling and was away in the country most weekends, doing up an old cottage that he'd bought.

"So what did he say to you?" asked Fergus.

Millie thought for a moment about how to reply. "Not much really. He said if love came knocking on my door would I even recognize it?"

"And would you?" he said, unlocking his car.

"Of course." As she got in Penny, Fergus's old Labrador, jumped up at her, wagging her tail.

"She looks better," she said, patting her and getting in.

"They removed her tumor but the cancer could come back. As I've got the afternoon off, I went and collected her. I wondered if you wanted to go for a walk up the mountains. Maybe grab some lunch in a pub?" he said with a smile.

Millie stared out of the window as she considered it. "Actually I've got my staff appraisals to do next week. I might head back home and plan them."

Fergus gave her an odd look, which she couldn't make out. He looked back at the road, started his car and drove off. Within ten minutes he parked outside her apartment and turned the engine off. "Please come, Millie. It could be fun."

She squeezed his arm. "I'm tired and I really should prepare those appraisals. But thanks for the lift and for coming to rescue me, even though I didn't need it," she said with a laugh.

As Millie got out of the car, Fergus's eyes lowered.

"See you Monday," she said, closing the door and waving as he drove off.

Millie walked into her hall and seeing her answering machine flashing, pressed Play. A male foreign accent said, "I shall be in Dublin on Sunday, staying at the Westbury. I have an hour spare in the afternoon and would enjoy your company. We'll discuss poetry and other forms of art. Come around three . . . This is Herman Feltz."

Millie's face lit up with excitement. *He wanted to see her again!* She replayed the message twice more and grinned broadly.

That evening, she sat in her armchair, sipping her wine and listening to the Love Zone, dreaming with renewed hope that love might actually come her way. Maybe it was finally knocking on her door. What was Ronnie Littlebrick talking about—of course she could recognize it.

———

ANNIE SPARROW lives in Dublin. She writes regularly for the *Irish Evening Herald,* and her first novel, *Said & Done,* was published in 2001.

Moving

Colette Caddle

Sara sat in the middle of the bedroom floor, pulling the contents of a drawer apart. At times like this she wished she were the tidy sort and not such a terrible hoarder. But she was. And as a result this drawer contained her Leaving Certificate results—seventeen years ago. The diploma she'd received from the secretarial college she'd attended three nights a week—sixteen years ago. Her first payslip—for the princely sum of £65. Photos from her debs ball—cringe! How could she have worn that dress? And as for the hair!

"Mama, Mama!" Molly pointed her fat little hand at the photo.

Sara handed it over. "There you go, honey. Hopefully you won't end up like that."

Molly beamed at her and proceeded to chew on the corner of the photograph.

"That's probably the treatment it deserves," her mother said dryly before turning back to the job at hand. Nearly all of the contents of this drawer belonged in the bin, but somehow Sara knew she'd end up keeping most of it. She smiled at the ultra-sound images of Molly and Gavin. They should of course be in an album. When she got to the new house she'd take care of it, she promised herself. There were yet more photos of her twenty-first, several holidays where she went from being a size 8 to a size 12, and, of course, her wedding day. There was one of her and Will standing under the tree outside the church. He was smiling broadly into the camera and she was staring off to the side. "I wonder what I was looking at," she murmured. Will looked happy and impossibly young. She looked—well—OK. Not exactly the radiant bride but happy enough.

Sara sighed guiltily. Here she was with two wonderful children, a devoted, handsome husband and a lovely four-bedroom house in the right part of Chelsea. Why was she only "happy enough"? Right now she should be ecstatic because in exactly three days she would be moving home to Dublin. But the truth was she wasn't sure she wanted to move. It would be great for the kids to grow up surrounded by their grandparents and dozens of cousins. But she wasn't sure that *she* relished the idea. She'd been self-sufficient for so long. What was it going to be like having her mother-in-law drop by for coffee? How would she feel when her own mother was looking over her shoulder and criticizing everything she did? And what about Will's sisters? Was she to get swallowed up into a babysitting pool? "You and Will go out this Saturday and you can babysit the girls next week." The whole idea of family was a little daunting. It didn't help her guilt that her mother was planning a huge welcome-home party.

"I'm sure it will be a great night," her husband had said not very convincingly. "And it's very kind of Grace to go to so much trouble."

"She's not doing it for us," Sara had said sullenly.

"Now, Sara, don't start. You're going to have to learn to get on with Grace. You'll be living in the same city after all."

The same city. Sara shuddered now as she gathered the photos into an untidy heap and picked up a battered envelope. "Oh my God," she breathed, sliding out the thin notepaper.

"Mama, mine!" Molly demanded imperiously.

Sara absently shoved the photos at her and stared blankly at the letter she'd received on the morning of her wedding. She didn't really need to read the words. They were imprinted on her brain.

> *Dear Sara,*
>
> *I just wanted to wish you well on your big day. I know you are doing the right thing and that you will be very happy.*
>
> *Remember me kindly.*
>
> *Love always,*
> *Tim.*

She pressed the paper to her face and closed her eyes. "Mummy! Come and see. Mummy!"

Sara put the letter quickly back into its envelope and shoved it into the pocket of her jeans. "Coming," she called out to her three-year-old son as she scrambled to her feet and followed the sound of his voice.

"I'm packing too," he said proudly.

Sara stood rooted in the doorway of Molly's room and surveyed the devastation that was Gavin's idea of "packing." All of the baby's clothes had been emptied into a pile in the middle of the floor and the diaper bucket was full of Molly's frilly knickers and socks. Sara picked it up and sniffed hopefully but, as she'd feared, she'd forgotten to empty it last night. Oh well, another load for the washing machine. God, there was so much to do and Will was about as useful as his son.

"Gavin, watch your sister, I'll be back in a minute." Sara hurried down the stairs with the bucket and bunged the clothes into the washing machine. As she was adding the powder she heard Will in the hall.

"Hey, I'm home. Where is everyone?"

"Daddy, Daddy!" Gavin hurtled down the stairs and threw himself into his father's arms.

"Hey, little man, how are you—Jesus!" Will bounded up the stairs as his daughter swayed precariously on the top step. "It's OK, Molly, I've got you. Sara! Where the hell are you?"

Sara hurried into the hall as her husband came downstairs, a child in each arm. "What is it?"

"What were you thinking of, leaving the kids alone upstairs? Molly could have broken her neck if I wasn't here."

Sara bit her lip, thinking that if Gavin hadn't run to greet his daddy, the two children would have played happily upstairs until she'd returned. "I only left them for a minute," she protested weakly.

"That's all it takes. Don't you know that most accidents happen in the home? You should be more careful."

"Well, it's not easy trying to do all the packing on my own and mind the kids at the same time," Sara shot back. "You promised you'd be home hours ago."

Will shrugged. "They had a bit of a do for me, I could hardly walk out."

"No, of course not," Sara said sarcastically. "That would have been rude."

"Oh, for God's sake, Sara, stop playing the martyr. The removal people will do all the work tomorrow."

"They're hardly going to go through all our personal stuff. I wouldn't want them to anyway."

Will sighed wearily. "Just leave it to me. I'll have it sorted in an hour."

"Great!" Sara grabbed her bag and the keys of the car and headed for the door. "But before you do, give the kids their dinner, then bath them and put them to bed. Oh, and don't forget to read them a story. Gavin likes *Thomas the Tank Engine* and Molly likes her book of nursery rhymes."

Panic crept over Will's face. "But, Sara, wait—"

Sara smiled brightly and blew her family a kiss. "Night-night."

14 February 1992, Dublin

"There's something I want to say to you, Sara." Tim leaned closer.

Sara gulped as she stared into his clear blue eyes, so tender, so earnest. This was it!

"Yes?"

He took her hand in his. "God, you're so beautiful."

"Is that what you wanted to tell me?" Sara teased.

He looked down and shook his head. "No, no it isn't. Oh, Sara, this is so difficult for me."

Sara's smile faded away. "What is it, Tim? Tell me."

Tim took a deep breath and looked her straight in the eye. "I'm married."

Sara felt as if she'd been kicked in the stomach. "Married?"

He nodded. "I'm so sorry, Sara, I should have told you before but I was afraid of losing you."

"You're separated?" Sara desperately tried to make sense of what he was saying.

"No."

"But you live alone."

Tim looked shamefaced. "The flat is only rented. I moved into it while our house was being renovated. Carol went to the States to stay with her sister. She gets back tomorrow."

Sara closed her eyes, waves of nausea threatening to overpower her. Carol. Somehow a name made it more real, more horrific. "You said you loved me," she said faintly.

"I do," Tim protested. "Oh, Sara, I've never done anything like this before. I'm disgusted with myself for being unfaithful to Carol, but I never counted on meeting you."

"Have you any children?" Sara was surprised at how calm she sounded.

He shook his head emphatically. "No, no kids."

"And are you . . . happy?" She stumbled over the word.

Tim shrugged. "We do OK."

"Only OK?" Sara probed, pushing her feelings of guilt firmly to the back of her mind.

"Maybe I expect too much," Tim said sadly. "I thought I would always be as madly in love as I was the day I got married." He looked at her hungrily. "But then I hadn't met you. Oh, Sara, I love you so much."

Sara's eyes filled with tears. "I love you too, Tim!"

"If only I'd met you first."

"Maybe it's not too late," Sara ventured, her cheeks reddening. "Couples separate all the time. I know you couldn't get a divorce but I wouldn't mind."

Tim stroked her hand lovingly. "You're so understanding, Sara, but I couldn't walk out on Carol. She's done nothing to deserve it and she would be devastated."

Sara's face fell. "Well, OK, but there are other ways . . ."

Tim shook his head. "I would never ask you to—"

"Be your mistress? The other woman?"

"No." Tim was adamant. "You deserve better. You deserve a man who can give you everything, unconditionally. I can't do that."

"So it's over." Sara's voice was barely a whisper.

Tim stared at her miserably, his eyes bright with tears. "It's for the best, Sara. Just remember me kindly."

15 February 1992, Dublin

"He's married." Sara sat on her friend's bed and stared mournfully at her reflection in the mirror. She had thought she'd met the love of her life in Tim Hutchins. She had thought they'd be together forever.

"What? You're kidding me!"

"Nope."

"I suppose he's told you he'll leave his wife when the kids are older," Ali said knowingly.

Sara looked away, embarrassed. "He doesn't have kids."

"So what's the story? Do they live 'separate lives'?" Ali's voice was laden with sarcasm.

She'd heard all the lines before.

"I don't think so."

Ali frowned. "I don't understand. What's his excuse?"

"He says he loves me but that he will never leave his wife."

"Oh." Ali looked confused. This was a new one on her. "But he wants to go on seeing you too, right?"

Sara's eyes filled up and there was a wobble in her voice. "No. He says I'm too good to be just someone's mistress, that I deserve better."

"Of course you do!" Ali said staunchly but groaned as she saw the tears spill over onto Sara's cheeks. "Oh, dear, you're nuts about him, aren't you?"

Sara nodded, unable to speak.

Ali sat down on the bed and put an arm around her. "At least he was honest with you."

"Yeah, but it's so unfair, Ali. I know he loves me. Why couldn't I have met him before Carol?"

Ali shrugged. "It wasn't meant to be," she said philosophically. "It means there's someone even better out there for you."

"Do you think so?" Sara said, unable to believe a man as wonderful as Tim existed on the entire planet.

"Yes, of course!"

"You know he brought me to The Four Seasons for this gorgeous meal last night. That's when he told me." She laughed harshly through her tears. "I actually thought he was going to propose!"

"And instead he told you he was already married. On Valentine's Day! His timing is something else!" Ali tousled her friend's hair. "Poor you. I'm so sorry, Sara."

Sara blew her nose loudly. "Hey, easy come, easy go."

Ali hopped up and threw open the wardrobe. "Let's get seriously dressed up and go out on the town."

"Can we get really, really drunk?"

"It's a prerequisite," Ali said solemnly.

"Well, OK then."

2 July 2001, Chelsea

Sitting in a corner of the dimly lit pub, Sara sipped her lager and lit a cigarette. She wouldn't really leave Will to do all the work. She'd just stay out long enough to make him sweat. She pulled Tim's crumpled letter out of her jeans and studied it. What on earth had made him write it? She hadn't even realized that he knew she was getting married. It had been over six months since they'd split up and though she'd heard snippets of gossip about him through mutual friends, it had never occurred to her that he might be keeping track of her too. Maybe he'd missed her. Maybe he'd realized he'd made a terrible mistake.

After their breakup, Ali had dragged her out clubbing most nights, telling her that the love—or more accurately lust—of another man was the way to get over Tim

Hutchins. Six weeks later, her determination paid off when Sara met Will Frost. They had been drawn to each other immediately and within weeks had slipped into a comfortable relationship. They were like old friends. Sara smiled slightly at the memory of Will's proposal. Not the most romantic, it had to be said.

"We're getting on really well, aren't we, Sara?"

"Yes, we are." Sara had nodded.

"I've never been able to talk to a girl the way I can talk to you," he'd admitted. "I think we could really make a go of this."

"Yeah?"

"Yeah. Let's get married, Sara."

She had spluttered into her glass of cider. "Sorry?"

"Well, why not?" he'd hurried on, beads of perspiration appearing on his forehead. "I know I'll never find anyone as great as you."

"Don't you think we're rushing things?" Sara had said.

Will had shaken his head. "Why wait? I know what I want, how about you? Do you think you could spend the rest of your life with me?"

"I, I don't know," Sara had stammered.

"Look, Sara, I've been offered this amazing job in London. Come with me. Marry me."

Sara had refused to give him an answer that night, but a few days later she said yes.

"Are you mad?" Ali had screeched. "I told you to get yourself a new man. I didn't say you had to marry him!"

"But I want to. Will's nice."

Ali had wrinkled her nose. "Nice?"

"Yes, nice," Sara had said defensively. It may not be good enough for Ali but it was perfect for Sara. She didn't want to be hurt again and she knew that Will would always look after her and protect her. So she'd left one very unhappy chapter of her life and moved on. She would never think about Tim again. And she hadn't. Well, only occasionally.

Sara finished her drink and wondered what Tim—now forty-one—would look like. Was he still gorgeous in that dark, overwhelming way? Was he still with his wife? Did he still think about her the way she thought about him? Sometimes his image flashed into her head when Will was making love to her. It consumed Sara with guilt that it should but Tim had made her feel like no man ever had before. It wasn't easy to forget that.

"Can I get you anything else?" The waitress looked inquiringly at Sara's empty glass.

Sara looked up, startled. "No, thanks." She put Tim's note carefully in the inside pocket of her handbag and stood up. It was time to return to reality. Time to forget that other life and concentrate on the one she'd made with Will and the children. It was a good life and, for the most part, a happy one. She could only put her current feelings of unease down to the move. Once they were settled back in Dublin she'd be fine again. Of course she would.

6 July 2001, Dublin

"I wish you'd come to the party, Ali," Sara groaned. "It's going to be an ordeal without you."

Ali grinned as she tucked the phone under her chin.

"Sorry, pet, but Jack is taking me to the K Club for the weekend. I couldn't really pass that up, now, could I?"

"I wish we were coming with you," Sara said enviously. Why couldn't Will be as spontaneous as Ali's husband? "It's years since Will and I went away together."

"You should do something about it," Ali told her. "It's about time you two had a second honeymoon."

"Huh, that's a laugh! If I brought him somewhere like the K Club, he'd just want to play golf all the time. Having me along would be more of an inconvenience."

"My, we are feeling sorry for ourselves!"

Sara flicked absently through the bills on the hall table. "Sorry. I'm just exhausted after the move and the thoughts of this party—"

"Oh Jeez, I forgot to tell you!" Ali interrupted excitedly. "You'll never guess who I met during the week."

"Who?" Sara brightened at the smell of gossip.

"Tim Hutchins."

"You're kidding me!"

"I'm not."

"Did you talk to him? Did he ask about me?" Sara looked at herself in the hall mirror and touched her hair self-consciously. "How did he look?"

"Yes, yes and OK if you like that sort of thing." Ali laughed.

"Where did you meet him? Was he on his own?"

"It was at a reception in the National Art Gallery and no, get this, he was with his new wife!"

Sara sank onto the bottom stair. "New wife?"

"Yeah, Abigail, gorgeous and twenty-five at most."

"Bitch," Sara said automatically. "I can't believe it. He told me he'd never leave Carol."

"Word is that she left him."

Sara closed her eyes. "That's incredible," she breathed. "Do you know when?"

Ali sighed at the misery in Sara's voice. "Oh, Sara, you're not still carrying a torch for the guy, are you? I'd never have told you if I thought—"

"No, of course not!" Sara forced herself to laugh. "I'm just curious, that's all."

"Yeah, well, I don't know all the gory details, I'm afraid."

Sara suppressed a sigh of frustration. "That's OK, I forgive you. Look, I'd better make a start on dinner. Have a great weekend."

"Thanks, pet. I'll call you when I get back. And enjoy the party!"

"Yeah, right!" Sara hung up the phone. He's married again. It might have been you if you'd waited for him. If you'd given him some time—

The phone shrilled and she pounced on it. "Yes?"

"Hi, love. I've been trying to get through for a while."

"I was talking to Ali," Sara told her husband defensively.

"Oh, how is she? Is she coming to the party?"

"No, she's going away for the weekend."

"Pity. Listen, I'll be home at about seven. Why don't I pick up some takeaway en route and you can have a break from the kitchen?"

"That would be nice," Sara said guiltily. "Don't forget to get some chicken for Gavin."

Will laughed. "As if I would! You know that child is going to sprout feathers one day! Seeya later."

"Seeya." Sara replaced the handset and went to check on the children. Molly was curled up like a puppy in a corner of the lounge, fast asleep, her thumb in her mouth. Gavin was pounding around the room growling and baring his teeth, pretending he was a dinosaur.

She looked at the two of them, her eyes bright with tears and wondered once more why she was only "happy enough."

7 July 2001, Dublin

"Great to see you back!" Gerry Nolan raised his bottle of beer and winked broadly at her.

"Thanks," she said, feeling that her jaw would break if she had to smile for much longer.

"Having a good time, love?" Her dad pressed another glass of tepid white wine into her hand.

"Great, Dad, but I wish Mum hadn't gone to so much trouble."

Joe Kavanagh glanced around the packed room. "Ah, sure you know your mother. She loves giving parties. Moans like hell about it, but loves it all the same."

Sara studied her mother standing in the center of the room chatting to a neighbor. Grace Kavanagh looked completely wrapped up in conversation but Sara knew that she'd be taking in everything going on around her. Who was talking to whom, had the catering company skimped on the vol-au-vents and were her family all playing their parts? Joe caught his wife's eye and sighed. "I'd better go and talk to Nigel or your mother will never forgive me. See you later, love."

Sara watched her father approach the idiosyncratic investment analyst who lived in the largest house on the road. Her mother was always trying to court him and though he often attended her "do's" he never returned the compliment. "Miserable old sod."

"Who's that?" Kath asked, taking a gulp from Sara's wine glass.

Sara pulled the glass away from her little sister. "Nigel."

Kath rolled her eyes. "Oh, *him.*"

"Do you think he's gay?" Sara mused.

Kath smirked. "If he is, Mum will be devastated. She's smitten."

Sara snorted. "Smitten by his big house and bank balance, you mean."

"Now, now, that's no way for a prodigal daughter to talk about her mother."

"God, I feel like I never left," Sara said with feeling. "Nothing much changes around here, does it?"

"At least you don't have to live here," Kath moaned.

"And neither do you, you're just too bloody lazy to move. I don't know, twenty-nine and still living at home!"

"Ah, but the food's good and the laundry service is even better."

"You're a user."

"Mum needs someone to fuss over," Kath protested. "I'm doing her a favor."

"You're all heart."

"Where's Will?"

"Around." Sara looked vague.

"Is everything OK with you two?"

"Yeah, sure, why wouldn't it be?"

"No reason," Kath said innocently. "Just thought that you might have hit the seven-year itch."

"We're married eight years," Sara replied dryly. "And only men get 'the itch.' "

"God, you're so old-fashioned! Haven't you heard of equality? Anyway, Will would *never* get the itch."

"What do you mean by that?"

Kath shrugged uncomfortably. "Well, he's too . . . too . . ."

"Boring?"

Kath flashed her a look. "I was going to say settled."

"Same thing," Sara said morosely.

"Sara?" Kath was all concern.

"Oh, don't mind me. I'm just feeling sorry for myself. I'm absolutely knackered after the move and the last thing I needed was this!" She gestured at the room full of people whom she barely knew.

"It's only one night, Sis, and it makes Mum happy."

"Yeah, I know," Sara said guiltily. "I'm an ungrateful cow."

"You're just too sober," Kath said cheerfully. "Let's get sozzled."

Sara looked disgustedly at her wine. "On this stuff?"

"God, no! Follow me. I know where the gin is stashed."

Sara giggled. "Lead on."

"Sara? Sara, wake up!"

She groaned as Will turned the light on. The gin had definitely been a mistake. "What are you doing? What time is it?"

"Around five. Look, I want you to take a look at Molly. She seems a bit hot to me."

Sara shot up in the bed. "Is she crying?"

Will led the way back to the nursery. "It's more like she's moaning. I'm not sure whether she's awake or not."

Sara turned on the night light and leaned over the baby. Tiny tendrils of dark hair stuck to Molly's forehead and she was tossing restlessly. Sara quickly put a hand to her head, then to her stomach. "You're right, she has a temperature."

"Should we wake her up and give her something?" Will always let Sara make the decisions where the children were concerned.

"I'm not sure. She doesn't seem that upset. Let's sponge her down and open a window and see if that helps."

Will hurried off to get a cloth while Sara gently opened Molly's babygro. "Oh, God—Will!"

Will raced back in as Sara turned on the light. "What? What is it?"

"She's covered in a rash. We need to get her to a hospital."

Will leaned over to inspect his daughter. "It doesn't seem too bad. Maybe we should call a doctor."

"We don't have a bloody doctor," Sara hissed worriedly. "I haven't had time to register with anyone."

"That doesn't matter. We're back in Dublin now. Any doctor will come out in an emergency. Let me get the phone book."

"But Will—"

"Sit with her, sponge her down and leave it to me," Will said firmly.

Sara obediently turned back to her daughter. As she sponged the tiny body she found herself remembering Molly's birth. She could vividly recall the first time she'd held her. The look of wonder and tenderness on Will's face when he saw his daughter. Gavin's rather mixed feelings about having a sister. "You're going to be OK, sweetheart," she whispered now. "Mummy's here. Everything is going to be OK." Molly stirred and her eyelids flickered but she didn't wake. God, maybe she was in a coma. "Please, God, make her better. I'll do anything, anything at all. I'll never complain about being bored again. I'll never complain about my life again. Just make my baby better!"

Will came back in and put an arm around her. "He'll be here in about twenty minutes. Don't worry, love, I'm sure she's fine."

"How do we know if this doctor is any good? I can't believe you just picked a name from the phone book."

"I didn't," Will replied calmly. "I phoned Mike Collins—a guy from the office. I'd forgotten that he lived in Sutton too. He called his own GP for me."

"Oh, Will, that's great. I'm sure it's probably nothing but I'd still feel a lot better if a doctor checked her out. Do you think we should do the glass check?" she added nervously.

"Why not?" Will went to fetch a tumbler from the bathroom. It wasn't the first time that he and Sara had held a glass against Gavin or Molly's skin to check for meningitis. Each time they did, they both held their breath. Sara held the restless child still as he pressed the glass against her tiny arm.

"Oh, thank God," Sara breathed as the rash disappeared.

Will smiled. "She'll be fine. It's probably just some bug she's picked up. I'll go and check on Gavin."

Sara looked startled. "Oh! You don't think—"

"I'm sure he's fine, Sara. I just want to check on him."

Molly stirred and started to sob.

"Why don't you sing to her," he said gently. "That always calms her down."

Sara nodded and reached in the cot to pick up her daughter. She walked up and down the room crooning softly, her mouth against the baby's head. "Twinkle, twinkle, little star . . ."

Will quietly left the room and went to check on his son. Gavin was sleeping peacefully, one arm flung across the bed, the other tightly clutching his Bob the Builder Truck. After satisfying himself that Gavin's temperature was normal, Will smoothed his son's hair and went back to the nursery. "Sleeping like a baby," he reported in answer to Sara's questioning look. He stood and watched Sara rock the baby until he heard the crunch of tires on the gravel outside. "That will be the doctor," he said unnecessarily and hurried down the stairs to open the door. "Thank you so much for coming, Doctor."

"No problem." The doctor looked as if he'd just fallen out of bed. "Greg Berry," he introduced himself.

"Will Frost." Will shook his hand and led the way back upstairs.

"Now, tell me about your daughter."

"Her name is Molly. She was one three weeks ago."

"Is she normally in good health?"

"Absolutely."

"And does she eat well?"

Will grinned. "Everything we put in front of her."

"Good, and has she had all her inoculations?"

"Yes, including the latest meningitis one. Oh, and we've just moved back here from London." Will pushed open the nursery door and stood back.

"OK, then." Greg went in ahead of him. "Hello, there." He smiled at Sara. "Hello, Molly."

"She's very hot," Sara told him, too anxious to even manage a hello. "And the rash is on her back, arms and stomach."

"Let's take a look. Has she been asleep the whole time?"

Sara nodded. "Yes, do you think she's in a coma?"

Greg took Molly in his arms and started to examine her. "No, I'd say she just wants to sleep, Mrs. Frost."

"It's Sara. Molly has had all her inoculations—"

"Yes, your husband filled me in."

Sara looked at her husband in surprise. She wouldn't have thought Will would have even known. She had always taken care of the children's health visits.

Greg finished his examination and handed Molly back to her. "I'll give her an injection and then I'll write you a prescription. I'm sure she'll be fine in the morning but come in and see me on Monday if you're still worried. And now, I think we should wake this little one up. It would be better if Mum did that. She'll get an awful scare if she looks up and sees me!" He put a hand to his uncombed, unruly mop of hair.

Sara smiled weakly. "Molly? Molly? Wake up."

"Shall I turn on the music box?" Will suggested.

"Oh, yes, good idea," Sara said gratefully.

As the light tinkly music filled the room, Sara gently tickled Molly's tummy then held her upright. "Come on, Molly, it's time to wake up now."

Molly's eyes flickered, then she yawned and after a quick look at the doctor threw back her head and roared.

* * *

"Do you really think she's OK?" Sara asked Will again.

"Of course she is! Just look at her!"

She looked down at her daughter sitting on the floor surrounded by Gavin's trains and clapping her hands happily as the whistle blew. Gavin scrambled eagerly around her—now that he'd woken up properly, he was quite enjoying the adventure.

"That injection seemed to do the trick." Will leaned down to touch his daughter's cheek. "I'd swear her temperature is on the way down already."

"And she doesn't seem to be in any pain," Sara admitted. "But I just hate it when they say, 'Oh, it's probably just a virus.' Just! I was scared stiff!"

Will hugged her. "Me too. God, what would we do without the pair of them? What would I do without you?"

Sara smiled shyly. "You were great tonight."

"All I did was call the doctor."

"No, you stayed calm. I didn't."

"You're her mother, Sara. And you're such a great one too. Of course you were upset. Don't be so hard on yourself. I love you."

"Me too," Sara mumbled into his chest, choked with guilt as she thought about the way she'd been feeling about him lately. If only he knew.

"I'm sorry about the last couple of months," he said suddenly, as if reading her mind.

"What do you mean?"

Will shrugged. "I haven't been much good to you since I was offered this new job."

"You've been under a lot of pressure," Sara replied.

"Yes, I have, but so have you. You organized our whole

move. You got everything packed up and pretty much sold the house on your own. And now you've turned this place into a home already." He looked around him at the cartoon characters Sara had painstakingly applied to the nursery walls on the night they'd moved in. Molly had slept through, oblivious, and woken the next morning delighted to be surrounded by her favorite characters. "Sorry, for leaving you to deal with so much."

"That's OK," Sara said, feeling really guilty now. Would he be so nice to her if he knew that she was dreaming about other men—well, one man, but that was nearly worse.

"Are you happy to be home, love?" Will asked.

Sara looked down at her children's dark heads pressed together and her heart lurched.

"Yes, of course I am."

He kissed her gently on the lips. "Good. Because you know, if you wanted to go back tomorrow, I'd do it."

Sara raised an eyebrow. "And walk away from your six-figure salary?" she teased.

"Tomorrow," he repeated, deadly serious. "If it was what would make you happy."

Sara looked up into his eyes and smiled. "It would make me happy if we got these two to sleep and went back to bed."

Will's eyes twinkled. "I'll have them tucked up and fast asleep in ten minutes, leave it to me!"

23 July 2001, Dublin

Sara kissed her mother goodbye. "Thanks for lunch, Mum."

"You're welcome, dear. Now remember dinner at eight on Saturday. Oh, and did I say? Nigel's coming."

"You said," Sara smiled. *At least five times*. "We'll be there."

"And don't forget to tell the children that we're having a day out next week," her mother continued, oblivious. "I think I'll take them to the zoo."

Sara gawped at her. "They'd love that."

Grace Kavanagh nodded. "Good, then that's what we'll do. Goodbye, darling. Love to Will."

As Sara strolled back down Grafton Street she thought about how good it was to be home and how amazed she was that it *was* good to be home. She was getting on better with her mother than she ever had in the past.

"You're older now and a mother yourself," Will had said when she'd remarked on this new development. "You've got more confidence. Grace doesn't intimidate you anymore."

"You think she intimidated me?" Sara had asked in surprise.

Will had laughed. "That woman intimidates everyone! Even Gavin eats his greens when she's around."

Sara smiled as she remembered the conversation. It was true that Grace was a force to be reckoned with but she didn't needle Sara the way she used to.

"Sara? Sara Kavanagh?"

She swung around to see who was calling her name and the smile froze on her face.

"Tim!"

Tim took her hands and smiled down at her. "Oh, Sara, it's so wonderful to see you. You haven't changed a bit!"

Sara looked at his linen suit and flamboyant silk tie. "Neither have you." She could scarcely believe her eyes. Tim Hutchins was standing in front of her after all this time.

"It must be at least six years."

"Nine," she corrected with a tremulous smile. "I believe you met Ali."

"Yes! Isn't it amazing? After all this time I bump into the two of you in the same month! She was telling me that you have children."

"Yes, two. Gavin is three and Molly is one."

"Are they as beautiful as their mother?" he said with that wonderful smile that had always made her toes curl.

"They're actually the image of their dad," Sara admitted, "but yes, they're beautiful."

Tim looked thoughtful. "You look wonderful—in fact radiant."

"How are things with you?" she asked, trying to keep her voice steadier than her hands.

"Good, everything's good."

"Ali told me your news. Congratulations."

Tim had the grace to look embarrassed. "Oh, right, thanks. You must have thought it odd but you see—"

"Tim! I wondered where you'd got to." The tiny blonde who'd just emerged from a nearby shoe shop put a possessive arm through Tim's and shot Sara a challenging look. "They didn't have my size."

Sara took a deep breath and held out her hand. "Hi. You must be Abigail."

The girl tittered. "Eh, it's Rachel, actually."

"Rachel's a colleague," Tim said hurriedly.

Rachel licked her lips and smiled up into his eyes. "Yeah, that's right, I'm a colleague."

Sara looked from her triumphant grin to his sheepish one. "Right. I see." And for the first time she saw Tim for what he was. Not her devoted lover desperate to do the right thing. Just another guy who was out for what he could get. "Well, it was nice to see you again. Like I said, Tim, you haven't changed a bit."

Tim touched her arm as she turned to go. "It wasn't like that, Sara—"

"It really doesn't matter, Tim," Sara told him and realized she meant it. "Just remember me kindly." She winked at him and strode off down Grafton Street with her head in the air. *How come I'm not in floods of tears?* she thought. *Shouldn't I be devastated to find out that I was just one of many?* But she felt—nothing. She'd told Tim it didn't matter and it was true, she realized. It really *didn't* matter. Tim Hutchins was history. She'd been in love with a myth.

"So what did you do today?" Will asked as they sat in their local Chinese restaurant that evening.

Sara took a sip of her wine. "I spent a fortune on this dress and had lunch with Mum."

Will gazed appreciatively at her plunging neckline. "Worth every penny," he murmured.

"Oh, and I met my ex!"

"Who's that?" Will wrinkled his nose. He remembered that Sara had broken up shortly before they met but he couldn't remember the guy's name.

"Tim, Tim Hutchins," Sara told him.

"Oh, I remember. The married guy." Will tut-tutted

disapprovingly. "So, what did he have to say for himself?"

"Well, I was just congratulating him on his new wife when his bit on the side appeared beside him."

"You're kidding! God, that was a lucky escape! Aren't you glad you married me now?"

"I am," Sara answered a lot more fervently than the flippant question required.

"Can I get you some dessert?" The waiter appeared at her side, pad and pen at the ready.

Sara consulted the dessert menu in front of her. "I think I'll have some of that wonderful chocolate ice cream."

Will nodded enthusiastically. "Oh, yes, I'll have the same and two Irish coffees, please. So tell me more about this boyfriend," he said teasingly when the waiter had departed.

Sara shook her head, smiling. "No, he's not important. Tell me about your day."

COLETTE CADDLE's first novel, *Too Little, Too Late,* was published to enormous success in Ireland in 1999 and remained at the No. 1 bestseller spot for four weeks. This was followed by two further bestsellers, *Shaken & Stirred* and *A Cut Above.*

Colette Caddle lives in Dublin with her husband and son.

Playing Games

Catherine Dunne

I asked myself, not for the first time, how much longer I could keep this up. What sort of humor would Delia be in tonight?

I circled the block twice, getting lucky at the last moment. A very young man wearing shades and a superior expression eased his silver Lexus out of a tight parking space. He made great show of his power steering, nonchalantly caressing the wheel with just one hand. He barely glanced in my direction, but still, I knew he was conscious of his audience. Come on, come on, I thought wearily. It's not bright enough for sunglasses and I'm way too old to be impressed.

I reversed slowly, carefully, the back wheel of my ancient Mitsubishi Colt just nudging the curb. I straightened her up, unlocked my seat belt, clicked off the lights. I checked my handbag once more to make sure I had my reading glasses: it could well be another one of Delia's dictionary nights. I noticed with satisfaction as I put on the alarm that I had managed to park right under a streetlamp. A double deterrent for any would-be car thief.

The Victorian house in Ranelagh where Delia lived had made no concession over the years to modernity. She had refused adamantly, on more than one occasion, to open up her driveway to provide a parking space. Years back, Mr. Doyle, her next-door neighbor, had approached me, nervously, offering to fund the transformation of my aunt's unkempt garden into parking spaces for his three adult children. Delia had been outraged. Why should she give up something that was hers purely for the convenience of others? I couldn't disagree with this sentiment in the abstract; however, I did point out that Mr. Doyle was willing to pay, not only for the construction, but also a yearly rental for the relief of escaping from the city's encroaching clearways. Privately, as her only surviving relative, I also thought it would add greatly to the value of the house, when that time came. But Delia had stood firm. Knowing her as I do, I could see the glint of delight that she had had the opportunity to refuse. Behind the outrage was her satisfaction that she had put Mr. Doyle firmly on the back foot: the only comfortable place for one's neighbors.

I rang her doorbell, using our familiar signal, and waited; then I inserted my key into the lock. Some nights, she managed to shuffle her way down the hallway, and would be indignant if I let myself in before she'd had the chance to reach the front door. Not tonight. There was no sign of her, no sound of the shush-shush of her slippers on the polished linoleum. I glanced at my watch. Six minutes past eight.

"You're late, Norah," she says, as I open the sitting-room door. I sigh. A blast of gassy, dusty heat slaps me in the face, making my eyes water.

"Hello, Auntie Delia," I say brightly. I can drop the "Auntie" a bit later, once we're back on easier, familiar territory. For now, though, there is the ritual, the ceremonial beheading to be gone through.

"Eight o'clock is eight o'clock, you know. Not five minutes past, or five minutes to. Your mother was the same."

She addresses her feet as she speaks, her hands cupping the bony rounds of her kneecaps.

I say nothing. No excuse can ever make a difference, anyway: and certainly not one about the lack of parking spaces. And as for Mother, I have long since given up hope of hearing anything positive from Delia about that elusive figure in my life.

"You're looking well," I remark. Joy, from down the road, has obviously been in. Delia's fine gray hair has been curled so tightly I can see the tender pink scalp, shiny in between where the rollers have been. I feel sorry for her: those baby-pink places make her seem suddenly vulnerable, where before she has seemed merely old.

I rummage in my handbag. I am normally a tidy person, but I can also be an indecisive one. With a small handbag, I fret that I may have eliminated too many possibilities, cut off some area of choice. So I use a big one, and bring everything I might possibly need in an emergency. I pull out a bottle of Jameson, still in its box.

"A present for you. I noticed last week you were getting a bit low."

"Why, thank you, dear," she says, sounding genuinely surprised. I've been bringing her a fresh bottle every two weeks for over fifteen years now, ever since I first started to visit. I had sought her out, when I'd learned that a stroke had almost killed her. After all, no matter what, she was family. She smiles at me now, and I can almost hear the ice melt.

Delia shifts a little in her seat, making the old springs creak. She clears her throat, and there is the sound of the executioner sheathing his sword. A reprieve.

"You'll join me in a Jemmie," she says.

I allow her certainty; it is only to be expected.

"Thank you, Auntie. Shall I get the water?"

I have learned over the years never to say *no,* or *well, just the one, then: I'm driving.* Anything that smacks of moral judgment and Delia's high horse is immediately saddled. I have sat for whole evenings in her company when she refused to touch her drink; it would have been pointless to explain to her that, later on, she would be driving nothing more dangerous than her walking stick.

I pour a large one for her, a much-diluted one for me, topped up with lots of ice. I watch as she compares the levels of the two drinks, peering through her glasses with pale blue eyes that miss nothing.

"Busy at work?" she asks, making, for her, a hugely polite opening gambit.

"Very busy: it's coming up to auction season. It's good to relax."

And I smile warmly, reassuring her that Friday nights

here are the only reward I crave after a long week's toil in the mortgage department of the EBS. It's not a great job: it pays the bills. My childhood was one long lesson, by way of bad example, regarding the importance of financial security. Beyond achieving that, I've never had much ambition.

Delia reaches for her cigarettes. The gesture is deliberate, an almost elaborate movement, but I'm not sure what she's trying to tell me. Tonight, the packet of Sweet Afton is given unusual prominence: placed, center stage, on a small lacquered Chinese table. One of the many souvenirs of my grandfather's travels, the table has, for as long as I can remember, been hidden by towering library books, crosswords, Sunday supplements and the ever-present deck of cards. Now it seems almost unfamiliar in its bareness. It is as though I have never seen it before: never understood its significance as a prop. And I am, I admit, curious about the Sweet Afton, and have been for weeks. I didn't even know that this particular brand was still to be had. The yellow and gold pack is, of course, already familiar to me from childhood. Both Kenneth and Mother were inveterate smokers.

Delia leans forward now and lights a spill in the almost white flame of the gas fire. Recently, she's been smoking her way through ten, every Friday night, until my clothes stink from a combination of airless gas-fire heating and strong tobacco. Her milder brand—doctor's orders—is no longer in evidence. Perhaps she has decided it's time to dice with death. It seems to me that she lights up tonight with unaccustomed relish.

"Would you like me to get you some of those for next week?" I ask, nodding toward the open packet.

I don't expect her to tell me, but she and I both know that my question is designed to elicit information she is not prepared, yet at any rate, to give. However, it will satisfy her that finally, after three weeks, I allow that she has aroused my curiosity. It is the right card to play: there is a sudden light in the watery blue eyes.

"Not at all, my dear," she says. "You do quite enough for me already."

The answer does not please me. Gratitude is not one of Aunt Delia's virtues. There is something more here, some strategy I don't fully understand. There is a lull, when all I hear is the hiss and suck of her cigarette, the steady hot hum of the fire. Finally, she taps on the arm of her chair with impatience.

"Shall we have a game?" she says, archly.

I nod, as though I would never have thought of the idea myself.

"Yes—why not."

I stand up, and make my way to the shelf under the television where all the board games and thousand-piece jigsaws are kept.

"Scrabble?" I say. "Ludo? Snakes and Ladders?"

My aunt's board games do not go beyond the nineteen-fifties. I spent a fortune one Christmas when Trivial Pursuit was all the rage, and we never played it, not once. It simply disappeared. With my Aunt Delia, you don't ask.

"Scrabble," she says, after a moment's thought.

I set up the board, and she gets to go first.

"Double-word score," she says triumphantly. "That's sixteen points."

I put on my reading glasses. She has placed the word "house" across the starred center of the board. She is in good humor now; she always likes to go first. I begin to unwind; the evening is progressing just as she likes it. I continue to make feeble three-letter words, miss the occasional double- or triple-word score that could easily have been mine, keep everything nice until it's time for supper. I don't miss every opportunity, though—she's far too smart for that. She wins, but only by a margin of six points. She's pleased with that—any more and she accuses me of not trying; any less and she gets agitated, worries about how close she's come to losing.

"Tea?" I ask, glancing at the clock.

She suddenly stiffens.

"No, thank you. I haven't been sleeping too well, lately. Dr. Collins says tea keeps you awake."

So does whiskey, I think. But I say nothing.

"Milk, then?"

She shakes her head in an abrupt, dismissive way that seems to mean: go away now, the evening is over. I'm puzzled. This is new: a part I haven't seen her play before. It's not as though she has anything else to do, anywhere else to go, and she's just won the game. I've gone to the trouble of crossing the city, bringing whiskey and homemade apple tart with me. And I've managed to lose to her at Scrabble. But it doesn't do to get huffy with Delia. She can out-huff anybody, anytime.

I hesitate. Should I stay until she's safely in bed?

As though reading my mind, another uncannily accurate skill of hers, she answers my unspoken question.

"You go off home now, dear. I'll sit up a while longer. I'm not quite ready for bed, yet."

I stand up. There seems to be no point in doing anything else.

"Well, if you're sure," I say, picking up my handbag, having a moment's tussle with myself as to whether to leave the apple tart or take it with me. I leave it, and immediately regret it.

She shuffles with me to the door, her cane noiselessly sinking into the layers of green speckled linoleum on the hall floor. She never throws anything out: the old lino serves as a bouncy underlay for the new. Together, we ignore the potentially treacherous creases, rising here and there like small glaciated folds; pretend not to notice the skewed door saddles. She had it laid on the cheap. I stoop to kiss her dry, lined cheek. She smells faintly of Johnson's Baby Powder. Just then, she plays her trump card, or it is played for her.

The telephone rings. The sound is so unusual in this house that its sudden explosiveness genuinely shocks me. None of your purring tones here: this is genuine, black Bakelite, in-your-face shrillness. She doesn't move. Hasn't she heard?

"The phone, Delia—would you like me to get it for you?"

"No, thank you, dear," she says firmly, almost pushing me out onto the porch step. "He'll wait until I answer."

And the door closes. I cannot move. The porch light and the hall light are simultaneously extinguished. I stand on the checkered tiles, trying to come to terms with the fact that I have just been ejected. There is nothing else for it: I start to walk toward my car, but my legs seem suddenly to have gone numb. The only bit of spite I can muster from the depths of my shock is to leave her garden gate wide open. I know how much she hates that.

* * *

It played on my mind all over the weekend. Who was "he"? I'd had fifteen years of listening to Delia telling me how I was the only one she had, in tones that varied from self-pity to downright bitterness or scarcely veiled contempt, depending on the mood she was in. All her acquaintances, it seemed to me, were women, apart from Mr. Doyle next door. Ever since the unpleasantness over the parking spaces, Delia had deliberately gone out of her way not to speak to either Mr. Doyle or his wife. Young Joy, who did her hair, was indisputably female. Margaret, Delia's long-time carer, was a stout woman, on the wrong side of middle age, one who made no secret of her disapproval of me. She told Delia time and again that I should take her to live with me in my small house in Marino. This patently delighted Delia. Margaret's indignation put me in a bad light, and gave my aunt numerous opportunities to remind me of my inadequacies. At the same time, it afforded her even greater pleasure to continue living on her own, sitting on a property worth in excess of half a million. And so, Friday's phone call disturbed me: "he" was a mystery player, and there was nothing Delia enjoyed more.

Years back, when I used to visit her first, she would tell me over and over again how well-off she was, how efficiently she had looked after her old age, how very fortunate I was to be her only heir. Your mother, she'd say to me, was a very foolish woman. (She was also Delia's only sister: why did I get all the blame?) A spendthrift, a flibbertigibbet, a glamour-puss. And once, more recently, when she'd heard the word on one of those awful American sitcoms she watched, an *airhead*. She nearly spat the word at me, nodding her head once in my direction, triumphantly. I almost laughed out loud: the word, so redolent of youth and *Friends*-generation Americana, had seemed bizarrely out of place in her high-ceilinged, potentially elegant drawing room.

But I didn't reply. In my heart, I agreed a little. Mother's marriage at nineteen to the devastatingly good-looking Kenneth, ten years her senior, was not built to endure. They had beauty, lots of it, and romance and excitement, and travel and excess—while it lasted. I had always thought of him as Kenneth, rather than my father: fathers, in my book, stayed around long enough to see their children grown. He was gone by the time I was five. To say that Mother stayed would be overstating the case. Over the next ten years, she devoted herself to fading away out of my life, and out of her own. I have impressions, rather than memories, of her vague affection for me. I don't think she was an unkind woman, but I have spent most of my life feeling the indignity of being both an only child, and an abandoned one.

When she was being particularly savage, Delia liked to remind me that I look nothing like either of my parents.

Margaret called me early on Tuesday morning of the following week.

"Your aunt," she said, "has had a very bad night. I called Dr. Collins. He wants to talk to you."

And she put the phone down. I have had perhaps four conversations with Margaret in my life, all of them like this. I called Dr. Collins. My aunt was distressed, he said. Acute case of irritable bowel, in his opinion—but a visit to a specialist was advisable, just to be sure. Irritable bowel? Why be so specific regarding location?

I left work early, drove in the snarling evening traffic to visit her. She was sitting, as usual, beside the gas fire; the room was stifling.

I put on my best sympathetic voice.

"Auntie Delia—I'm so sorry you're not feeling well."

She turns and looks at me, and I am shocked by her appearance, although nothing on the surface has changed, at least, not for the worse. Her eyes have a strange light, almost an excitement to them, and the index and middle fingers of her right hand are stained darker than ever with nicotine: I notice how the ugly shadow is now creeping, yellowly, up her fingernails. I wonder why she's so nervous.

"We've an appointment with the specialist for Friday—an *emergency* one."

Is this why she looks so animated? Could she, perhaps, be one of those people from the planet *Munchausen*—those who fake medical conditions in order to get attention? She certainly looks healthy enough—the same tough old bird as ever. Delia the indestructible.

"I'll bring you, of course," I say. Immediately, I want to bite my tongue. The look she gives me is full of rancor. I can see "it's the least you can do" blazing in blue lights across her forehead. I've slipped badly here. I blunder on, regardless.

"What time have we to be there?"

We agree that I'll pick her up at three. The appointment is in Beaumont, right on the other side of Dublin, which means I'll have to cross the city twice. I have a moment of mild panic. I'll miss two monthly-status meetings, and have to spend all afternoon, as well as all evening, in Delia's company.

Not for the first time, I curse my parents, each of them in turn: Kenneth for his fecklessness, their reckless spending, and for simply never being there; Mother for her early death. They've left me doing all this . . . stuff, which is the only legacy either of them ever bequeathed me.

Doctor, sorry, *Mister* Murrough McCarthy was a dapper little man, in an elegant dark suit, gleaming, Daz-ad white shirt and a bow tie. I made to retire discreetly, before Delia's consultation began, but she surprised me by insisting I stay. Did I make out a flash of fear behind the thick lenses, or was it the glimmer of another emotion, one I didn't recognize?

Her medical history was uneventful enough, just as unremarkable as I remembered. I hated hospitals. They reminded me that my fifth decade was drawing to a close, and I hadn't even begun to do all the things I thought I might have liked to, had my life been different. I let my eyes drift along all the framed statements of professional success on the consultant's wall. FRCS, diplomas from London and Toronto, certificates from just about everywhere—when suddenly I sat up, jolted into an acute awareness of my aunt, myself, my surroundings.

"Yes, I'd surgery twice," she was saying, the voice no longer wavering. "I'd my tonsils out when I was twenty-five. And I had a Caesarean section when I was twenty-eight."

I could not move. Her calmness was astounding. Did she realize what she'd just said? Was there a woman in the world who'd confuse a section with any other sort of medical procedure? Incision? Exploration? Operation? Complication?

Mr. McCarthy simply nodded, writing away with his elegant, navy-blue Mont Blanc fountain pen. That was all I could focus on: his hairy hand, moving methodically across and down the page. She must have been confused. My spinster aunt? Yes, certainly, she was confused.

We drove back to Ranelagh in silence.

I go into cheerful-niece mode the moment the hall door closes behind us.

"You must be hungry," I say. "You put on the fire there, and I'll make us something."

For once, she does as she's told. I escape to the tiny kitchen, put on the kettle, take bread out of the freezer. Margaret's been shopping. At least there's something to make sandwiches. I can't stop the speeding of my heart every time I think of Delia's—what? Admission, confession, mistake? If it's true, then where did the baby go? I can hardly take in all the implications.

(I'd like to say that my first concern, my first sympathy, was for my aunt and all that she must have suffered, if this were true. But I am fundamentally an honest person. I'd have to say that my first emotion was fear. I had a too-clear vision of four-bedroomed, bay-windowed, semidetached Victorian splendor in desirable location deflating slowly, almost imploding, like a withering balloon after a party. And, true or not—for I had to keep in mind that this was Auntie Delia telling a story—how could I ever bring up such a subject again? Was it a magnificent lie in the face of her own mortality, or a truth kept hidden for over fifty years?)

Something starts to niggle at me as I pile sandwiches onto the plate, like the scratchy feeling I get at the back of my throat before a bad cold. She's calling me. I dismiss it, whatever it is, and hastily pour boiling water on the tea leaves.

"Coming!" I call.

"So," I say, once the tea ceremony is over, and Delia has finished grumbling about the extortionate fifty pounds *Mister* McCarthy charged her for *less than twenty minutes.* "What'll it be? Scrabble?"

I really don't want to play the word game tonight; losing cleverly takes too much effort. I'd prefer the randomness of Snakes and Ladders or Ludo, or even the total focus demanded by a thousand-piece jigsaw of galleons at sea, puppies in baskets, or some such. I hope that by mentioning Scrabble as my first choice, she'll opt for something different. It's never failed yet.

She surprises me for the second time that day by choosing Scrabble.

This time, I get to go first. I've decided not to cheat for her. Today has made me feel reckless. We are playing for higher stakes than usual.

She stares at her letter tiles for a long time.

"Your mother," she says suddenly, "*always* got what she wanted."

I am startled. Delia only ever mentions her these days in order to berate me for the twin evils of hopeless time-keeping and overall lack of life-organization, both of which I seem to have inherited from Mother.

"Spoiled," she continues, shaking her head, still not lifting her eyes from the little wooden stand on which her tiles are perched. "Had to have everything she fancied—never mind that it belonged to someone else."

I am almost holding my breath. This is as close to personal as I've ever been with Delia. The whole room has grown stiller; even the gas fire is hissing less than usual.

"Huckle," she says suddenly.

"Pardon?"

"Look it up," she says testily.

It takes a second to realize that we are no longer talking about Mother. I reach for the dictionary, privately hoping there is no such word. I want her to go back to where she was a moment ago, back to the land of Mother, far away from any word game.

"Huckle," I read aloud, disappointed, "hip; haunch; huckle-backed: humpbacked . . ."

"That's enough," she says. "I've got what I wanted. You should do more crosswords."

There is no return to the only topic that now interests me. I feel angry, let down, as though Delia had just made a promise and refused to deliver. I can't help the feeling that everything, including today, is somehow connected to Mother.

I am angry enough to beat her. I win by twenty-four points. Her mouth is pulled tight, looking like an asterisk. I don't care. I am finally tired after too many years of this: circling the block, appeasing the executioner, playing at word games. I'm going home. I sweep the tiles into a plastic Ziploc bag, snap the board shut and stand up.

"He was mine, you know," she says softly. Her face has crumpled a little, looking as it does whenever she loses at Scrabble, only more so.

"Who was?"

I know my tone is sharp, but I really, truly, cannot play by her rules any more. I am dangerously close to tears. If she wants to be bitter and twisted, blaming me for how her life turned out, playing God with what's left of mine, then she can sit here on her own, right to the end of her days, as far as I'm concerned—

"Kenneth. Your father. He was mine. We were going to get married—until he saw Polly."

Polly. Mother's pet name. Girlier, prettier than Pauline. I have a blinding vision of her, of the one photograph which mysteriously disappeared years back from the drawer in my kitchen. Some dinner-dance in Sutton, over half a century ago, Kenneth by her side. She's looking at the camera over one shoulder, chin resting on her interlocked fingers. She has a flower behind her ear, her long dark hair is waved and glossy, eyes huge and smoky. I remember her lips as being a faded pink. I think the photo had been tinted afterward. I suddenly miss my mother with a hunger that only Delia can assuage. And she's right—I look nothing like that photograph.

"Tell me."

For once, I feel that I have the upper hand. There is a change in Delia: I think she knows she's pushed me too far, that now she needs to behave. Do I really sense fear in her: that if she doesn't tell me the truth, whatever it is, I might go for good? Despite my anger, I feel a little nudge of sympathy for her, a reluctant atom of goodwill.

"We were the same age, Kenny and I. We met at work. All the girls wanted him, but he chose me."

She lights another Sweet Afton, blows the smoke away from my face this time.

"He chose *me*. And your mother"—here she stabs the cigarette in my direction—"couldn't bear it that I had something, someone, that she didn't."

I say nothing. Everything Delia says matches somehow the information I have filed away on the back wall of my skull. I've always known it to be there, but I've never cared to pull it out and look at it. My scant memories of Mother are all of her tending to herself, rather than me. I know I saw myself off to school each day, and returned, more often than not, to find her still in bed, leafing through magazines, surrounded by overflowing ashtrays. At some point, she would hurl the magazines away from her, as though whatever she saw there made her furious.

"She stole him. It's as simple as that. She had to have him, and I never took anything away from her, not ever. I've never forgiven her."

That last bit is true. Tonight is not the first time I've floated across the deep, wide pool of bitterness that separates my aunt from all memories of Mother.

The half-thought, almost-memory that had niggled at me in the kitchen comes back to me, scratching more loudly now.

"Is that why you went away?" I ask her gently, my head filling with one of the last pictures I have of Mother. We are sitting in a small garden somewhere, I am reading a book, she is smoking. I have finally managed to pluck up the courage to ask her why we never visit Auntie Delia. As usual, I am hurting over my lack of family. Nothing else in those days set you apart quite so much from other twelve- or thirteen-year-olds as the lack of family. It was somehow judged to be your fault— nobody liked you enough to want to live with you. I can see Mother's face as she draws deeply on her cigarette. I know that the glass of orange juice beside her contains more than vitamin C—her eyes are already getting that hooded, dreamy look I came to know so well. She is telling me sadly how Aunt Delia refused to be her bridesmaid, how she went away before the wedding, all those years ago, out of sheer jealousy and spite. How she was still jealous.

"Is that the reason, Delia?" I ask again. "You couldn't bear to see them married?"

She looks at me, almost surprised.

"Yes," she says, nodding, as though convincing herself. Then, "Yes, that's why I went away," and that's the end of it. I can feel it as keenly as if she'd let a curtain fall between us. She looks suddenly tired. I feel real pity for her again, pity without anger—just as I did the previous week when I saw sudden, raw vulnerability in her tightly curled hair. I also have a strange feeling of incompleteness—as though I'm somehow missing something—some carefully placed clue that I've failed to pick up on. The moment for it—whatever it is—has now passed. Delia yawns decisively.

"Would you like to go to bed?"

She shakes her head.

"No, I'll sit up a while longer. You go off home, now, you've been here long enough."

I can't decide whether that means long enough for me, or long enough for her. I stand up, impatient with her again, with myself.

"Right, then. I'll call the hospital on Monday to arrange for your tests, and I'll let you know when we need to go back."

She nods. I kiss her cheek.

"Thank you, dear," she murmurs.

For once, I think she might actually mean it.

I see myself out, and just before I close the front door behind me, I think I hear her voice, calling me back. I wait for a moment in the porch, just in case. But there is only silence. I must have been mistaken.

Three o'clock that morning, I suddenly got it. I'd been dreaming of her and Mother together, in one of those crazy, mixed-up stories that would give any psychiatrist a field day. I suddenly woke, knowing that there was something in the dream I wanted to hold on to, some explanation that made everything—life, love, the meaning of the universe—absolutely clear. Of course, it faded almost at once, and I was left awake in the darkness with my heart thumping.

I made my way down to the kitchen for a glass of water, and stood by the window drinking it. The first faint streaks of dawn were already in the east. I was glad it was Saturday; the unaccustomed luxury of a morning on my own. As I stood there, wondering again about the dream and Mother's missing photograph, the clue I'd been missing suddenly etched itself sharply onto the brightening sky. It really was like a lightbulb going off above my head, just like the ones you see in cartoons, or one of those speech bubbles with "Idea!" in the center.

Frantically, I rummaged in the drawer for a pen and paper. I couldn't even sit I was so agitated. I worked it all out—dates, memories, allusions, the lot. I was sure I was right. All that remained now was to confront Delia.

* * *

I arrive without phoning. It's just after ten o'clock; I know she'll be up. I ring the doorbell as usual, but this time I don't give her any opportunity to shuffle down the hall. I insert my key into the lock and push. I push again. The Chubb is on. We have an agreement that she only uses this security lock when she's going to be out for some time—say, to the pictures or to tea with Margaret—never when she's on her own inside. Mrs. Doyle is clipping away at her hedge.

"Oh, you've just missed her, dear," she says sympathetically. "The taxi is only gone about ten minutes."

Taxi?

I try to act casually.

"Oh, it's just something I forgot to give her last night. Did she happen to mention what time she'd be back?"

There is something in the woman's expression I cannot read.

"Why don't you come in and have a cup of tea?" she says.

And so I discover that my Auntie Delia is gone away; gone for good. Mrs. Doyle is embarrassed; I, for now, feel absolutely nothing.

"It was all perfectly fair, perfectly legal," she is saying nervously, pulling at the beads around her neck. "Your aunt got three valuations for the house, and our son and his wife agreed to pay the highest of all of them. She got a good price."

This last is said somewhat defensively. I raise my hand to stem the flood of words I can almost see hovering behind her carnation-tinted lips.

"I don't doubt it for a moment, Mrs. Doyle. It's just, well, you'll appreciate that this is something of a shock. I was with her all day yesterday, and she said nothing."

Even in my dazed state, I am struck by how true, and yet absolutely untrue that last statement is. As it transpires, Delia said more yesterday than in the previous fifteen years.

The woman nods her dyed head sympathetically, eager to please now that she has been relieved of any burden of guilt on my behalf.

"She was always a little . . . eccentric."

I smile.

"Yes, she was."

Even now, I'm speaking about her in the past tense. My future hangs in front of me, sagging like one of Delia's old cardigans. Just one last throw of the dice:

"Did she, by any chance, leave a forwarding address?"

Mrs. Doyle shakes her head vehemently.

"No. She was absolutely adamant about that. Said this was a new life for her, that all her ties here were finished with."

For some reason, that hurts.

"All the contents are to be sold, for charity. The valuer was here yesterday afternoon. I let him in myself . . ."

Here, her voice trails off. I suddenly wonder how Mrs. Doyle must see me, sitting here in her kitchen on an ordinary Saturday morning, cups of tea growing cold between us: a dutiful, shocked fifty-year-old woman, outsmarted and abandoned? Someone she can sympathetically click her tongue over when her husband comes home from golf? Or a greedy relative, one who visited only out of grim-jawed duty, one who's just got her comeuppance?

I have to hand it to Delia—the hospital visit was a master-stroke. She knew I was a plodder, that it would take me some time to put two and two together and make a resounding four, without her ever having to show more of her hand than she cared to.

"Did she say . . . who she was going to?"

But I already know the answer. Mrs. Doyle is tight-lipped.

"To her son?"

Somehow, I just know Delia's baby isn't a daughter.

Now the woman looks amazed.

"Yes! You knew about young Kenneth?"

I nod.

"I knew, but she never told me. He's the one who's been sending her the Sweet Afton."

She looks mystified at this, and I don't explain. My life suddenly feels very empty. I even begin to regret my lack of ambition in the EBS. But all of this has a certain neatness, an economical snipping away of loose ends. Mother takes Kenneth from Delia; Delia takes Kenneth from me. A brother; half-brother—what do fractions matter? At least I do have family, out there, somewhere. At least there's some comfort in that. Not that he'll ever know.

"Oh—she left a parcel for you."

I take it and leave. I don't even bother shaking hands.

I open the brown-paper parcel in the car. Scrabble, Ludo, Snakes and Ladders, playing cards, four hideous jigsaws, probably all with pieces missing. A miniature chess set I've never seen before.

Checkmate, Delia.

CATHERINE DUNNE is the author of three highly acclaimed novels, *In the Beginning, A Name for Himself* and *The Walled Garden*. Her fourth, *Another Kind of Life,* was recently published.

She lives on the northside of Dublin with her husband and son.

Girls' Weekend

Marisa Mackle

*L*ots of men went away without their girlfriends. Or wives. It wasn't unusual. No, no, it wasn't unusual at all. And just because you went away didn't mean you were going to be unfaithful, did it? Even if there *was* going to be an obscene amount of drink around. And women. With very little on. Because of the heat.

It was quite normal to want to get away with ten of the lads for a break, wasn't it? It was a male-bonding thing. Golf and all that. And contacts. Yeah, contacts were very important these days, weren't they? Emma didn't object. Not at all. No, not at *all*. She would have done exactly the same with the girls herself, she told herself as she sat on the sitting-room sofa. Alone. The girls. Hmmm. When had she ever gone away with them?

Not very often.

Hardly ever.

Never.

In fact.

You see, the "girls" didn't really see the *point* in going away without the "lads."

Funny that, wasn't it?

Seeing as the "lads" didn't think twice about going away without the "girls."

Anyway what was the use in analyzing it all? Martin would be back in five days and sixteen hours and forty-five minutes if the plane wasn't delayed. And then it would all be over.

The holiday.

He *had* phoned, of course. Like he'd said he would. Which was great really. After all, another man might have forgotten.

Only he'd phoned from a pub. Which wasn't that nice. Because she hadn't really been able to hear him properly. And one of the lads had grabbed the phone and burped into it. Which was pretty disgusting really.

And it had sounded like there were women in the pub. Which shouldn't have been *that* surprising. After all they were hardly in a "men only" bar. But maybe the women shouldn't have been so close to the phone. So close that Emma could pick out their thick Scandinavian accents.

They were probably really tanned. And blond. The sort that whipped off their tops on the beach. Oh God.

The phone rang.

Please God it would be him.

Maybe ringing to apologize for the night before.

"Emma?"

Oh God. It was Annette. Her best friend. The only one of her friends who thought men were a complete waste of time. Emma's heart hit the floor. She just wasn't in the mood for a "need to get a life" lecture.

"What are you doing?" Annette demanded.

"Nothing much."

"Let me guess. You're watching TV."

"Why not? It's Monday."

"Yeah, but that's what you did all day yesterday and Saturday and Friday. Jesus, if Martin asks you what you were up to for the week he's going to think you're an awful sad case."

"Don't care," Emma mumbled.

"You're not drinking, Em, are you?" Annette was sharp.

"Just a glass of red wine."

"I don't really trust you when you drink, Em," Annette said doubtfully. "You're not to do anything daft."

"Like what?"

"Like, you know . . . ring Martin."

"I'd love to know if he's getting on with everyone all right."

Or getting off with everyone more like, Annette thought grimly. What Emma saw in that eejit of a man, Annette would never know. It was terrible the way he'd turned her fun-loving friend into an insecure fruitcake.

"Listen," she began pragmatically, "you've got to pretend to Martin that you had some kind of life while he was away, OK?"

"Right," Emma agreed, then hesitated. "So . . . er . . . how are we going to do that then?"

"Well, it will be hard, I admit," Annette said, "but a

weekend away might just save you from this nutcase existence."

Emma thought about it. A weekend away. God, she hadn't had one of those in years. Maybe it wouldn't be such a bad idea.

"Where would we go?"

"Dunno," Annette shrugged. "Galway is always good for a break but I'm open."

"Galway . . . mmm . . . I'd have to ring Martin though."

"For what?" Annette could feel her blood pressure rising.

"Well, um, just to let him know where I am, you know, in case he's ringing. He might be wondering where I am."

"That would be good though, Em."

"Do you think?"

"Let him sweat. Now I know it'll be hard but it will be worth it in the end. He'll be mad for you when you get back."

"Oh," Emma almost smiled. "Do you think so?" It had been so long since Martin was mad for her that she'd almost forgotten what it felt like.

"Absolutely," said Annette, not quite believing it herself. The only Martin she knew was mad about himself and himself alone.

"Right then," Emma agreed. "I'll leave it to you to go ahead and book something. Imagine! This might be my last girls' weekend ever."

"How do you mean?" Annette sounded suspicious.

"Well, you know . . ." Emma said bashfully.

"Know what?" *Had Emma got some big secret she was*

keeping from her? "Don't tell me you and Martin have discussed . . . have discussed . . . you know?"

"Well, listen, if I tell you something will you promise not to tell anyone?"

"Right." *God, what now?*

"Just before he went away, Martin said that he needed time to think about things."

"Really?" *Did Martin think? What a surprise!*

"Yes," Emma answered. "So I reckon if he thinks things through, he'll, you know, want to move things along."

"Would you *like* to end up with Martin though?" Annette was skeptical. "I mean what makes you so sure he's the one? Are you sure you're not just panicking in case you're left on the shelf?"

"Martin *is* the man for me." Emma sounded hurt. *Why did nobody ever seem to believe her?*

"OK." Annette decided to drop it. "So will I go and book a B&B in Galway then?"

"Do."

"And you're not going to go and change your mind or anything?"

"No," Emma promised.

Annette booked a B&B near the center of Galway. She was looking forward to getting out of Dublin. Weekends in the city during the summer were hot, sweaty and made her feel claustrophobic.

Annette couldn't see what Emma saw in Martin.

At all.

But then she was often accused of being a tad unromantic.

Her last boyfriend, Anthony, had been dying to get hitched. But it just hadn't felt right. It wasn't enough to be "in like." She had to be crazily, madly in love. Or nothing.

"I'd look after you," Anthony had suggested at the top of the Eiffel Tower on a romantic trip to Paris.

Annette had felt dizzy.

Not with desire . . .

She was afraid of heights.

"Right," Annette had said.

"You wouldn't have to do anything."

"I see."

"I'd provide for you."

"Huh?"

"You wouldn't have to lift a finger again for the rest of your life."

"But Anthony, I *want* to work. I love my work. You know I do. I'm not just saying this."

He'd turned all serious all of a sudden.

"But Annette," he'd said, "I would prefer you not to work."

What did he think she was, an invalid?

She'd decided there and then that she never wanted to be supported, provided for or anything for. She was well able to do all that for herself. All she wanted was a laugh. A bit of fun. And whatever it was that Emma thought she shared with Martin, it didn't seem much like fun.

It was nearly eleven o'clock when Emma realized she hadn't thought about Martin once since she'd woken up. Was that a sign, she wondered.

"Emma? Wakey wakey, are you coming for a coffee?" asked Lorna, the other PA in the office.

"Sorry, Lorna," Emma smiled, "I was just thinking about something."

"Some*thing* or some*one*?" Lorna probed.

"He'll be back on Saturday."

"And you'll be out at Dublin airport waving the plane in if I know you," Lorna grinned.

"No," Emma said defensively, standing up from her computer, "I'll be away."

"Huh?"

"Yeah, I'm going away on a girlie weekend."

"You're going away with a girl? Are you all right, Emma? You're not sick or anything are you?"

"Why?"

"Well, it's just that you've spent the last few months moping over this holiday that Martin's on and the fact that he was going away without you . . ."

"Yeah, well I've changed," Emma answered.

She didn't want to tell Lorna too much. She was the nosiest person Emma knew. Lorna was on speaking terms with the whole of Dublin. She made it her business to be like that. If you wanted to keep something a secret you'd be better off putting up a notice in the canteen rather than telling *her*. That was the problem with Dublin, Emma thought, as she followed her colleague into the canteen. It was too small. Dublin was a village when it came to hot gossip. A village.

"There's Suzie. She must be back from sick leave," Lorna muttered as she dropped a spoonful of sugar into her tea.

"Oh," said Emma without interest. "What was wrong with her?"

"What *wasn't* wrong with her, if you know what I mean?" Lorna said out of the side of her mouth. "Sick, me foot."

"I don't understand," Emma said.

It was true. She *didn't* understand. In fact she didn't "get" office gossip at all. What was the fun in bitching about people from work? It was the reason she'd stopped going out with the girls. Office nights out were the pits. Knives being stuck in colleagues' backs.

Colleagues who weren't in the pub at the time.

Obviously.

"Apparently Suzie went on a six-week bender."

"What? You mean Suzie had a . . . has a . . . drink prob—"

"Ah Jesus, Emma, what planet have you been living on at all? Sure she went bananas altogether when your man ran off with your woman."

"What woman?"

"Your woman, you know, from the telly."

"Telly?"

"Ah, no one famous or anything," Lorna sniffed. "It's that oul one who does that knitting program, you know the one that no one watches."

"Oh right."

"But still."

"But still, yes."

"I wouldn't like to be her though . . . with everyone talking . . . you know."

But everyone isn't talking, Emma thought. *Except you.*

"Anyway, any other news?"

"Er, no," Emma mumbled and looked at her watch. "Gosh, is it time to go back up already?"

God, roll on Friday.

"Christ, I hate Enfield," Annette screamed as they'd sat for about half an hour in bumper-to-bumper Friday evening traffic. "This is ridiculous. How can they get away with just one lane on the Dublin to Galway road?"

"Once we're past Enfield and the road widens we should be all right though," Emma pointed out. She was delighted to be getting away. To get out of Dublin. Away from the office and Lorna the office snoop. "Listen, Annette, thanks a lot for suggesting this. I was really becoming moronic thinking about Martin all the time— as if that was going to bring him back sooner."

"Well, I'm glad to hear it," Annette said. "Look at the horse in that field over there," she added, just in case Emma decided to start yet another conversation about Martin. Conversations about Martin tended to be never-ending. And it wasn't like he was even an interesting guy.

"I think there's something really special about the west of Ireland, don't you? Martin would love it here."

"Sure he was here not so long ago himself," Annette said like lightning. "Remember Paddy Naughton's stag?"

"Oh . . . yes," Emma said quietly. "Yes I'd forgotten."

"Well, this is really a lovely B&B." Annette flopped down onto one of the huge beds. "It reminds me of a holiday I had as a kid. We stayed in a place just like this."

Emma smiled coyly. "It reminds me of a weekend I once spent with—"

"Do you mind if I use the shower first?" Annette jumped up. "I feel a bit sticky after the long journey."

Emma got the message. *I've got to stop thinking about Martin,* she told herself as she lay on the bed, shut her eyes and imagined his tanned body lying on a beautiful beach.

Imagined him drinking exotic cocktails.

Under palm trees.
Without her.

"God, this place is wild." Annette came back with two pints of beer and plonked them onto the table. "You won't believe how many fellas tried to chat me up at the bar."

"How many?"

"Well . . . one." Annette laughed. "But many more looked like they *would* have if I'd given them half a chance."

"But you're not really looking to score though, are you?" Emma questioned. "I mean we're only here for the laugh, aren't we?" she continued somewhat alarmed.

"I remember," Annette lowered her voice and leaned toward her friend, "I remember when you thought scoring *was* a laugh."

"For fuck's sake there's two of them," one fella said out loud as they walked into the second pub.

"I presume that's supposed to be a compliment," Annette laughed as she strode past, Emma in tow.

They grabbed two stools.

It wasn't long before they were joined.

By a lone man.

A drunken lone man.

With red hair.

He was from Northern Ireland.

"What do you call a girl standing on a tennis court?" he roared with laughter when Annette eventually told him her name.

"Do you know you're the first person ever to ask that?" Annette made a face. She scanned the crowded bar. There was plenty of talent here. Just a pity it all seemed to be over on the far side of the room.

"Ach, where's your sense of humor?"

"I left it back in the B&B along with my tolerance for people like you."

"Here, I was only being friendly." The guy's smile disappeared.

"We know," Emma cut in diplomatically. It wouldn't do to start a fight before the evening had even started to get going, she thought. Annette had a habit of getting fairly hot-headed once she had a few drinks in her. "How about trying out that bar next door?" she suggested to Annette. "It looks good as well."

Annette shrugged. "One bar is as good as the next," she agreed. "Come on, let's go."

And that was where they met Dave. In the next bar.

He had dark hair and huge dark eyes hidden behind black-rimmed glasses. Emma thought he had the most extraordinarily beautiful face she'd ever seen. He turned around from the bar counter and locked eyes with hers across the blurred sea of faces in the crowded smoky room.

She wasn't sure how it happened exactly. Emma *never* caught men's eyes. It just wasn't something that she did. And so she quickly decided she wasn't going to start doing it now. She turned her back so as not even to be tempted to catch his eye again. And she reminded herself how much she loved Martin. *Martin.* Her true love, she thought uncertainly.

She studied her second (or was it her third?) pint thoughtfully. She refused to look up. Because that would only confirm that she fancied that dark-haired guy. Which she didn't. Not at all. At *all*. He was just some bloke. He could be anyone. And she had a long-term boyfriend. *Long-term*. Hmmm. Did that sound good or bad?

"Where are you girls from?" OhmiGod, he was standing beside them. He was chatting them up. He wasn't wearing his glasses anymore. How cute. He must have taken them off because he felt self-conscious. He must have thought he was more handsome without them.

But he was looking at Annette. Which was . . . you know, *good* . . . because Annette was . . . well, single . . . and she herself was . . . you know . . . taken.

"We're from Dublin," said Annette and gave him a huge smile. Which was extraordinarily unlike her. She must be keen, Emma thought. *Wildly* keen. "Where are *you* from?"

"Originally from Cork but I've been living in London for the past five years. I'm based in Dublin now."

"Right, oh I see. So, you lived in London . . . I love London. Love it . . . go there all the time. It's mad."

Emma suppressed a smile. The only time she remembered Annette going to London was when she was a kid. To see the Tower and Madame Tussaud's and all that.

With her mum.

"Are you girls here on holiday?"

"Just a weekend really." Annette fiddled with her glass playfully. "A girls' weekend."

"You left the guys at home, I suppose."

"Well, *I* don't have a boyfriend," Annette was blunt. "But Emma here has one."

"And you left him at home?" His eyes met Emma's. "Independent woman."

Emma smiled coyly. He really was something.

"Oh no," Annette cut in. "Emma's boyfriend is away on a golf trip. We wouldn't be here otherwise, isn't that right, Em?"

Emma felt her cheeks burn. God, Annette was making her out to be really pathetic. Is that how she came across to people in general? Oh God! Did people really think she was that sad?

Maybe they did. Of course they wouldn't *say* anything. *Of course* they wouldn't. Not to your face anyway. But what about people like Lorna? What did *she* say about her in the canteen to the others when she wasn't there? Emma gave a slight shudder. It was best not to think about things people might say about you.

"Anyway, I'm Dave."

"I'm Annette and this is my best pal Emma."

"My pal is over at the bar. Do you mind if I bring him over?"

"Not at all," Annette said like a shot. "We'll make some room for him."

"Push over—the friend can sit beside you . . ." She nudged Emma when Dave had gone. "So, do you think I'm in there?"

"Sure," Emma tried to sound brighter than she felt. What was wrong with her? She should be delighted for Annette. Not sitting there like a jealous cat because someone was chatting her friend up. This was ridiculous. "I think he likes you," she lied. "You should go for it."

"Maybe you might go for the friend."

"I'm taken, remember?" Emma gave a watery smile.

Until now Emma had always loved saying that to people. *"I'm taken"* had a comforting ring to it. Or *"I'm* involved," "I've already got a boyfriend," "My partner and I . . ." or simply "We."

Now it sounded very off-putting and un-fun.

Suddenly she wanted to shout something really mad like "I'm free!" "I'm game!" or "Could all the single men in this bar please stand up!"

Stop it, she told herself. Stop it right now. Deep down you know how lucky you are to have Martin.

So lucky.

Well, maybe not.

Because if she was lucky she'd feel *happy* when she was with Martin, wouldn't she? And *secure*. And *comfortable*.

And she never felt any of those things.

With Martin.

"What can I get you girls to drink?"

Dave was back. With friend. Who was absolutely bombed by the look of things. Then again, lots of people in the pub looked the same way. Emma tried to remember the last time she'd got absolutely hammered. She couldn't.

God, wouldn't it be great to get really drunk again?

Martin didn't like her to drink.

No.

He preferred her to drive.

"I'll have a Bacardi and Coke," Emma said. *What the hell.*

"Same for me," Annette piped up.

"JD for me. Go easy on the ice," said the friend. He introduced himself as Ben.

Emma held out her hand. He went to kiss it. And fell.

Annette screamed with laughter. "He's hilarious so he is."

Emma wasn't sure if she agreed.

Dave was back. He took a seat beside Annette. *So what?*

Emma sipped her Bacardi. It was strong. Good.

Sometimes it was hard to tell if they'd put in any Bacardi at all. The taste of Bacardi reminded her of Spain.

She wondered if Martin was drinking Bacardi in Spain.

Ben said, "So what are two gorgeous girls like yourselves doing here?"

"Same as you two gorgeous lads," Emma said back.

"Galwaysh great craic, ishn't it? You been here before?"

"Many times," Emma said and noticed how red Ben's eyes were. He was going to have a desperate head in the morning.

The girls ended up at a packed nightclub where everyone seemed to be either a student or a tourist. The place was flying. The drink had shot straight to Emma's head. She couldn't wait to hit the dance floor.

"Wait until we get a few more drinks into us," Annette said.

Emma didn't object.

It wasn't like she had to get up in the morning.

"Where did the lads get to?"

"They're following us in later," Annette explained. "They decided to stay on for a few."

"So do you think you'll get it together with Dave?" Emma tried not to sound too interested.

"You remember his name?" Annette pretended to be amazed. "Gosh, Em, you're going through a major bloody transformation here."

Emma made a face as she tried to grab the barman's attention.

"He fancies you."

"Who? The barman?" Emma looked confused.

"No . . . Dave does."

Emma paled. She mustn't have heard right. No, she couldn't *possibly* have heard right. Sure hadn't Dave been chatting Annette up for the last hour while she had struggled to try and follow Ben's nonsensical ramblings.

"I'm telling you, he fancies you."

"But, what about you?"

"Listen there's no need to be condescending," Annette said.

"Sorry . . . I didn't mean . . . I meant . . ."

"Hey, don't worry about it." Annette began to laugh. "I was only teasing. Besides I've just seen my future hubby."

"Huh?"

"Yeah, see your man over there with the blond hair? He's mine."

She was off.

Emma stared after her friend in amazement. God, wouldn't it be great to be like that? To do stuff just on the spur of the moment and not care.

"Hi there."

She swung around. She was face-to-face with Dave. Wow. Talk about being hit between the eyes. She tried to drag her eyes away from his. Couldn't. Couldn't stop staring. This was ridiculous. She wasn't a teenager.

"What are you drinking?"

"Er . . ." Emma hesitated. Should she go for another Bacardi? Or was it time for a Coke?

On its own.

Maybe.

"Bacardi," she said.

She watched him stand at the bar as he waited patiently to give his order. He had soft skin, she noticed, and his eyes were captivating. They seemed to be able to read her soul.

It was unnerving.

As he walked away from the bar, she saw him collide with a smooching couple. She heard him apologize. He looked mortified.

"How did that happen?" she giggled as he handed her a drink.

"I just didn't see them," Dave said.

"You're as blind as a bat, aren't you?"

"I am quite shortsighted, yes."

"Well, leave your glasses on then."

"Do you think I should?"

"Of course I do. I adore men with glasses."

"Does your boyfriend wear them?"

"No."

What if? she thought. What if she were to snog somebody else? Someone other than Martin? Who would ever find out?

Nobody.

Probably.

The thought filled her with excitement and anticipation. Imagine if she just went for it?

"Drink up." Dave was smiling at her.

She smiled back.

What if?

* * *

"Oh my God, this is my *favorite* song." Emma fell into Dave's arms. About seven Bacardis later.

The room was spinning.

Or maybe it was just her.

It was hard to know.

Annette was back.

With Declan.

The blond's name had been established.

Annette had a drunken, questioning look on her face.

Emma ignored it.

"Wanna dance?" Declan roared in Annette's ear.

They disappeared.

Again.

Dave took Emma's hand. His touch sent shivers up her spine.

And that was only his hand.

God!

They sidled through the dancing crowd. Hand in hand.

As if in a dream.

She never wanted to let go.

She felt hammered.

Dave's arms wrapped themselves around her waist.

He had strong arms.

She tried to relax.

But couldn't.

Was as wound up as wheels on a high-speed train.

Loved this song.

She moved her head toward his. She could feel his breath on her mouth. She pressed herself against him.

If she'd let go she might have fallen over.

"Why don't you kiss me?" the drink spoke.

"Because you've got a boyfriend," Dave said.

"But no one would know."

"We would though." He kissed her forehead. "We would know."

"Is this *your* B&B?"

"Yeah, I think it is." Emma wasn't sure. It was dark. She was drunk. She fumbled in her bag for the front-door key.

"Here, I've got a key." Dave laughed.

"How come?"

"I stole yours."

"Did you?"

"No." Dave pretended to look shocked. "This is my B&B too. I can't believe it. I'm staying here too."

"Oh . . . not in my room though. Ha ha. Sherioushly though . . ."

"Hey, what do you take me for? I wouldn't even kiss you, remember?"

"Hmmm."

He opened the front door and saw her to her room.

His glasses were off again. He must want to kiss her.

She paused outside and leaned her back against the door.

"Well," she fluttered her eyelids. God, she could barely see.

"Well, good night," he said.

He was gone.

Just like that.

The nerve!

Emma was flabbergasted.

Who did he think he was? Not even *trying* anything?

Of course she wouldn't have let anything happen. But that wasn't the point. The point was . . . the point *was* . . . Oh God . . . what *was* the point?

"No, I'm mortified." Emma dropped a second aspirin into her glass of water.

She felt like someone was hitting her head with a brick.

"So you're definitely not going down for breakfast?"

Emma shook her head.

"No nice scrambled eggs?"

"God, I feel sick. I really do. Please stop talking about eggs. I swear I'm never drinking again. I mean it. It's just not worth it."

Later that evening . . .

"So, a Bacardi and Diet Coke, is it?" Annette was heading for the bar.

"Just a Diet Coke."

"Are you sure?"

"Yeah."

"How about just the one?"

"Oh, all right then."

"Another Bacardi?"

"Sure. God, I can't believe I'm locked again."

"Is that your phone?" Annette was wondering.

"Huh?"

"Your phone. Your mobile's ringing."

"Hello? . . . Martin. God, you're back. Er . . . welcome back . . . darrrrrling. No, of course I'm not drunk . . . haha."

"Tell him you'll call him tomorrow," Annette hissed.

"I'll call you tomorrow, yeah? . . . Yeah? Do you love me? Do you? Do you? . . . I can't hear you . . . the line is . . . oh for fuck's sake."

"Oh God, Martin sounded really pissed off that I wasn't at home."

"Why though? It's not like you're doing anything wrong. By the way, Declan said he'd join us later," Annette announced.

"Did he ring you?"

"Yeah, he just rang my mobile while you were in the Ladies. You don't mind, do you?"

"Suppose not," Emma said. *But wasn't this supposed to be a girls' weekend? When had the rules suddenly changed to suit Annette?*

"I think he's really nice," Annette enthused. "By the way, your man Dave left a message at reception to say he'd call into our room at nine. Imagine. As if we were going to be sitting there waiting for him!"

"How do you know?"

"The landlady told me."

"But why didn't you tell me?"

"I . . . um, forgot . . . sorry."

"But it's a quarter past nine now," Emma panicked. "Maybe we should go back."

"What? Don't be silly, Emma. Martin's back in Ireland. You'll be seeing him tomorrow night."

"Yeah, I suppose you're right," Emma said uncertainly. Martin hadn't sounded too pleased to hear her voice though. Actually that was a bit of an understatement— Martin had sounded bloody furious. It was as if he couldn't really believe that she actually had the nerve to do anything without him. She was sure Dave wouldn't go on like that . . . if he had a girlfriend.

Declan arrived. With a friend for Emma. So *that's* why Annette hadn't passed on the message. Everything was beginning to make sense now. Before long Annette and Declan were snogging.

"So what kind of music are you into?" the friend asked Emma.

"Oh, a bit of this and that," Emma replied and suddenly wished she were anywhere but here. She was too hungover to get pleasantly drunk. It felt like she was drinking just to get an even worse hangover. What was the point in that?

She'd had enough. She just wanted to go back to the B&B.

"You have *got* to be joking." Annette was clearly annoyed.

"I'm sorry, Annette, I just don't feel well."

"OK, fine."

Emma got a taxi back.

There was no sign of Dave.

Well, he had hardly come to Galway just to sit in a B&B, now had he?

There was a note under the door.

Waited until half past. Understand that you mightn't have wanted to see me. If you were mine, I wouldn't want to let you out of my sight. Best wishes, Dave.

Emma read the note about twenty times.

What a sweetie.

What a pity she hadn't been here earlier. Then again, what did she think she was playing at? She'd be back in Martin's arms tomorrow night. So why wasn't that prospect cheering her up? She was just tired. And confused. She'd sort everything out in the morning.

In the morning Dave was gone.

"What?" Emma couldn't believe it.

"I'm afraid they checked out pretty early," the landlady said.

"I see," she said, distraught.

"What's for you won't pass you," Annette said encouragingly on the way home.

"But sure I'll never see him again."

"What about Martin?"

Emma sighed. "What about him?"

"So I know it might sound like I'm being a bit of a prick, but I'm just being cruel to be kind." Martin lit a cigarette and inhaled sharply.

Emma just stared at him, dazed. It was going to take a while for all of this to sink in. She noticed his nose was peeling. He should really put some after-sun lotion on it. He should really . . . my God, what was it he had said again?

"Let me get this straight," she began. She might as well be reciting words in a play. Everything just seemed so unreal. "You met some girl on the beach. She's moving in and you want me to move out."

"In a nutshell."

"But . . . but . . ."

"Don't make this more difficult for me than it already is . . . please, Emma."

"Difficult for you?" Emma was stunned. *Difficult for Martin?* Had he always been this selfish? Had she really never noticed? Was she that stupid? She took a long hard look at him. For the first time ever she noticed he was heavier than the average man. He had a beer belly. And his eyes were too small. His hair color was really nondescript. And he had a most unattractive nasal voice.

"I've decided to give you a week to get yourself sorted," Martin said. "It's only fair."

"Thank you so much," Emma spoke like a robot, "but I'll only need twenty-four hours."

"Right, well, if you're sure that's not too much trouble. And, Emma, I know this might sound weak but in the future I hope we can at least try to be friends. After all, we spent nearly three years together."

"Oh yes," she said.

Over my dead body, she thought. *The bastard. And for your information it was four and a half bloody years.*

"And I'm sure you'll meet someone."

"I will." She paused. "In fact . . . in fact, Martin, I already have."

"What?"

"Yes. In Galway."

"Did you . . . did you . . . did—?"

"Yes, I did."

"You—?"

"Yes. It made me realize what I'd been missing all these years."

"God, you're a bitch."

"Sometimes you have to be cruel to be kind, do you know what I mean? Now, if you'll excuse me, I've packing to do."

*   *   *

"Well done," said Annette. "No, really well done. I never thought you had it in you."

"I still can't believe what's happened, though. How am I going to face everyone at work?"

"You were able to take on Martin, so you can face the girls at work. I'm proud of you, Em. But, listen, there's just one more thing you've got to do."

"What?"

"Find Dave."

"Hi." Emma tried to sound bright. "I . . . er . . . we, er, stayed in your B&B over the weekend and we . . . er (God, this was so sad!) . . . we met these two . . ."

"Oh, is that Emma?"

"Yeah, that's right. Wow, you've a great memory."

"Well, I don't actually—it's just that, believe it or not, that young fella called Dave was on earlier on wanting to know if I'd a surname for you. But your room was booked under Annette Krane. I couldn't help him any further, I'm afraid."

Oh God, Oh God!!! "Did he leave a telephone number or anything?"

"I'm sorry, he didn't and they paid with cash so I didn't get credit card details or anything but do you want to leave me your number now in case he rings again?"

"Sure," Emma said. *But realistically what were the chances of him ringing again?*

Monday came.

The sky was gray and depressing.

The thought of going into work was even more so.

Emma stood at the bus stop and tried not to cry.

Lorna pounced on her as soon as she arrived in.

"EMMMMAAAA!!! Tell us *everything*. What did he bring you home? Did he miss you? Come on down to the canteen and I'll get us two coffees."

"I feel sick," said Emma. "If you don't mind I don't think I'll go down."

"Nonsense," Lorna said loudly. "You'll come down if I have to drag you by the hair of your head. And besides," she gave Emma a wicked grin, "I have some photos I have to show you."

"Of what?" Christ, Lorna was always showing her bloody photos of her friends and relations.

As if anybody gave a damn!

"We've split up," Emma told her.

"Oh my God, I don't believe it! Who broke it off with who?" Lorna's eyes widened. Gosh, this was the most exciting piece of news she'd heard in ages! Who ever said Mondays were boring?

"He did." She might as well be honest.

"And how are you coping?"

"Great," Emma answered, knowing how much that would disappoint.

"Oh well, plenty of fish and all that . . . Now *wait* until I show you the pictures of my little prince. His name's Adam. You can tell me what you think."

Emma mechanically took the photos off her.

"So what do you think?" Lorna squealed.

Emma looked at the first photo. Her heart hit the canteen floor. Oh Jesus. Oh no. She didn't think she could stomach this. The guy in the photo was . . . *Oh Christ, why did life have to be so cruel?* . . . It was Dave.

"He's . . . he's really . . . he . . ." Emma felt like she was going to faint.

"What?"

"He's great," Emma whispered as the walls seemed to close in on her.

Lorna leaned over. "Not him," she screeched. "God no, not the fella with the glasses. Ha ha. Here, gimme the photos. There he is, that's him."

"I see," Emma sighed with relief. "And who . . . who's the other guy?"

"Oh that's Dave, who lives with Adam. Quiet guy. Not really my type. Keeps himself to himself."

"So he's not involved . . ."

"No. Why? Are you keen? I'll tell him you're interested, ha ha . . . now that you're back on the shelf ha ha."

Emma looked at Lorna. "Yeah, tell him that." She wasn't smiling. "Go on, make my day."

Lorna looked baffled.

But Emma didn't care. Thank God she worked with someone who knew everyone, she thought, chuckling to herself.

Thank God Dublin was a village!

Born in Armagh, Northern Ireland, MARISA MACKLE now divides her time between Dublin and Marbella. Her first novel, *Mr. Right for the Night,* was published in May 2002. She would like to dedicate this story to her best friend, Roxanne Parker, with whom she's shared many girls' weekends.

The Union Man

Tina Reilly

ere it comes, I thought, trying my best not to look completely indifferent.

"Oh, my boy's a great boy," Mrs. Long said on cue, gazing proudly at her one and only offspring. "You're a very lucky girl, Laura."

Her one and only offspring, who also happened to be my husband, smiled modestly.

The three of us, me, Peter (the great boy) and his mother, were ensconced in Mrs. Long's "good" room. A dark, furniture-laden chamber where polish seemed to be the only smell allowed.

Peter had bought me a bunch of bedraggled roses for Valentine's Day and I was meant to be going all gaa-gaa over them. I smiled stiffly, knocked back some more tea and refused to look at the mutual admiration that was going on between Peter and his mother.

"He's always so thoughtful," his mother went on, her voice getting more saccharine by the nanosecond. "I remember when he got his first wage packet he went out and bought me a state-of-the-art . . ." she paused, took a deep breath and said reverently, "iron."

"Really?" I'd heard all this before. I heard it every time Peter bought me a present in fact.

Beside me Peter preened himself.

"Oh yes," Mrs. Long nodded vigorously. "It was like a bird the way it glided across all the clothes." She made a flowing motion with her hands and then sighed. "Oh, but sure that was when I had ironing to do." Sad look, bravely replaced by another high voltage beam at Peter. "Oh, I do miss him. But sure he has his own life to lead now. He's a great lad, so he is."

Peter reached over and patted her hand. He threw a triumphant look at me. *See,* the look said, *someone appreciates me.*

I knew nothing was expected of me. All I had to do was smile and nod. Oh, I'd come a long way in four years. My mind drifted back to the first time I'd heard Mrs. Long's mantra about how wonderful her son was.

Twenty, fresh from college, dying to get a job and earn a few bob, I ended up working in a law firm, typing and filing. The craic was great, the money was not and so one fine day someone somewhere decided that we should strike.

Peter was our union rep. He was the reason most of us went to the union meetings, he was the reason we voted to strike. Peter, with his impassioned speeches, blazing eyes and fabulous grin, turned us weak at the knees. This was a guy who would get things done and even if he didn't at least it meant he'd be around a lot *trying* to get things done. He made us all feel important as he talked to us, telling us we were too valuable to be wasted on crap wages.

"Honestly," he'd say, as he pinned us with his glittering eyes, "yez *need* more. Yez deserve more. I'll get yez more!"

His fist would pound the air and we'd cheer.

Ohhh God!

And the way he walked. Hands half in, half out of his jeans. Slow, easy, nonchalant strut. Head down as he looked at the world from under thick black eyelashes.

Sex just waiting to happen.

Despite Peter's speeches and our determined stance— determined mostly by lust, it has to be said—we lost the strike. Despite the fact that Peter told us we'd get more, we actually didn't. He told us it didn't matter. He hadn't lost, he said. He was just going to find another route to victory.

I couldn't have cared less. I was young, besotted and eventually after much marching in the rain in crippling shoes, tight tops and short skirts, Peter noticed me. It was hard not to. Whenever he came into earshot, I'd shout, "Whatda we want!" And everyone else would shout, "A shag with Peter."

Peter would grin, blow me a kiss and at last, the final day of the strike, he asked me out.

He spent our first date talking about the union, about how he was their main man on the ground, about all the wonderful things he was going to do.

A few dates later, I was brought home to meet his mother.

She spent the evening talking about Peter's union, about how he was their main man on the ground and about all the wonderful things Peter had done, was doing and was going to do in the future.

My life continued like this for some months. Soon I was talking to everybody about Peter's union, about how he was their main man on the ground and about all the wonderful things Peter had done, was doing and would be able to do.

"Yeah," Marcella, my flatmate said, "but is he good in bed?"

"Mmm," I answered. "He is. He doesn't snore and he never hogs the bedcovers."

Marcella nodded and skitted a bit. "Keep it to yourself then, smart bitch."

I honestly didn't know what she was talking about.

Anyway, to cut a long story short, in this brainwashed state, I was convinced that I was marrying God. Only there was no way God would have been as good-looking. Or as funny. Or the union's main man on the ground.

And so our big day arrived.

Peter promised me a limo to bring me to the church. A mate of his knew someone's uncle who knew someone that had one. Only the "someone-that-had-one" obviously hadn't got one at all because at two o'clock, when I was meant to be making my way to the church, I was sitting at home, trying not to cry while my father rang up every taxi rank in the area.

He wasn't having much joy as Ireland were playing

a big match that day and taxis were thin on the ground.

At two forty-five, when I should have been married, I was climbing into an abused-looking taxi, while my father attempted to tie a red ribbon onto the aerial.

"Aw now," the taxi man protested, "dat dere ribbon is going to ruin de reception on de radio. Dere's a match on today dat I wand to hear. Yeh'll have to take it down."

My father gave a jovial smile. "Look, it's my daughter's wedding day and—"

"And I've a bleeding bet on dis match. Take—de—ribbon—down." The driver climbed out of the car, all twenty-odd stone of him. "Now," he added menacingly.

So, minus the ribbon, the taxi trundled and farted its way toward the church.

Twenty minutes later—with a very dour-looking priest who gave a sermon on the value of dependability in a relationship extending to all areas of our lives—we were married expresso-style. Hymns had to be cut as there was another wedding at four. Prayers of the faithful were gone, which resulted in Peter's godchild howling the place down because she'd been practicing for months. And to top all that, Mrs. Long gave me a look that would have deep frozen the Gobi Desert. "You're a very lucky girl that Peter didn't leave," she muttered over dinner. "Honestly, my poor boy at the top of the church on his own. I never felt as sorry for anyone. I think he thought you weren't going to turn up."

At that stage I was still in blind love mode. "Of course I'd turn up," I exclaimed. "I love him."

"That's what I told him," Mrs. Long said. "I said, she's a girl that knows what way up her bread's buttered."

And I replied, "I do. You're right."

* * *

We bought a house. A semi-D in suburbia. A semi-D that had a garden that needed to be done. "We'll have a water feature over here," Peter said authoritatively the day we moved in. "And I'll build a garage down at the far end."

Cor, I thought. *Build a garage.* I couldn't wait to see him, gorgeous body bathed in sweat, lifting blocks and cementing them together. Doing big strong man things.

And to give him his due, he went out and bought a shiny shovel. But wouldn't you know it, the ground in our back garden was very hard. God, he'd never dug ground as hard in his entire life, he said. And his back . . . jaysus, don't *mention* his back! So after a day's digging, which resulted in a large hole and major backache, he put the shiny shovel carefully away underneath the stairs.

Oh, I was promised extensions, attic conversions, open-plan rooms, cobble-lock, painting, wallpapering, varnishing, sanding. You name it, he promised it with a sincere face, a sexy grin and a wink that still got me weak at the knees. In fact, Peter promised me so much, our house would have rivaled the White House if it had come to pass. Everything was promised with the "T" word.

Tomorrow.

Only, as I was to discover, tomorrow was always a day away.

It was the Valentine's gift of manky roses that did it. You see, in my total innocence—or was it stupidity?—I'd actually got excited when Peter turned down my offer to buy him dinner on Valentine's Day.

"Naw," he said, looking all cagey, "we're, eh, heading out somewhere else."

"We are?"

Peter nodded mysteriously and tapped his nose.

"Aw, go on, tell us," I begged.

He shook his head. "Nope. And stop asking—nosy women are very unattractive." He tweaked my nose, kissed my cheek and made a face. "Jaysus, the wallpaper in here is manky, I'll have to do something about it soon. Maybe tomorrow."

Normally I'd have slagged him over that comment but I was too excited to bother.

I told all the girls in work, I begged them to try to find out what Peter was up to. I bought new clothes. Got my hair done. Even invested in some nice makeup. When Valentine's Day came around, I was in a tizzy of excitement. Peter arrived in our bedroom that Sunday morning. Clad in boxer shorts, he looked good enough to eat. In one hand, he held a small white envelope.

"Good goods in small parcels," I tittered.

"Thanks," he muttered, offended, as he looked down at himself.

"No, not you. The envelope," I laughed.

"Oh yeah, right." He tossed the envelope onto the bed where I pounced on it.

I felt it for clues before opening it up. A voucher? Or maybe it was plane tickets? Or a holiday booking?

It was a card. *To my wife on Valentine's Day.* A picture of flowers. Inside it read: *Happy Valentine's Day.* He'd signed it, *Love Peter.*

"Thanks," I smiled, still optimistic. From underneath the mattress, I drew out an enormous card and gave it to him. He opened it and laughed at the poem I'd made up especially for him.

Roses are red
Violets are blue
Why do it today
When tomorrow will do?

"It's a joke, the poem," I explained hastily, just in case it offended him.

Peter grinned good-naturedly. "It's good," he said. "Kinda strange though."

Kinda true, more like, I wanted to say. But of course I didn't. At that stage he was still a legend in both our minds.

"I gotcha some flowers too," he said then. He grabbed my hand and pulled me from the bed. "They're in the kitchen."

Going out somewhere *and* flowers? Peter was excelling himself. I even had a daft vision of the whole room being covered in flowers.

Four withered roses tied with a ribbon stood in a see-through milk jug on top of the press.

"Bought them from a guy last night in the boozer," Peter sounded delighted with himself. "Here, have a smell." He shoved the roses almost halfway up my nose. The only smell from them was smoke.

"Lovely," I managed faintly.

"Fifty pence each, special offer."

I wasn't falling for this. Something else was going to happen and he was only teasing me.

We had our breakfast.

Our lunch.

Peter had to go to a quick meeting.

OK, part of my mind said—the part that lived in a

permanent state of denial—he isn't *really* going to a meeting, he's going somewhere else to get my surprise ready.

I changed clothes and did myself up just to be prepared.

Two hours later he arrived home. "Ready?" he asked. "Got your coat?"

I attempted to look as if I hadn't been expecting this. "I'm just getting it now."

I put on my new coat and gave my hair a final brush. As I arrived out to the car, Peter looked me up and down admiringly. "Did you do something to yourself? You look very nice."

"Thanks."

"Can't wait to show me mother what a gorgeous wife I have."

It was as if I'd just landed on a runway with no wheels. "Your mother?" I said slowly. "We're going to your mother's on Valentine's Day?"

"Didn't I tell you?" He attempted surprise.

For the first time since I'd met him, I was furious with him. And it wasn't just because he was bringing me to his mother's. It was everything. The fact that our house looked like a barn, that our garden looked like Beirut, that I was such a stupid eejit.

I was about to say something when it hit me.

Of *course* we weren't going to his mother's. No way would he do that. It was all part of the surprise.

I gave a knowing smile and turned away from him.

"I meant to tell you," he said innocently. "She's awful lonely and Valentine's Day brings back thoughts of Dad."

"Yeah. Right." Just how stupid did he think I was?

Even when we turned into his mother's driveway, my

mind refused to believe that I'd spent the last month preparing for *this*. It became increasingly difficult to keep up the denial, however, when his mother enfolded him in a huge bear hug, told him accusingly that he'd lost weight and, with a curt nod in my direction, linked his arm and chatted and laughed all the way into the house.

I kept my composure all through the meal which, incidentally, was his favorite. Shepherd's pie and ice cream.

Who cared that I was vegetarian and ate neither shepherd's pie nor ice cream?

On the way home, however, I didn't talk to him. It was about as effective as drowning a fish. Peter just took it as his opportunity to talk about himself and how wonderful he was. He was normally worse after visiting his mother. She inflated him with a huge sense of self-worth.

In that moment I knew that I'd had it with him and his empty promises. I'd had it with having the mankiest house on the street.

Tomorrow was coming and I was ready for it.

Tomorrow arrived for me a few weeks later. Peter was heading to a conference for four days.

"Making more promises you don't keep," I said dryly. Our relationship by now was consisting of him talking, of me being sarcastic and of him not noticing.

"I don't make promises," he said as he buttoned up his shirt, "I say what we hope to achieve." His voice patronizing, he added, "There *is* a difference."

"Not that I can see," I muttered. "Your promises achieve nothing and neither does your union."

"Is it your time of the month again?" Peter asked, trying to sound sympathetic. "I dunno. They should call it time of the fortnight." With that comment, which typified him so completely, he left (after having the *nerve* to kiss me).

Once he was gone, I dressed at speed, tidied the house (as best I could) and waited for THE DECORATOR to come.

I'd hired the decorator the day after Valentine's Day. He'd hummed and hawed about coming out on such short notice but after I offered him a fee that would have fed the Third World for a month, he eventually capitulated.

I didn't care about the cost, I'd promised myself that if Peter wasn't going to get stuff done, well, I bloody well was. It was the start of the new me. The one that didn't wait around for a particular man to do man stuff. Any man would do.

Clinton Blake, the decorator, was a nondescript, balding, short man of fifty-odd years.

As he came with his ladders and pasting board into our shambles of a hallway, his first question was, "Why did you choose me? Did ya hear about me from someone? Or was it the Yellow Pages?"

Actually it had been his name. I'd pictured Clinton Blake as a "heave-ho" kinda guy, not this vertically challenged man standing in front of me. "Yellow Pages," I muttered, flushing slightly.

"Good," Clinton nodded, obviously pleased with my answer. "I'll renew my sub next year so."

He gazed around my hall. "Wow," he mumbled. "What a challenge."

After downing three cups of tea, he set to work with a

vengeance. He pasted and papered and painted. I stripped (wallpaper) and sanded and polished.

By the time Peter was due back, the hall and kitchen had been done. I told Clinton that when I won the lottery I'd give him a call to finish the rest of the place. It was a joke, but Clinton seemed to have been born missing his ironic gene.

"Chances of winning the lottery are," he screwed up his rather screwed-up face and threw out a figure. "You're better off putting a few bob aside each week and saving that way," he advised.

"Thanks," I muttered.

Then exit Clinton and enter, a few hours later, Peter.

I have to say, I felt a bit sick before Peter arrived. All sorts of doubts crowded my head. Maybe it wasn't right to get stuff done behind his back? Maybe he'd throw a wobbler? But then I remembered the four manky roses and the trip to his mother's and all the promises he'd made which had never come to fruition.

Jesus, I couldn't wait to see his reaction.

Bastard.

At ten o'clock, he arrived back. Hearing his car pull up outside, I opened the front door to him. In he came with his fancy holdall. He stepped into the hallway and froze. His eyes flitted from the walls to me and back to the walls. Looking puzzled, he stepped outside, looked at the manky garden and reassured himself that he'd obviously come home to the right place. He stepped back inside again.

The look of puzzled bewilderment on his face would have been funny if my heart hadn't started pumping about like mad.

"What happened here?" he asked.

"I got it done while you were away," I said as if it was a regular occurrence. "D'you like it?"

"It's pink."

"No fooling you—is there, Peter?"

"Did you do it yourself, like?" There was a grudging admiration there somewhere.

"Nope." I braced myself. "I had a man in to do it. He said he'd come on Tuesday and, *imagine*, he came on Tuesday."

"A man?" Peter's face grew dark. "What sort of a man?"

"A decorator. Clinton Blake." I let my voice dwell on the words of the name, drawing them out in a sort of orgasmic appreciation. Then I added, "He did it in a day."

"Clinton?" Peter guffawed. "Jaysus, with a name like that, no wonder the hall is pink."

"And what's more, I'm getting him to do the rest of the house," I snapped. "At least he's dependable."

I saw him flinch before he asked in his best union man's voice, "And how much did Clinton charge?"

I gave him a sanitized version of the figure.

"That much?" Peter gawped at me in disbelief. Then he went and counted all the sheets of paper and calculated how much he'd charged per sheet. Then he proceeded to point out nonexistent bubbles. "You were done," he proclaimed finally.

"No, Peter," I said, voice shaking with fury, "the hall was done. The kitchen was done. The only time I was ever done was when I believed all the shite out of you!" With that brilliant quick-thinking comment, I stormed upstairs.

* * *

He came up to me later and asked gruffly why I'd got in a decorator. Why hadn't I waited for him to do it?

"You say it yourself, Peter," I sneered. "If you can't win one way, you've to find another route to victory."

He laughed a little at that. "A union man's wife to be sure," he teased, nibbling my ear.

I wasn't having any of it. Pushing him off, I spat out, "Unfortunately."

His teasing eyes grew somber. "I would have done it," he said quietly.

"Yeah, when?"

"Look, I'm the union's man on the ground, I'm busy doing other things."

"Yeah. Making promises you can't keep." I pulled the bedcovers over my head. "Piss off and let me sleep."

The next morning, Peter stunned me by ringing work and announcing that he was taking a few days off. Then he rang my work and told them that I was taking a few days off too.

"Sorry?" I gawped at him.

"So you should be," he snapped. "Getting a guy called Clinton to paper our house in pink. Pink!" He scoffed before saying stiffly, "We're going to head out and choose some paper for the rest of the rooms. I'll show you that when Peter Long says he's going to do something he means it." With the sort of determination he usually reserved for organizing doomed strikes, Peter strode out of the house, leaving me to catch him up.

We visited every paper, paint and tile shop in Dublin. Peter went through samples, discussed shades and textures with me. I was like a zombie, terrified to wake up properly in case it was all a glorious dream.

The car was fit to burst by the time we bought a final twelve rolls of wallpaper for the dining room. Single-handedly, Peter carried them to the car. "I'll bet Mr. Do-the-Hallway-in-Pink-Clinton couldn't carry twelve rolls of paper under one arm, could he?"

I doubted Clinton had ever tried, he wasn't that juvenile. But Peter had this anxious little boy look on his face that endeared him to me all over again. I shook my head. "No way." Then knowing what would keep him sweet, I added, "You're *so* strong, Peter."

If he had been the sun, he would have blinded the whole human race with the shiny smile he gave me. "I'll bet Clinton was a right arsehole, wasn't he?"

I shrugged. "He was able to paper the hall in a day, though."

Peter's smile disappeared. He threw the wallpaper into the boot and got into the car. "You haven't seen me in action," he muttered.

That much we *could* agree on.

He worked like a man possessed. He hadn't a clue what he was doing but that had never stopped him before. Bubbles abounded and in the boxroom the paper we'd picked with rabbits on it (in case any children were unfortunate enough to be born to our union) was all over the place.

"But the rabbits all look like they're mounting each other," I muttered when he asked me what I thought.

"That's what rabbits do," he said sullenly.

And he had a point, I guess.

As the days went by, he got more efficient. He even took out a stopwatch and timed how quickly he could measure, cut, paste and hang.

"Five minutes," he scoffed at one stage. "Betcha Clinton Flake took longer."

"Yeah, but he didn't hang it upside down."

Apparently that small detail didn't count.

It was on day three of this frantic activity that it dawned on me why he was so committed to doing the house up. He was jealous. Madly, insanely jealous. Some guy called Clinton had come into his territory and impressed his wife. Peter had been the only man in my life up to this and I'd believed him to be wonderful. He'd never had competition from any quarter. In fact, in the whole of his life, Peter had never had competition. Women swooned all over him and his mother doted on him.

In fact, it chilled me to realize that my relationship with Peter was very much the same as the one he had with his mother.

The thought sent a cold shiver right through me.

Life for this man was going to change.

I played hot and cold. I dropped breadcrumbs of praise into our conversation when he was least expecting it. Hungry for some hero worship, he'd feast on it for a while until he got fat and cocky again. Then the larder would dry up until the next time.

The next time usually happened when he'd pulled out all the stops to impress me.

I don't know how he felt about it, I didn't ask. One time he'd told me that he wasn't going to put up with my sneering.

So I'd sneered some more.

The way he'd bent over backward to win some approval was lovely.

My life was lovely.

It was lovely until the day I found him digging the garden. He had resurrected the shiny shovel from its place under the stairs and was excavating piles of earth at a furious rate. My first thought was that it was brilliant. Even though Peter had kept up his decorating, he'd never tackled the garden. The most he did was cut the grass. The grass mainly consisted of weeds and the odd daisy. Plus, of course, the huge hole for the garage that had never got built.

The night before I'd dropped a casual remark about hiring a man to do the garden. "There's this great guy," I said, "and he's brilliant. Monica swears by him."

"What?" Peter had said grumpily. "I didn't know Monica slept with gardeners."

"Pardon?"

"You said she swears by him. What does she say? 'Oh God, shag me again' or what?"

"Funny Peter." (It was a day when I wasn't giving him compliments and that included not laughing at his jokes.) "No, seriously, I'm thinking of getting a man in to do the garden."

He'd looked sort of panicky and hurt and I longed to cuddle him but it would have been fatal. Nothing would get done then.

So I left it.

And it had obviously worked or he wouldn't be digging the garden with the shiny shovel. Digging as if his life depended on it.

"Going to tackle the garden now?" I asked, doing a great job of sounding impressed. Then, just in case I was being too nice, I added, sarcastically, "Are you going to put in the water feature you talked about six years ago?"

"Maybe," Peter shrugged. "But for now, I'm going to build an extension."

Sweat glistened on his brow and tender and sexy thoughts raced at speed through my head.

"An extension?" I murmured, really genuinely impressed. "But how?"

"It's all thanks to you." Peter put down the shovel and came toward me. He smelled of earth. His lips brushed mine and my heart began to race. Give me a sweaty physical man anytime.

"Without you, I don't think I'd ever have tackled the house. I didn't like it that you got that Clinton guy in to decorate that time. It made me mad, I didn't want you thinking he was better than me."

"Oh, Peter," I pulled his face down to me again for another kiss, "no one is better than you."

I could literally feel him swelling with pride. Or was it with something else?

"No one," I whispered.

He pulled away from me and shrugged. "I dunno if I believe that," he said darkly. Then resuming his digging, he said, "But anyway, I did the house and now I'm doing this."

"You can do it," I said, already beginning to plan what it'd look like.

"And my mother will love it."

"I'm sure she will," I said dryly. "She loves everything you do."

"She's so lonely on her own, she'll be only too happy to move in."

Abrupt end to sexy tender feelings. "What?" The world lost its honey glow. "What?"

"Well, I'm going to try to build a granny flat for her."

"But . . . but . . . you can't build." I adopted my sneering voice, the one that normally had him fawning like a puppy dog. "Don't be ridiculous."

"You won't say that when it's up and running," he said back. "And my mother thinks it's a great idea." He looked sad for a second. "She always supports me in everything."

It was loaded. The way he said it was loaded.

In the last year, I had turned from a stupid adoring wife into a streetwise clever woman and he couldn't take it. He needed his stupid adoring mother more than ever now. He needed her to reassure him how wonderful he was.

Hoisted by my own petard.

"You can't build," I spluttered again.

"It's thanks to you that I've the confidence to try," he said back with chilling logic.

Blown apart by my own petard.

That's Peter.

He never loses, just finds another route to victory.

A union man to the last.

———

TINA REILLY is the author of the bestselling *Flipside* and *The Onion Girl*. Her third women's novel, *Is This Love,* was published February 2002.

She writes a weekly column for *The Evening Herald*

and under her married name, Martina Murphy, she has published a number of teenage books—*Livewire, Fast Car, Free Fall* and *Dirt Tracks*. *Dirt Tracks* was shortlisted for both the Bisto Book Award and the RAI reading award, while *Livewire* won an international White Raven Award.

Tina runs a drama school and lives in County Kildare with her husband, two kids and a cat.

An Independent Woman

Morag Prunty

Bridie tipped a little of the brown goo onto a dampened sponge, just as she had been instructed by the magazine, and began to spread it across her thin white skin using "gentle downward strokes."

Lovely, she thought, a much smoother finish. Now, why didn't I think of wetting the sponge myself? I must tell Sharon about it the next time she calls around. Sharon was Bridie's daughter. The truth was she was calling around less and less these days. She still kept a room at her mother's small semi in Kingsbury, but preferred to spend time at her boyfriend's flat in West Hampstead.

"Kingsbury is such a dump, Mum," she had said on one of her rare visits home. "You should sell up and get a studio flat in West Hampstead—I'm sure you could afford one if you took out a small mortgage. You'll never meet a rich man hanging about here."

It was true enough, thought Bridie. Single rich men were thin on the ground in Kingsbury—although there were some very nice houses in Mill Hill and Hendon, but they were mostly families she supposed. No, Sharon was right. However, she was reluctant to disturb all the belongings she had gathered over the years. The collection of porcelain animals she had gradually picked up in airports on her trips to America to visit her brother. The Denby dinner service it had taken her twenty years to complete. The determination with which she had kept a neat and, to her mind, stylish home was all the more cause for pride, thought Bridie, because she had never been married. Her brothers and sisters-in-law in Ireland and America had all been given ready-made homes when they got married. People didn't think to buy household objects for a single mother. I have done it all myself, she thought. I am an independent woman. A London woman. Like you see in the magazines—a woman who juggles her life.

Her brother Jack, who was a priest in America, had bought the house outright for her in 1964, when Sharon was born.

"You'd be happier in London," he said. "There are lots of single mothers there, free love and all that." Of course, he had tried to talk her into adoption—and she had thought about it. Had she known that thirty years on she would still be single, Bridie might have given Sharon up. But she didn't think about that now. "Look forward," that's my motto, she thought.

Jack had regularly sent checks to London over the

years, and so Bridie had never really needed to work. They had had enough to manage, but when Sharon needed to raise the money to do her beauty therapy course, Bridie had got herself a job in a local chemist's shop selling cosmetics. She had enjoyed the job at first, trying on all the new products. Lancôme one day, Max Factor the next; she thought it was important to show off each range to potential customers. After a few months, however, she had tired of selling corn pads to weary pensioners and chasing teenage girls who came in to pilfer cut-price lipsticks and hairbands from the baskets that cluttered the cosmetics counter. "Too many black women come in," she had said to Sharon one evening as the two of them tucked into a Weight Watchers Chicken Korma. "I never know what colors to sell them," she said, backing up her complaint with a little quip. Sharon didn't think it was funny.

Sharon's current boyfriend was black. Well, sort of black, Bridie explained to Jack when he made one of his regular phone calls from Boston. Not fully black, you understand—more of a light brown really. I think his mother is Spanish, she said by way of an excuse.

"We must be tolerant of people from all races, Bridie," Jack had replied. She didn't really know what he meant, but then Jack had always been a bit odd.

"I suppose," she conceded and went on to tell him about the new life Sharon was leading in swish West Hampstead. Her boyfriend had a bright red car, one of those sporty things. And Sharon said it wasn't really a flat he had—it was a "penthouse apartment." Sharon hadn't really had the chance to make her stamp on it yet, Bridie told him, but she kept some of her things there.

"What does he work at?" asked Jack.

"Sharon says he's a 'self-employed businessman.' "

Drug dealer, thought Jack.

"Well, tell her to be careful and not to move too far from home."

"Sharon thinks I should sell this house and move to a smaller place down there. It's a much nicer area."

Jack said nothing.

"Well," Bridie said, "I suppose it *is* very expensive." She had hoped that Jack might make one of his helpful suggestions, but he stayed quiet. Bridie tried to keep the bitter note out of her voice, but the conversation ended awkwardly. Jack said he would send her the tickets to America as usual this year. Bridie mumbled a cursory thanks. Truthfully, she was sick of her annual trips to visit her siblings in Boston. She knew that her brothers found her silly, and their wives were all so glum and ordinary. No glamor or spark to them at all. Too interested in their children, and not, she mused, interested in their appearance at all.

"Take Kevin's wife, Sue," she had said to Sharon after her last trip. "I mean, she's one of those attorneys—earns plenty of money. But her suits—all gray and drab. I told her she should get a perm, 'get those roots *up*, Sue,' I said."

She could tell Sharon wasn't listening. She listened less and less to her mother these days. Bridie missed her.

Bridie picked out a flowery blouse and decided to wear her Jaeger suit. It was from the Not Quite New Boutique in Hendon Central. All the rich Jewish ladies left their clothes there. As she got older, Bridie had found she needed to wear more subdued, well-cut clothes. Much of her North London life had been spent scouring Wembley and Burnt Oak markets for cheap clothes that could be dyed or altered into "something special." But the markets had changed, and the brightly colored saris and flimsy imported clothes were not to Bridie's taste. Even the fruit and vegetable stalls had changed. Fragrant herbs banked up against the swedes and carrots. Huge green bananas, giant pink rocks that looked like potatoes but which weren't potatoes at all.

"Look at those great big brown lumps of vegetables—they look like you-know-what," she had said to Sharon one day as they picked their way through the crowds on their Saturday shopping trip.

Sharon shouted at Bridie when they got home.

"You're a racist!"

Bridie was hurt. "I am not," she said, "I just want to be able to get a decent head of cabbage and know what I'm buying, like I used to."

It was still only six o'clock and Bridie had an hour to go. She'd get a minicab, she decided. Treat herself. Besides, the cheap beige sandals she was wearing were uncomfortably high, but they were the only ones which went with her suit.

She went downstairs and poured herself a small sherry. May as well settle my nerves a bit before the big event, she thought. The ad sat on the smoked-glass coffee table and she read it again. Searching for more clues.

"Gentleman doctor, early 50s, seeks charming lady for serious relationship. N.S., G.S.O.H., E.O. Age not important."

It was her friend Sheila who had suggested she look through the papers. Sheila lived in a mansion block around the corner. She had been at school with Bridie, and they had met up again recently when Sheila had moved to the area after her divorce. Sheila was a teacher, and her children were now grown up. She was always nagging at Bridie to get a job and lately Bridie had become irritated by her persistence. A few weeks ago, when Bridie had been complaining about there being no good shops in the area, on account of all the foreigners, Sheila had said, quite out of the blue, "You should go back to college, Bridie. You have too much time on your hands."

It was a deliberate dig, Bridie felt. Sheila was just jealous because she had to work and wasn't as well preserved as her friend.

Still, Sheila had given her the lead about the ads.

"If you are serious about finding someone, Bridie, you should take a look in the *Hendon Times*," she said. "There are plenty of small ads there every week."

"I couldn't," Bridie said, but the thought was already forming in her mind.

Bridie had been confused by all the initials at the end of the ad. She thought they might be the doctor's qualifications, so she had taken them around to Sheila for an explanation.

"N.S., G.S.O.H., E.O. Non-Smoker. Good Sense Of Humor. E.O.? I don't know what that means. Eating Out maybe?"

Good, thought Bridie. I like eating out. She had done a night course in elocution and etiquette when she was younger. She was good at eating out. She knew which cutlery to use.

She had sent in a photograph of herself and a short letter giving her age as five years younger, as a precaution. She hadn't expected a reply, and when the phone call came, Bridie was flabbergasted. She had managed to ask a few pertinent questions such as where did he practice?—she knew that was a doctoring term—and she found out what street in Hendon he lived on. She walked up that road on her way to the Not Quite New. Not mansions, but nice big houses—better than where she lived. She felt a thrill as she imagined him looking out of his window and seeing her by chance. A mystery lady whom he had yet to meet. She fantasized that he might have already admired her in passing, felt stirred by the swing of her Weight Watchers bottom neatly tucked into a smart red skirt.

They had arranged to meet at The Orange Tree in West Hendon at seven. A doctor. Imagine! A date with a doctor. She had tried to contact Sharon to tell her, but her boyfriend's mobile phone was switched off. "Sorry, the customer you are calling has their unit powered off. Please try later." It had been a couple of weeks now since they had last spoken. Bridie felt a little annoyed. She'll be sorry she missed this one, she thought. Maybe, Bridie said to herself bitterly, I won't bother telling her at all.

At exactly three minutes past seven, Bridie walked through the front door of The Orange Tree. She had been there once before when her brothers had been over on holiday, for a Sunday morning drinking session. She didn't like her brothers very much. Jack was useful enough, but critical and controlling. The others were coarse and ignorant, she thought. Untidy and unsophisticated, for all their money and education they had very bad manners. She disliked their loud raucous laughter at jokes which she did not understand; and they still had those common Mayo accents, she complained to Sheila one day. "I would have thought that university might at least have taught them to speak properly." ·

"I think accents are nice," said Sheila. "I still have mine."

"Oh no," said Bridie reassuringly, "you've lost yours almost completely. You have a lovely cultured voice."

Sheila looked a little crushed. Bridie didn't notice.

He had told her that he would be wearing a light-colored suit and carrying a copy of the *Telegraph*. Oh yes, Bridie thought, the *Telegraph*. He's *definitely* a doctor. "Light-colored suit," she liked the sound of that. Clearly this was a man of style and taste. She tried to contain herself as she walked in, not get too excited. Tried not to imagine herself swanning into his surgery with two Harrods bags swinging under her arms, or sitting in a fancy restaurant ordering hors d'oeuvres, or arranging her porcelain figurines on his mantelpiece. Trinkets to remind her of her past life. The dull thud of loneliness as she woke to face each hollow day in Kingsbury. The empty fear of growing old and unlovely, alone.

He had asked what she would be wearing and she had said, "A Jaeger suit—beige." It was good to get the Jaeger bit in, let him know what kind of a woman she was. Clothes said so much about a person, she thought.

"That sounds nice, Bridie."

Polite, gentlemanly, nothing nasty or smutty in his tone. He had used her name. That was a good sign.

She had asked him what his name was.

"Pat," he said. No surnames yet. That was informal, friendly—although he hadn't sounded Irish. His accent had been rather marked in its Englishness.

Bridie looked around. The bar was almost empty, early Wednesday evening was not a busy time, but the bar was nice, it felt safe enough, not like some of the noisy pubs in Cricklewood and Kilburn where she had spent so many of her early years in London. There was lots of wood and old artifacts, and artificial orange trees in large wooden boxes at each side of the door. Very elegant, Bridie thought. There were two young women sitting at the bar, and a few couples scattered around the place. In one corner was a group of young men in suits—talking business she supposed, and next to them in the corner was a little Indian man reading the paper. It was unusual to see an Indian in a pub, she thought. But then, they were everywhere these days.

Bridie decided to wait at the bar, get herself a dry white wine. She'd buy the first round tonight, she thought. Show she was an independent woman, not just some young bimbo after his money. Give him the right impression.

It was five past. He was late. Bridie paid for her drink and took a self-conscious sip. She examined her nails. Pink Pearl Mist, subdued and feminine—nothing brassy tonight. She looked around her anxiously. Six minutes past. Maybe he wasn't going to turn up. The humiliation! No, he had sounded reliable. Maybe she was in the wrong pub? Maybe there was another Orange Grove pub nearby that she didn't know about. Had she got the name wrong, perhaps? Orange Grave? Orange Cave? London was so big, there were so many places with the same name! She wished she had brought one of her crossword magazines with her as a distraction. Maybe the whole thing was a big mistake. Maybe she was making a fool of herself . . .

"Excuse me."

She turned around and the little Indian man she had seen earlier was standing behind her. With her being perched up on the stool he barely reached her shoulders.

"I'm waiting for someone," she snapped. This was really too much. The cheek of it. Where was Pat? Why was he late? This little Indian obviously thought she wanted to be picked up. She began to feel afraid.

"Are you Bridie?"

He knew her name! What was going on? She had read about things like this in the papers. This Indian man must have been following her. A stalker! A pervert! Maybe he worked in one of the markets and had heard Sharon use her name. This was horrible! And what would Pat think when he arrived, would he think that she knew him? This wouldn't be a good start. She must get rid of him quickly, but she couldn't move a muscle. She just stared at him blankly.

"I'm Pat," he said.

Bridie looked him up and down. Beige linen-mix suit, light-colored, copy of the *Telegraph,* which he now held up to her.

He smiled. Mascara met mascara as she blinked with embarrassment.

"Look, the *Telegraph.* I am so sorry that I missed you coming in, I became absorbed in my paper. That was most remiss of me. Won't you come and sit down? I see you have already bought a drink."

Bridie got down off her stool in a trance. This was mortifying. She was too shocked to take it in for a few seconds, and it wasn't until they were sitting down that she began to get ahold of herself. This was ridiculous. She would finish her drink and then leave.

"This is really a very nice place. Have you been here before?"

"No." Bridie was getting annoyed now. He was chatting away as if everything was normal.

"They have good food in here too. I often come in for a roast dinner at lunchtimes during the week."

Roast dinner? Curry more like. Bridie was really starting to boil.

"My surgery is just around the corner. Do you live nearby? Kingsbury, I think you said in your letter?"

"You didn't say you were an Indian," Bridie blurted it out and then flushed. She was annoyed at herself for having said anything at all. She should just keep her mouth shut and get out as quickly as possible.

"Oh. Well, indeed I am."

"You said you were a doctor."

"I am a doctor."

"Yes, but you're an Indian. You didn't say you were an Indian."

"Is it important?"

His face fixed hers, silently waiting for a reply. He might get annoyed, thought Bridie, who knows what could happen then?

"No. But, well, it's just not what I was expecting, that's all."

He looked a little disappointed.

"Pat. Well that's an Irish name."

"It's short for Patel. I studied at Trinity and my friends shortened it as a kind of a joke. You thought I was Irish?"

"Well, no. Well, yes, maybe I did."

Patel erupted into a fit of giggles. Bridie thought he looked rather foolish. Like a small brown boy. A spluttering puppy.

"Oh well now, I'm sorry. But that really is very funny."

"Well, I don't see what's so funny about it. You said you were a doctor and your name was Pat, what was I supposed to think?"

Bridie felt convinced people were looking at them. He was making fun of her. She didn't like that. *Him* making fun of *her*—the cheek of it!

Pat pulled himself together.

"I did say I was E.O. in the ad. Ethnic Origin?"

"I thought that meant something else."

"What did you think it meant?"

Bridie didn't want to tell him. He might want to take her out for a meal.

"Nothing. I didn't know. I just didn't know you were Indian. I thought you were a doctor."

"Well, I am. A doctor and an Indian. All at the same time."

This is not fair, thought Bridie. She was bristling with the injustice of it.

"I thought it meant Eating Out."

Pat laughed again.

"Ah, but I do like eating out. I'm a sort of a genius. I'm a doctor, *and* an Indian, *and* I eat out," he said smiling broadly. "I believe the youngsters today call it multitasking," and his shoulders shook with another little fit of mirth.

"Well," Bridie said, straightening her back and trying her best to look haughty and superior, "you were right about one thing."

"What's that?"

"You have a Good Sense Of Humor."

Pat became apoplectic with laughter. Bridie was sure people were looking now. After a few minutes, which seemed like an age, he composed himself.

"Bridie, are you hungry? There is a very nice Italian restaurant around the corner from here."

Bridie wanted to get out of the pub. A restaurant would, if nothing else, mean a quiet table where no one could see them. Besides, she was a little peckish and it was a long time since she had eaten in a proper restaurant. After all, a meal didn't mean anything, and at least they weren't in Kingsbury where the neighbors might see her.

Bridie had temporarily forgotten that she didn't know any of her neighbors anymore. They were all Indian.

The restaurant was a disappointment. Small and quite brightly lit. Not nearly as posh as Bridie had briefly hoped. Pat didn't order a starter, and Bridie followed his lead, so she didn't even get the chance to show off her cutlery skills. On the way there it started to rain and Pat opened his umbrella. Bridie was in a dilemma between getting her freshly blow-dried hair wet, revealing the bad perm she had so painstakingly disguised, or standing in what she considered to be too close proximity to the little Indian man. She was afraid he would smell of curry. In the end she relented and walked with her knees bent to compensate for his lack of height. She was surprised to

discover that he was wearing a rather healthy portion of
Chanel Pour Homme. Bridie recognized it from her days
in the chemist's. It was her favorite. "You can't go wrong
with Chanel, madam. It's expensive, but then you always
have to pay for a touch of class."

They sold very little of it. Most people favored those
artificial deodorants in cans these days. No style. The
kind of tacky fragrances her brothers would wear, if they
ever bothered about themselves at all.

"Of course, I don't really consider myself Indian anymore."

Bridie was enjoying her meal. Spaghetti bolognaise.
She made it herself at home sometimes, but she cheated
and used the packet sauces. No point in bothering when
you're on your own. This was the real thing. Very nice.

"I was educated here, and then in Dublin. My parents
sent me to boarding school when I was eleven, then I
decided to go to Trinity. I liked Ireland, but London felt
more like home, so I came back."

"You don't have an Indian accent anyway."

"You don't have an Irish one."

"Thank you."

Who cares, thought Bridie. I may as well chat as say
nothing. It's a free meal anyway. It felt cheap to be thinking such things, but Bridie was feeling cheap. Cheap and
cheated. She supposed it wasn't really this man's fault—
although he had seen her picture and should have realized. She was disappointed, irritated, but in another way
she didn't really care anymore. She certainly wasn't concerned with impressing him. Despite herself, Bridie found
she was beginning to relax. In less of a hurry to get away.

She would have pudding and one of those modern cappuccino coffees. Sharon had a machine for making them at home, but Bridie didn't know how to use it.

"Oh, I sometimes think it's a shame to get rid of your accent," he said. He had dark brown eyes and very long eyelashes. Like Omar Sharif.

"I don't," Bridie snapped back.

"Why not?"

Why did he keep asking her all these questions?

"Because I think accents are common. English should be spoken with a proper English accent."

Bridie finished her plate of spaghetti, and wiped the corner of her lips with a napkin. Paper, she noted disparagingly.

"I suppose you're right. When I started at school, no one could understand me. In Ireland it didn't matter so much, at Trinity. People are very tolerant to foreigners in Dublin."

"That's because there aren't any living there."

"I suppose."

Bridie flushed despite herself when she realized what she had just said, and tried to be nice.

"So when did you lose your accent? I mean how? Was it hard?"

"Well," Patel said, looking a little sheepish, "I'm not sure I should tell you. It might put you off."

Bridie almost laughed herself then. Put me off, she thought. As if I could ever be "on" in the first place.

"Well, if you don't want to tell me . . ."

"No, all right then, I will. After a few years working in London, well, I decided that this was where I would be spending the rest of my life."

More's the pity, thought Bridie.

"I like the culture here, you see. It suits me. I had been living in England since I was a child, and my Indianness—well, it was nearly all gone. Many of my contemporaries were moving back to India, getting more and more in touch with their heritage, their own history. Me? Well, I made up my mind to stay, form my own little rebellion if you like."

Yes, yes, yes, thought Bridie. Get on with it. I can do without the life story.

"And so, I'm nearly too embarrassed to say. Oh my Lord, this is difficult."

"Like I said, you don't *have* to tell me."

"No, it's important. Well, here goes. I went for elocution lessons."

Bridie smiled. Not the clenched, difficult smile she generally reserved for photographs and shop assistants. A real smile.

"Oh really?"

"There, I told you it was embarrassing."

"Where? Where did you go?"

"Oh, to a woman called Clarissa Partridge . . ."

"Hampstead Library, Elocution and Etiquette . . ."

"Yes . . . how do you . . . ?"

"I went there too, in 1977."

"1975 . . . we missed each other by two years . . ."

"Wasn't she *marvelous!*"

Bridie didn't know herself after that. They chatted and laughed and seemed to talk about everything. How to address a member of the Royal Family. The problems of seating arrangements at dinner parties—neither of them had ever even held one. They had a laugh over that. The little things in life that were important. Bridie was charmed to discover that Pat agreed with her wholeheartedly about men opening car doors and pulling back chairs for ladies to sit down. Surprisingly, Bridie found that they shared many of the same political opinions. Pat was a staunch conservative and believed that the immigration laws in Britain were far too lenient. "This is England, after all. Why should foreign cultures take over our traditional street markets? Our shops?" Sunday shopping, they both agreed, was entirely the fault of the Pakistanis. Pat explained to Bridie that he was not, by any stretch of the imagination, a Pakistani. That in fact the Indians and the Pakistanis hated each other. Something to do with land, she didn't really understand it, but it was very interesting nonetheless. He asked her about the political situation in Northern Ireland, and Bridie was surprised at how much she could recall from school. She couldn't remember the last time she had talked so much, had a proper conversation. It made her feel like quite the intellectual. Both agreed that it was important to respect the country you were living in. Bridie told him how when she had first come to London she had gone to the Irish pubs and clubs, "But they are all so rough. All that drinking and singing and no appreciation for the finer things in life."

She preferred the company of English people, she said. Pat agreed.

They even talked about clothes. About the importance of looking smart, and how difficult it was to get good quality fashions at the right price. Bridie felt so at ease, she found herself coyly confessing to where she had bought her suit.

"I know the owner well—Mrs. Cohen," Pat said, and

then he whispered conspiratorially, "The truth is I am always nagging her to open one for men." He asked if he could feel the fabric and Bridie said he could. His fingers did not linger untowardly on her arm, but Bridie felt a small tingle nonetheless. His hand was not really black, she noticed. More of a light brown. It could almost be a deep tan. His nails were clean and buffed to a clear shine. She liked that.

Pat told her about his arranged marriage to a young Indian girl which had dissolved ten years and three children later, much to the upset of his family. It had gutted him financially, he said, although, he was quick to assure her, he was back on his feet now. He listened nicely then as Bridie told him about Sharon and her new boyfriend. Your children all grow up and leave you, they agreed. It was lonely, but it was the way of the world. Pat assured her that she was right to stay in Kingsbury. He had lived in West Hampstead himself once and told her, "It's not all it's cracked up to be."

"That's an Irish expression," Bridie said.

"Oh," he replied cheekily, "Clarissa wouldn't approve of *that*," and they both laughed.

They stayed and talked until the restaurant closed. The owner knew Pat and came politely to present the bill. "Sorry Doctor," he said and Bridie felt a thrill as Pat flipped him an American Express card. She had drunk over half a bottle of wine and was feeling a bit giddy. As they were leaving Pat told Bridie about a factory warehouse that he knew where you could get designer clothes at factory prices.

"They cut the labels off," he said, "but it's exactly the same stuff as you get on Bond Street. I know the owner. He's a patient."

Bridie was very impressed, and he arranged to pick her up that coming Saturday afternoon. His car was in for servicing at the moment, that was why he had arranged to meet somewhere close to home this evening. Bridie had wondered about that.

"What kind of car have you got?" It was a brazen question, but Pat didn't mind.

"A BMW," he said, "G reg."

Bridie took a mental note. She would ask Sharon if that was good. Sharon knew more about cars than she did.

Pat walked her to the local minicab office. It was still raining, but she held the umbrella this time.

"Because I'm taller," she said. "On account of my lovely long legs," and they both laughed.

"It has really been a pleasure to meet you, Bridie," Pat said as he leaned down, having opened the cab door. "You really are a very funny, charming lady."

Bridie blushed.

"See you on Saturday, then."

As the driver drove off she said to him, "His name's Pat, you know—but he's not Irish," and she smiled at her own joke.

———

MORAG PRUNTY, London-reared of Irish parents, edited several young women's magazines in London, including *More!* and *Just Seventeen,* before moving to Ireland in 1990 to relaunch *Irish Tatler.* She is now a full-time writer and lives in Dublin with her husband and son. Her first novel, *Dancing with Mules,* was published in 2001.

DOWNTOWN PRESS
PROUDLY PRESENTS

"A TRUE ROMANCE"
from
SCOTTISH GIRLS ABOUT TOWN

SHARI LOW

Now available in paperback
from Downtown Press

Turn the page for a preview of
"A True Romance" . . .

Friday morning. The Kilcaidie Advertiser *Daily Horoscope. Sagittarius: Despite a bumpy start to the day, positive aspects will forge a new beginning mid-afternoon. Don't turn away from new ideas or challenges as your future happiness might just depend on them.*

Dee placed her cup of tea and bacon sandwich down on her desk and switched on her PC. There was no putting it off any further. In the last hour she'd considered and dismissed every conceivable excuse to avoid sitting down and doing some work today. Excuse number one: raging hangover. Dismissed on the grounds that it was self-inflicted so therefore not a credible reason to avoid doing paid labour. Number two: a mountain of ironing so high that a Sherpa would get vertigo just looking at it. However, ten minutes searching for the iron had proved fruitless. It was probably underneath the pile. Desperation started to creep in. Number three: it was nearly a fortnight since she'd visited her mother. She could nip over for a couple of hours. After all, she was already feeling atrocious, how much worse could it be? She sighed in resignation, then gritted her teeth. Sod it. It would be less painful to sit down and put in a few hours' work. Her mother's dulcet tones on top of the hangover from hell would have her speed-dialling the Samaritans.

She blinked hard, trying to clear the fog. Which of her

literary hats would perch most comfortably on her pounding head today? Did she feel like being Desdemona White, the True Romance Book Club's novelist of the month, esteemed author of such romantic classics as *He Came, He Conquered* and *His Throbbing Heart?* Not for the first time, she gave an involuntary shudder. How *had* she managed to assume the identity of someone whom her mostly aged, single readers imagined lounging on a chaise-longue, wearing an apricot kaftan and patting a shitzu while she wrote her love classics on parchment with an antique fountain pen? If they could only see her now . . . She'd be evicted from the House Of True Romance quicker than a bigamist with body odour.

A flashback seared through her trance-like state. It had all been Trudy's fault. But then, everything always was. It had been Trude's idea to write romantic slush to supplement their meagre grants at uni. It had been Trude's theory that creating personas in keeping with the True Romance Book Club's average reader would give their manuscripts a better chance of being accepted. Thus Dee became Desdemona White, a fifty-year-old spinster who passed her days in a picturesque cottage in a blustery Scottish village, tending to her four cats and her petunias as she awaited the arrival of her God of Love, who would one day, she was sure, come and conquer.

It was also Trude's fault that even now, ten years after leaving university at the age of twenty-two, Dee was still penning her fluffy pink prose for a paltry income, instead of being the hard-hitting investigative journalist that she had always aspired to be. Well, okay, so that wasn't Trude's fault at all, but in her present tender state it made her feel better to pretend it was. In more lucid moments she would admit that the truth of the matter was that she just hadn't wanted it enough. No matter how many times she'd planned the move to London or composed applications to the more respectable tabloids and the lofty broadsheets, she never quite made it to the train or put her CV in the post. Finally, in a moment of clarity on her twenty-fifth birthday, she'd grudgingly acknowledged what everyone around her had always known: she was staying in Kilcaidie. And what's more, she was happy about it.

Three train stops and thirty minutes on a good day from the centre of Glasgow, Kilcaidie was notable only for the fact that, defying a long Celtic association with the merits of alcohol, it was the only dry village left in the West of Scotland. Not a pub for fifteen miles. It was therefore completely understandable that Dee was in this fragmented condition today, she reasoned. After all, you had to make the most of a trip to Glasgow and that's exactly what she and Trude had done on yesterday's shopping-cum-eating-cum-drinking-cum-rousing-three-other-passengers-and-a-dog-into-a-sing-song-on-the-last-train-home excursion. At her age she really should have known better. But then that was the story of her life, she mused. Common sense had never been her strongest personality trait. If it were, then she wouldn't have a career pretending to be a post-menopausal spinster on heat, earning a salary that was barely above the poverty line (not including, of course, a heady £100 bonus for being voted Author of the Month in September 1998), which she had to supplement by being Auntie Diana, author of the *Kilcaidie Advertiser*'s agony column, and the in-house astrologer, Madame Donatella, predictor of the population's daily fortunes. Multiple personality disorder was more a career choice than a mental condition.

Indecision furrowed her brow. Auntie Diana it was. It

was a warming thought that reading about other people's trials and tribulations would undoubtedly make her feel better about her present sorry condition.

Bacon sandwich in one hand, she manoeuvred the mouse to the Outlook Express icon and clicked. It pinged as it opened the program. Ouch! Good God, when did that ping get so loud? It was vibrating round her head so violently that her eyelashes started to tremble.

She quickly slid the mouse to the volume control and reduced it to mute, before switching to the "Advertiser—Auntie Diana" profile and clicking send/receive. The screen flashed up its progress. Dialling. Verifying password. Checking mailbox. You have twelve new messages. Dee groaned. Kilcaidie was a troubled place this week. Normally there weren't more than three or four letters in a week and they generally consisted of a lonely heart, a couple of neighbourly disputes and a complaint from George the hypochondriac about skateboarders on the high street inducing his panic attacks.

She automatically clicked on the most recent arrival.

Dear Auntie Diana,
I'm very concerned about my best friend. I think she has a serious drinking problem—every time she indulges in alcohol she has an irresistible urge to sing Beach Boys songs really loudly on public transport. Is there a support group for this condition? Please advise as to the best course of action.
Yours in deep concern,
Trudy

An amused snort escaped as Dee started typing.

Dear Trudy,
Pretend she's a horse with a broken limb and put
her out of her misery—with the severity of her current headache she'll thank you for it. And thank
you for your concern.
Auntie Di

Two minutes later the phone rang. Ouch. Dee snatched it
from the table. The caller spoke before she did.

"Sorry, mate, I haven't got a gun. How's your head?"

"Don't ask. And stop bloody sending e-mails to Auntie
Di—she's overworked as it is. How are you feeling this
morning?"

"Like I've spent two weeks marinating my head in
gin." Pause. "But enough fantasizing. I've got a proposition for you."

Dee groaned out loud. "Whatever it is, you can forget
it. I'm not going to start yoga classes at the community
centre, donate my eggs or do a sponsored slim in aid of
Save the Whale. No matter how ironic that is."

"Nope, it's none of those. Although, and I'm telling
you this strictly in the spirit of a best friend who only
wants what's best for you—your thighs could definitely
benefit from a session or six of Ashtanga. Anyway, the
proposition. How would you like to join Dave and me
tomorrow night for a veritable feast of dishes from around
the world as featured in the new Jamie Oliver bible of
home cooking?"

"What's the catch?"

"Why does there have to be a catch? Can't I just invite
my best friend for dinner without there being some dark,
ulterior motive? I'm *so* offended."

"It's a proposition, Trudy, therefore there's a catch. Who is he this time?"

"Okay." Trudy sighed in a tone pitched somewhere between resignation and defeat. "It's Dave's new boss. He's just moved up here from London, so we thought we'd do the hospitality bit and invite him over. Can't beat a bit of grovelling to authority in the name of career advancement."

Dee put her head in her hands. Or at least she tried to, but her aim was off and she succeeded only in imprinting her keyboard on her forehead. This was the last thing she felt like doing this weekend. Dave, Trudy's fiancé of four years (he didn't like to rush things), worked in some obscure department of Glasgow City Council. He had told her about his job a couple of times but Dee's tendency to zone out after the first two minutes meant that she was none the wiser. Another internal groan. Dinner with the remnants of a hangover (this was definitely a three-day headache) and two civil servants, one of them trying to impress the other—was this some cosmic punishment for over-indulgence last night?

Trude sensed her hesitation and resorted to blatant pleading. "Come on, Dee, if you do this, I'll never mention your cellulite again. Please."

"Okay, okay. But I'm warning you, this had better not be a set-up. The first whiff of a blind date and I'm out of there, Trude."

"It's not a set-up, I promise. It's just a fine example of good old Scottish hospitality."

Somehow, Dee doubted that.

Saturday morning. The Kilcaidie Advertiser *Daily Horoscope. Sagittarius: Today is a day for rest and recuperation and taking quiet time to recharge your batteries. For those Sagittarians who do have to venture out, avoid new social interactions arranged by friends—despite their well-meant intentions, they don't always know what is best for you.*

Dear Auntie Di,

I'm very worried about my best friend. She is in her thirties now and is still single despite numerous attempts by me to introduce her to suitable men. In fact, she was downright rude when I last sprung a blind date on her (I mean, what's so bad about a nervous twitch, a train-spotting hobby and mild halitosis—nobody is perfect) and threatened to amputate my limbs if I repeated the exercise. What can I do about her anti-social tendencies and her threatening behaviour?

Yours in mortal fear,

Trudy

Dear Trudy,

Maybe your friend is perfectly happy with her single status and as her friend you should support her in this lifestyle choice. Perhaps there is something sadly lacking in your life that prompts you to take such an avid interest in other people's relationships. I suggest you look into taking up a hobby, such as basket-weaving or origami.

Yours sympathetically,

Auntie Diana

PS: Trude, you promised that tonight isn't another set up. If it is, I'll have to kill you.

Dee stared at her reflection in the full-length mirror. She should have asked Trude what to wear tonight but she hadn't wanted to appear adolescent or apprehensive. She was a cosmopolitan woman of the world. One with no dress sense, she reflected. It was so difficult trying to dress for occasions like this. If she were too casual, Dave's boss might take offence, especially if he was one of those late-fifties, dress-for-dinner, formal types. On the other hand, Trudy and Dave's kitchen dining table, which doubled as a table tennis table and, in times of decoration, the wallpaper pasting area, didn't exactly lend itself to cocktail dress and diamonds.

In the end she settled for the middle road. Dark blue hipster jeans (size 12—who needed yoga?) with a black, low-cut T-shirt, supported by breast-enhancing bra. She clipped diamond studs into her ears and twisted up her long auburn hair, leaving some tendrils loose to frame her face. She couldn't decide if it looked Julia Roberts classy or been doing housework all day messy. Anyway, why was she caring? She was just there to make up the numbers and to reinforce the theory that Dave was a decent, normal guy who was a credit to any workplace. After all, it wasn't as if this was a date or anything . . .

The very thought sent her eyeballs rolling and a shiver down her spine. She *so* wished that Trudy would just let her get on with living her life the way she wanted to. Why must everyone on the planet be shackled up to a member of the opposite sex to ensure everlasting happiness? Why was a man (or another woman for that matter) crucial to self-esteem, image and sense of worth? Dee shrugged her shoulders. She just didn't get it. She'd tried to analyse her feeling many times over the years (especially after a few libations and in between the Beach Boys' greatest hits) but the truth was she didn't care enough to delve too deeply. Maybe it was the fact that she'd been an only child and was therefore used to enjoying her own company. Perhaps it was because the things she enjoyed doing most—reading, lying in the bath pondering life, and running in the mornings with her walkman on full blast—were predominately solitary pursuits.

She had never had her heart broken and had never crushed anyone else. And no, it wasn't down to deep-rooted self-loathing, a pathological aversion to commitment or some deep psychological scar tissue on her soul. It was simply a fact of life. Dee Statton was happy being the word that was greeted with fear, horror and loathing amongst other women of her generation: *single*. She didn't want children, she didn't want to be married and she enjoyed only emotionless flings with members of the opposite sex. As soon as they demanded any form of commitment deeper than occasionally borrowing her toothbrush after they'd spent the night, Dee would trot out the "going too fast, maybe we should have a break" speech.

Meaningless sex and someone to be her partner at weddings, funerals and the odd trip to the cinema—that was all she wanted in a man. Was that too much to ask? And anyway (she was perched on her metaphorical soapbox now), why was it that a single, attractive thirty-something male with a job, financial security and the freedom to change partners at a whim was revered and envied by his peers, yet a female in the same circumstances was almost unanimously pitied by hers? It was one of life's little idiosyncrasies, she decided. Like why men automatically scratch their nether regions in times of deep concentration, bravado or when they think no one's watching them. God was definitely having a laugh when he created human beings . . .

Trudy opened the door and physically dragged Dee inside. "He's here and he's *gorgeous,*" she stage-whispered through the hand that was trying to cover the grin stretching from one gold hoop to another. "I promise, Dee, this wasn't a set-up. But he's thirty-five, was married for three years to a female who sounds like a major bunny boiler. Anyway, she ran off with the plumber who was installing their en-suite. Marble. Cream. He's been divorced for six years. No children. Earns over fifty grand a year. Likes football, rugby and tennis, but isn't obsessed. Hates cricket. Listens to soul, Motown and also likes rock. Favourite group Oasis. No obvious halitosis or strange hobbies. Likes to travel, go to the flicks and Italian food is his favourite." She paused for breath. "Sorry, that's all I could find out. He's only been here five minutes."

Dee laughed, despite an overwhelming premonition of doom. "You forgot his inside leg measurement."

"Thirty-four and a half inches, give or take a fraction. And you know I'm never wrong about these things."

That summer job in the gent's tailors had left its mark.

Dee followed Trudy into the kitchen, mentally noting that she seemed to have got her outfit just right. Trudy too was wearing jeans with a black top, her blonde hair pulled up into a high ponytail. That was no surprise. Ever since their virtually inseparable childhood, they would arrange to meet and then invariably both turn up in almost identical clothes. They liked the same music, the same movies, excelled at the same sports . . . Sometimes it was almost as if they had one brain, just with extra arms and legs.

Thankfully, though, there was one area in which they differed, Dee thought, as she entered the kitchen and Dave stood up to kiss her. Men. To Dee, Dave had all the appeal of a big teddy that looked good in the corner of a room and might occasionally warrant a cuddle in times of severe stress or depression. He was sweet, cuddly and cute, but didn't set the bells ringing in her brain, or any other part of her anatomy for that matter. Still, he loved Trudy and she adored him and that was all that mattered. And one day they'd give her gorgeous adopted nieces and nephews to play with. Ones that she could hand right back at the end of the day.

"Hey, Dee, you look gorgeous," Dave smiled as he kissed her cheek. None of this air-kissing nonsense. North of the Watford Gap, you got the full saliva-leaving, make-up-smearing, deadly suction smacker. It's been known to result in bruising.

She returned Dave's kiss, then turned to face the new-comer. He put out his hand and shook hers. "Hi, I'm Greg, pleased to meet you."

"Dee," she replied superfluously.

"I know. Thirty-two, natural hair colour, journalist and author, single, never been married, likes *ER*, re-runs of the *Sweeney* and had a childhood crush on Tony Hadley. Hates seafood, likes Japanese, Chinese and Indian food and going to the cinema."

Dee closed her eyes in embarrassment.

"Oh, and inside leg thirty-one and a half inches," he concluded.

She opened one eye and contorted her face into what she hoped was an apologetic expression. Trude should carry an early warning alarm.

She half expected him to make a run on his thirty-four

and a half inch legs, but no, he was still standing there with a lopsided grin. Trudy hadn't mentioned that he had a killer smile.

There was a pause, then the ludicrousness of the situation seemed to descend on all four of them at the same time and they creased into laughter.

Can't beat a bit of ritual humiliation to break the ice, Dee thought, as she offered her hand to his. "Erm, pleased to meet you," she laughed. And she was.

Dinner passed in a comfortable, lots-of-laughs and four-bottles-of-red-wine kind of haze. Dee made a mental note to apologize to her liver—no alcohol for a month then two blow-outs in the one week. She was going to feel like road-kill in the morning.

They ran the usual gauntlet of discussion topics. Dee was pleasantly surprised to find that other than the information Trudy had forcibly extracted from the defenceless Greg, they actually had loads more in common too. Maybe there was a bit of potential there after all. There was, if she was reading the signals correctly, definitely the hint of a mutual attraction going on. It was the little things: he listened with a smile when she spoke, was interested in everything about her and didn't cringe when a spoonful of chow-mein missed her mouth and landed in the cleavage created by her push-up bra. By midnight she'd decided that the wine was fantastic and dinner parties were great! And so was Trudy, for obviously fixing her up with this lovely man. She must remember to thank her in the morning. Good old Trude, what a star!

At one o'clock, Greg called a taxi just as she announced that she was heading for home.

"Let me drop you off," Greg offered.

"No, there's really no need. But thanks."

"Look, I insist."

"Thanks, but honestly, I'm happy to walk. It's really not far," Dee persisted.

Greg refused to listen, so eventually Dee shrugged her shoulders and succumbed. Five minutes, lots of kisses and so much winking from Trudy that she now had repetitive strain injury in her right eye, they were ensconced in the back of a Mondeo.

"Thirteen Thistle Drive," Dee said with only a slight slur.

The driver looked at her quizzically. "But—" he started to say.

Dee put up her hand. "I know, but humour me. Thirteen Thistle Drive, please."

The driver shrugged his shoulders and released the handbrake, shaking his head.

Greg looked momentarily confused by the exchange, but obviously put it down to too much wine or a taxi driver with attitude. As the car pulled away, he turned to Dee.

"I wanted to take you home because I thought we could talk on the way there without the relationship sheriff monitoring our every move," he confessed with a smile.

Dee said nothing.

"You see, the thing is—" He was caught in mid-sentence as the driver slammed on the brakes. What was wrong with this guy?

"Thirteen Thistle Drive," Schumacher announced.

Greg looked confused and Dee couldn't suppress a giggle.

"I told you there was no need. I live only three doors down from Dave and Trude."

She almost felt sorry for causing his flabbergasted expression.

"But—" he stuttered. Dee cut him off by leaning over and kissing his cheek.

"Call me," she said with a wink, as she alighted from the Mondeo and started up her path. "Trudy will give you my number," she continued without turning round.

As she closed the door behind her, she heard the taxi take off down the road.

Maybe there was something to this blind date thing after all . . .